"I need more books like *The Nanny*, stat. A smart, educated heroine (Yes, please!) meets a driven, career-focused single dad. Sparks fly . . . and fly, and fly. Seriously, this book is like if Ali Hazelwood and Tessa Bailey had a smutty baby. I devoured every page and was sad to see it end. This is the spice BookTok wants! Now I need Lana Ferguson to work faster, because I want to see everything she writes."

—Ruby Dixon, international bestselling author of
the Ice Planet Barbarians series

"Smart, fun, sexy, and sizzling with romantic tension, *The Nanny* is a mouthwateringly delicious take on second chances, with a healthy dash of steam. I can't wait for more from Lana Ferguson!"

—Sara Desai, author of *To Have and to Heist*

"*The Nanny* is sweet, beautifully sexy, and Aiden is the single Zaddy you want in your life. An amazing debut."

—Elena Armas, *New York Times* bestselling author of
The Long Game

"Ferguson makes the will-they-won't-they sing with complex emotional shading and a strong sense of inevitability to her protagonists' connection. . . . Rosie Danan fans should snap this up."

—*Publishers Weekly* (starred review)

"This steamy romantic comedy puts a modern spin on traditional tropes, bringing the falling-for-the-nanny and secret-past story-lines into the twenty-first century. . . . Readers who enjoyed Julie Murphy and Sierra Simone's *A Merry Little Meet Cute* will adore this positive, upbeat, sex-filled romp." —*Library Journal*

"Everything about *The Nanny* is enjoyable: the plot, the pacing, the characters, and especially Ferguson's wise and funny voice. It's also refreshing to see sex-positive characters who approach intimacy with maturity. . . . If you're a fan of dirty talk and slow-burning chemistry, you'll love *The Nanny*."

—*BookPage* (starred review)

"If you're looking for a heartfelt romance that knows how to bring the heat, look no further than *The Nanny* by Lana Ferguson!"

—The Bookish Libra

PRAISE FOR

The Fake Mate

"Lana weaves fantastically the elements we love from a paranormal romance (namely, attractive shifters with extremely interesting drives), with the humor characteristic from the best contemporary rom-com you can get your hands on. This book is addictive, epically smutty, and the breath of fresh air the romance genre didn't know it needed."

—Elena Armas, *New York Times* bestselling author of *The Long Game*

"What begins as a typical fake-relationship story quickly slides into a delightfully endearing study of two people overcoming expectations."
—*Publishers Weekly*

"This fun, steamy romance has interesting, well-drawn characters who happen to be shifters. . . . Fans of fake relationships will appreciate Ferguson's . . . paranormal twist on the trope."
—*Library Journal*

"A steamy, worthwhile romance with plenty of banter, tapping into the popular grumpy-meets-sunshine trope."
—*Kirkus Reviews*

"Charming. Funny. Primal. Ferguson's paranormal romance manages to be sweet and spicy at the same time, with two likable leads who can't ignore their wolfish urges. . . . Readers will tear through this omegaverse novel."
—*Booklist*

"With lots of laughs, feelings, and love, *The Fake Mate* reminded me . . . why I love reading. Five wolfy stars from me!"
—Heart's Content

"Holy smoke does Lana Ferguson deliver the steam in her new werewolf romance book. . . . So much fun to read."
—She Reads Romance Books

The Game Changer

LANA FERGUSON

BERKLEY ROMANCE

NEW YORK

BERKLEY ROMANCE
Published by Berkley
An imprint of Penguin Random House LLC
penguinrandomhouse.com

Library of Congress Cataloging-in-Publication Data

Names: Ferguson, Lana, author.
Title: The game changer / Lana Ferguson.
Description: First edition. | New York : Berkley Romance, 2024.
Identifiers: LCCN 2023056200 (print) | LCCN 2023056201 (ebook) |
ISBN 9780593816837 (trade paperback) | ISBN 9780593816844 (e-book)
Subjects: LCGFT: Romance fiction. | Novels.
Classification: LCC PS3606.E72555 G36 2024 (print) |
LCC PS3606.E72555 (ebook) | DDC 813/.6—dc23/eng/20231211
LC record available at https://lccn.loc.gov/2023056200
LC ebook record available at https://lccn.loc.gov/2023056201

First Edition: July 2024

Printed in the United States of America
1st Printing

Book design by Daniel Brount

To me, actually, for not letting this book make me its little bitch.
It sure as hell tried.

The Game Changer

One

DELILAH

See?" I wink at the camera as I pull the tray from one of the double ovens on set, making sure they can get a good view of the flaky, browned goodness there. "I bet most of you at home were thinking this was impossible when we started, but look how easy that was." I set the tray on the cooling rack, pulling off my branded oven mitts and making a show of inhaling from the still-hot pastries. "Mm. Look at us. Who would have thought? Making pain au chocolat with stuff we already had lying around!"

I blow on the pastry gently before taking a small bite, making appreciative noises for the camera's benefit. Not that it isn't delicious, because it is, but honestly, my stomach is still a little sour thinking about the meeting I have waiting for me after I finish filming this episode.

"Okay," I say, licking the remnants of chocolate from my finger and setting the half-eaten sweet back on the tray. "If you can stop at just one of these, you're better than me. I will be shamelessly sneaking seconds the moment those cameras turn off.

Don't forget my hot tip about making your dough the night before and letting it chill overnight, and be sure to tag me in your attempts on social media! I love seeing everyone and their creations."

I glance at the unfinished dessert on the tray, biting my lip before grinning at the camera. "Okay, I have to finish that, I can't just let it *sit* there!" I shove the rest of the pastry into my mouth, *mmm*ing loudly. "Wow. That really is so good." I put on my brightest smile after swallowing it down, zeroing in on camera one. "Next time, I'm going to show all of you how to make éclairs at home with mascarpone." I hold out my hands. "Trust me, you're going to want to see what that's about. But until then, just remember that baking"—I make sure to accentuate the next bit with a practiced twirl of my finger—"is whisk-y business."

"*And cut.*"

I relax from the pose I'm holding, blowing out a breath.

"That was great, Dee," the floor manager, Greg, tells me.

I pull my apron over my head, frowning at the bits of flour that escaped the hem to cover my chest—a common occurrence, with my . . . ample landing zone. Everybody wants huge tits until there's flour involved. "What about that egg I dropped?"

"Nah, we can definitely cut that out in post."

"Perfect," I tell him, dropping the apron on the counter and moving away from the stage kitchen.

"Hey, Delilah, you want the rest of these?"

I glance back at the pain au chocolat still sitting on the cooling tray, our boom operator, Dante, standing beside them with a hungry look. Normally, I would be snatching up the leftovers and hoarding a few for myself before passing them around to the crew, but as it is, I just shake my head.

"They're all yours."

I hear a muted collection of *yes*es behind me, heading for the little table where we keep bottled water and snacks. I screw the cap off a bottle and guzzle down half in one go, trying to settle the sensation of bees buzzing in my stomach.

"Take a breath, girl," Ava laughs beside me. She's tall enough that I have to crane my neck up at her, but at five foot four, that's nothing new for me.

I shake my head, taking another swig before screwing the cap back on. Ava Carmichael is our junior producer—but more than that, she's become my best friend over the three years that I've been doing the *Whisk-y Business* show. I know that she's well aware of the meeting that's happening far sooner than I'm prepared for, so I think she knows exactly why my face scrunches with frustration.

"Kind of wanted to throw myself in the oven, not gonna lie," I tell her.

"Stop." She places one hand between my shoulder blades, rubbing there. "It's not going to be as bad as you're building it up to be in your head."

"Ava," I sigh, running my hands through the thick mass of my chestnut waves. "We both saw the numbers for last month. It's probably going to be *worse* than I'm building it up in my head."

She tugs on her blond braid absently, something I know means she's more worried than she lets on, her pert nose scrunching in thought. "I mean, it's not like they can cut the show, right? You still have the rest of this year on your contract."

"Yeah, *this* contract," I point out. "They could absolutely decide they're not going to extend it."

She frowns as if she hadn't allowed herself to entertain that possibility. "But everyone loves you! I mean, *Whisk-y Business* basically paid for the new studio. It sure as shit wasn't Courtney's *Apples to Apples*." She snorts. "How anyone didn't have the foresight to see that the girl was going to run out of things to make out of apples after six months is beyond me."

"I mean, at least she's moved on to pears now," I offer.

"Yeah, which is really good for branding on a show built around apples," she mutters. She waves the thought off. "Whatever. All I'm saying is, your show is the headliner of the entire network."

"Yeah, but . . ." I bite my lip. "The numbers just keep seeming to trickle down. It's like people are losing interest. I keep dragging out harder and harder recipes, but it doesn't seem to be making any difference. The social media manager has noticed a downtick in interactions there also."

"Right, but . . ." Ava frowns. "You really think they would cut the show?"

I shake my head. "I have no idea. That's why I feel like I want to throw up."

"Fuck them, honestly," she huffs. "You could make doughnuts in your basement and get a ton of views on YouTube without them."

"Your faith in me is inspiring," I remark dryly. "Also, as the junior producer of the show, I feel like you should probably *not* be writing off the higher-ups."

"Yeah, yeah, whatever. I'm fine with working in your basement if I have to."

"You know I live in an apartment, right?"

"Shh. I'm being supportive."

My phone starts to vibrate in my back pocket, and I reach a hand behind me to fish it out. Ava gives me a *go on* motion as she gestures vaguely behind her, which I guess is a signal that she has things to do in that general direction. I watch her lithe form saunter off as I put the phone to my ear, hearing my brother Jack's voice shouting on the other end.

"Oh, come on!" His voice is at least ten decibels louder than is appropriate for a call, and I tug the phone away quickly to prevent hearing damage. "Oh, fuck off with that shit. Offside!"

"Jack," I try, met with more shouting. I clear my throat. "*Jack*."

"Oh, hey. What took you so long to answer?"

"It didn't take—" I purse my lips, deciding against reasoning with him. "Did you need something?"

"Wow. Your big brother calls you on the darkest day of your life to offer encouragement and unyielding support, and he's met with cold indifference. Our parents would be ashamed."

"I cannot deal with the dead-parent jokes today, Jack," I huff. Jack and I have very different methods of coping about being orphans. "Also, I don't think calling it the 'darkest day of my life' while trying to be supportive is helpful for morale."

"Maybe."

I hear the distinct sound of crunching.

"Are you watching replays of your games again?"

"Whabotit?" He manages through what I suspect is a handful of Cool Ranch Doritos. I hear him swallow. "Have you talked to them yet?"

"Not yet," I mutter. "I'm heading up to their office now."

"Remind them that you're an orphan."

"Not all of us use the orphan card for everything."

"You totally should," he says seriously. "It's really handy. Chicks dig it too. I'm basically Batman with a hockey stick." He snickers. "Hockey stick in my p—"

"Please don't finish that sentence," I groan. Sometimes I wonder how it is that he's five years older than me. Emotionally, there's a good chance he's still sixteen, not thirty-three. "Did you take your meds today?"

"What my Adderall and I do in the privacy of my own home is no one else's business," he answers primly.

"Take your fucking meds," I sigh. "I don't want to find you in your closet 'cleaning' it again."

"Hey, it got clean."

"Only because you had everything you took out of it lined up in your bedroom while you 'reminisced.'"

"I took my damn meds," he grumbles. "Worry about your own shit. What's your plan?"

"I'm just going to remind them of all the good this show has done for the network," I tell him, for his benefit or mine, I'm not sure. "Just because the last few months have been slow doesn't mean that the ratings won't pick back up. We can brainstorm some ideas to boost the viewer numbers."

"Too bad I have this busted arm," he laments. "I could come by and swing my hockey stick around." He is quiet for a beat before saying, "My actual one, mind you."

"Oh, because that would solve everything."

"Um, yeah? This is Boston, my dude. The Druids just won the Stanley Cup. Pretty sure you could make beer-battered cheese fries and people would watch if I was there."

"Your humility is inspiring," I deadpan.

"It's just one of my many positive attributes."

"Of course."

"Oh, hey, I was also calling to tell you the good news."

I pause by the elevator that takes me up to the higher floor, pressing the button. "What good news?"

"Ian is back."

I hover outside the doors of the elevator for several seconds after they open, only remembering myself when they start to shut again, and I realize I'm standing there without having gotten inside. I shake off the mountain of memories that just crashed down on me, clamoring onto the elevator and quickly hitting the correct floor.

"Oh? Is that right?"

More crunching. Fucking Doritos. "Ya. Heesh stayn wiff me."

"Don't talk with your mouth full, you goblin," I grunt. "Why is he back? Is he coming back to the team?"

"That's the plan," he says when his mouth is free of chips. "We're getting up there, you know? Retirement isn't too far off. He wants to finish out his career here at home. Thank God. He's been up there in the frozen wasteland for way too long."

"Calgary is hardly a frozen wasteland."

"Eh. I assume everything above the border is snowed in."

"That's wildly inaccurate. You literally play there sometimes."

"Yeah, and it's always cold as fuck."

"Back up. Ian is staying with you? So he's there? Right now?"

"Nah, he's flying in tonight. We have to be at the training center tomorrow." He scoffs. "Well, *he* has to be there. I'll be on the sidelines playing cheerleader with this stupid sling."

"Yeah, well, that's what you get for trying to do an axel while drunk."

"Sanchez dared me!"

"And yet it's *Baker* in the sling."

"Yeah, yeah," he mumbles. "Anyway, I figured we should all hang out soon. He's probably gonna feel weird being back, after the divorce and all, and I just thought that we—"

Jack's voice fades in the background, the reminder of Ian's marriage and then divorce all those years ago still making my chest twinge even after all this time. I've always reasoned that it's perfectly normal to feel something when your first crush and star of all your teenage fantasies marries and moves on—but I've never quite pinned down how to feel about everything that came after his marriage fell apart. Especially since he packed up and left right after to stow away in Canada for the following six years, something that even now I can't really figure out. I mean, sure, I know what the headlines said. I know that he supposedly left to keep the team out of the media circus that he found himself in, but I still don't know how his parents could just allow one of their top players, and more importantly, their *son*—to uproot his entire life instead of showing him support. I mean, they own the damned team, and his father had always been so *proud* to have his son playing for his team; it's all he ever talked about when he popped up in the news.

So how could he let him go?

"Dee? *Hello?* Delilah! You listening?"

"Hm? Oh yeah. Sure. Hanging out. We can do that. I'll have to see how things go today. I might be busy if they hear me out about brainstorming for new ideas on how to bump up the numbers."

"Well, pencil us in. I'm sure Ian has missed you. It's been forever since we've all been together."

I'm sure Ian has missed you.

It's incredibly stupid what that one sentence can do to my

heart. As if *I'm* sixteen again and not twenty-eight with over a decade between me and my pathetic pining. I hate the way a part of me perks up, as if I haven't purposefully avoided all things Ian since he left, for the sole reason of knowing he probably *wouldn't* miss me all that much, since I was never more than Jack's little sister in his eyes.

"We'll see," I manage, since I can't bring myself to commit any more than that. I have enough going on without throwing Ian Chase into the mix. I don't think I could tackle that even if my plate were entirely empty.

"Fine. Tell me how it goes, yeah? Don't be afraid to flash that orphan card. It really does—"

"K, thanks. Call you later."

"Kisses, Dee."

I hang up and shove my phone back into my pocket as the executive producer's office comes into view, lingering outside of it for a moment as I steel myself for whatever happens on the other side. I wipe my hands that are only slightly sweaty against my jeans, sliding them over the curve of my hips in an anxious gesture. It doesn't help that I have to go in alone, since my agent, Theo, got held up in another meeting. I always feel better when he's here.

You're Delilah Baker, I tell myself, attempting a pep talk. *You studied under Olivier Guillaume in Paris before you were twenty-five. You've got this.*

I knock gently, pushing the door open when I hear my EP bidding me entry. Gia is on the phone at her desk, and she holds up one perfectly manicured finger, signaling me to give her a second. I study her face to try to gauge her mood; her rich brown skin is smooth between her eyes, devoid of the singular wrinkle that sometimes pops up there when she's particularly stressed, and her bright red lips are still perfectly vibrant, which means she hasn't spent the afternoon going through Red Bulls as she is wont to do when things are going bad. I let these little things give me a glimmer of hope that this won't be as disastrous as I've been assuming it will be.

Gia hangs up her phone call after only another minute or so, blowing out a breath as she rubs her temples. "I swear, if I have to talk about budgeting one more time this week, I'm quitting to manage TikTok influencers."

"Frank giving you shit again?"

"When is Frank not giving me shit?" She turns in her chair then, eyeing me warily. "Speaking of . . . I assume you've gathered that's why I called you up here."

"I had an idea," I admit.

"I take it you've seen the numbers these last few months," she starts carefully.

I nod grimly. "I know they've dipped a bit."

"Twenty percent in the last four months," she says. "Now, this could be due to a lot of things, but . . . it's definitely a problem."

"I've had consistent numbers for the last two years," I point out. "My ratings have always been solid. I know the revenue the show brings in, and I think that's important to remember."

"Of course it is," Gia assures me. "I don't want you to think this is some sort of ultimatum here, but it is a concern. You know I love you, but upstairs . . . All they care about is numbers. We need to really figure this out and find a way to turn that needle so I can remind them that *Whisk-y Business* is a valuable commodity."

"I know," I sigh, sinking deeper into my chair. "I've been dragging out more difficult recipes, trying to make it more of a wow factor when I simplify them for the people at home, but . . ."

"People are fickle." She nods in camaraderie. "They're wanting flashier and flashier hooks every day. It's all about competitions in cooking now."

"You know I don't want to do that sort of thing."

"I know, I know. But that means we have to think of some other way. People love you, that hasn't changed. You're the girl next door, the sweetheart of the Boston baking scene, and that will always be true."

I suppress the urge to frown. I don't *hate* being known as the proverbial good girl, it's just a brand, after all, one that I suppose looks fitting with my small-but-curvy frame and my freckles and my big brown eyes that Jack and I share. Although, he uses his for evil far more often than for good. Still. It almost feels backward to lean into the whole Suzy Homemaker schtick.

I remind myself that I need the views.

"We could do specials focusing on particular cultures?" I cross my arms over my chest, thinking. "Or maybe I could get in contact with Olivier for some sort of collaboration?"

"Do you think he'd be willing to come to the States?"

I grimace, remembering hours upon hours of conversations that ended and started with: *you Americans.* "Ah . . . maybe not."

"I do like the idea of collaborations though. We could do crossovers with other shows on the network? What about Courtney?"

I make a face. "She refuses to do anything that doesn't involve fruit."

"People like fruit!"

"I guess," I huff. "But I think two bakers isn't really much of a wow factor, if I'm being honest."

Gia frowns. "Fair point." She taps a nail against her lower lip, thinking. "Well, we need something quick to give us a boost. I need some solid reasoning as to why we need to put the fate of your show on the back burner for a little while. Just something that will make that needle move enough to give us more time to come up with a more permanent solution. What can we do that will get the people of Boston excited about baking again?"

Her phrasing pings a memory, my brain grasping at straws before settling on the conversation Jack and I had before I came in here.

This is Boston, my dude.

My lips part, an idea forming. Although, whether or not it's a good one or a terrible one remains to be seen.

"Hockey," I blurt out, already regretting this, since it will mean I owe my brother for the half-assed idea he accidentally pitched as a joke. "What about hockey?"

Gia is visibly confused. "What?"

"My brother plays for the Druids, well, not at the moment, since he's on medical leave for a fractured ulna—dumbass decided to try figure skating while drinking—but regardless, I have an in with the team."

"And you think that will get us views?"

"I mean . . . I could chuck a rock on the sidewalk and hit at least three hockey fans in this city. Get one of my brother's teammates on here in their gear? A big hockey player making little pastries? People would eat that shit up. No pun intended."

She arches her brow. "It's not . . . a terrible idea. Bad puns aside."

"I hate to admit it, since it was technically a rambling from my brother I brushed off, but it might be a great idea. Even if it's just for one special. Training camp is about to start for the new season, so it would be great buzz for the both of us. At least, that's what we're going to tell their PR team."

"And you really think they'll agree to this?"

I think of the hundred or more favors that Jack owes me from the years of saving his dumb ass from one stupid thing or another, smirking. "I have a good feeling."

"Hm." Gia chews on the inside of her lip as she mulls it over, tilting her head back and forth in thought. "I mean . . . I'll have to run it by *our* PR team, but . . . I like it. I think it could be what we're looking for."

Relief floods my chest, knowing that this isn't a permanent solution, but at least it will give me more time to figure something out that will help long-term. Gia is already grabbing for her desk phone and punching in numbers, and I let myself relax just a little in my chair, feeling marginally better, at least. Even if I'm already regretting my brother's big fat *I told you so*.

Man, Theo is going to have a lot to say about this.

Two

IAN

> *Former Druids player Ian Chase was rumored to have at-*
> *tended the wedding ceremony of his ex-wife, now Mei*
> *Garcia, last week, fueling speculation about whether or*
> *not Chase is trying to win Mei back. People will remember*
> *the disastrous divorce between Chase and Garcia, ending*
> *what the media dubbed Boston's "fairy-tale romance"*
> *between an NHL legacy player's son and an up-and-*
> *coming artist. Mei Garcia, contemporary artist seen at*
> *galleries like Canvas and Interior Mosaic, offered no com-*
> *ment on Chase's attendance. Six years ago, photos of*
> *Chase and a mystery woman circulated social media*
> *when the couple were freshly separated, sparking rumors*
> *that the hockey star and his wife ended things because of*
> *unsavory—*

I shove my laptop away, grinding my teeth. Six years. Six fucking years of this shit trailing after me, finding me no matter how far

I run. I've long learned the lesson firsthand that anything on the internet stays there forever.

"I told you not to look," Mei says gently from the other end of the phone that I'm gripping too tightly against my ear.

"Yeah, well," I huff. "I've never been very smart."

"Shut up," she chides. "We both know they don't know the whole story. You should have let me make a statement."

"No." I scrub a hand down my face, my stubble scratching against my palm. It's gotten too long in the last few weeks. "You're on your honeymoon. You shouldn't be worried about my bullshit. Besides, they didn't believe you when you defended me last time, so why would this time be any different?"

"I just don't understand why they're dragging things back out," she says. "It's been years. Don't they have better things to talk about?"

"Who knows," I muse. "Maybe it's because I'm coming back home. Maybe it's because you got remarried. People love bringing up old shit. I probably shouldn't have come to the wedding."

"Oh, fuck that," she scoffs. "There was no way you were missing my wedding."

"Yeah, well, now they're turning your big day into a circus." I raise a hand to flag down the flight attendant, needing a drink if I'm going to keep from coming out of my skin while we wait for them to clear the plane to leave the tarmac. Because a delay is just what I needed today. "How is Bella, by the way? Still a dick?"

"I heard that, you asshole," Bella's voice chimes. "You're on speaker."

"Oh no, now you'll think we can't be friends," I chuckle.

"You wish your friends were as cool as me," she tosses back.

It's true, if I'm being honest. Isabella Garcia is cool as hell. As far as people hooking up with your ex-wife, I really couldn't have asked for better. Even if I do enjoy giving her shit. Thankfully, she gives as good as she gets.

"How is Fiji?"

"Hot," Mei complains. "I'm going to look like a tomato when I get home."

"Mi pobre esposa," Bella coos. "She's so delicate."

"Not everyone can be blessed with an eternal tan," she grumbles.

Bella gives an exaggerated sigh. "It is a gift."

I can practically hear Mei rolling her eyes. "Anyway," she says, addressing me again. "How long are you going to be stuck on the tarmac?"

"Pilot says another half hour, at least. Runway has ice they need to clear."

"Wow, I bet you won't miss that."

"I don't know. The snow has kind of grown on me."

"But being back in Boston will be great, right? We barely got to see each other at the wedding with everything going on. You'll have to come by the new house for dinner when we get back."

"Sure, that will be great," I tell her honestly.

"Don't worry too much about those people online," she tells me. "They're just bored and need something to gossip about. It will die down."

"We thought that last time, and I ended up in fucking Calgary."

"You didn't *have* to take the trade."

I don't argue with her, even knowing that isn't entirely true. I grit my teeth, reciting the same approved reasonings I've given anytime my trade is mentioned.

"Every time the Druids played a game, the press would rather talk about my damned love life than how many goals we scored. It wasn't fair to the team."

"Your parents own the team! They could have done more. They *should* have."

Again, I keep my mouth shut. It's true; my grandfather owned the team first, passing ownership to my mother when he died, and subsequently to my father. It's a legacy that has always hung heavy over my head growing up—being raised by a hockey great *and* the owner of an NHL team, meaning that every step I've taken in pursuit of the sport has been monitored, watched. Meaning that I had all the more eyes on me to fuck everything up.

"They did all they could," I mutter, not knowing what else to say.

"But six years? Why didn't you come back sooner?"

Another question I don't know how to answer. I know that I could tell Mei everything, that she'd never repeat it to another soul—but I can't bring myself to. It doesn't feel like her burden to bear. Not after everything she's already shouldering. Besides, deep down, I think a big part of the reason as to why I didn't fight harder to come home for so long was what I knew was waiting for me. What secrets I left behind that were easier kept from a distance.

"I don't know," I answer her, not entirely lying. "But I'm thirty-three. I've only got a couple years left in me. I don't want to retire in Calgary. I want to finish back home. So I guess my reasons aren't important now."

"Of course your reasons are important," she says softly.

There are seconds of silence that stretch between us, and I know exactly what's going through her head before she gives it a voice.

"You could just tell the truth, you know," she tries gently.

I clench my jaw. "We both know that's not an option."

"It is though," she presses. "You don't owe it to anyone to bear everything on your own. What if you spoke to Abigail, and—"

"Mei," I interrupt, a little more harshly than I intended.

Another beat of silence before, "I'm sorry."

I let my head thunk back against the headrest, closing my eyes.

"Don't be," I sigh. "It's not on you."

"It's not on *you* either," she urges. "This is *your* life. Not mine, not your father's, and certainly not Ab—"

"I know," I interject quietly, not wanting to hear her name again. All it does is dredge up old problems. Ones I still don't have solutions for, even after all this time. "I know that. I'll think about it, okay?"

I won't though. There's too much at stake. Too many people to disappoint. I think she knows it, too, but she thankfully doesn't push me on it anymore.

"Well . . . regardless. I'm happy you're coming home. We've missed you."

"No, we haven't!" Bella calls from further away.

I smile despite everything. "I miss you guys too."

"Is Jack going to pick you up from the airport?"

"Yeah," I tell her. "He'll be there when I land."

"Go out for dinner! Don't stay at home moping about the internet."

"We'll see," I mutter back.

"Babe!" Bella shouts. "Beach! You promised you'd let me put sunscreen on your ass, and I'm collecting."

"Wow," I groan. "That's not what you want to hear about your ex."

Mei giggles, and to be honest, I love hearing her happy. "Call me when you're settled, yeah?"

"I will," I promise. "Have fun over there."

I tuck my phone back inside my pocket after we hang up, sinking deeper into my chair. I've just resolved myself to a nap when a throat clearing from the next row up catches my attention, and when I crack open one eye, I notice a guy not much older than me eyeing me with excitement.

"Hey, sorry. You're Ian Chase, aren't you?"

I give him a thin smile. "Yeah, man. I am."

"So sorry, but could I get your autograph? Big fan."

"Sure, of course." I take the napkin and pen he hands me, scribbling my name. "You a Wolverines fan?"

"Nah, Druids, actually. I'm super stoked about you going back."

"Ah, well. I've missed playing at home, for sure."

"And I never bought all that bullshit they say about you online," he says earnestly as I hand the napkin back. "You never seemed like the cheating type to me."

It's a little harder to hold my smile, but I manage somehow. "Right. Yeah."

"Anyway, good luck next season, yeah?"

"Sure. Thanks, man."

I close my eyes again to discourage any further conversation, irritation simmering in my skin.

Six years. Six fucking years, and absolutely nothing has changed. I'm still defined by rumors and speculation, my entire life a show for others to pick apart. And I'm flying right back into the heart of it all, certainly in store for more of the same, maybe even worse. All for the sake of finishing my career on my terms.

Home sweet home, I think irritably.

— — — —

"Man, it's so cool to be back here with you," Jack says beside me, practically bouncing with excitement.

He's been the same ball of energy that he's always been in the twelve hours since he picked me up from the airport last night—the only difference now being the garishly pink sling his arm is wrapped in. Even if he hasn't shut up for a single minute that he's been awake since picking me up, it's still incredibly good to be with him again. Jack is just as much my family as the one I share blood with. Hell, all the Bakers are.

"I have to admit," I say, "there was a time I didn't think I'd ever be here again."

"Nah," Jack scoffs. "I always knew you'd be back. Boston is in your blood, man."

He's not wrong there.

"Well, I'm happy that someone's glad to have me back."

"Fuck off," Jack snorts. "We're all stoked. Coach especially. Fuck what Twitter says. That place isn't real, anyway. You can't put stock in something owned by Elon Musk."

"I think Tesla investors would argue with you."

"Shut up."

"Also, I think they renamed it."

"Yeah, but it's stupid. I don't know what that guy's obsession with naming things with just letters is."

He throws his good arm around my shoulders, an easy feat since we're both relatively the same size at six foot four. He flashes me a wide grin, one that hasn't changed in all the years since I've known him; Jack has always been the more approachable of the two of us—his shaggy, chestnut hair, deep brown eyes, and easy smile have always been a helluva lot more inviting than my perma-scowl that's constantly hidden under the red scruff I can't ever bother to shave completely off. Jack used to joke that I was entirely too gruff for a ginger. That we're supposed to be "sunshine-ier," and now that I've grown my hair out so long, he says I give off "Viking vibes." Whatever the hell that means.

"So . . . meeting with Coach and Leilani, huh?"

"Leilani is the new PR agent?"

"Mhm. She's cool. Tiny thing, but she'll stick those pointy fucking heels up your ass if you mention it."

"Good to know."

My worry must show on my face, because Jack nudges me with his good shoulder.

"Dude, it's going to be fine. They already signed you back, yeah? Everything else is just gravy."

"Right," I answer, nodding to myself as if this can wash away my nerves. "You're right."

"We'll get through this first week, and then maybe we can grab dinner with Dee this weekend, huh? She'll be excited to see you again."

That gives me pause. "Lila?"

"Yeah. You've caught her show, right?"

I shake my head. "We don't get the channel in Calgary. Not really big on TV, anyway."

"Dude. You have the internet though. It's a big deal! I can't believe you haven't given it a watch. I mean, I don't watch it religiously, but I still DVR the episodes."

"I know," I say with a frown. "I need to remedy that now that I'm back."

"Well, we can all catch up, regardless. She's going to kick your ass when she finds out you haven't seen her show."

I grin at that, trying to imagine the tiny scrap of a girl I remember with her freckles and her constant coating of flour kicking my ass. "It's been too long since I saw the kid. It'll definitely be good to hang out."

"Don't let her catch you calling her 'kid,'" he says.

I can't help but flash another smile. "Yeah. I better head back to Coach's office. I'll see you on the ice, yeah?"

"From the sidelines," he grumbles.

"Ian!"

I freeze at the sound of my mother's voice; I'd known she'd be here but still wasn't prepared to see her. Not quite. I turn to catch sight of her coming down the hall, her expression bright and her more-silver-than-blond hair tied back in a twist. I try to focus on her, try to keep my smile pasted on my face for her benefit, but I can already see the larger figure looming just behind her, the presence of my father like storm clouds rolling in, impossible to ignore.

My mother's tiny frame collides with mine, her thin arms wrapping around my middle and squeezing tight. I smile into her hair, which boasts the familiar scent of roses courtesy of her favorite shampoo, reveling in the comfort it brings. Even if only for a moment.

"Oh, I missed you," Mom says. "You haven't been to visit in far too long! You didn't even come see us after Mei's wedding."

"He had a lot of other things to worry about, it would seem," my father adds, forcing me to acknowledge him.

Bradley Chase and I look a lot alike; his dark red hair is almost identical to my own, save for streaks of silver at the temples, and his gray eyes are the same as mine, but with a hardness to them, a calculating gleam that has always put me on edge.

I nod my head. "Dad."

"Good to see you, son," my father says. "I wish it were in better circumstances."

My mother smacks his chest. "None of that, Bradley. We said we weren't going to mention it."

"*You* said," my father responds gruffly. "We have to think about the backlash to the team. I advised him not to go to that wedding, and it looks like I was right, as usual."

Forbid me to go is more like it—I'm sure that's why his eyes look harder than usual; I'm sure he wishes we were alone so he could tear into me. I'm grateful that with Jack and my mother around he will choose to hold off for appearance's sake, but I know it's coming. He's already had a go at me via text when I wouldn't answer his calls, but he's always preferred to look me in the eye when he's cutting me down.

"He can't live his life worried about what the internet might think," Jack chimes in, his voice lacking its usual cheerfulness. "It's not his fault."

Jack is the only person who knows the more sordid details of the complicated relationship between my father and me, something that I am almost positive my father suspects, but nothing he can prove, thankfully. I know if he could, he would have had Jack off the team years ago, if for no other reason than he's never really liked the way Jack says whatever thought pops into his head, and it is only because of my mother's much kinder heart that he hasn't interfered.

"Whether or not he's at fault is debatable," my father snaps coldly. "Now we just have to deal with the consequences."

"And you're good at that," I snort. "Aren't you, Dad?"

My father narrows his eyes, and for a moment, I feel like a little boy again, being scolded for doing whatever I'd done that day to disappoint him. I have to remind myself that it doesn't matter now, that it doesn't affect my decisions. Well, any more than it has to.

"Please don't fight," my mother sighs. "Can we just be happy that we're all back in the same city? We have people to handle this sort of thing. That Leilani we hired is a real shark. She's got gumption, that one. I'm sure she'll figure out a solution."

"She'd better," my father mutters.

"Christine," Jack says, touching my mother's shoulder with his good hand. "Have you seen the new practice jerseys yet? They just came in the other day. The stitching on them is fucking awesome."

"Language," my mother chides.

"Right," Jack replies sheepishly. "The stitching is . . . cool? Anyway, come see while Ian deals with scary old Leilani."

I give Jack an appreciative look, and he winks back at me as he loops his good arm through my mother's and starts to lead her away. I notice my agent then, Molly, waving at me from the hall that leads further into the building, and I throw one back her way before she disappears, indicating I'll be right behind her.

"We'll catch up later!" my mother calls from over her shoulder. "We'll have dinner soon, okay?"

"Sure," I tell her, glancing at my father, who is still eyeing me sternly.

"We *will* talk later," he says, his tone not allowing any argument. "Call me tonight. And you do whatever Leilani says to make this right, okay?"

"Okay," I answer, my jaw clenching.

"Bradley!"

My father turns his head to my mother, who is gesturing that he follow her and Jack, shooting me one last look that promises a headache-inducing conversation later—but that is later me's problem. I watch him follow after Jack and Mom, making a mental note to buy Jack dinner as thanks after we're done here.

I take a deep breath to steady myself as I head toward the entry that leads to the locker room, making the same path that I remember even after all these years that leads to Coach Daniels's office. I knock at it twice before letting myself in, Coach waving me inside as he finishes up a conversation with a petite woman with golden skin, long black hair, and a pantsuit that screams *don't fuck with me*.

I notice Molly already seated on the other side of Coach's desk, and she tips her chin at me, her hair that is only a few shades darker than mine pulled up tight in her signature bun and only just beginning to gray. She's also a tiny thing, but like the PR agent, she has the "don't fuck with me" vibe down pat. It's why I've stuck with her all these years even from a distance.

"Ian," she says in that throaty tone that comes from years of the menthols she's partial to. "Good to see you."

"You too," I tell her. I haven't seen her in person since last season. "Thanks for coming."

She waves me off. "Of course."

The PR agent turns her attention to me then. "Mr. Chase, glad to meet you."

"Hey," I greet, offering my hand. "You must be Leilani."

"Leilani Kahale," she says back with a nod as she shakes my hand. "It's good to have you back, Ian."

"Sure as hell is," Coach says with a grin. His beard has gained a lot more gray in the years since I've been away—almost stark white against his ebony skin. I know from experience, though, that regardless of how he looks, he could probably kick my ass if he felt inclined to. He stands from his desk, coming around it to pull me in for a hug. "Good to have you back home, son," he says, squeezing me.

He's an inch taller than I am and just as wide. It's like hugging a brick wall, fifty-seven or not.

"It's good to be back," I tell him, clapping him on the shoulder before pulling away. "I just wish I could have come back a little more quietly."

Leilani frowns then, gesturing to one of the chairs across from Coach's desk. "That would have been ideal, but we don't count on wishes around here. We deal with what we've got."

"I like the sound of that," I say.

"So do I," Molly agrees.

"The internet can be a madhouse," Coach sighs. "I wish it was only about hockey, but people like a story. Everything has to be sensationalized nowadays."

"I thought after so much time away, maybe things would have blown over, but I guess with my ex-wife getting remarried . . ."

Leilani nods. "It's unfortunate, but not impossible to deal

with. I've dealt with old scandals before, and usually the best approach is to give the people something better to talk about."

I flinch at her calling everything that happened a *scandal*—but I guess to an outsider, that's exactly what someone would peg it as.

I nod stiffly. "Sounds reasonable. I don't suppose winning games would suffice?"

"We've got six weeks until the season starts," Coach says.

"Right," Leilani agrees. "The last thing we need is for people to spend our entire training camp spreading negativity in regards to the team, which is exactly what a smear campaign against you will be. I know everyone likes to say that all press is good press, but the truth is—giving potential attendees a bad perception of you, and, by association, the team, could hurt ticket sales."

I nod. "So . . . if we can give them something positive to talk about . . ."

"It will hopefully boost the public's perception of you, and again, by association, the team as a whole."

"Okay," I tell her. "I'm open to any ideas you might have. I want to make sure the focus stays on our game, not my past."

Leilani's smile is Cheshire cat–like, looking pleased by my answer. "That's perfect, because as it turns out—we've already got a great start lined up for you."

"Oh?" I arch a brow, looking between her and Coach, who chuckles at my perplexed expression. "What's that?"

"We got a call from BBTV this week, and they were interested in a collaboration of sorts."

"BBTV?"

"The food and home network based in Boston," Leilani explains.

"I don't understand," I admit.

"You've got a good rapport with your teammate Jack Baker, right?"

I turn to look at Molly, but she just shrugs.

"Yeah?" My brow creases. "We grew up together. What's that got to do with anything?"

"Does that mean you know his sister, Delilah, fairly well, then?"

"I . . ." The mention of Lila throws me, mostly because it makes me feel oddly homesick. I spent the better part of middle and high school—even the beginning of college—having Lila Baker tail after me and Jack, and now after having not seen her for so many years, it's odd to have her mentioned twice in one hour. "I mean, it's been a while since we've spoken; we sort of grew apart when I got drafted. Then there was getting married, getting divorced, moving to Calgary . . ." I frown. "I haven't seen her in a long time."

"Well, you'll have the perfect chance to catch up," Leilani says brightly. "Because they want to have a player on her show, and we think you're just the man for the job."

"Me?" My nose wrinkles. "I don't know shit about baking."

Coach laughs. "That's the whole point, son. It'll be endearing."

"Endearing," I scoff. It seems ridiculous, but I suppose in my situation, I don't really have room to be picky. "And Lila is okay with this?"

"It was her idea," Leilani says.

That takes me by surprise. Lila wanted me on her show? I mean, I'm grateful that she'd be willing to help me out, but I can't say that I'm not thrown by it. Given that we haven't had a real conversation since I got drafted—it seems like a stretch.

But then again . . . Lila was always a fucking saint.

I turn to Molly, her expression cool and her lips wrinkling slightly with the way she has them pressed together. "Molly? What do you think?"

"It's a good idea," she admits. "If you're still against making a public statement—"

"I am," I interrupt firmly.

Molly nods. "This is a good alternative. Give the internet some cute shit to talk about. What's cuter than a ginger giant in an apron?"

I have to force myself not to wince at the image. I'm going to look ridiculous. But . . . I guess it's better than the alternative. Besides, what choice do I have?

"All right," I tell them, seeing little other choice even if I were opposed. "I'm cool with it."

"Great," Coach says, slapping his hands together. "We'll have other things lined up for you, but this is a great kickoff."

I nod aimlessly, still feeling nerves flutter through me at the thought of being in front of a camera working with flour and sugar and God knows what else. Definitely not how I imagined reconnecting with Lila again.

I can't help but smile. At least there'll be one good thing to come from all this shit.

I've definitely missed the kid.

Three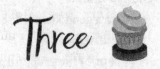

DELILAH

can't believe you didn't consult me first," Theo hisses beside me at the conference table the team is gathered around. "Hockey players are brutes. What if they say something stupid?"

I cock an eyebrow. "Brutes? You never seem to mind Olsson being a brute when you're lusting over him while we watch the games."

"That's different," he mumbles, his pale cheeks darkening. "I can appreciate their brutish form aesthetically without asking them to knock bowls off your counter or take out their teeth on camera."

"I don't actually know that many players who are missing their teeth," I tell him. "And I have met *most* of the players on the Druids at some point or another."

"Whatever," he huffs. "I just wish you'd have run it by me first."

"I panicked! You weren't there."

"I know. We should have rescheduled."

"It's fine," I assure him. "Really. I think people are going to love this."

The network's PR rep, Ben Carter, raps his knuckles on the table. His watery eyes always make him seem like he's either suffering from perpetual allergies or on the verge of tears—but you learn to focus on other things after a while when he has your attention. "Hey, Delilah, still good? Did you have a chance to look at the proposal?"

"Yeah, it looks good to me," I tell him. "Pretty straightforward. I'm glad we went with just one hour-long special for now. I'd hate to be contracted for more if this ends up being a disaster."

"I thought the same," he says with a nod. He glances at Theo, biting his lip. "Hello, Mr. King."

"Hey," Theo answers curtly.

There's a beat of awkward silence before Ben shuffles away to talk to Gia, and I elbow Theo in the ribs. "You're such a dick. He likes you!"

"He also looks like he's been hotboxing his Prius. Seriously, someone needs to put some Visine in his stocking this year for Christmas."

"Such a dick," I echo under my breath.

Theo shrugs. "You don't pay me for my preference in men."

"Thank God."

Gia checks her watch as she clicks her heels across the linoleum floor to take a seat on the other side of Theo. "They should be here soon."

"Oh." Strangely, the question on my tongue only occurs to me at this very moment. Maybe because this whole thing has been kind of a whirlwind of a week. "Did we ever hear who they're sending? Sanchez is nice—the dumb to my brother's dumber, but nice. Olsson has always been cool too. Either of them would be great."

"Oh, actually," Gia says with a slight frown, "I forgot to mention. They're sending a return player. He's been gone for a while. Apparently, he needs some good press."

A shiver runs down my spine—from nerves or excitement I can't tell. Nerves, I decide. Definitely nerves. Because with only a few sentences, I already have a fairly good idea who's about to walk through that door, even as Gia says his name. Even as a knock sounds at the door and the handle turns to let a small entourage spill inside.

And as big of a space in my head that Ian Chase's name takes up—his actual presence is a hundred times worse. Or better. I'm not sure.

He's changed since I last saw him; his hair is longer, his gray eyes are harder—but even with the years between the last time I saw him and now, that small smile he gives me still does the exact same thing to my insides that it did when I was sixteen. Earlier than that, if I were really being honest.

"Lila?"

The recognition in his eyes is colored with a touch of confusion, which is fair, given that the last time he saw me, I was just a knobby-kneed teen with braces whose boobs hadn't come in yet. He's not the only one who did some growing up since we last saw each other.

"Hey, Cupcake," I answer, pushing up from my chair and feeling my lips curl as I cross the room to meet him.

He makes a face. "We're still on about that?"

"You don't just *forget* someone eating half a dozen cupcakes and then throwing them up on my aunt's favorite rug."

He groans. "Serves me right for being your taste tester. Haven't eaten a cupcake since."

I laugh, and for a moment, we're both just standing there, neither of us entirely sure what to do with the other. It never used to be awkward between us. Before, he'd have already picked me up and spun me around until I threatened him to put me down.

Finally, he extends his arms, pulling me into them. "Get over here, kid."

Kid.

That really shouldn't sting as much as it does. *Kid.* Seems ridiculous since my boobs are currently squashed against his abs like overfilled water balloons. If the awkward pat between my shoulders is any indication, I think he might be picking up on that fact also. I snort before I can stop myself, and he cocks his head at me as he pulls away.

"You do realize I'm two years away from thirty, right? I don't think the whole *kid* thing applies anymore."

He frowns, a wrinkle forming between his eyes as he considers this. For a moment, he looks almost uncomfortable. Like he's just now considering that I'm *not* the kid he knew. My ego doesn't know what to do with that. His eyes widen a fraction, and I feel the weight of them as they move over my face, flicking down the length of me so quickly I might almost miss it, but long enough that I feel a flush at the back of my neck. I watch his throat bob with a swallow, his lips turning down in a slight frown.

"I guess you're right," he admits quietly. "Habit."

"Yeah, well." I jut out my chin. "Definitely grown up now."

There's a beat of silence before, "Yeah, I guess you are."

It's an innocent statement, but it gets me all flustered just the same. Not very good for my argument about being all grown up.

"It's good to see you," he tells me.

I nod, my smile tight but miraculously still on my face. How did a beard and a few creases at the corner of his eyes somehow make him hotter?

"You too."

"We're so glad we could make this work," Ben says behind me, busting up the meager moment we were having.

Ian glances over my shoulder to give him his attention, and ridiculously, I almost pout at the loss of it. What the fuck is that about?

A woman not much taller than me with graying, auburn hair shuffles past Ian, plopping down into one of the conference chairs. "Let's get the paperwork signed. I have another meeting."

Ian catches my eye, smiling at the look on my face. He leans in, lowering his voice. "My agent. Not big on nonsense."

"Ah." I chuckle. I hitch a thumb over my shoulder at Theo, who is alternating between trying to put distance between himself and a moon-eyed Ben and getting my attention to come be his buffer. "Mine. Very big on nonsense."

"Better get this out of the way," Ian says. His fingers touch my elbow then, my skin tingling from the contact. "Wanna grab coffee after? Catch up?"

He expects me to compose myself with just the two of us? Has he looked at himself in the mirror lately?

My mouth is a little dry, but somehow, I manage to get the words out. "That would be great."

Another smile that I have to pretend doesn't make my stomach flutter, and I mentally chide myself for acting like the kid he still thinks I am. I'm not sixteen anymore, and Ian has lived a whole life since I saw him last. Fanning the flames of an ancient crush is a recipe for disaster. Best to shut it down quickly.

I watch Ian take his seat, trying to ignore how his shoulders fill out the soft-looking gray cotton of his henley or the way his hair brushes against his collar.

Easier said than done.

— — — — —

Don't be weird. Don't be weird. Don't be weird.

As many times as I repeat it in my head, I can't ascertain whether it's actually helping or not. The meeting went fine; Ian and I didn't get much of a chance to chat anymore while our respective teams hammered out the details of the agreement and pointed out where we needed to sign, and save for a stilted exchange about where we could grab coffee—we've spent most of the walk from the studio in awkward silence.

I think it's that we're both realizing how many years have passed between us, how much life we've lived apart, how different we're bound to be . . . It's difficult to navigate. Neither of us can seem to figure out how to step back into the space we once shared.

"It's just up here," I tell him, pointing at the wooden sign hanging over my favorite coffee shop.

His head bobs with a nod, his long hair sliding against his shoulders with the movement. I can't pretend that I haven't been sneaking glances at the thick, red mass of his hair in the last hour. When he was still in college, he used to keep it shorter, more clean-cut. I've seen plenty of coverage of him during games, so I knew he had let it grow out—but every time I've caught glimpses of him over the years, it's been under a helmet. Without one, it falls back like it's perpetually fresh from a good run-through by his own fingers, tumbling over his ears and touching his shoulders in barely-there curls that elicit a strong urge to touch. More than once I've wondered what it might feel like if I were to run *my* fingers through it.

The smell of fresh coffee hits my nostrils when I step through the door that he opens for me, and it's a bit of a balm for my frazzled nerves. The place is crowded, and falling into line means being shoved further into Ian's side against both of our wills.

"Sorry," I mutter. "They're busy today."

"It's fine," he tells me. "Place looks cool."

"They make these blueberry scones that are basically better than sex," I say offhandedly, immediately blushing when I realize what I've said. "Wow. Sorry."

Ian's cheeks tinge pink when I peek up at him, but he smiles regardless. "They must be some really good fucking scones."

"The best," I assure him.

God. It's unfair that his smile looks like that. Beards are supposed to be for woodsy types and old men. On him, all it does is accentuate how white his teeth are, how perfectly straight. Not to mention the way it frames his lips. Which are plush and pink and entirely too soft-looking for my liking. It's been *years*. It's criminal that he got *better*-looking in that time.

"So, your show. Big star, huh?"

I roll my eyes. "Hardly. It's a local network. It's fun though."

"A local network is still more than a lot of bakers are doing back in their kitchens. Don't sell yourself short."

I can't pretend I don't like the praise, but that could just be an echo of the girl who used to hang on his every word begging for scraps.

"Yeah, well . . ." I rub my arm. "It is pretty cool. A dream, really."

Someone bumps into me then, jostling me to the side, and I teeter for a second before I feel Ian's warm, strong hand bracing at the small of my back to steady me. I feel the weight of it as if it were touching me skin to skin rather than through the cotton of my shirt, tingles shooting up my spine from the contact.

This is getting ridiculous.

"You okay?"

I nod tightly, still hyperfocused on where his fingers are resting against my back. I thought I was prepared for this, thought that seeing Ian Chase again was just going to be a normal, easy thing, that my old crush was just that. Something that would be good and buried after all this time. Apparently, it wasn't buried nearly deep enough.

I can see the moment that he realizes he's touching me; his lips part and the pads of his fingertips press a fraction harder against my shirt, his hand flexing with movement before he lets it fall away. He clears his throat, breaking eye contact and letting his gaze scan the space around us casually.

"Really is crowded in here," he mutters.

"I'm gonna hit the restroom," I blurt out, real cool-like. "Order for me?"

"Sure. What do you want?"

I shake my head distractedly. "Whatever. I'm not picky."

I'm already walking off before he can question me further, my cheeks hot and my body hotter. Just from a stupid fucking *touch*. An innocent one at that.

I don't stop until I'm bent over the bathroom sink, splashing some cool water on my neck and telling myself to get a grip. I have to remind myself that Ian has never seen me as anything more than Jack's kid sister. Hell, he's still calling me kid *now*, after all this time. So obviously, nothing has changed. It would be utterly stupid to let an old crush have me acting like a fool.

I give myself a pointed look in the mirror, taking note of my freckled nose and my big brown eyes that make me look younger than I am, my full mouth forming a pout. No wonder he still sees me as a kid. I glare down at my even fuller chest.

"You guys were supposed to help me out when you filled in," I mutter bitterly. "So much for that."

I sigh as I grip the sink, shaking my head.

Stop being stupid. Ian is your friend. You've had plenty of time to get that through your head. Go back out there and act like a normal, twenty-eight-year-old woman and not a lovestruck teenager seeing a cute boy for the first time.

I nod to my reflection, vowing to do just that.

With my new resolution in mind, I feel more confident when I step back out of the bathroom. Ian waves me over to the little table he's settled at, and I flash him a bright smile that isn't awkward or stiff, because I *can* be normal around him, damn it. I *can*.

But my smile falters when I get to the table.

"What's that?"

He follows the point of my finger to the drink he's bought for me. "What?"

"The drink." I eye the caramel-drizzled mountain of whipped cream, noting the sprinkles scattered over it. Not to mention the chocolate drizzle on the inside of the cup. "What is it?"

"You don't like them anymore?" He looks confused. "This shit was all you drank back in the day."

"You remembered my drink?"

His brow arches, looking even more confused. Like *I'm* the silly one for thinking him remembering something as arbitrary as a disgustingly sweet drink I used to indulge in once a week over a decade ago is unfathomable.

"I . . . yeah?"

I actually feel my heart beat faster.

That's when I realize I'm in real fucking trouble.

Four

Shit, have I already fucked up?

It felt like a nice gesture, getting her old drink, but the way she's looking at me—lips parted and a little furrow between her brow—makes me wonder if it was weird.

She pulls out the chair on the opposite side slowly, sinking into it while eyeing the sugar-loaded monstrosity warily. "I can't believe you remember my drink."

"Kind of hard to forget sugar coma in a cup," I scoff.

Her mouth twitches in a smile. Her smile causes the cute little dimple she's always had to deepen, and I'm struck with the realization that while it used to make her face more babyish, more angelic even—now it just accentuates how stunning she's become. It makes me feel strange to acknowledge that, even in my head.

Not that it's kept me from noticing, because *fuck* have I noticed.

The Lila I remember was all elbows and skinny legs, but *this* Lila—it feels almost wrong to refer to her as a kid, even for nostalgia's sake. This Lila is pouty lips and luscious curves and a smile that makes me wish I were wearing tighter underwear, and fuck *me* these are not thoughts I should be having, but my brain hasn't gotten the memo yet that this is *Lila*. Jack's little sister and my old friend.

I try to think back to the time when I last saw her—she had to be, what, seventeen? Between the draft and her going to college out of state, and then moving to France . . . it feels like a lifetime since I sat this close to Delilah Baker. Looking at her now, it seems like she's *lived* a lifetime since I last sat across from her. Save for her big brown eyes that are just as wide and clear as they were back then, I can't see much left of the scrawny kid I used to know.

This Lila isn't a kid at all, that's for damn sure.

"You know," she chuckles, tearing me out of my inappropriate tumble of thoughts, "I haven't had one of these in forever."

"Finally started caring about your glucose levels?"

She rolls her eyes, pulling the plastic cup closer. "In France, it's all about espresso. I got addicted to it."

"Oh, I can get you something else," I try.

She shakes her head. "This is good. Really."

She wraps her lips around the straw, and I watch for a second too long as she takes a drink. I clench my teeth as I force my eyes away toward my own cup, bringing it to my mouth to sip if for no other reason than to distract myself from the urge to stare.

"Mm," she hums. "Okay. So that's still amazing."

I glance up, but the sight of her pink tongue flicking out to catch some stray whipped cream on her lip sparks that same strange feeling in my chest. My heart rate seems to be as slow on the uptake as my brain, if the way it jumps at the sight is any indication.

I clear my throat. "So . . . France? That must have been a trip."

"Oh, it was amazing. A fucking dream, actually. The pâtissier I studied under—Olivier—total grump, but he's brilliant. I think I saw him smile maybe . . . twice? In three years? But the man can bake macarons that'll make your taste buds orgasm."

My ears heat, and I have to hope that they're not peeking out of my hair. It's the second time in fifteen minutes that she's made a sex reference to food. It's doing nothing for the me who's trying desperately to rein in my brain's confused reaction to her being so . . . grown up. I don't know how to navigate little Lila making sex references of any kind.

My eyes flick to her chest as if they have a mind of their own, and I have to hold back a snort.

Little. Right.

"That sounds great," I mumble, tilting my cup again for another swallow of my coffee. I rattle the ice after awkwardly. "Your brother sent me a few pics when you first left, but you know how Jack is with keeping up with people."

Maybe I would have been better prepared, I think bitterly.

She laughs, her dark brown eyes glinting. "Yeah, he came over my first year. I'm surprised you got that much. I bet it was the worst photo too."

"Half your head was cut off."

"That tracks."

"It was a very cute half of a head," I tease.

She visibly stiffens, and it takes me a second to hear what I've said. It's something I would have said to her when she was a teenager and sulking. Innocent. Without meaning. Does it sound like flirting now? Jesus. It's been too long since I've interacted with a woman outside of a meaningless one-night stand. The easy air between Lila and me that we once had is dryer now, harder to manage. Maybe it's simply because it's been so long? It sure as hell isn't helping that she looks like . . . Well, that she looks like the way she does.

I clear my throat. "Was the language barrier an issue?"

"Oh God," she says in a sort of laugh-scoff. "It took me *months* to even be able to have a decent conversation. Olivier *refused* to talk to me in English. He always said: 'If you want to cook like the French, you have to speak like the French.'"

"He sounds like a dick."

She shakes her head, smiling. "No, he was brilliant. I think most brilliant people tend to be a little eccentric."

"Is eccentric a nice word for 'kind of a dick'?"

She laughs again, and I can't help but enjoy the sound. Lila laughs with her whole body; she throws her head back, and it comes from deep down in her stomach, her entire face lighting up like she's not thinking about how she looks or what she sounds like—Lila laughs like she's happy to just *be*. It's infectious.

It's also hard to ignore how it makes my chest feel too warm.

"But you got it, right? I mean, you must have, eventually."

She nods. "I'm still not going to get snatched up as anyone's interpreter, but I get by."

"Well, go on," I say with a wave of my hand. "Talk French to me."

I say it as a joke, mostly, which means I could never anticipate the way my pulse quickens when she opens her mouth, sounding every bit a native to the French tongue in my very limited experience as her soft tone shapes softer words.

"Tu es mignon avec tes longs cheveux."

Jesus.

My fucking dick twitches. *Twitches.* Because Lila Baker just said God knows what to me in French. What the hell is that about? I clench my teeth, mentally sending down a message for my cock to settle the fuck down.

"What um"—I have to clear my throat again, because it's suddenly dry—"What did you say?"

Her smile is just a bit wicked as she leans to prop her chin on her fists. "Wouldn't you like to know?"

I would. I really would.

"Brat," I manage with a tight laugh, and I don't miss the way her eyes round slightly with the word, which is interesting. It's also something I shouldn't be noticing, probably. "You sounded pretty French to me."

"Well, I was there for three years." She twirls her straw in her cup. "What about you? Big change from Calgary to Boston. Do you miss it?"

"Parts of it, maybe?" I shrug, desperate for the distraction. "But Boston is home, you know? I'm really happy to be back."

Her mouth turns into a thin line, and I can see the flash of pity in her eyes, even if it only lasts a moment. It's still long enough for something sour to settle in my stomach. I know where her mind is, because it's written all over her face. I can't say why it's so upsetting to know that Lila is thinking at this very moment about all the reasons I left, but I don't like it.

"I didn't read the stories," she says quietly, confirming what I already knew. "I know they're bullshit."

And weirdly, I believe she believes that. Lila always did have an overinflated opinion of me. She thought I hung the moon when we were kids. Even after all these years, I don't like the thought of marring that image, even if it was always misguided. When we were younger, sometimes it felt like I could do no wrong in her eyes, and in turn, that used to give me the confidence sometimes to feel the same way, as silly as it sounds. I used to think it was because she was so much like a sister to me. Now that thought feels . . . odd.

I can't meet her eyes, focusing on my cup instead. "Yeah. Well."

"I still can't believe people are stirring it all back up again," she says irritably. "You would think they had better things to do."

"Yeah."

Apparently, I've been reduced to monosyllables.

I could tell her, I think fleetingly. Jack knows, after all. There's no reason why I couldn't tell Lila. I don't even know what's keeping me from doing so right now. Maybe it's just that it's too much, after so long. Dumping my problems on her after seeing her for the first time in practically a decade is probably a weird move.

"Well," I say instead, "hopefully I don't embarrass us too badly on your show, and people get something better to talk about."

She smiles again. Which means more of that fucking dimple. I try to take another drink, only to realize that I've already downed it all. Great.

"I won't let you burn your fingers off," she teases. "You wouldn't be able to hold a stick again, and then *I'd* be the one in the hot seat."

I can't help but grin. "I doubt they'd miss me too bad. I'm old news now."

"Shut up." She rolls your eyes. "I watch your games when I can. You've still got it, Cupcake."

There's a flicker of warmth in my chest, but whether it's from her silly nickname or her praise, I can't be sure. "Well, let's hope Boston agrees with you."

"They will," she assures me.

She brushes one thick tendril of her chestnut waves over her shoulder, and my eyes follow the silken movement in a way that just feels too *aware* for my best friend's little sister. My attention feels like the kind I would give a beautiful woman I saw across a bar, and I realize it's because I *would* if I didn't know her. If we didn't have the history we do. What the fuck?

I don't even realize I'm still staring until she talks again.

"So . . . Mei got remarried, huh?" she asks casually, not looking at me. "How do you feel about that? Are you okay?"

I feel a wave of genuine confusion. "Okay?"

"Yeah, you know . . . It must be weird."

"Not really," I tell her honestly. "I'm happy for her. They're great together."

I get the feeling that Lila must have at least seen the headlines from the last couple of weeks. Regardless of what she believes me to be capable of, it's clear that the possibility is still floating around in her mind that I might be hung up on my ex-wife, that I might have tried to sabotage her wedding . . . whatever else the news outlets have spat out lately. She gives me a strange look, almost like maybe she doesn't believe me when I say I'm fine with Mei being off the market again, but it feels odd to try to reassure her. I mean, what would be the point? It doesn't matter if Lila might think I'm still torn up over Mei.

"This is weird, right?"

My train of thought falters as I give her my attention, watching as she leans back in her chair and crosses her arms loosely over her stomach.

"What's weird?"

"Talking after so long. It didn't used to be weird."

"Oh."

I consider this, taking in all the things that have changed with her; her soft mouth, her softer curves, the spray of freckles over her nose that have gone from endearingly cute to sinfully enticing—all the things I shouldn't be noticing about her but can't help but notice, anyway.

"It's just been a while."

"You're different," she says with a crease on her forehead.

"Am I?"

"You used to smile a lot more," she points out. "You seem more serious now."

My mouth curls down. "A lot has changed, I guess."

"That's fair," she reasons. "I can't say I haven't changed a little bit myself."

She says it offhandedly, probably just trying to commiserate, but my eyes tilt down to the stretch of her T-shirt over her chest compulsively—it's an easy mistake, I think, given that her crossed arms make everything above them more prominent—too quickly for me to even realize what I'm doing, but not quick enough that I don't notice *her* noticing I've done it.

What the fuck is wrong with you? This is Lila.

I've never been more grateful for growing my hair out. There's no way my ears aren't red.

"You've definitely changed," I mutter distractedly, only making the moment weirder.

Fucking hell.

I rattle the ice in my now-empty cup. "I'd better be getting back to Jack's," I blurt out. "He mentioned going over some game footage before we start training camp."

"Of course he did," she says with a breezy laugh.

When the fuck did I become so conscious of dimples?

She stands, taking her cup with her, and I do the same, hovering awkwardly and making a point to keep my eyes on her face, where it's safe.

"I'll see you next week, though, right?"

I nod, all too aware of how I tower over her standing like we are. I don't know why it matters.

"Yeah," I tell her. "I'll see you next week."

She surprises me by reaching out with her arms, and for the second time today, I'm subjected to the softness of her body pressing against mine. It's nothing we haven't done before. We've hugged a thousand times in our lives. There's no reason for me to be so damn on *edge*. Maybe this really is weird, like she said. Maybe we just need time to readjust. Eventually, my brain has to catch up and remember that it shouldn't be having all these weird thoughts about her. Right?

I hold my empty cup in one hand to loop my arm around her shoulders, returning the hug as the scent of her lavender shampoo and a lingering sweetness underneath it that must be all her assaults my senses, just as soft as she has come to be.

She really isn't a kid anymore, I think distantly.

I have no idea what to do with that.

— — — —

Jack is sprawled out on the living room couch when I get back to the apartment, his hair wet from what I assume is a recent shower and his arm in a different sling—lime green this time.

"How many of those do you have?"

He glances down at his sling. "I don't know. Seven or eight, maybe? The standard ones are just navy or black. Shit is boring."

"Heaven forbid," I murmur, locking the apartment door behind me before heading to the fridge and grabbing a beer.

"How was the meeting?"

I unscrew the cap from the amber bottle, taking a drink before giving Jack a shrug. "It went okay. We got everything signed, at least. Molly made sure that I won't be pushed into any shirtless nonsense at the last second."

"Better not be getting naked around Dee," he says with mock indignance. "How was she, anyway? Did you two catch up?"

I can only hope that my face doesn't betray the twinge of guilt I feel when my mind immediately wanders to her dimple and her too-soft curves that shouldn't even be on my radar. They *aren't* on my radar, I chastise myself.

"We got coffee after the meeting," I answer flippantly. "She told me a bit about her time in France."

Jack makes a face. "Fucking hated it there. No one liked me!"

"Wow, that must have been a novelty for you."

"Damn right it was. I'm lovable." He juts out his chin in a way that reminds me of his sister. Now *that's* an odd thought. "Dee had this douchey boyfriend for a while. I met him once when he came back for Christmas with her. God, he was a tool. He acted like wine drinking was some kind of religious experience and was appalled when I had the gall to offer him a Michelob."

It makes no sense that I bristle at the mention of Lila's past boyfriend—I'm sure she's had several over the years, with as gorgeous as she's grown to be. I tell myself it's a lingering sense of protection for a pseudo–little sister. Even if it feels off.

"She seeing anyone now?"

Jesus Christ. What the fuck, Ian?

Jack arches an eyebrow. "Why?"

"Just realized I forgot to ask her," I say as casually as I can muster. "No big."

Appeased, Jack shrugs. "She hasn't had a boyfriend for a while. Thank fuck. I hate thinking about some meathead boning my little sister."

My shoulders tense.

Okay, this is getting ridiculous. What the actual *fuck is wrong with me?*

"Yeah, I hear you," I toss back. "Weird that she's not a scrawny kid anymore."

"Tell me about it," Jack huffs. "She turned into a Grade A hottie, which means I have to worry about dicks sniffing around her all the time."

"Is it weird that you refer to your sister as a hottie?"

Jack smirks. "Nah. We have the same genetics, after all. Just an informed opinion from an objective standpoint."

"They should have put your head in a sling," I snort. "It's gotten too big."

"That's what she said," he laughs.

I roll my eyes. "You still want to watch that footage?"

"Yeah. Pittsburgh got a new center last year. He was a rookie, but he had a killer season. We play them first thing when the new season starts. You need to see him play."

"We should just slap a coach's jersey on you," I muse, dropping onto the couch beside him. "You're almost as bad as he is."

"Someone has to make sure you guys can still win a game with me out of commission for another two months."

"Right," I deadpan. "How will we go on without you?"

"Don't act like you're going to mope when you skate back out as our left wing and look to your right and I'm not there."

"I'll try to hold back my tears."

"You're excited to be back, though, right?"

"Mostly, yeah," I tell him. "I could do without the stupid-ass internet chirping, but it does feel good to be back home."

"Did you talk to your dad again?"

I can feel myself grow immediately tense, a common occurrence when my father is involved. My official relationship with my father is that publicly, we're solid, but privately? He can fuck right off. Not that it stops him from calling every so often to try to critique my performance even though I was playing for *another* team. And now that I've up and gone against his wishes and taken Mom up on her prodding to get me to take the trade back home . . . things are even more tense.

"He's still not happy I'm back," I admit. "Especially since everyone is making it their business to try and suss out why I was at Mei and Bella's wedding."

"Because there's no way you could have just been invited, obviously," Jack snorts.

"Dude, I have read everything from I tried to object when the minister called for it to me cornering her in her honeymoon suite, demanding an audience."

"Bella would have kicked your ass."

I nod. "Absolutely she would have."

"Well, good thing he doesn't have the final say in where you play," Jack says smugly. "He'd have a lot of explaining to do if he pushed you too hard on it."

"But so would I," I point out with a sigh.

Jack frowns, no doubt trying to think of what to say to that. I wave him off.

"It's whatever," I tell him. "I just have to keep my head down until this shit with the press blows over. Once we start winning games, Dad won't give a shit where I am as long as I keep my mouth shut."

"And Abigail?" Jack prods gently. "Have you talked to her since you've been back?"

I grind my teeth together. Abby's name always elicits strange emotions inside me—ones that are usually colored with guilt. "Just some texts here and there." I shoot him an apologetic look. "I gave her your address in case she wants to visit. I hope that's okay."

"Shut up." He waves me off. "Of course it is. I'll add her to the list with the doorman so she can get up without any fuss." He eyes me warily. "Sorry," Jack offers, clearly seeing how tense I've become. "I wasn't trying to rehash old shit. I was just curious."

"It's fine." I shrug. "Let's just watch your footage."

"Sure. Yeah."

He fiddles with the remote, flipping through recordings in the DVR, making a face that is equal parts concentration and worry. It's funny—I've seen Lila make the same one. The reminder of her inadvertently causes my mind to wander back to our visit at the coffee shop, the scent of lavender and sugar still lingering in my senses.

"I was really surprised by how different Lila looks," I say offhandedly. "You should have sent more pictures and prepared me while I was away."

"You know I suck at pictures. You should use social media like a normal person."

"You know why I don't."

"Ah." He looks sheepish, no doubt remembering the onslaught that awaits me on social media on any given day. "Right. Sorry."

He frowns then, peering at me from the side. "Wait. Are *you* trying to say that my sister is a Grade A hottie? Because that's weird, dude."

"I didn't say that," I say a little too quickly.

"But you're thinking it?"

"I'm not thinking anything! I'm just saying she grew up, that's all. It was a surprise."

A knock you on your ass surprise, that's for sure.

Jack narrows his eyes for a moment, finally turning his attention back to the TV and grumbling, "Don't be getting any ideas about my sister. That would be weird as fuck. Practically incestuous."

I want to argue that Lila and I are absolutely *not* related—but I imagine it would do nothing to help my case. Besides, it doesn't *matter*, because for all intents and purposes, he's right. It would be weird for me to think of her like that.

It *is* weird.

"Wasn't thinking that at all," I argue feebly. "Chill, man."

I guiltily remember my body's reaction to Lila and her little French lesson, one I desperately wish I could remember the words from so I could google what the fuck she said.

"Mhm." He hits a button, bringing up the recording, and his short attention span saves me from any more grilling. "Oh shit. This right here. Watch this. Fucking wild what this kid can do with a stick."

I force myself to focus my attention on the screen, but admittedly, I'm still turning over Jack's words in my head, almost like they're stones that I expect to yield something new beneath them if I shuffle them around enough.

Stop being weird, I tell myself. *You're just surprised by how much she's changed. That's all. You could never think of Lila as anything other than the kid sister you never had.*

And those are exactly the reins I'm going to tie around my thoughts, because that's exactly what I should be thinking. There's no good reason to entertain anything different. In fact, it would be better to just not think of Lila at all. Obviously, my brain is being too weird for that.

And yet, for all my reasoning . . . none of it stops me from thinking about her smile.

Five

DELILAH

I'm double-checking my measured ingredients when I hear footsteps on the stage behind me, glancing to my left and relaxing when I see that it's only Ava.

"Girl." She gives me a pointed look. "Why didn't you tell me that you had a hot-ass hockey player in your back pocket?"

I roll my eyes. "He's not 'in my back pocket.' He's just an old friend."

"You've never mentioned this 'old friend' before."

"Yeah, well . . ." I shrug, giving my attention back to the little measuring bowls on the counter. "He's been gone for a while. We haven't really been in touch for the last few years."

"I hope distance makes the heart grow fonder, because . . ." She fans herself exaggeratedly. "Wow."

I know she's just teasing, so it makes no sense for me to feel a pang of irritation at her obvious thirsting for Ian. I mean, can I really blame her? The man is sex on legs. Always has been, really.

The years have only made him better. Ian Chase ages like Gouda, and I love me some fucking cheese.

"I'm practically a sister to him," I mumble, tamping down the thought. "It's not like that."

She narrows her eyes, leaning in to study me in that freakish way of hers that lets me know I'm being entirely transparent. "But you'd *like* it to be like that, huh?"

"I didn't say that," I protest weakly.

"Oh, honey." She pats my shoulder. "How long have you had it bad for the ginger giant?"

I frown, my hands stilling over a bowl of cherries. "Pretty much since puberty?"

"Fuck," she says, her tone more sympathetic. "Is this all awful for you? I know he was married before. It's gotta suck having him back around after already going through him being taken off the market."

I wave her off. "Please. It's not like I've been waiting at the door for him. I've dated plenty since he left. Good sex has a way of making you forget things."

"Yeah, but . . . I mean, you never forget your first love."

I snort. It's a silly notion. I didn't *love* Ian. What I felt for him was just teenage hormones and a too-intense crush on the first boy who ever gave me attention—romantic or not. That's all.

"Seriously, it's not that big of a deal," I assure her.

She doesn't look convinced. "Mhm."

"Don't you have something you're supposed to be doing?"

"I'm checking in with the talent," she says matter-of-factly. "Part of the job."

"I'll bet."

More footsteps sound behind her, heavier ones this time, and when I turn my head to peer over her shoulder, Ian meanders on set wearing his Druids jersey and a disgruntled expression that looks insanely good on him.

"Hey," I call, the word coming out as more of a croak.

Ava turns her body, glancing at Ian for a moment and then back at me to where I'm surely gaping like a stranded goldfish. A smirk colors her mouth, and I have to rein in the urge to elbow her in the gut.

"Hey, Ian," Ava says as Ian steps closer to the counter where we're gathered. "Dee here will give you another rundown of the takes we're getting first. I have . . . stuff to do. Over . . . there."

She brushes past us, shooting me a thumbs-up and winking like she's just been incredibly smooth. Normally, I would be calling her out, but as it is, I'm doing well not to drool over the aforementioned ginger giant who looks perturbed and cranky, which somehow makes him even *more* endearing.

"I didn't know they were going to put makeup on me," he grumbles.

"Your toxic masculinity is showing," I remark dryly.

He scoffs. "I don't give a shit about that, but she said she wanted to make my lips *kissable*. What the fuck does that even mean? They're all shiny and sticky now. Feels weird."

My eyes dip down to the lips in question, finding he's absolutely right. And they *are* kissable, so much so that the urge to lean in and taste them is as powerful as it is wrong, and I manage a tight smile instead.

"That's show business, Cupcake."

He eyes the ingredients laid out in front of me. "What are we making, anyway?"

"A cherry clafoutis," I tell him. "It's a French pastry."

"Another thing you picked up over there?"

"Among other things."

"Speaking of picked up." He makes a face. "Jack told me all about some douchebag you dated over there."

"Jack is biased," I laugh. "Etienne was nice." His frown deepens, and some hopeless part of me wants it to be jealousy that has him looking so sour, as silly as that is. Maybe that's what leads me to say, "Plus, he was really hot. Dirty talk is ten times better in French."

The only reaction Ian has is a barely-there clench of his jaw, but that could just be him feeling awkward. Most likely is, if I'm being honest with myself. I can't say why I feel the urge to keep pushing his buttons.

"Definitely not something I need to hear about, I think," he says quietly.

God, I wish it was more than just seeing me as a sister. I really do. And here I am telling Ava how over Ian I am. Maybe I really believed that, before I saw him again. Maybe you really don't forget your first love. *Crush*, I correct. *Crush*.

"Anyway," I say, reaching to the other side of the counter and grabbing the pink cloth there. "I have your apron right here." He eyes it like I've just asked him to put on a Speedo in the studio, and I can't help but laugh. "You don't give a shit about your male ego, remember?"

"Yeah, yeah."

He takes the apron from me—just like mine, with the show's name embroidered over the front—gripping the looped neck in his hands and lifting it to pull it over his head. The pink totally clashes with his hair, but the sight of him in it takes him down from smolderingly sexy to comfortably cute. I should make him wear it more often so I can have an easier time not turning into a simp whenever he's within a ten-foot radius.

"Dee!" the cameraman calls. "They want to know if you're ready to get rolling."

"I think so," I call back, checking my ingredients again to make sure that, yes, they're all there and accounted for. I peek over at Ian, who looks a little queasy as he grimaces at the large camera being rolled up closer to the stage. "You ready, Cupcake?"

His face is still sort of pinched when he meets my eyes, but he nods, albeit warily. "Let's just get this over with."

"That's the spirit," I laugh.

Thirty minutes into filming, and things are going far better than I expected them to go, admittedly. Ian has never shown any sort of aptitude in the kitchen, from what I remember, and I half worried he might drop a bowl or stick his hand into the batter or something. He's engaging if not quiet in front of the cameras, answering my questions and asking plenty of his own as I walk him through mixing the ingredients, and all of it reminds me of summers in my aunt's kitchen with him impatiently waiting to taste something I was trying out. It's distracting, but not enough that I can't maintain my normal camera persona.

"So, that should do it for the batter," I note, checking the consistency. "How are my cherries?"

Ian peeks into the baking dish that he's been meticulously arranging cherries into with some slivered almonds, as if they needed to be *just* right at the bottom. "They're in there."

"Julia Child would be so proud," I laugh.

His brow furrows, eyeing my bowl. "That looks like cake batter."

"It's similar," I tell him. "The almond extract makes it a little nuttier."

I dip my spoon into the bowl, bringing the edge to my mouth to taste as flavors explode against my tongue. "Mm."

Ian makes an almost imperceptible noise, almost like clearing his throat but softer, and I notice his big body shift a little beside me.

"You're not supposed to eat the batter," he scolds.

"Okay, Dad," I scoff. I smirk in his direction as I deliberately give my spoon another lick to catch the lingering bits of batter I missed. "But it's the best part." I wink at the camera after I slide my spoon from my mouth. "Listen, I know raw batter is bad, but sometimes being bad is worth it." I *mm* exaggeratedly. "Life is short, or as the French say, 'la vie est trop courte pour boire du mauvais vin.'"

Ian's mouth is turned down into a frown, but his eyes aren't on mine, instead fixed on my mouth. I can almost imagine a slight heat to his gaze, and if I let my eyes linger too long on his face, I can almost tell myself his cheeks are slightly flushed. It makes me want to whisper more French nothings in his ear. Dirty talk really *is* better in French, honestly.

Ian is still looking at my mouth, and it's stupid, the idea that pops up into my head, and they're definitely going to cut it from filming, but the tight look on Ian's face makes it irresistible.

"Oh, come on, Cupcake," I coo. "Live a little."

My heart hammers a bit as I grab another spoon and dip it into the batter, holding it out with my hand underneath to catch any drippings so that Ian can taste it for himself. There's a moment where I think he'll refuse; his lips are pursed and his eyes are hard to read, and I'm seconds away from pulling the spoon back and laughing it off as a joke when his wide palm reaches to cup the back of my knuckles, his fingers curling around the hand holding my spoon and enveloping it in his warm grip.

The inhale that rushes past my lips is short and quiet, but as close as he is, I can't help but wonder if he hears it. His eyes hold mine until the last second as he pulls the spoon in and lets his plush lips taste some of the batter he'd just been scolding me over, but I can't even bring myself to point out this hypocrisy with the way my skin is tingling beneath his touch.

"It is good," he admits, his fingers still holding my knuckles. "Still bad for you though."

I swallow, something that wasn't all that difficult prior to about seven seconds ago, pulling back my hand and both mourning and celebrating the loss of his touch for the havoc it wreaks on my system.

"Right," I laugh shakily, trying to compose myself. I manage to look sure when I glance back at the camera—I think so, at least—but I can't help but wonder if they can see my pulse hammering in my throat even from the other side of the lens. "Ian has always been a stickler for the rules."

I don't look at him as I set my spoon on the rest nearby, focusing on the bowl of batter that has just become the bane of my existence.

"Let's pour this over the cherries, huh?" I remember the whole appeal of "big hockey player trying to bake" then, giving Ian my brightest smile that I can only hope doesn't betray my racing heart. "Or do you want to do the honors?"

"I can do it," Ian says quietly, nodding as he reaches for the bowl.

I nod at the sleeves of his jersey. "Unless you want a dry cleaning bill, I suggest you roll those up."

"Oh." He glances at his wrists. "Right."

I watch as he reaches to grip the fabric of one sleeve, starting the slow process of rolling it up, and my tongue suddenly becomes glued to my mouth.

Oh.

My.

God.

My eyes move greedily over the corded, lightly freckled muscle of Ian's forearms, drinking in the swirls of ink that cover each one.

When did he get those?

I can make out some shapes and a block of script that I can't read at this distance, and my fingers itch to explore, to see how far they go. Does he have them anywhere else, I wonder?

He continues to roll each sleeve right up over his elbow, and I can see more dark ink creeping up his biceps, making them all the more lickable. My brain actually fizzles a little. Someone could ask me right now what the hell it is we are making, and I might honestly not be able to tell them. It could be a goddamned soufflé for all I know.

"Here," he says, his sleeves effectively rolled and my mind effectively blown. "Let me."

I nod mutely as he takes the bowl from me, and I know I should be explaining something, giving a fun fact about the dish and where it originated—but I am helpless to do anything but watch him pour batter over a bowl of cherries as if it's the sexiest thing a man has ever done. Honestly, at this very moment, it very well might be.

Ian looks pleased when he's done, giving me one of his rare-ish smiles that is full and open, and it's too much, really. Baking, ink, and full-blown smiles? They're going to be paying me workers' comp after this for stress-related injuries. I don't realize I'm just standing there gawking like an idiot until I hear Ava quietly saying my name, a gentle way of telling me to snap the hell out of it.

My cheeks flame, and it takes absolutely *every* bit of willpower to smile at the camera and pretend that whatever . . . *that* was didn't happen, but I'm fully aware that the studio and Ian all saw me lose my mind for about four seconds.

And we haven't even gotten the damned thing in the oven yet.

- - - - -

"Cut! That was great, guys. We've got plenty to work with here."

I shoot Greg a smile before peeking to my left to check on Ian, finding him already wrestling the apron over his head only seconds after the camera has stopped rolling.

"Wow, you were counting the seconds down until you could do that, weren't you?" I laugh.

He rolls his eyes, tossing the garment on the counter before reaching to rub at the back of his neck. "Damn string was irritating the shit out of me."

"Sure it was." I pull my own apron off, chancing a glance at my chest and confirming that, yes, there is flour there. "How did you manage not to get a single thing on your jersey?"

He peers down his front. "Maybe I'm just less clumsy than you are."

"Oh, fuck you."

His lips twitch. "You're the professional here. How do you manage to get so dirty?"

"Well, when you're carrying the team . . ."

He rolls his eyes. "I helped."

"You did," I chuckle. "You didn't burn anything down, at least."

He follows me when I step away from the set, his heavy footsteps not far behind mine when we move from the raised platform of the stage to the refreshments area set up nearby. I grab a bottle of water and then offer one back to Ian, eyes lingering briefly on his hands as the memory of what his sleeves are hiding flit through my thoughts.

"So," I say as I unscrew the cap on my water, "I never pegged you as being into tattoos."

He looks thoughtful for a brief moment before he shrugs. "My mom always said that you can't get just one, because you'll become addicted. I guess she was right."

"I only got one," I counter. I take a swig from my bottle before adding, "Haven't had the urge yet to get any more."

He cocks one eyebrow at me, perching his fists on his hips to give me a stern look that absolutely *doesn't* have me repressing a shiver. "You have a tattoo?"

I beam back at him. "Sure do."

"What is it?"

"A better question would be: *Where* is it?" I wink, and I notice a slight flush of color at his cheekbones. Wow. Okay. I like that reaction. It almost makes me believe that I might eventually get him to see me as *Delilah*—not Lila, the kid sister of his best friend. "But I'm keeping both a secret. For now."

He still looks a little stunned by my boldness, and to me, it feels like a small victory. Sure, I'll never get to play out all the fantasies I've entertained of Ian Chase over the years—ones made marginally worse after that bit of spoon-feeding not even half an hour ago—but at least I can give him back a fraction of the discomfort he's caused me in my young life. It's only fair, I think.

"Hey, guys!" Ava practically skips toward us, holding a clipboard and looking cheerful. "That was amazing. I was totally sure that Ian was going to burn himself at one point—"

Ian scoffs. "What is it with everyone thinking I am going to burn something?"

"—but, you guys did great," Ava finishes, ignoring Ian's grumbling. "Did you plan that moment with the spoon? Because it was totally hot."

"What?" Ian looks taken aback. "It wasn't hot."

My lips purse. "Ava . . ."

"What?" She crosses her arms over her chest. "It *was*. I guarantee viewers are going to eat that shit up. I thought for sure you planned it."

"Of course we didn't," Ian asserts, sounding almost irritated. "We're friends. We don't want to give people the wrong idea."

There's *no* reason for that statement to sting, considering it's true, but there's still an irritating sensation in my chest when he says it. Especially since he looks so uneasy right now—shifting his weight from one foot to the other, his lips twisted in a frown.

So much for him ever seeing me any differently.

"Right," I answer tightly. "It was just spur of the moment. It didn't mean anything."

"Whatever." Ava waves us both off. "It was still hot."

Ian still looks positively uncomfortable, and even with the long stretch of years between the me today and the me who used to follow him around begging for crumbs of his attention—seeing the physical proof that he still thinks of me as the dumb kid who clung to his ankles . . . It's not the best feeling in the world. Actually, it's downright awful.

I turn to Ian, patting him on the arm. "You did great, Cupcake. I'm really glad we did this. And we should catch up again soon, yeah?"

His brows turn down. "You got somewhere to be?"

"Oh, you know . . ." I shrug noncommittally. "Just have some things to check on. But I'll talk to you soon, okay?"

He nods stiffly, still looking at me strangely. Probably because I am *acting* strange. Or maybe I'm acting normally, and it just feels strange to me. I turn away from Ian and Ava to leave them standing at the refreshments table, heading for nowhere in particular, just wanting to put space between Ian and me and let my brain breathe. I can't believe that after all this time, Ian can still make my head a mess like this.

It stays messy for the rest of the day, even much later when I'm sitting safe in my apartment and staring at a text that came through from Ian while I was in the shower.

IAN: I had a lot of fun today. Let's hang out again soon.

I've typed out a few innocuous replies that all sound stupid in my head, finally settling on a generic: I had fun too! Definitely!

I know that if Ian is back for good, I am going to have to get a handle on these old feelings rearing their ugly heads, that I'll have to figure out a way to navigate them if there's any chance of slipping back into a friendship with the guy whose name I used to doodle in my notebook margins with little hearts.

Maybe some distance is the best answer. It's not like I *have* to hang out with Ian again anytime soon. Some time to get my head in order would probably be just the thing to figure my shit out and stop acting ridiculous.

Yes, I think. That's definitely the right call. I'll just make sure to only spend time with Ian when there's a good amount of buffer. One-on-one is definitely off-limits.

I cling to that resolve through brushing my teeth and readying for bed, halfway managing to convince myself that it will work, that I'll start to feel less crazy in his presence as time goes by.

As I crawl into bed, I actually feel mostly optimistic about the whole thing. I close my eyes for the first time since Ian blew back into town, not thinking about his voice or his eyes or his deep laugh that makes my stomach clench.

Well, mostly.

Six 🧁

IAN

"All right, men, remember this drill!" Coach Harris shouts from near the goal line. "We're getting a tip-in early, right?" He points at Sanchez. "Good feet! Pull that puck around and let's look for a fall."

Practice might be over, but Coach has apparently not let up on his insistence of after-practice skill drills immediately after our usual session. He has us all lined up at the neutral zone, ready to skate in one after the other for some rapid-fire shooting.

For the first time being out with the rest of the team, I'm fairly pleased with how well I've meshed. I expected there to be some pushback or even some good-natured hazing of the "old guy" returning, but most of the players who I didn't already know have been all right. Not that we've had a lot of time to shoot the shit with the way Coach is working us.

I move into a ready position when Olsson takes his shot, my muscles sore but my adrenaline high as I keep my eye on the goal line. I let my skates glide over the ice like muscle memory; at this stage in my life, being on skates is second nature. I keep my fingers tight on my stick, waiting for the lineup and bursting the short distance to the dropped puck before swiping at it hard. It skids over the ice at rapid speed, clinking against the inside corner of the goal post but sliding into the net just the same.

"That's a good shot, Eighteen," Coach calls before turning his attention to Kennedy. "Twenty-Four! Open up! I want to see that transition backward and forward."

Jankowski nudges me when I fall back in line, offering me a friendly grin. "Doing pretty good, Old Man."

I chuckle, shrugging. Jankowski is only a few years younger than me—we actually played together before I left for Calgary—so I know he's just giving me shit.

"Knees are being good today, thank fuck," I laugh.

Rankin snickers. "Do they even make walkers with blades on them?"

"Fuck off, Rankin," Vasilevski groans. "I saw your baby ass fall on the ice last week."

"Dude, I was just fucking around," Rankin grumbles.

I laugh despite it all. I missed this. I mean, it's not like I didn't like my team back in Calgary—they were a great group of guys, after all—but this feels like *home*.

"All right, guys, let's huddle up!" Coach hollers. "Over here."

The entire team works across the ice to crowd around where Coach is standing, and he nods good-naturedly, looking among us. "That's good work today. Like always, we're having some details, doing everything full speed—I'm looking at you, Kennedy—finishing plays, falling toward the net . . . There were a lot of good handles out there." He slaps Olsson lightly on the chest, grinning at all of us. "Way to work, guys. I'll expect everyone back Monday for the first official day of training camp, yeah? I have a good feeling about this season. You boys be good till then."

We break, and people skate off toward the locker rooms, but I coast over to the sideline where Jack is currently hanging over the railing where he's been shouting encouragement for all of practice. His sling is a pale purple today, and even though he's still out of play, he's got his practice jersey on in full support.

"Looking good out there, Old Man," he teases. "How are the knees?"

"You do realize you're only two months younger than me, right?"

His cheek dimples with his smile, so similar to Lila's it's uncanny.

Not that I'm thinking about Lila. Not that I've been actively forcing myself *not* to think of her all week.

"Yeah," he chuckles. "But I'm young in spirit. By at least a decade. Your spirit was probably a passenger on the *Titanic*."

"Dick," I mutter.

Jack just laughs again. "I told you it was going to be great. Everyone was cool, right?"

"Yeah, I think so," I tell him. "Rankin likes to bust my balls, but he's harmless."

"Rankin is practically a rookie still," Jack snorts. "He's just battling little-man syndrome."

"He's six four," I point out.

"His spirit is little," Jack amends.

"All right, Miss Cleo," I laugh. "I'll be sure to come to you when I need my fortune told."

"Mr. Chase?"

We both turn to see a man not much older than either of us standing next to what I assume is his teenage son. It's not uncommon for people to come sit in on practice sessions; the facility is open to the public, after all.

I return the smile he's wearing, noticing that his son looks like he's ready to shit himself. "Hey, man, how are you?"

"Good, good," the guy says cheerfully. "You looked good out there. We're stoked you're back home." He clasps the boy on the shoulder. "My son was too nervous to come over and say hi; he's a huge fan. He's watched every single game you've played, even when you were in Calgary." He laughs then. "Put some strain on our household. We're die-hard Druids fans, you see."

I nod, smirking. "It's a good choice."

"Well," the dad says as he gives his son a little shove. "Go on then."

"H-hey," the kid stammers. "It's awesome you're back in Boston. You're the best left wing they've ever had."

He can't be more than fifteen, so I don't know if he's the expert on the history of the Druids roster, but with the way his eyes are filled with admiration, I don't think it's my place to question the compliment.

"I really appreciate that, man," I tell him. I point to the jersey he's wearing—*my* jersey. "I could sign that for you, if you want?"

His entire face lights up. "Shit, really?"

"Blake," the dad scolds, lightly smacking his son on the back of the head. "Language."

I chuckle as I take the marker the dad has already dug out of his pocket, gesturing for the kid to turn around and kneel down so I can sign my name and a little message on the white fabric where my number is. I cap the marker and hand it back to the kid's dad after, feeling a swelling warmth in my chest at the obvious excitement the kid is experiencing from something so simple.

"Thanks, Mr. Chase," he gushes. "Thank you so much!"

"Ian, please," I tell him.

The kid, Blake, looks like he might throw up a pile of emoji hearts at any second, he's so happy. "Right. Ian. Wow. Okay. Thanks, Ian."

"Really cool of you, Ian," the dad says. "We're all really glad you're home. I bet your old man is thrilled to have you back on the team, yeah?"

I do my best not to let any emotions show on my face, forcing a tight grin instead. "Yeah, he and my mom are stoked."

Jack asks him a question I barely hear with the blood rushing in my ears, and they chat for a second about his recovery time, telling him he can't wait to see him play again, and they both give us a pleasant goodbye as they stride further down the other side of the railing.

"You good?"

I nod, shaking off my irritation. "Yeah, it's not his fault my dad is a prick."

"Still. Sucks that you have to pretend he's not a tool."

I wish that I could say that after all these years, I still don't feel the weight of his expectations, that I still don't hear his voice in my head whenever I make even the slightest mistake, but it would be a lie. Bradley Chase is many things, but easily forgettable is not one of them. He'd never allow that to happen.

"Gotta keep the legacy alive," I mutter bitterly.

It's the only thing he's ever cared about, after all.

"But hey, see?" Jack says with a wide smile. "I told you people were excited you were back."

"*Most* people," I mutter.

Jack waves me off with his good hand. "Fuck those dicks on

social media. They just want something to gossip about. They'll get bored."

"Not a minute too soon."

Jack must notice my creeping melancholy at the mention of all the people still clamoring about my supposed villainy online, giving my shoulder a light shove with his good hand.

"You notice he didn't ask *me* to sign his jersey?" he pouts, changing the subject.

I smirk back at him. "Probably didn't want to lower the value of it."

"Now who's a dick?"

"I learn from the best."

Jack scowls at his sling. "I can't wait to get this fucking thing off."

"It'll fly by," I tell him. "Maybe next time you'll think twice about attempting figure skating while under the influence."

"You sound like Dee," he grumbles with a roll of his eyes.

The mention of Lila makes me pause; I haven't spoken to her since she texted me the night after we filmed the episode earlier in the week, even though I've wanted to. I keep trying to think of something to say to her, something that doesn't feel weird, but everything I type into our message thread *feels* weird, and I can't even pinpoint why. I keep telling myself it's because we've both grown up so much. So much time passing between two friends is bound to make reconnecting a little awkward.

"How is Lila?" I ask casually.

Jack cocks an eyebrow. "Didn't you just see her?"

"Well, yeah, while we were filming. Didn't get much of a chance to talk to her after."

"So you could just text her," he says. "If you wanna know how she's doing."

I tap my hockey stick idly against the lower railing, averting my eyes. "Oh, well . . . I don't want to bother her. I know how busy she probably is."

"Why are you being weird?"

I tense up. "I'm not being weird."

"You're second-guessing texting Dee to see how she's doing. That's weird."

"We just haven't really spoken in a long time, okay? It's strange seeing each other again after so long."

"It's just Dee," Jack huffs. "You've seen her in her underwear."

"Yeah, when I was twelve," I splutter. "She was seven!"

"Eh. Whatever. You still grew up together. Don't be a weirdo."

I would love to continue to argue that I'm *not* being weird— but that wouldn't be entirely true. A decade ago, I wouldn't think twice about texting Lila to check in on her. Hell, I did it at least once a day. Why is it strange to consider now?

My mind inadvertently goes back to that moment during filming—as it has unfortunately done several times in the last few days—of her small hand in mine as she stood impossibly close, watching me lick some batter I can't even remember the taste of from her spoon. Why the fuck did I do that? I've been mulling it over again and again, and I can't come up with a good reason why I played into it. I don't even want to *consider* the tremor of satisfaction that had run through me with the slight widening of her eyes, the small hitch in her breath.

Seriously, what the fuck is wrong with me?

A ping in Jack's pocket distracts me from spiraling into my thoughts too deeply, and I turn my head to watch him attempting to wrestle it from his pocket one-handedly, finally managing to grip it with his palm and slide it unlocked.

"Oh, hey, you have a new alert on Google," he says.

I groan. "I told you to turn off my Google alert."

"But how would I keep tabs on all the hot goss? We gotta stay on top of that shit."

He squints as he scrolls with his thumb, his expression twisting into one of confusion the more he reads. He glances up at me with that same pinched face, looking at me like he's trying to figure something out.

"Is there something we need to talk about?"

Now it's my turn to look confused. "What?"

"Is there something going on between you and Dee?"

I rear back, at a loss for words. "The fuck are you talking about?"

"I'm talking about this."

He turns his phone so I can read, met with an article that has a glaring caption above a picture of Lila holding that damned spoon up to my mouth, my eyes boring into hers with an intensity I hadn't even realized I'd had and hers meeting mine with an equal amount of interest. We look . . . Well. The headline isn't as out of left field as I would like. Not with a picture like that right underneath it.

IS SOMETHING COOKING BETWEEN BBTV'S DARLING AND RETURNING DRUIDS HEARTBREAKER?

The article continues on to speculate about something romantic between us, entirely based on this one photo that has . . . admittedly a lot of tension. It touches on Lila's career and our shared history and even my complicated past—and it feels raw seeing our lives intertwined in this weird way. I don't like it. I don't like knowing that my bullshit might taint Lila in some way.

"Jack, I . . . I don't know what this is, but—"

"Chase!"

I rip my head to my right, seeing Leilani sticking her head out of the entrance to the inner workings of the arena. She's got her phone pressed to one ear, gesturing at me wildly to come to her.

I turn back to Jack, who is still looking at me like I've grown a second head, and I raise my hands in what I hope is a placating gesture.

"Listen, Jack, I don't know what's going on, but that's bullshit. It was just a weird out-of-context thing. I promise, okay?"

He nods slowly. "Okay."

"Chase!"

"I'm coming!" I call back to Leilani. I shoot Jack a serious look. "I'll be back. Don't go anywhere."

I rush to the exit from the ice in a blur, pausing only for a brief moment to shuck off my skates as I practically jog to the inner doors and pace toward the coach's office past the locker rooms.

Leilani is already there when I push inside, pacing from one end of the office to the other while speaking rapidly into her cell phone. Coach is scratching at his graying beard as he scrolls through something on his computer screen, giving me a stiff nod and gesturing for me to sit.

I sink into the chair and give Leilani a wary glance, watching as she ends her call and shoots me a look. "Is there something going on with you and Delilah Baker?"

What the fuck? Is everyone going to think we've got something going on now?

"No," I tell her firmly. "We're friends. We have been for a long time. That picture is just an out-of-context screenshot from her show. It doesn't mean nearly as much as people are trying to make it."

Leilani narrows her eyes as if trying to figure out whether or not I'm lying, finally huffing out a breath through her nostrils and shaking her head. "Delilah's PR team are saying the same thing. This article is just the first of many. You guys have already got a ship hashtag going on."

"A ship hashtag?"

She nods. "*DelIan.* It's not the worst one I've ever heard, but regardless, the internet is all abuzz about the possibility of hockey's 'bad boy' being in a relationship with his childhood friend. I mean, they call her the 'darling of baking.' What a shit show."

"I'm not hockey's 'bad boy,'" I snort. "For fuck's sake, there was a guy on Nevada's team that had an underground gambling ring last year. I don't think old relationship drama qualifies me to hold the title."

"Whatever, I didn't give you the moniker, Ian, I'm just here to deal with any possible blowback."

"Okay, so, we just make a statement that Delilah and I are friends," I say. "Easy."

"We all know that the internet doesn't always care about the truth," Coach says gently.

My mouth presses into a thin line, knowing he's right. "Do you have a better suggestion?"

"I might," Leilani answers, "but I don't know if you're going to like it."

"What?"

She taps something into her phone, turning it around and handing it to me to show me an open social page. There are a flood of comments under the aforementioned "ship tag," and I feel my brows shooting up as I read through some of them.

@gingerbreadgirlboss: I am LIVING for this couple? Childhood friends to lovers?? Hello??? Someone call Shondaland right now. I need the movie. #Dellan

@sopuckinghornyrightnow: dude but like they are really hot together #Dellan

@justhereforthepuns: why do hockey players work at bakeries during off season? they're great at icing the cake. #Dellan

@bakemeacake: okay but I want someone to look at me the way Ian looks at Delilah my boy is smitten #Dellan

I frown back at Leilani. "What am I looking at?"

"Well," she starts. "For the most part . . . the internet kind of loves this."

"But it's not true," I counter, handing her phone back to her.

"Right, and I know that, but . . ." She bites at her lower lip, shrugging one shoulder. "I mean . . . they're *finally* not talking about you and your ex."

"But it's not *true*," I repeat more firmly.

"I know that. I *know*." She reaches to rub the space between her eyes, sighing. "Listen, I was speaking to Delilah's team, and we think we have an opportunity here."

I narrow my eyes. "What kind of an opportunity?"

"I just mean . . . if the internet continues to think that some-thing *might* be going on between the two of you, it's a chance to kind of reshape your public opinion, given how popular the idea of it seems to be with the general public."

I feel my mouth part in surprise as I process what she's say-ing. "You want me to . . . lie?"

"Not lie," she says quickly. "We don't want you to make any official statements. Nothing like that."

I can tell by the look on her face there's more to it. "But . . . ?"

"*But* . . . we might think it's a good idea to . . . encourage the rumors."

"Encourage the rumors," I echo dumbly.

"Yes! You know . . . You're friends, right? Just be friends. Exactly like you would otherwise. But just . . . be friends out in public. Be seen together. Keep people talking about something *other* than your past."

I can feel myself actively gaping. Is she serious right now?

"That's not much different than lying," I counter weakly.

"It's distinct enough to make sure we can't be held liable for anything." She cocks her hip, looking down at me where I'm sitting from the high vantage point her sharp heels give her. "You have to admit, it's a simple but effective idea."

I weigh her words in my head, letting them simmer as I try to see things from her point of view. On the one hand, the fact that the internet is talking about *anything* else but my history with Mei is fantastic, but on the other . . .

To exploit Lila like that? It feels . . . wrong.

"This isn't fair to Lila," I say finally.

Leilani shakes her head. "On the contrary, her team thinks it's a great idea. Good for ratings and viewer boosts. This could be great for her show. The episode you did has only been out since last night, and it's already the highest-viewed episode they've had since her first six months on air."

Damn. I haven't watched the episode yet; I haven't been able to get myself to while still feeling awkward about that spoon incident, worried that if I saw it played back I might reexperience all the strange feelings I felt in the actual moment. I can't pretend the idea of helping Lila doesn't make my chest swell though.

"And Lila? What does she say about all this?"

"They're calling her in to discuss it now, but they're confident she'll agree. Her show really needs the boost. There's been talk of cuts."

My pulse thuds angrily. "They want to cut her show?"

"It's just talk," Leilani corrects. "For now."

I consider that, staring into my lap. "And you think this could help?"

"We think this could be great for *both* of you," she stresses. "And you're friends, right? It's a no-brainer."

Friends. It feels like a complicated word, even though it should be simple. *Friends* don't think about each other the way I haven't been able to make myself stop thinking about Lila since I saw her again. I can only imagine that any level of *encouraging rumors* about there being something between us can only make those feelings worse.

"For how long?"

"At least until training camp is over," Coach cuts in, leaning onto his elbows, which are braced against his desk. "Once everyone starts to see you playing for us again, once they remember what you can do for Boston, they won't give a shit about your love life."

"That's the idea," Leilani adds confidently.

I cross my arms, staring at my socked feet that I hadn't bothered to put regular shoes on while rushing back here to see what the fuck was going on. Again, I can't pretend I'm not a little thrilled at the idea of the internet shifting its focus from my past, there's no denying that. And to think that doing something like this could help Lila as well . . . It should be a no-brainer. Because we *are* friends. It would be easy and harmless if it weren't for the weird awkwardness that seems to hang between us now. Mostly on my part, I think. And now I'm going to be gallivanting with her in public to perpetuate rumors that there might be something between us? That's sure to make things even stranger.

Still. I'm not sure there's another option here. Especially if Lila wants it. Especially if it could help her.

But the question is . . . *Will* she want to agree to this? I find the possible answer to that question is more important to me than it should be, for reasons I don't quite understand.

"I'll want to speak to Lila," I tell Leilani. "After her team. I want to make sure she's okay with it."

"Of course," Leilani answers. "She's heading into the studio now. You could meet up with her after."

I nod. To myself more than to her. "Okay. I'll do that."

"So . . . you'll do it? If she agrees?"

Do I really have a choice here?

"Yeah," I say, feeling a little insane. "As long as she agrees."

Leilani has a gleam in her eye that feels predatory; this woman really loves what she does, I can tell. But my mind is far away, wondering what the hell Lila is going to think of all this. Will she think it's crazy? Will she even think twice about it at all since we *are* friends first and foremost? Why do these thoughts make my head spin slightly?

Just be friends. Just like you would otherwise.

It sounds so simple. And it really should be. It *is*, I tell myself.

Fuck, I think with a groan. *Jack is going to be a pain in the ass about this.*

Seven

DELILAH

've been scrolling for the last fifteen minutes, and with every post, the strange, roiling sensation in my gut seems to get worse. I'm used to a small level of notoriety, nothing major, I mean this is just local cable, after all—but seeing thousands of people speculating over my possible sex life is . . . odd. Especially since the other person being discussed is someone I've never even seen naked; not for lack of imagination, of course. My brain can do some pretty amazing things with memories of a younger Ian shirtless by the pool. Current me has had a nice time also working into the mix the new knowledge of all his tattoos.

"So," I say finally, drawing out the *o* as if the extra few seconds will force my brain to catch up to the situation. "Everyone thinks Ian and I are . . . together?"

"They're *speculating*," Gia corrects.

I frown. "Right, I can see that."

"You sure you didn't plan that spoon bit?"

I twist my neck to glare at Ava, who is shrugging from the corner of Gia's already-crowded office. "No. It wasn't even a thing! It's nothing that hasn't happened a million times before with cooking duos."

"Right," Theo snorts. "Except the duo in question is hot."

"You're not helping," I hiss.

Ben clears his throat from the edge of Gia's desk, where he's been contemplating quietly in between stolen glances at my agent. "Like I was saying, Delilah," he starts, "this could be a good opportunity."

"Yeah, you said that, but I don't even know what that means." I throw up my hands. "What exactly are you asking me to do here?"

"We're not *asking* you to do anything," Gia stresses carefully. "We would never ask you to do anything with your personal life for the sake of views."

"Oh, but she could *strongly* advise it," Theo snorts.

Gia's eyes narrow as she shoots Theo a withering look, masking it quickly as she gives me a—what I assume is—pacifying smile. "All we're saying is that we have an opportunity to capitalize on the buzz this is getting."

"I have yet to hear anyone spell out what sort of opportunity is not being suggested," I sigh.

Ben taps his fingertips together like some sort of anxious cartoon character. "All we're suggesting is that it might be beneficial for you not to . . . quell these speculations."

"Like, you're saying I don't deny it."

Ben nods. "You don't have to officially address anything."

"So, what, you just want me to pretend to be dating Ian?"

"No, no, nothing like that," Ben assures me. "All we're saying is"—he glances at Gia, who gives him an encouraging look like a parent encouraging a toddler to admit they did something wrong—"that you could let them continue."

"And how would I do that? We already released the episode."

"And it was the highest-viewed episode in a long time," Gia points out.

I like Gia, I really do, but she could be a little less subtle.

"I understand that," I say slowly. "But that still doesn't give me any sort of opportunity to improvise another apparently sexy spoon-feeding."

"You and Ian are friends, right?" Ben pipes up with enthusiasm. "Surely it wouldn't be a struggle to just . . . spend time together."

"Spend time together," I parrot.

"Out in the open," Gia tacks on.

I can feel the frown tugging at my lips; sure, it's entirely possible that Ian and I would spend time together at some point, especially since he's *living* with my brother—but since I *just* resolved to put a little friendly distance between the two of us, this feels a bit like cosmic irony.

"What does Ian think about this?"

"I've spoken to the team's PR manager," Ben says. "Ian is completely on board as long as you are."

I feel a faint flutter in my stomach at this news. I know that Ian is probably looking at this from a PR standpoint only, and that he's most likely assuming that it will be a piece of cake to hang out with his best friend's kid sister like old times, but that doesn't mean I don't get all squirmy anyway, thinking about him agreeing to be in any sort of romantic rumor mill regarding me.

"I'm sure he is," Theo grumbles. "With the way the internet is still hounding him about the fiasco with his ex, I'm sure he's chomping at the bit for a way to take the heat off."

I feel my pulse skyrocket, a rush of blood in my ears as a weird urge to fight the entire internet washes over me. "Are you saying this could help him with that?"

Theo gives me a *look*, one that I don't want to analyze in the slightest because it's probably laced with sarcastic disapproval. "It's something positive attached to his name. People are really into the idea of there possibly being something between the two of you considering your history, so I'm sure Ian and his team are happy to further any sort of discussion that doesn't surround him or his past."

I consider that, my hands twisting in my lap. It's completely idiotic to entertain this, given that my not-so-dormant crush is still hanging around—hell, it's practically a stage-five clinger—but I've never been very good at saying no to Ian. Even when he's not outright asking me to do anything, apparently.

Who am I kidding? If Ian were standing here right now, asking me to help him out, I would throw away every single worry I had in regard to my own feelings and dive in headfirst.

And that's definitely an issue I need to look deeper at, I think.

"Can I think about it?"

Gia purses her lips. "We'll want to jump on this pretty quickly. The internet has a short attention span. Something else could come along and make this old news."

"Of course she can think about it," Theo practically growls, like a mama bear. "You're kind of asking her to rearrange her whole personal life for God knows how long—"

"Just until the start of the new season," Ben corrects. "A month or so at most."

Theo's nose wrinkles in distaste, and I know it's taking everything he has not to be rude to Ben; he's probably only keeping himself in check because everyone in this room and, hell, probably this city, knows that Ben has a crush on Theo, and Theo isn't as mean as he'd like people to think he is.

"*Still*," Theo goes on tightly. "She can have a fucking day to think about it."

Gia taps her manicured nails along the top of her desk, sighing. "Look, Dee, you know we would never even suggest something like this if we didn't think it could be helpful to you and the show. We all know how the numbers have been . . ." She trails off, but the implication is clear. She shrugs lightly. "We just don't want to look a gift horse in the mouth."

I know she's right, and if it were any other man with any other connection to me—it would be a no-brainer. But it's not. It's Ian, leading role to every teenage fantasy I had before I even knew what to do with them. Hell, pretty sure Ian led to my first attempts at masturbation. It's a wonder I can even look the guy in the eye.

"Give me the night," I say, inserting every bit of confidence I don't feel into my voice. "I'll talk to Ian, and I'll give you an answer in the morning."

Ben nods eagerly. "Of course. Yes. Think it over. You can get back to us in the morning."

Ben and Gia begin murmuring back and forth, and Ava comes up from her little place in the corner to pat my shoulder. "You sure about this?"

"Doubtful," Theo huffs.

I shake my head. "Not really. But I have to consider it, right?"

"Fuck that," Ava says lowly, so that just the three of us can hear. "Don't let the network pressure you into anything."

I chew at the inside of my lip, finally taking a deep breath and blowing it out slowly. "I need to talk to Ian."

Ava looks sympathetic, and I sort of wish I'd never even mentioned my pathetic crush. Theo just looks disgruntled, but that's sort of his baseline.

I pull out my phone to send off a text to Ian before I can lose my nerve, surprised to find one already waiting for me.

IAN: Can we talk?

So much for one-on-one being off-limits.

－ － － － －

I tell Ian to meet me at the same café we went to last time, thinking that the bustle of it will be a nice buffer for the awkward conversation that surely awaits us. Especially now that I apparently have to be looking over my shoulder, worrying about the possibility of someone snapping a photo of us together and analyzing it to death.

Of course, this *would* be the one day, the one hour, that the place is totally dead.

Ian is already sitting at one of the little tables in the corner when I come in, his head tipping up from where he'd been scrolling on his phone to watch as I step through the door. His thick, red hair is pulled back in a half bun that has *no* business being so fucking attractive, and I swear to God, when he tucks a piece of it that's escaped behind his ear just before giving me a little wave— my stomach twists up like a balloon animal.

I summon every bit of confidence I possess as I move across the startlingly empty café to join him at the small table, trying not to greedily take in his bare arms and their shaded grays and sharp-lined blacks. No long sleeves today, because that would just be too easy on my poor nerves—no, Ian has opted for a worn green denim jacket that is slung over the back of his chair. I can tell just by looking at it that it looks amazing on him, that it goes great with his hair. I'm torn between wanting him to put it on so I can see him in it and hoping it stays right where it is.

"Hey," Ian says, almost shyly, which isn't like him at all. "Thanks for coming."

I can't help it, a laugh tumbles out of me. "'Thanks for coming'? You sound like you're about to break up with me or something."

"Fuck," he says with a chuffed laugh of his own. "This is really weird."

"Agreed."

"Did you read any of the, ah, posts?"

"Yep. Loved the one that had a poll on how long it would take you to put a bun in my oven. Very on topic." Ian's eyes bulge, and for a second, he looks a little pale, and I laugh harder without meaning to. "If we're even going to think about agreeing to all this bullshit, we'll need to learn to laugh about it."

He scrubs a hand down his face. "Yeah, well, *you* didn't just come from a stern discussion with your brother."

"Oh shit. How did *that* go?"

"Can you imagine Jack giving anyone the 'hurt my sister, and I'll kill you' talk?"

"He didn't."

"He sure as fuck tried."

My laugh sounds more like a snort now. "He didn't even do that with Etienne, and he hated that guy."

"Yeah, well, apparently our history makes the idea of"—he

looks lost for a second, frowning, finally gesturing between us vaguely—"*this* even more wrong."

I have to will my face not to scrunch up. I love my brother, but he is a total cock block. Granted, he doesn't *know* this is a cock I might not want blocked, but still. Not that it matters anyway, since Ian looks like he kind of wants to die just talking about this.

"So I guess you got the same spiel as I did about this being good publicity?"

Ian nods. "Anything to get people not talking about me and my bullshit, apparently."

His tone sounds almost defeated, and it takes all I have not to reach across the table and grab his hand if only to try to comfort him. I've done my best over the years to avoid the gossip about Ian, and suddenly, I'm wondering if that would have been time better spent on a burner account kicking social media ass on his behalf.

"Well," I say, my voice teasing, "I could always take out the naysayers." I punch my open palm. "Handle the problem."

"No," he snorts. "I know how you 'handle problems.'"

"If you're talking about Kevin Powers—they never proved it was me."

He arches a brow. "Are you saying you *didn't* put a dead fish in his duffel bag?"

"He fractured your collarbone!"

"During practice! It's hockey," he laughs. "People get hurt."

"Yeah, well," I grumble. "He was always too rough with you."

"His jersey smelled like fish for weeks."

"Well, *whoever* put that fish in his bag was probably justified."

That forlorn expression is gone now, and in its place is a warm smile that I know too well. It's half the reason I was so obsessed with him. It's hard not to be, when he smiles like that.

"You made like three dozen cupcakes to cheer me up."

"I was just trying new recipes," I sniff. "It was totally coincidental."

He arches a brow. "Oh, was it?"

"Okay, no," I admit. "I was totally trying to cheer you up."

"But then I threw up all over Bea's rug. If I didn't have the fracture, I think she would have whooped my ass."

"No one told you to eat seven in one sitting, *Cupcake*."

His grin widens, setting off a flurry of little flutters in my stomach.

"Well, I was very grateful that *someone* had my back," he says softly.

I nod, feeling my cheeks heat. I don't say that I'll always have his back, because it sounds lame even in my head. I focus my attention on a bit of chipped nail polish on my thumb, going for casual. "So, what do you think?"

His brow cocks. "What do I think?"

"Yes. About all of this. Is this something you want to do?"

"It's not just up to me, Lila, it's up to you too."

"That's not what I asked. I asked if it's something *you* want to do."

I don't know if it's my tone or my words that take him by surprise, but I can tell it does from the small part to his lips, the widening of his eyes. I watch a dozen emotions play across his face as he considers the question, finally looking resigned and somehow small despite his massive frame when his shoulders slump.

"I won't lie to you and pretend it wouldn't be nice not to hear about strangers picking apart all my bad decisions for once, but I mean it when I say it's not just up to me. My team tells me that this could be good for you with views and all, and if that's true, then yeah, I think it's great that we could help each other out. But that being said, I would never want to push you into something you're not comfortable doing. We haven't really spent the sort of time together that we used to in a long while. We're just getting our footing back in this friendship, and if you think this is too weird, then I will stand by that one hundred percent, our teams be damned. I'll tell both of them to go fuck themselves before I let them pressure you."

I feel stunned by his confession, and a little touched too. He looks so serious, so sure of himself that he would handle all of this if it's not something I want. *That* is definitely the Ian I remember. He was always one breath away from diving into a problem headfirst if it meant making sure someone he cared about didn't have to. It's just one of the many reasons I was always so gone for him. Still, the mention of his own troubles and the buzz about his past tugs at my heartstrings.

I want to ask about it, want to in a way I have for years but have been too chickenshit to do so—but I keep my mouth shut instead, thinking. Logically, I know that agreeing to this farce wouldn't actually require us to *do* much. Hanging out, being seen a little bit, teasing the public, as it were—it's nothing. Or it should be nothing, if you don't have complicated feelings for your partner in crime. And would it even work? Would anyone *really* care if Ian and I looked a little *too* friendly?

Movement catches my eye outside the window we're sitting in front of, and I notice a couple of girls standing across the sidewalk, not-so-surreptitiously taking a picture of the pair of us with their phones. When they notice me watching, they both have the grace to look sheepish, quickly scuttling away.

Guess that answers that.

I blow out a breath. "I think we should do it."

"What?"

"We should just do it." I nod, trying to convince myself even as I'm speaking. "I mean, what's it really going to mean? We hang out a little? Maybe I stand a little too close? Laugh at your dumb jokes a little too loudly?"

His eyes narrow. "I don't have dumb jokes."

"You barely have jokes at all anymore, from what I've seen," I tease. "But when you did, I do remember them being kind of dumb."

"Brat," he huffs.

My stomach twists again.

You have no right to be turned on by that, I tell my nether region. *Down, girl.*

"I really don't see what we have to lose," I reason. "You get some good press, I get some buzz that will bump my views . . . Seems like a win-win."

"It could work," he muses, his gaze far away as he considers. "As long as I can manage not to do something to fuck it up."

I *do* reach across the table to grab his hand then, sensing his melancholy, and the second my fingers touch his, his entire body flinches.

"You're going to have to practice not being so jumpy, if we're going to do this," I chuckle. "You're acting like you've never touched a girl before, Cupcake."

I can see a spark of defiance in his eyes, an old flame of endless competitiveness that I doubt either of us ever really grew out of. He almost makes *me* jump when his hand grips mine tighter, his thumb making a slow sweep across my knuckles, and his teeth flash in triumph when I suck in a breath.

"Maybe *you* need practice," he murmurs.

Memories of stupid dares and foot races and a dozen more childish things that used to fill our days flash through my mind, and I lean in, smirking. "You don't want to play that game with me, Ian. You'll lose."

"Whatever," he laughs, letting my hand slip from his and having no clue just how much I'm mourning the loss of it. "Nothing makes me uncomfortable. You'd tap out way before I did."

I feel my lips curl, daydreams about paying Ian back a little for years of clueless feeding into my silly wants bouncing around in my head. Because one thing is for certain, I am *not* that little kid anymore. Ian has no idea who he's dealing with.

"We'll see," I say with a sly grin.

He looks serious again. "So we're really doing this?"

What the hell, I think. *When will I ever have a chance to indulge in all my old fantasies like this? Maybe it will finally give teenage me some closure.*

"Yeah," I say with a nod. "I guess we are."

Eight

IAN

Kennedy, you're lagging! Get your ass across the line! You need training wheels?"

Jankowski nudges me. "Who's gonna be the one to remind Coach that skates don't have training wheels?"

"Not it," Rankin snorts. "He's already riding me like he's paying for it."

"Oh?" Sanchez leans on the end of his stick as we hang back in the neutral zone, watching Coach run defense through a drill. "And how much would you charge him?"

"Fuck off," Rankin mutters.

A chuckle escapes me, watching Sanchez give Rankin a good-natured shove. "Don't worry, babe, you won't be a rookie forever."

"I'm not a rookie now!"

Sanchez shrugs. "You're a rookie till we get a new rookie. I don't make the rules."

Rankin skates off mumbling curse words under his breath,

and Jankowski shoots me a conspiring grin. "Coach gonna give us a break anytime soon, you think?"

"He's never been big on breaks, as I recall," I point out.

"Fair," Jankowski concedes. His grin turns sly then. "You wanna tell us about this *situation* with you and Baker's sister?"

"You know damn well there's not actually a situation."

"That's what you and Jack are singing, but seems like a waste to me. Dee is hot."

I feel a prickling sensation in my chest, tamping down an influx of bad feelings that don't make any damned sense. "Watch it," I warn.

"*Ooo*," Sanchez chimes in gleefully. "Sensitive subject? You know we don't step on another man's territory. Team rules."

"There's no *territory*," I huff. "We're just doing this to help each other out."

"I can think of a lot of ways you could help each other out," Jankowski says, waggling his eyebrows.

That prickling feeling intensifies, and I scowl back at him. "You want to finally lose a few teeth? That's Jack's sister you're talking about."

"Mhm." Jankowski's eyes are practically sparkling. "That's all it is, I'm sure."

"Hey!" Coach shouts from the other side of the rink. "If you have time for chitchat, you have time to get your asses over here and run speed drills!"

Another elbow nudged in my side as Jankowski laughs. "Come on, Old Man. Let's get shit done so you can get home to your sweetheart."

"Is it cheesy to say you're on thin ice?"

Jankowski gives me an innocent look. "Dude, I was talking about Jack."

I glide after him over the ice as he takes off, cackling, and I have to remind myself that I *like* Jankowski.

"*Fuck*, I'm sore," Sanchez groans.

"I think even my balls are aching," Olsson gasps, bent over at the waist. "Is Coach trying to kill us on day one?"

"Funny, I feel fine," Rankin pops off, his hair drenched in sweat and his face startlingly red.

Sanchez shoves him, nearly knocking him off-balance. "Fuck off."

"Knees still good?" Jankowski teases me.

I roll my eyes. "They're holding up. If you don't stop acting so concerned for me, I might start to think you have a crush on me."

"You're not my type," he answers. "I'm saving myself for Coach." He perks up, clapping me on the shoulder. "But speaking of types . . ."

I follow the nod of his head to the railing on the edge of the rink, spotting a familiar mass of brown waves piled high above what I know to be bright eyes and a brighter smile. It's been less than twenty-four hours since Lila and I agreed to our little PR endeavor, and even though I know there's nothing real about this thing we're doing, I still feel a tiny flutter in my stomach at seeing her so soon. Like I haven't had enough time to properly figure out how I'm going to approach the whole thing.

Jankowski straightens, smirking at me. "Think I'll go say hi to Dee."

God, I really do like the guy, but he's asking for an ass kicking with this shit.

My body moves on its own to follow him, so quickly that it's like my brain has no say in the matter. Jack gives me a bit of side-eye when I sidle up next to Jankowski below the railing where he and Lila are huddled together; we had a long talk last night about everything that's going on, and I know (or at least, I *think*) he's cool with it, but I get the sense that there's still a bit of weirdness he's sorting through. He's definitely not the only one.

Lila immediately brightens when I approach, her lips curling into a wide smile and her eyes crinkling at the corners, and the electricity of it paired with the knowledge that there are a few dozen people meandering around the arena with their eyes on us has that flutter in my stomach intensifying to something that feels like it's crawling up my throat. Her tight jeans and her soft green sweater make her look delicate, the color making her already big brown eyes seem wider, sweeter even. Not to mention her smile. And that goddamned dimple.

"Hey, Cupcake," she greets me, her voice sweet and musical and entirely too loud to be calling me that. "Looking good out there."

"I'm sorry," Sanchez snorts, skating up behind me. "*Cupcake?*"

I groan, narrowing my eyes at Lila, who looks like she knows exactly what she just did. "Really?"

"What?"

She winks at me, and for reasons beyond me, I feel the innocent gesture as if she reached out and touched me. Me suddenly acting nervous around her just because we made a formal agreement to spark some rumors makes no sense. The only thing that

I can fathom is the added microscope it's putting me under, even if it's a slightly more positive one.

"*Cupcake* played great," Jankowski coos.

"Oh," Jack snorts. "I actually just decided I am going to like this whole thing between you guys."

I roll my eyes. "So happy everyone's on board." I arch a brow at Lila. "What are you doing here?"

"Oh, you know." She shrugs, giving me another sweet smile. "Being seen. Perpetuating rumors. That sort of thing."

I take a quick look around, and sure enough, there is more than one phone pointed in our direction. "Looks like it's working."

"Anything for the team," she laughs.

I turn my head again when I see a flash go off somewhere to my right. "I can't wait to see whatever the internet is going to be saying tomorrow."

"You'd better get used to it," Lila hums. She leans over the railing, hanging between my arms—which are reaching up, hands clasped there—and extends her arm until her finger closes in on my nose, giving it a boop. "We're the talk of the town, Cupcake."

It's little more than a brush of her fingertip against the tip of my nose, but I feel the heat of it spread through my face in a way that surely must show on my fair skin; am I embarrassed or amused? I don't allow myself to consider anything else I might be possibly feeling about it.

"Perfect," I mutter.

Jack scoots closer to his sister as Sanchez and Jankowski start arguing about some play they didn't quite get down during practice, looking between us pointedly. "You tell him about the play day?"

I cock a brow. "Play day?"

"Dee's thing. She got it going a few years back. We do it every year now at St. Michael's."

It takes me a second to place the name, but only a second. Jack and Lila didn't spend more than six months at that orphanage before their aunt got full custody after their parents' accident, but I have to imagine it was long enough to leave an impression.

"What is it?"

Lila looks almost shy for the first time since seeing her again, her cheeks turning a sweet shade of pink as she reaches to tuck a stray tendril of hair behind her ear. "It's nothing too crazy," she says. "Just an event I pitched a few years ago that stuck. The kids really love it."

"She's being modest," Jack tsks. "She worked her ass off organizing it. Still does. Every single year. She put together this huge fundraiser when she got back to the States, right? Raised enough money to get the kids a bona fide hockey rink built behind the orphanage. Every year, me and some of the guys take the day to run drills with the kids, play around, you know, nothing too crazy. Dee always comes out with her shit and teaches them how to bake something. The ones who don't want to play, that is. It's always a huge hit."

Lila still looks embarrassed during Jack's praising speech, but I feel a swell of pride coursing through me. Everything about what he just told me sounds *exactly* like something my Lila would do.

My Lila?

I mentally rear back. Where the hell did that come from?

"That's really great," I tell her, meaning it. "Seriously, Lila. It's amazing."

Her blush deepens, her teeth pressing against her lower lip, accentuating the fullness of it and drawing my eye for a second longer than is appropriate.

Without my consent, there are flashes of images in my head of that same soft mouth touching me in places that are entirely inappropriate. Those same teeth biting into my skin. They're so quick and so vivid, I don't even have the time to mentally kick my own ass over them.

I tear my eyes away when she finally speaks.

"The kids really love it," she says quietly. "And I love doing it. The guys always seem to have a good time too. I was thinking that it would be a good place for you to be seen. I mean, if you're not too busy. I don't want you to feel like you have to—"

"Of course I want to help," I tell her firmly. "Are you kidding? Even if we didn't have this whole shit show on the internet. Sign me up."

Her smile is so wide that it makes *my* face hurt, but that might just be a general ache from how hard it is not to stare.

"Awesome. Thank you, Ian."

"I mean, I'm terrible with kids, but still."

She chuckles. "You'll be fine."

"Oi!" Jack shouts suddenly. "The fuck are you doing over there?"

We both watch him stomp off toward the other end of the rink, where a few players are roughhousing against the rails.

I shake my head. "Dumbasses are going to hurt themselves. No plexiglass around the practice rink."

"Leave it to Jack to play rink mom," she laughs.

I huff a laugh through my nostrils. "He's very good at it."

"You really don't mind helping out at the play day?"

"What?" My brow furrows. "Of course I don't mind." My

mouth twitches. "Besides, when have I ever been able to say no to you?"

She rolls her eyes. "It's been a long time since I've put that to the test."

"Definitely a lot of wheedling to catch up on."

"Don't worry, I won't abuse my power too much."

"Somehow I highly doubt that," I snort. "You were always a needy little shit."

She folds her arms over the railing, resting her chin against them as she smirks. "I think *you* were just a bit of a pushover."

"Oh yeah?"

"Total pushover," she affirms. "I could play you like a fiddle, Ian Chase."

I don't tell her I have a sneaking suspicion that she still could, if she wanted.

"That right?"

"One hundred percent, Cupcake."

I narrow my eyes before letting them drop to her legs, doing the first thing that comes to mind, wrapping my arms around her thighs and pulling her downward until she slides under the railing with a squeak. She falls into my arms in a laugh that sounds more like a squawk, my arms landing under her knees and her shoulders just as her hands wind around my neck to steady herself.

"What the fuck, Ian?"

"Seems like you're a bigger pushover than I am," I deadpan.

She snorts as she wiggles out of my hold, grumbling as she falls to her feet on the ice. I hold her steady with an arm around her waist so she doesn't slip, feeling smug. I should probably be thinking about how it looks, what I've just done, but it's something

I wouldn't have thought twice about ten years ago, so I try not to let myself do that now. Even if she feels much softer and much more . . . grown-up against me now.

Lila looks flushed, and I can't help but tease her. "How's that for being seen?"

"You think you're so slick."

"I have my moments."

I only have a split second to register the calculating look in her eyes before her hand slips under my arm, weaving its way over the back of my jersey until her fingers are teasing the sweaty ends of my hair sticking out of my helmet.

"I told you not to play this game with me," she says coyly. "You'll lose."

With the slight tremor that runs down my spine with the weight of her against me, I have to admit she makes a solid argument.

Suddenly, she gives my hair a sharp tug that I feel all the way down in my balls, and I only have about four seconds to form a solid "What the fuck was that?" thought before thudding footsteps and Jack's shouting voice blast through whatever the hell just happened.

"Okay, okay, that's enough canoodling," he grouses. "It's weird as fuck." He crouches and offers a hand out when I finally manage to tear my gaze away from a still-smug-looking Lila, watching as she slowly unwinds herself from me to take Jack's hand. "And what are you doing on the ice? You trying to break your neck?"

"Doing dumb shit on the ice is your department," she fires back, hoisting herself up over the ledge and crawling back under the railing.

I resist the urge to watch her ass as she goes, and to the surprise of no one, it's incredibly difficult.

Seriously, what the fuck, Ian?

"Save the touchy shit for public spaces," Jack huffs.

I frown. "This is a public space."

I hear him muttering something under his breath that sounds suspiciously like: *fucking weird*, and I have a feeling he would be losing his shit on me if he knew the weird thoughts I'm having right now.

But Lila seems entirely unfazed.

"So I'll see you next week at the play day, then?"

It takes me a second to realize this is directed at me, and I manage to nod dumbly as I try to remember how to make words while the sensation of her tugging on my hair still racks through my body.

"I'll be there. For sure."

Another blinding smile that I feel in a more PG-rated part of my body, and then she gives Jack a stern look. "You too. You might be useless right now, but you can be my assistant."

"Assistant, my ass," Jack snorts.

She wiggles her fingers at us, looking breezy and unbothered like she didn't just leave me with weird thoughts and even weirder feelings about them. "Bye, guys."

Jack waits until she's out of earshot to say, "She's such a pain in the ass."

I'm nodding at him, mainly because I'm only half listening, but I can't say that I agree in the slightest.

"Gonna be weird as fuck watching you two pretend to be into each other." He makes a gagging sound. "Training camp can't be over fast enough."

I'm nodding, again, because I'm still only half listening, and again, searching every corner of my brain . . . I can't find any shared irritation to this situation to match his.

Even if I have no clue as to what that means.

Later, when the guys are talking shit in between changing out of their gear, I'm still lost in my own head. Every time I think about Lila's hands on me—of her small, delicate hand grabbing a fistful of my hair and making me feel it in places I have no business feeling—there's a tingling awareness that creeps along my skin. Like my body refuses to let me forget just how much I *felt* that mostly innocent action. It's confusing as hell.

"Yo," Sanchez calls from across the locker room, drawing me out of my thoughts. "You coming out for beers?"

I shrug. "I don't know. I'm kind of tired."

"Dude, we always get beers after the first practice of training camp," Jankowski says seriously. "It's tradition."

"Is this a superstition thing?"

"Hey," Olsson says. "We don't judge you for keeping that shaggy-ass haircut."

I frown, running my fingers through my sweaty mop. "I cut it . . . after the season ends."

"Don't worry," Jankowski says, puckering his lips. "You're a total hunk."

"Fuck off," I mutter.

Sanchez crosses his arms. "So, beers?"

"Yeah, yeah, fine," I relent. "Let me shower and see where Jack is at."

"Oh, he's already there," Olsson says. "Saving us a table."

"We'll wait for you outside, yeah?"

I nod at Jankowski. "Sounds good."

They all start to file out, and I peel my base layer over my head before rolling my shoulders as the cool air touches my sweat-drenched skin. A shower sounds fucking fantastic, actually.

I'm just peeling off the last of my layers when my phone starts to chime in the pile of my discarded clothes. I riffle through the fabric, trying to find the trilling device, my thumb swiping across the answer button before I actually see who it is.

"Shit."

I considered hanging up for a second and claiming it was an accident, but I know I can't avoid him forever.

"Hello?"

My father's voice is exactly as it always is—gruff and laced with irritation. Probably aimed at something I did, most likely. "How was practice?"

"It was . . . practice. Same as always."

"Don't get smart with me," he scoffs. "How is the team treating you? Anyone giving you shit?"

"No? And what if they were?"

"Well, we'd take care of it, obviously."

"I don't need you to take care of anything," I huff. "I do just fine on my own."

"Yeah, well, tell that to your piss-poor point average last year," he laughs scornfully. "You could be on the all-star team if you just applied yourself."

I shut my eyes, my jaw clenching. I don't tell him that I don't give a shit about that, because I know from experience it would fall on deaf ears. My opinion has never really mattered to him, not when I was a child and certainly not now, so I let him rant for a moment about all the things I could do to be a better player, only speaking again when he seems to tire himself out.

"How's Mom?" I say, ignoring everything he's just said.

He makes a disgruntled sound. "What the hell do you mean? She's the same as she always is. Maybe if you came and visited her once in a while, you'd know that."

I also don't comment on the fact that I would visit a lot more if every single instance didn't end in him berating me for every perceived slight he can think of in regard to "his game." I know there's no point in arguing with him. You can't argue with someone who won't entertain the idea of being wrong. Even if I *did* make the all-star team, even if I visited every other day—I'd still be a disappointment somehow.

"I'll try to come visit soon," I say instead. "I gotta get in the shower. The guys are waiting on me."

"Just make sure to keep your nose clean, you hear? I've been filled in on the details of this scheme with you and the Baker girl, and I can't say I'm a huge fan of it, but if it gets the vultures talking about something other than you and those damned pictures, I'll allow it."

I'll allow it. His echoed words in my head make my face heat. As if *he* isn't just as complicit in this mess as I am. As if every step I've made in the last six years hasn't kept *his* ass out of the spotlight. I would love to say that his *concern* is of the fatherly sort, but it would be a lie. It's his reputation he cares about. The fact that the only *problems* that plague me in this town are the ones he created for me. Not that he'll ever admit it.

"It will blow over," I manage tightly, praying that it's true.

"It had better," Dad scoffs. "Don't make me regret letting you come back."

Letting me come back. I have to *actually* bite my tongue.

"Sure, Dad," I force out. "I'll do my best."

I hang up with my father, feeling the same as I always do after we talk. Tired, mostly. Tired and simmering with a sort of anger that feels like old coals. Hot, but also died down, just waiting to be stoked by the next jab.

I'm about to throw my phone back into my pile of clothes when it vibrates with a text, and I almost ignore it on the off chance it's something my father forgot to throw in over the phone.

But it's not him, much to my pleasant surprise.

LILA: Thanks again for agreeing to the play day. It'll mean a lot to the kids.

I'm grinning as I tap out a reply.

ME: And you too, right?

LILA: Eh. I guess so.

I cover my mouth with my hand, my palm pressing into my smile as I picture the teasing tilt of her mouth as she typed it. Amazingly, all the bitter feelings that had been threatening to consume me dissipate in the wake of that imagined smile.

And I still have no clue what that means.

Nine

DELILAH

This looks like shit."

I choke on a laugh as I try to keep my expression stern, turning on the precocious twelve-year-old giving a disgusted look to a sugar cookie. "Jamie. I don't think you're supposed to be saying things like that."

"It *does* kind of look like shit," Corbin agrees, looking over Jamie's shoulder.

Jamie immediately elbows the larger boy in the stomach, causing the breath to rush out of him. "Shut up. Why are you here, anyway? Boys aren't supposed to be baking."

I drop my spoon into the bowl of icing I've been mixing so we can decorate the cookies, putting my fists on my hips. "Hey, none of that. Boys can do anything girls can do if they want to. And girls can do anything boys can do too. Got it?"

Jamie looks sheepish. "Yeah, okay."

"I don't like the skates," Corbin mumbles. "I can't stand up in them."

"And that's okay," I tell him, patting his shoulder. "Hockey isn't for everyone."

I feel a shadow cast over the table, turning to see my brother's smirking face as he leans over it, his turquoise sling matching his jersey pretty good. "You guys want to know a secret? My sister here busted her nose the first time she ever got on the ice. She looked like she had an eggplant on her face for like a month."

The kids around me all giggle, and I roll my eyes. "You want to tell them why you're wearing the sling, Kristi Yamaguchi? Or should I?"

"Rude," he tsks. "What are you guys making?"

"Sugar cookies," Brittany, one of the older teens, says in a bored tone. "Duh."

Jack is unbothered, shooting her a grin. "Sorry, they don't pay me for my brain."

"Good thing," I laugh. "Your income would be significantly lower."

"I will refrain from responding in front of the children."

"That means he was gonna call her a bad word," I hear Jamie whisper, followed by a soft laugh from Corbin.

I tilt my head toward the rink on the other side of the open-air building, trying not to let my eyes linger on a particular jersey, something I've been perfecting for the last hour or so. "How is it going out there?"

"Well, Sanchez hasn't run any kids over," Jack snorts. "So that's something."

I avert my eyes, grabbing the bowl of cookie icing and my spoon and giving it an absent stir. "And how's Ian doing?"

"Boyfriend's fine," Jack answers with only a hint of sarcasm. "He hasn't yelled at any of them yet."

I roll my eyes. "He wouldn't yell at a kid."

"Says you. The little one likes to chirp."

"Chirp?"

"Trash talk. He's determined to trip Ian."

My lips curl in a smile at the image of my massive hockey player tumbling on the ice because of some tiny little boy. Well, not *my* hockey player, but whatever.

"I'm going to go check on him," I say, handing Jack the bowl. "Stir this."

"Stir this?" He looks at the bowl like I've handed him a bomb. "What do you mean 'stir this'?"

"That spoon there? Pick it up and turn it clockwise."

He's still shouting at me when I start to walk off. "I've only got one hand!"

"Bet it doesn't stop you from doing other things!" I toss back, laughing.

I can hear the kids start to volley questions at him as I pace away, their voices growing fainter and the much louder ones of the five hockey players who volunteered superseding them as I get closer to the rink. I lean over the railing as Jankowski herds a group of preteen boys to the crease to show them some defensive moves. I watch them for a moment, trying to pretend I didn't come over here to get a glimpse of one player in particular, but it's futile really.

Ian is huddled close to a small boy who can't be any older than seven—Kyle, I think his name is—his expression serious and his hands gesticulating wildly as he explains something about his stick. I watch him straighten to his full height and bend at the waist as he shows Kyle how to strike at the puck; he's showing him how to attempt a slap shot, I realize. I rest my chin on my folded arms as I watch them, and it takes several seconds for me to register the soft smile on my mouth as I do so.

Ian hands the stick to Kyle, folding his arms over his chest as he watches the little boy study the puck with all the intensity of a full-grown man. He bends just as Ian did, pressing the end of his stick to the puck and rearing back before suddenly slapping the shit out of it and watching it fly across the ice.

Ian's face transforms into a blinding grin, clapping Kyle on the shoulder and nodding fervently as his mouth moves in what I assume to be praise, given the way the boy lights up. The entire exchange makes it feel like my ovaries are being tied up in a knot like a fucking cherry stem.

"Looking a little flushed there, Dee," a voice says coyly.

I turn my head to catch a familiar face grinning at me. "Fuck off, Sanchez."

"Wow." He clutches his chest. "In front of the children?"

"How are they doing out there?"

"I think they're having fun," he says. "How's the baking?"

"I've got Jack manning the icing station."

Sanchez cackles. "Wow, I need to take my skates off and get over there. I gotta see that."

"Make sure he doesn't break something else," I chide. "He always seems to when you're involved."

"It was *one* time," he argues. "And he totally bragged that he could do a double axel."

"Whatever helps you sleep at night," I tease.

He narrows his eyes. "Jerk. I'll leave you here to enjoy the view."

"You know it's not like that."

"Yeah, yeah, I heard the PR spiel." He leans in close, pinching my cheek. "Hasn't stopped the big guy from glaring at me for the last sixty seconds."

Sanchez is already skating off when I whip my head back to where Ian was working with Kyle, catching his eyes on me for only a second before he tears them away. Even from a slight distance, I can see his face get a little red, his lips pressing into a tight line.

Well, that is interesting.

I move from my spot to wander closer to the other end of the rink, wiggling my fingers in a wave that Ian returns before saying something to Rankin. Rankin comes closer to take over with Kyle, and then Ian is gliding my way, coming to rest just on the other side of the railing that I stop in front of.

"Looking good out there, Cupcake."

"You keep saying that," he says. "I'm going to start thinking you're just flirting with me."

My eyes round for only a second, recovering quickly as I flash him a lazy grin. "Would you like me to flirt with you, Ian?"

"No, I didn't mean—" His throat bobs, and his cheeks darken with something that has nothing to do with exertion, I suspect, and his eyes dip down to his skates as he chuckles. "Damn it, Lila."

I tilt my chin toward the rink. "You *did* seem like you were having fun."

He looks embarrassed, scratching at his neck as he shoots another glance back at Kyle and Rankin, who are still working on shooting. "The kid's doing pretty good. He's got some raw talent."

"But are you having *fun?*"

He pushes back the hair, which is darkened with sweat, from his face, his expression almost shy and his smile even more so. "Yeah," he admits. "I am. It's a really cool thing you've done here, Lila."

It's so stupid that something as simple as a nickname that literally no one else uses would do weird things to my insides, but it's more about the way his voice sounds when he says it, I think. It's the way his tone always, *always* softens a fraction, the way his mouth shapes the syllables like he wants to be careful with them.

Or at least, that's what my crush-addled brain chooses to believe.

"It just felt right to me," I tell him honestly. I turn my head to let my eyes wander over the different groups of kids in various stages of fun, smiling. "I know we weren't in here long, but I remember how lonely it was. That feeling like no one was coming for you. Fuck, like no one *wanted* you. I just figured if I could distract them from that for a day . . ." I shrug, feeling embarrassed myself now under his scrutiny. "I don't know. It just felt right."

I was far too young when the crash took my parents to really remember much about them, but I *vividly* recall feeling so alone. Even at a young age, feeling like you have no one sticks with you. I was fortunate enough to at least have Jack and my aunt Bea and even Ian, for a while, but these kids? Some of these kids have *no one*. All of this is nothing compared to that.

"It really is amazing," he says, actual reverence in his tone that makes me feel like I'm flying a little bit. "But you always were."

My cheeks heat, and I know there's no special meaning to what he's just said, but fuck if it doesn't have me biting back a grin.

"Says the pro hockey player," I laugh.

He rolls his eyes. "Hitting a puck doesn't hold a candle to all this, Lila. Take the compliment, brat."

Fuck. What is it about that word? Is it just because it's Ian? I have a sick urge to make him keep calling me that, and I've never felt that once in my entire adult life.

"You keep saying that," I say with a grin, "I'm going to start thinking *you're* flirting with *me*."

There's less surprise this time, replaced instead by a glimmer of challenge in his eyes as he clears his throat. "Would *you* like me to flirt with *you*?"

"I mean"—I shrug one shoulder, leaning over the rail to reach for a damp tendril of his hair, twirling it around my finger—"isn't that what we're supposed to be doing?"

His eyes narrow, but there's a twitch of his lips like he wants to smile. "Are you trying to one-up me, Lila?"

"I'm just playing the part, Cupcake," I answer sweetly.

His hand envelops mine suddenly, yanking me closer so that he can lean in, his lips brushing my ear and causing me to shudder. "Two can play that game, brat."

"Fuck," I say on a stuttered exhale, and I feel Ian tense against me.

He draws back, his mouth parted slightly as he studies my face. I know he can see how flushed I must be, since my cheeks are on fire, and amusement colors his features as his mouth curls into an impish grin. "You good, Lila?"

"Fine, you win this time," I grumble.

He laughs fully then, releasing me, and I immediately feel the loss of his touch.

"I should get back out there," he tells me. "Gotta make sure Rankin doesn't end up on his ass. That Kyle is sneaky."

"Big scary Kyle," I chuff, willing my knees not to wobble from the lingering sensation of how close he just was to me. "I'd better go make sure Jack hasn't locked himself in the oven."

"I want to say that that sounds unlikely, but I know Jack, unfortunately."

"We love him for his personality," I say seriously.

Ian makes a face. "Debatable."

"Come see me when you finish up, yeah? I want to show you something."

He looks confused for a second, but then he nods. "Sure. Okay."

"Watch your knees," I warn. "Wouldn't want Kyle to take you out."

He gives me a look that feels downright dirty, or maybe that's just the way my brain chooses to perceive it, but thankfully he skates off quickly enough that he doesn't see the actual shiver that passes through me, one I can't exactly explain away, given that it's pretty warm today.

I let my eyes linger on him for longer than is appropriate, probably, watching his broad shoulders wrapped in black and teal square up as he skates up alongside Rankin, knocking forearms with him before flashing a grin down at a focused-looking Kyle.

"Dee!"

I turn my head back toward the baking station, catching sight of Jack waving his one arm at me and wearing a helpless look as well as a good bit of bright pink icing down the front of his jersey.

Yeah, that's about right.

——— ———

I'm cleaning up when Ian finds me; the kitchen I oversaw the construction of on the other side of the building is pretty open, which means that I can hear him when he approaches, the kids having all gone back to the main building to get ready for dinner after a long day.

"Hey," he says. "Where'd Jack run off to?"

"He's next door with the others, sniffing around to see what the kitchen is putting out for dinner. The kids really like getting to hang out with them." Speaking of, I notice Ian isn't alone. "Hey, Kyle." I address him with a smile. "Did you have fun?"

The little boy nods seriously. "Ian said I could kick ass someday."

Ian immediately flushes, looking sheepish. "Don't repeat that."

"Okay." Kyle gives another solemn nod, his little brow furrowing as he peers up at Ian. "Can you come practice again?"

"I—" Ian looks momentarily thrown, recovering quickly as his lips quirk and his large hand comes to rest against Kyle's blond curls. "Yeah, buddy. I'll come back soon, okay?"

"Okay," Kyle says with another nod, his expression entirely too serious for his angelic face.

"Why don't you go on over and see what they're having for dinner?" I tell Kyle. "Ian is going to help me finish cleaning up out here."

Ian laughs. "Oh, am I?"

"You're a pushover, remember?"

Ian shakes his head, giving Kyle's shoulder a gentle nudge. "Go on, buddy. I'll catch up."

We both watch him trod off, his hair bouncing with each step.

"Someone made a friend," I say.

Ian is still smiling softly as he watches Kyle go back inside the building. "He's a good kid. Really does show some promise. You think they'd let me come back sometimes to work with him again?"

"You really want to?"

Ian gives me a look like it's a silly question I've asked, and my heart melts a little. "Not like I have a lot else going on."

"Besides being a pro hockey player and feeding tabloid gossip, you mean?"

He rolls his eyes. "I noticed a couple of reporters hanging around earlier. Had those big clunky cameras."

"I can't wait to scroll through our ship tag tomorrow."

He purses his lips. "You're enjoying this entirely too much."

"Maybe a little," I chuckle.

"What did you want to show me?"

I nod toward the sink. "Finish washing those dishes first."

"Oh, so you were serious about helping clean up."

I arch a brow. "If you want one of those cookies I see you eyeballing, then you're going to have to get your hands dirty."

"Such a brat," he grumbles.

My lips curl.

Oh, he has no idea.

- - - - -

"I didn't know this was back here."

Ian's fingers trail along an old chain attached to one of the swings, tweaking it thoughtfully.

I brush past him, plopping down into the rubber seat. "Jack and I used to play out here a lot while we stayed here." I push the toes of my shoes against the ground, propelling myself back and forth and giving him one arched brow. "He would always push me."

Ian chuffs as he moves behind me, giving my back a gentle shove. "Subtle."

"Got what I wanted, though, huh?"

"Did you just bring me out here to get me to push you around?"

I tilt my head back to smirk at him. "You'd know if I was trying to get you to push me around."

His fingers still at my back for a second, and I feel a tiny thrill course through me at having tripped him up, even if only a little.

"It's always strange coming back here," I murmur, my eyes sweeping over the empty playground. "Brings back old memories."

"Then why come back?"

"I guess . . . because I know how much it means to these kids to have someone show up for them. Sometimes just showing up can make all the difference."

"That's . . ." He clears his throat. "That's really great, Lila."

"Yeah, I guess so." I let the tips of my shoes scrape across the dirt as I swing. "I really just wanted to see how you were doing with all this."

"All this?"

"You know. The PR shit, the training, all the jerks on the internet . . . We haven't had a chance to talk about it."

"What's there to talk about?"

"Don't do that," I huff. "It's been a fucking whirlwind, Ian, and you know it. Even with all the good chatter on social media lately, I know people are still talking. I know it has to bother you."

"I'm used to it by now."

"Yeah, well, you shouldn't have to be."

He stops pushing, his hands curling around the chains on either side of me. "Why are we talking about this?"

"I don't know . . ." I let my head drop back again to meet his eyes. "I guess I feel guilty that we never have."

"We've both had lives, Lila," he says. "It wasn't your responsibility."

"Still. I feel like I could have reached out. When everything happened. We were close once."

He looks contemplative, his full lips pressing into a tight line. "I was a mess, anyway. I'm not sure that I would have been very receptive to anyone trying to help."

"We could still talk about it, you know. About Mei and the pictures. You know that I'm always here to listen."

I watch as his jaw clenches, a wrinkle forming at his brow before he suddenly gives my back another push. "There's nothing to talk about, really. It's old news. People just haven't figured that out yet."

I want to push it, for my own curiosity as well as my worry for his feelings, but I can tell when I'm being shut out. I can't even say why I'm so eager to talk about it in the first place. Is it just because I want to know more about him? To understand him better? And why is that? It's not like there's *actually* anything between us.

"When I saw the pictures of you and that woman, I swear I never thought that you would ever—"

He stops pushing altogether, making a frustrated sound and stepping away from the swings. "Lila. We seriously don't have to talk about this. It's not important anymore."

"Okay." I hang my head, feeling my face heat. "I'm sorry."

"No, don't—fuck," he mutters. "Hey." He kneels down at my feet, peering up at me. I suck in a breath when his hand reaches to press his fingers to my chin, tilting it up to force me to look at him. "Don't be sorry, okay? I just hate the idea of you thinking about this shit. I can take everyone else thinking I'm garbage, but not you."

But not me?

My brain is already reading way too much into that.

"I don't think that," I assure him quietly. "I've never thought that."

His mouth quirks, and his eyes are warm, and there's a barely-there swipe of his thumb against my jawline before his expression changes, and he stands abruptly. "Good," he grunts. "You were always as much of my friend as Jack was. I hope you know that."

His *friend*.

Fuck, that word sours my stomach now just as much as it did back then.

"Right," I answer softly. "Of course."

His gaze lingers on my face for a second more, his expression unreadable but his eyes still soft. "We should probably get back. Everyone is going to be looking for us."

"Sure," I say, sliding out of the swing and landing on my feet.

Like this, the disparity of our heights is glaringly obvious, and being this close makes me feel tiny, dainty even—thick thighs and all. It makes the lizard part of my brain wonder if he could simply slide his hands under my ass and pull me up against him without a second thought.

I try to cut through the awkward tension between us by shaking off my desperate thoughts and bumping my hip against his, forcing a grin on my mouth. "Come on, I'll race you back."

"What?" His nose scrunches. "I'm not going to—"

I take off at a dead run, laughing, and it hardly even takes a second for me to hear the heavy falls of his footsteps close behind me, an answering laugh in the wind.

Idly I wonder if I can go fast enough to outrun all the conflicting emotions Ian makes me feel . . . but somehow I doubt it.

Ten

IAN

The picture that circulates on the internet in the days after the orphanage isn't one I thought it would be. It isn't glimpses of Lila talking to me at the rink, or me helping clean up after, not even the moment where I whispered in her ear that still makes me heat up when I recall it—all things that would have been perfectly good rumor-feeding photos—no, the picture that trumped them all is the one I hadn't expected anyone to nab.

It's not the first time I've looked at it, not even the first ten, if I'm being honest—mostly because there's something about seeing myself crouched in front of her while she looks down at me from her perch on one of those old swings that strikes me as odd. Or maybe it feels odd because of how *not* odd it feels. I can't be sure. My fingers are gentle against her chin, and there's a serious expression on my face that is completely at war with the soft one she wears, and the entire scene as a whole is . . . It's fucking believable, is what it is. It sure as hell doesn't look like just two friends.

And we hadn't even been *trying*.

My only explanation is that I had felt such a strong need to comfort her, to let her know that I wasn't at all upset with her—because I had meant what I said to her. I can handle strangers thinking that I'm a piece of shit, or even just that I used to be, but for some reason, the idea of Lila viewing me that way turns my stomach. When we were younger, her obvious affection had always felt so warm and right, so much so that I found myself seeking her out anytime I came around, just to experience it. Lila has always been a comfort to me, and even if she's grown up now and different from the girl I knew—it's obvious that nothing about that has changed. I still feel that urge to be close to her, to protect her, to make her laugh, and when she was a child, that felt totally natural, but with the woman she's become . . . something about it feels different now.

Which leaves me all sorts of confused.

A knock at the front door of Jack's apartment startles me out of my own musings, and I turn my head to peer over the couch, noticing that the bathroom door is still closed as the faint sounds of Jack's shower drift out of it. His showers take twice as long with that sling now.

I push myself off the couch with a grunt and pad over to the door, unlocking the chain and dragging it open, only to feel a complete rush of surprise barrel me over.

"Abby?"

Her mouth curves into a shy smile, her bright gray eyes looking nervous and unsure. "Hey," she says. "Sorry, I know I should have called, but I thought—" She looks up and down the hallway. "Can I come in?"

I haven't seen Abigail in person in years; there are phone calls here and there—awkward conversations that neither of us seems to know how to navigate—but the last time I saw her, the entire interaction ended up all over the internet, a catalyst to the implosion of my personal life. She's changed since I last saw her; her blond hair is shorter, framing her face in a stylish cut that makes her look older, despite her sweet-looking face.

I manage to get a handle on my shock, nodding dumbly and stepping aside from the open door. "Yeah, come in."

"Nice place," she notes as she steps inside. "You live here with your friend, right?"

"Yeah," I tell her, closing the door. "Jack."

She seems jittery—shifting her weight from one foot to the other as she busies herself with taking in the apartment. "I really didn't mean to barge in on you, I was just . . ." She blows out an unsteady breath. "I guess I needed to see a friendly face."

"What happened?"

She looks almost guilty when she turns to look at me over her shoulder. "I called him."

"Oh."

Tension seizes up my muscles; I guess it isn't all that surprising that she still talks to him, but something about it still makes me feel . . . strange. Even after all these years, I haven't gotten used to this fucked triangle we're in.

"You can sit down," I tell her, gesturing to the couch. "You want something to drink?"

She shakes her head. "I'm good." She lets out a huff of a laugh. "I don't even really know why I'm here. I should have just called."

"Why didn't you?"

She looks at me with a furrowed brow, and I shake my head.

"Sorry," I amend. "I didn't mean to sound like a dick, it's just . . ."

"I know," she offers. "This is totally out of the blue."

"Did something happen?"

"No, no, nothing like that." Her teeth press against her lower lip, her finger twirling one strawberry blond curl around and around. "I've just been doing a lot of thinking lately, and I don't really know what to do, and now that you're back in town, I just . . ."

I carefully cross the room and ease onto the side of the couch opposite her, eyeing her warily. "Thinking about what?"

"All of it," she says. "I think I'm . . . I think I'm tired of keeping secrets, Ian."

My eyebrows shoot up. "What?"

"I know it's not fair to you," she says quietly. "And I know I agreed to not say anything, but—"

My voice comes out harsher than I mean it to. "Have you thought about what will happen if you say something?"

"I have," she answers, nodding softly. "I know it would be a nightmare." She glances at me, eyes full of guilt. "For you too."

"Then why?"

She closes her eyes, looking older than her twenty-five years. "I'm tired of only having secret conversations when there's time for them. I'm tired of lying about who I am. I'm just tired of all of it."

I can't pretend that I don't understand the way she's feeling; I can only imagine the sort of hell she's been through, even more so than me, in some ways—but I also know what sort of bomb her coming clean would be to everyone involved.

"Abby, I—" I clench my jaw, trying to sort through my feelings on this. "I can't tell you what to do."

"But?"

"But I can't pretend it won't be a fucking shit show." I level my gaze with hers. "And not just for you."

Her eyes drop to her knees, and she looks so young and vulnerable that I feel an almost visceral urge to close the distance between us and wrap my arms around her. Something I don't even know if she'd want. After all this time, I still don't quite know how to maneuver our . . . relationship.

"I know," she says finally. "I know that. It's probably a stupid idea."

"I didn't say that," I try.

Her eyes are harder now. "But I'm sure you were thinking it."

"Abby," I sigh.

"It's fine," she says harshly, pushing up from the couch. "Fuck. I don't even know why I came. It's not like we're really . . ." Her lips press together, and she looks so . . . lost. "I'm sorry."

I move to stand, reaching out for her. "Abby, you don't have to be—"

"Hey! Did you know we're out of body wash? Had to use your weird bar. I hope it's not for your balls or anything. My skin is going to be dry as fu—"

Abby and I both turn to find Jack haunting the end of the hallway with just a towel wrapped around his waist, his eyes darting between the two of us. A glance at Abby shows her face full of surprise as her eyes widen, and then she's practically power walking to the front door, reaching for the handle and wrenching it open. She turns to linger in the doorway for a moment, giving me those same sad eyes.

"I'm sorry," she offers. "I shouldn't have barged in on you. Maybe we can talk later?"

I feel my nod, heavy and slow. "Sure."

And with that she's gone, the apartment door falling shut behind her as if she never had been here. The silence she leaves behind is palpable, so thick that the sound of Jack's breathing feels as if it's only steps away instead of all the way across the room.

"That was her, wasn't it?"

I can only nod. "Yeah."

"What did she want?"

"I . . ." I shake my head. "I'm not really sure, honestly."

It's not the whole truth, but it's not *not* the truth. She definitely seemed unsure of things.

"You need to talk about it?"

God. What is it about the Baker siblings and them wanting me to hash my shit out?

"I'm good," I tell him. "We gotta get going soon, anyway."

"Yeah." Jack gives me a wan smile. "Aunt Bea will kick both our asses if we're late to dinner."

Because there isn't enough confusion in my life right now, of course Jack and Lila's aunt has invited us all to dinner tonight, meaning that I will have to sit across a table from the woman who's causing chaos in my head in a home that always felt more mine than my own—all while pretending I'm *not* slowly unraveling. Add Abigail into the mix? My mind might as well be a basket of wet cats right now.

"Let me hop in the shower real quick," I say, "and then we can go."

"Okay," Jack answers. "We really are out of body wash, though, just a heads-up." I turn, catching the way his nose wrinkles in distaste. "The bar on the shelf *isn't* for your balls, right?"

My mouth quirks, and I shrug one shoulder as I head past him toward the bathroom. "Who can say?"

His mumbled "Dick" and the resulting laugh it pulls from me might be the most normal thing that has happened today.

－－－－－

It's both weird and completely easy being back at Bea's place.

The few times I've seen her over the years have all been out and about—at dinners with Jack or seeing her at games of his I caught—but I haven't been back *here* since I was twenty-two years old and on the cusp of being drafted into the NHL. Before that, I was in and out of her house constantly for the entire decade prior; I think I spent more time over here than at my own house. So it *actually* feels like coming home, sitting in her dining room as she sets out different food she's made.

"Now, I've got brownies in the oven," she tells the three of us. "I figure we can eat them with some ice cream after dinner."

Lila is sitting right next to me, her smile easy and frequent and hard not to return. Jack is on the other side of the table, already reaching for a roll with his good hand, only for Bea to smack it away.

"You wait until I get everything set out, heathen."

Jack pouts. "Dude, I'm injured."

"Well, you're about to be even more injured if you don't hold your horses." She frowns in his direction. "And I'm not your 'dude.'"

"Yeah, fine," Jack grumbles under his breath.

"Ian? You want some bread?"

"Sure, Bea," I say.

Jack makes an indignant sound. "Hey!"

"You shut up over there," she tsks. "He didn't reach."

Lila giggles softly, and Jack cuts his eyes at her, sticking out his tongue. It's so similar to a night from my teen years that I feel a wave of nostalgia wash over that unravels some of the tension I've been carrying. It makes me wish I'd come for a visit long before tonight.

We all fill our plates and settle into comfortable conversation, but I'm hyperaware of the way Lila's elbow brushes against my arm every so often. The way she smirks at me when I drop a bite of peas back onto my plate, a playful glint in her eye. Hell, I'm just aware of *her*, period. That's definitely different from the last time I was here.

"So," Bea says after the catching-up dies down, pointing her fork between the two of us. "What's this Jack tells me about the two of you acting like you're all lovey-dovey for the masses?"

I almost choke on my roll. Lila pats my back, clucking her tongue. "What the hell, Jack?"

"What?" Jack tries to look innocent with a mouthful of potatoes. "Didn't know it was a secret."

"It's not," I say, finally, managing to swallow my bite down. "It's nothing, Bea. Just something our PR teams cooked up."

The words feel heavy on my tongue. Not like a lie, per se, because it absolutely is pretend, but something about dismissing it still doesn't sit quite right. I don't really have time to assess those feelings, though, since Bea isn't done.

"Always hoped you two would get married," she says offhandedly, like it's not the equivalent of dropping an atom bomb into the conversation. "Then I could have all of you as my kids."

"*Aunt Bea*," Lila hisses, her face flushing. "Seriously?"

Bea cocks an eyebrow. "What? An old woman can dream, can't she?" She tilts her chin in my direction. "That one you married was nice though. How is she?"

"Mei's fine," I tell her. "She just got remarried. They're off on their honeymoon right now."

"Didn't she marry a woman?" Bea's nose wrinkles. "What did you do to her that she didn't want men anymore?"

"*Aunt Bea*," Lila repeats on a choked groan. "Oh my God."

"She's bisexual," I laugh. "Think she always leaned more toward women though."

Bea considers this, her expression thoughtful. "I imagine they're softer. Guess I can't blame her."

"I would like to very much not explore this conversation," Jack chimes in.

"So you two gonna have to kiss and stuff on camera?" Bea barrels on.

My mouth falls open, and I look to Lila for help; she seems just as thrown. The image of Lila's soft, pink mouth on mine thunders through my thoughts, making itself known, and it should be a curious thing, I think. It should be nothing more than a passing oddity that is just a result of Bea putting it there, but the effect it has on me . . . My pulse picks up, my ears heat, and the breath I'd been about to release gets caught in my throat, like my body can't help but hold it. It's definitely *not* a passing oddity. Not with the way my thoughts are practically tattooing it onto my brain.

"I don't think it'll come to anything like that," I manage thickly after far too many seconds. "The internet sort of makes their own rumors, you know? Once the idea is there, they pretty much don't need much to keep it alive."

I peek at Lila, and instead of seeing gratitude at my save, she looks almost . . . irritated. It's not something I'm used to seeing on her. It's gone too quickly for me to really analyze it though.

"It's just a silly game, Aunt Bea," she says finally. "It's only for a few weeks."

It's only for a few weeks.

Why does that make me want to frown? I can't seem to get a handle on my own head.

"Sure," Bea laughs. "Whatever you kids say." She points her fork at Lila. "You all up for a game of Farkle?"

"I fucking hate that game," Jack groans.

Bea smacks his good shoulder, causing him to yelp. "You want me to break your other arm? Watch your mouth."

"Why are you so mean to me?"

Bea rolls her eyes. "Oh, hardly." She looks between Lila and me. "Two of you want to go find the game? I keep them in Dee's closet. Top shelf. Might need Ian's help to get it down without causing an avalanche."

There's a twinkle in her eye that suggests she's up to something, but Lila is already standing, dropping her napkin on her empty plate. "Sure," she says. And then to me, "Come help me?"

"Okay," I say, standing from my own chair.

I know the way to Lila's bedroom; I've seen it many times, after all, but stepping inside it after all this time feels . . . different. Even if everything looks exactly the same.

"Wow," I say. "Bea hasn't changed a thing, has she?"

"I think it makes her feel better," Lila says over her shoulder as she crosses the room to her closet. "She gets lonely here living on her own."

"But you guys visit a lot, right?"

"Oh yeah. At least once a week."

I shuffle over to Lila's bed, picking up a stuffed rabbit resting against her pillows, a smile touching my lips. "I see this guy is still clinging to life."

"Who?" Lila angles my way, chuckling when she sees what I'm holding. "Ears will outlive us all."

I run my fingers over one soft ear the rabbit was named for. "I remember you couldn't sleep a wink without this damned thing."

"I was seven," she grumbles.

"Oh?" My mouth quirks, and I tilt the stuffed bunny back and forth. "And when did you stop sleeping with him again?"

Lila rolls her eyes. "Shut up."

"I remember the year you were obsessed with tea parties," I muse, setting the rabbit back on her bed and eyeing the little wicker table in the corner. "Jack and I drank so much fake tea, I'm surprised we didn't get sick."

She crosses her arms over her chest, arching one tailored brow, and my eyes are drawn to her smug expression, which makes her lips pout, taking my thoughts to places they shouldn't be. "You know, cool things happened here too."

"Oh yeah?" I chuckle. "Have a few ragers in here?"

She shrugs. "No, but I did try weed right there at that window."

"Wow." I fake a gasp. "Scandalous. What else did I miss in here, Outlaw?"

"Let's see." She taps her finger against her bottom lip, and it's an actual struggle not to let my eyes settle there for too long, feeling an urge hit me out of nowhere to run my finger there instead. "Well. I snuck a boy in here when I was sixteen."

I feel the fine hairs on my neck prickle; this is not news that should put me on edge, since I was twenty-one when this apparently happened, so why the fuck *does* it? Why do I suddenly hate this game we're playing?

"Did you."

"Yep." Her lips curl in a Cheshire cat grin. "Had my first kiss right there on that bed."

"With who?"

"Tommy Dalton," she tells me. "He was in my algebra class."

I grind my teeth. "Any good?"

"Not really," she laughs. "Too much tongue."

Why the fuck do I hate this so much?

"Poor Tommy," I mutter, absolutely not meaning it at all.

"Yeah, well," she says with another quiet chuckle. "I was pining for someone else, so the poor guy never stood a chance."

"Someone else?"

Her gaze finds mine, her mouth pressing into a line as she studies me. "Yeah. Someone older."

My stomach flutters with . . . something.

"Oh?"

"Mhm." She takes a step toward me, and I feel my heart begin to race. "Someone who just saw me as a kid."

I swallow thickly, watching her take another step. "I guess it never worked out, then, huh?"

"Nah. He was always going to see me as Jack's little sister back then." Her teeth press against her lip, and fuck if I'm fixated on the sight. "But I still think about him."

Fuck, does she mean . . . ?

I clear my throat. "Anyone I know?"

"Hm. You could say that."

She's close now, and her hand reaches to toy with the collar of my shirt, just a light touch that still causes goose bumps to break out along my skin. Without thinking, my hand shoots out to wrap my fingers around her wrist, watching her pupils dilate as I grip it tight, forcing her palm to press against my chest. I can feel the warmth of it through my shirt, and her eyes slowly move down to stare at my hand. They linger there for a second, maybe more, and when she tilts her head back up to meet my gaze, I realize I'm holding my breath.

"Lila, I—"

"You really never noticed?"

Her voice is barely a whisper now, and I feel like I'm under a spell, watching her lean in ever so slightly.

"I . . ." I struggle for words, because the implication is there, but to acknowledge it would be a game changer for the both of us. It would mean changing everything we've ever known, everything we've ever been—and is that really wise? Am I actually leaning in too? "Lila, I—"

"You two found it yet?" Bea calls from back in the dining room. "It's on the top shelf!"

Lila steps away from me lightning fast, the warmth from her closeness fading like it had never been there and a happy mask sliding over her features as she flashes me a grin. "Sorry," she says. "I just like seeing you flustered, Cupcake."

My mouth parts, only to close again, something deflating inside. She was joking with me? Really?

"Very funny," I manage dryly.

That glint of sadness is back in her eyes, and it comes and goes so quickly I might almost miss it, but I don't. I see it. I see it well enough that it makes me wonder if she was really joking. And if she wasn't, what does that mean for us and all the thoughts I keep having?

"Let's grab that game and head back," Lila says. "Bea gets cranky when you make her wait."

"Sure," I answer dumbly, my brain still reeling.

She points out the box with the dice and the score sheets for me to grab, hardly even waiting for me to pull it out before she's starting out of the room. I hold the game in my hand and watch her go, needing a second to collect myself before I follow after her.

You really never noticed?

I want to pull her back and ask her what those words meant. I want to know what that look on her face meant. I want to know if she was actually joking or if she meant everything that she just said. But mostly . . .

I want to know why I'm so disappointed by the possibility that she didn't.

Eleven

DELILAH

"And ... cut!"

I run my fingers through my hair as people on set start to move about after wrapping. I managed to keep focused during filming, but admittedly, only just. My mind wants to wander every time I let it off the leash for too long, and I suspect that it can all be traced back to a moment in my childhood bedroom that happened days ago now.

"You've got flour in your hair," Ava says, sidling up next to me.

I pick at a stray tendril and see that, yes, she's absolutely right. "Shit."

"The cutest little pastry ghost," she coos.

"Fuck off," I mutter.

"Oh, someone's cranky." She tugs me to the sink, leaning against the counter as I wash my hands. "Tell Mama all about it."

"There's nothing to tell."

"You're a terrible liar. You've been spacey all day." She waits until I've finished drying my hands, looping her arm through mine and leaning into me conspiratorially. "It doesn't have anything to do with a certain hockey player, does it?"

I can feel my face pinch, which is more than enough for Ava to latch on to.

"Aha!" She nudges me in the side with her elbow. "Spill. I want details. The pictures floating around are very . . . compelling."

"It's nothing," I say automatically, my stomach twisting with the words. "We're just friends."

"Did you even *see* that park photo? Man practically had stars in his eyes, and he was almost on his *knees* for you."

"That was taken out of context," I counter. "We were having a serious conversation."

"You tell yourself whatever you have to, girlie," she laughs. "I think there's some fucking chemistry there."

God, I wish that were true.

It's so much harder than I thought it would be, playing this game. Every time that I see Ian, spend time with him, I'm reminded of all the reasons why I was so obsessed with him to begin with. There's something so . . . comforting about him. Something solid and reliable that feels like stability and home and all sorts of other good things that turn me into a pile of goo whenever he's nearby.

It doesn't hurt that he's fucking hot either.

"I actually think I might have been weird recently," I admit, reaching the refreshments table and grabbing a water. "I've been too chickenshit to text him in the last couple of days."

"Details," Ava says with a snap of her fingers. "Right now."

"Well . . . We all went to dinner at Aunt Bea's this week, right?"

"Yeah, and?"

"It was going well. Felt just like old times, honestly. But then there was this moment in my bedroom—"

Ava gasps, clutching her chest dramatically, and I roll my eyes.

"—*where* we were grabbing a game for everyone to play, and we started kind of . . . reminiscing? I guess?"

"About?"

"Stupid things at first," I tell her. "Old memories and shit. But then I somehow started on about my first kiss happening in that room, and I just . . ."

I frown, looking down at my feet as I try to pinpoint what I'd been feeling at that moment.

"I guess it was a lot, you know? Having him in my room like that. It was like the beginning of every fantasy I ever had about him when I was younger, and suddenly there he was, in the flesh. I may have hinted that I wished he'd been my first kiss."

"*Girl*," Ava practically squeals. "Yes. I love this. What did he say?"

"I'm not even entirely sure that he picked up on it," I say dejectedly.

And why would he? I've always been so far outside his radar that I don't even ping as a possibility.

But the way he touched me . . .

I can't rationalize that part. Had it been a surprise? Had I made him uncomfortable? I want to tell myself that the look he'd given me was more than just catching him off guard, but I can't be sure of that. Which is why my head continues to spin in circles.

"Oh, honey," she says, her voice dripping with sympathy. "What did you do?"

"Played it off as a joke. I mean, what else could I do?"

"You could have just come out with it," she suggests. "See what happens."

"That would be a terrible idea."

"Would it?"

"*Wouldn't* it?"

Ava shrugs. "I mean, the worst thing that happens is he shows no interest, and you both move on and continue being friends, and you can once and for all put all of it behind you."

"Yeah and be horribly rejected in the process."

"But what if he didn't?"

"There's no way he wouldn't."

"But how do you know?"

"Because he's always going to see me as the dumb kid he knew over a decade ago!"

Ava looks surprised by my sharp tone, and I am too.

"Sorry," I say quickly, shaking my head. "I didn't mean to get snippy."

Ava raises her hands in acquiescence. "All I'm saying is that you're *not* that kid he knew all those years ago. You're a fully grown, hot-as-fuck woman who he'd be dumb as hell not to notice."

"You're not . . . *not* right," I mumble.

"You've got tits I'd kill for and an ass that won't quit, babe," she says. "Plus, you're, like, sunshine incarnate."

"Should I be offended by that?"

"Only if you strive to be a cynical asshole like moi."

"I don't know . . ."

She pats my shoulder. "Just think it over. He might surprise you. What have you got to lose, really?"

My pride, I think bitterly. *My dignity.*

"I'll think about it," I tell her only halfheartedly.

"Good." She flashes me a grin. "Now I can tell you that Gia wants to see you in her office."

I groan. "Why didn't you lead with that?"

"And send you up there looking like a kicked puppy? Had to sort out your shit first."

"I don't exactly feel 'sorted.'"

"Well, I'm a producer, not a therapist."

"Junior producer."

"A *friend* wouldn't correct me."

I feel a grin spreading on my own face now. "Yeah, well. You're an asshole, remember?"

"Fair." She gives me a shooing motion. "Run along." She pauses midstep before frowning at me. "And there's still flour in your hair, by the way."

I glare up at my forehead.

Of course.

─ ─ ─ ─ ─

Gia, to my relief, looks ecstatic when I plop down into one of the chairs in her office.

"Have you seen the buzz around you and Ian?"

She turns the monitor to her desktop to point out an article I haven't seen yet to prove her point, one that has a picture of Ian and me from the play day front and center—me leaning over the railing by the rink as he smiles down at me. Another flick of her fingers on the mouse pad reveals a shot where he leaned into my ear, and I would be willing to bet that if you zoomed in, you'd be able to see my goose bumps. It makes my chest feel gooey.

"Haven't seen that one," I tell her. "But I've definitely seen a few."

"Everyone is head over heels at the idea of the two of you," she says gleefully. "Also, it's spilling over into coverage of the show. I've already seen two articles stemming from one of the two of you highlighting *Whisk-y Business*."

"And the numbers? Have we seen any changes?"

"Slight uptick," she tells me. "Not as much as I'd like, not yet, but it's a good start." She gives me an assuring look. "It's only been a couple of weeks. At this rate, it's going to go just like we want it to."

"Let's hope," I say, still feeling a little bummed out at the idea of subjecting myself to more torture that is being close to Ian and knowing he'll only ever see me as a friend.

"I was actually hoping we could get Ian on for another episode," she says.

My eyebrows raise. "What?"

"It's just that the first one did so well, and now with all the buzz around the two of you . . . Another episode is *bound* to do better, numbers-wise. We could even play up the 'are they, aren't they?' more this go-round. A little more flirting, things like that."

It's a struggle, keeping my face passive and not letting it rumple into frustration like it wants to. "I don't know if Ian will have time for another."

"Oh, surely he will be up for it? The Druids are getting some good buzz from this too. Plus, I spoke with his PR manager just yesterday, and they're seeing a large decline in negative posts about Ian and his past. That alone will be enough incentive for him to agree, I think."

Fuck.

Part of me wants to refuse, even if just for my own sanity's sake. Flirting with Ian on camera? Can I really survive that, knowing that it's completely fake? But then again . . . How can I say no, knowing that this is helping him, that what we're doing is making his life a little easier?

"I can ask him," I say finally, my tone lacking even half of Gia's enthusiasm.

"Perfect," she answers brightly. "I was also hoping that the two of you could have some sort of outing soon."

Now I *know* I'm making a face. "Outing?"

"Yes, I was talking to Ben, and after all the pics following the play day, we think it would be a good idea if the two of you were seen again in public. Maybe just the two of you this time? Could make for some good press, which would mean more buzz."

"Like a date? Is that what you mean?"

"No, we can't ask you to go on dates for the network," Gia says with a nervous laugh, betraying that this is essentially what she's doing. "Just that you . . . spend some time together in public. We just want the two of you to be seen, remember?"

"I remember," I sigh. I consider it, coming up blank on what an "outing in public" with Ian would even look like. Are we supposed to go tandem biking in the fucking park or something? "Again, I'll have to run it by Ian. I don't want to agree to anything without talking to him first."

"Of course, of course," Gia says. "Talk it over with him tonight, if you can, and let me know tomorrow what the plan is so we can plant the appropriate leaks to the right people."

I don't even want clarification on everything she just said. I suspect I don't want to know the inner workings of network gossip and how they keep it rolling.

"Sure," I say instead. "I'll do that."

"Good. This is all going so great."

I try to match her excited expression, but it probably comes out strained. I know that she's right, that everything that's happening is exactly what we were setting out to do, that it's everything I agreed to, and I stand by my reasons for saying yes in the first place, I really do.

I just never imagined that it would be so damned hard.

I decide to visit Ian in person rather than talking over the phone about all this new nonsense the network has cooked up, so when he texts me that he's *home*—I make my way over to Jack's feeling more and more anxious the closer I get to their apartment. By the time I knock on the door, I'm practically sweating. Which I don't do. I don't fucking sweat over guys.

I'm giving myself a mental girlboss ass-kicking when the door swings open, and then I'm flummoxed by wet, red curls and stormy gray eyes and a dark navy T-shirt that is stretched tightly over a broad chest—the shoulders wet from his hair. He obviously just got out of the shower, which means my brain has effectively opened a window and let my entire ten-point speech on why we do *not* simp fly out on the breeze. It's gone now. Out there in the wind. I don't even have time to catch it since my eyes are gobbling up every bit of Ian they can reach.

"Hey," he greets me in that warm, low way of his. "Come in."

I step past him, swallowing around the lump in my throat and looking around the living room. "Where's Jack?"

"Physical therapy," Ian tells me, shutting the door behind us.

"Oh, duh." I'm nodding aimlessly as I sink down onto the couch. "I forgot."

Might have been nice to remember before you rode over here to be locked in this apartment alone with him.

Ian grabs a towel that had been slung haphazardly across the back of the couch, bringing it to his hair and rubbing it through the wet mass as he takes the end opposite me to sit.

"You said we needed to talk about something?"

"Right," I say, clearing my throat. "I met with Gia today, and she wants us to do another episode with you on the show."

His eyebrows raise. "Really?"

"Mhm. Apparently, now that we're hot goss, she thinks a repeat will do even better numbers than last time."

"Makes sense," he says thoughtfully, his hand slowing against his hair as he frowns down at his lap like he's thinking.

Which means that the bulge of his bicep is more prominent as he lazily works the towel against his hair, his skin wrapped in ink and still slightly damp in a way that makes me want to lick it.

"But only if you're comfortable with it," I add.

He shrugs one shoulder, giving up on the drying altogether as he drops the towel over the back of the couch again. "Guess it can't hurt." He smirks at me. "I told them as long as they don't try to get me naked on camera or something, I'm down for whatever."

Oh God. Do not think about him naked right now. He's wet, for God's sake. Do not think about him naked and wet.

I clench my jaw, nodding too quickly to be normal. "Awesome. I can let Gia know."

"You came all the way over here to ask me that?"

His voice is teasing, and I feel my cheeks heat in response.

"Oh, well, no. There was something else she suggested that I wasn't sure about."

"Oh?"

"The network feels that it might create more buzz for us to be . . . seen together again. Like the play day."

"Do they have an event in mind?"

"They would rather we have an . . . outing . . . with just the two of us."

He blinks at me for a second or two, and then, "Like a date?"

"They can't call it a date," I grouse, "but pretty much, yeah."

His hand reaches to let his finger trace along his lower lip, and my eyes are glued to that action, and I'm talking super, not Elmer's. It has me thinking about that stupid moment in my stupid bedroom where I said stupid things.

Which loosens my tongue to say even *more* stupid things.

"We'd probably have to be a little touchy-feely," I say quietly.

His finger stills against his lip, and his eyes lock with mine. "Yeah?"

"To sell it, you know?"

He nods slowly, still touching that fucking lip. "Makes sense."

"That's not going to be weird for you, is it?"

His brow furrows a fraction. "I can handle it if you can."

"Well, I can *totally* handle it," I fire back, hearing the challenge in his tone.

"And what sort of touching did you have in mind?"

"I didn't say I had anything particular in mind," I answer thickly.

His finger makes another slow back-and-forth against the seam of his mouth, his eyes thoughtful as they move over my face. "Probably hand-holding, at the very least."

"Probably," I answer, my voice sounding wrong. "I could pull the old hand-in-your-back-pocket move."

His brow arches. "People still do that?"

"Oh yeah. Loads."

"Hm." His eyes warm, and there's the barest hint of his teeth against his lower lip now, and I feel the same strange current of electricity I've been telling myself I imagined in my bedroom the other night. The one that had me word-vomiting in abstract in the first place. "I can handle whatever you can, Lila."

If I were standing, I think my knees might be wobbling right now. I don't know what I'm doing, I don't know what *we're* doing, but I can't seem to stop my brain from pouring words out of my mouth before I can stop them. Is this more of the silly game we've been playing? Or is it something else?

"Oh yeah? I'm pretty committed, you know. You don't want to sign yourself over to an impromptu make-out session."

Stop fucking talking, dumbass.

I'm holding my breath as Ian stares, his expression more locked up than Fort Knox. I'd give a whole tit just to know what he was thinking right now.

"I can handle," he says slowly, carefully, "whatever you can, Lila."

I feel my breath catch as my pulse triples, at least, my lips parting to say something, but what, I'm not sure. The air is thick and the room is too warm, or maybe that's just me, and I know I need to say something, say *anything*, really, and I—

Ian and I both startle when the door swings open behind him, Jack grumbling under his breath as he tries to balance his keys in the lock while holding a plastic bag with his bad hand, which is sticking out of his sling.

"Dude, we gotta get one of those keyless locks, this one-handed shit is for the—"

Jack frowns when he spots the two of us. "Every time I walk into this room lately, you've got a woman on my couch."

Something in my stomach sinks. "Oh, really?"

"Not at all what that sounds like, trust me," Ian says firmly, holding my gaze as he does so.

The charged air fizzles out around us, and despite the expression Ian is wearing, one that asks me to trust him when he doesn't owe me an explanation in the slightest to begin with, I feel heavy all of a sudden. Nauseous, even.

"I was just going over some stuff Gia suggested," I say flatly, standing from the couch.

"Lila," Ian says, following me.

I paste on a very wide, very fake smile. "I'll text you later about those outing plans, yeah? We can brainstorm ideas."

"Lila," he says again, looking irritated.

Why does he look irritated? It's none of my business who he has on his couch.

"You don't want to stay?" Jack says. "I got stuff to make nachos."

"I already ate," I toss back, moving toward the front door. "I have stuff to do at home, anyway."

"Suit yourself," Jack says with a shrug, blissfully ignorant to the energy of the room he burst into as he holds the door open wide to let me pass through it. "They're *not yo* nachos, anyway."

"That was awful," I groan, pulling him into a loose hug while I avoid his arm.

I purposely avoid looking at Ian.

"See you guys later."

I can feel Ian's eyes on me as the door closes, and I don't take a full breath until I hear the lock click into place. I've barely made it to the elevator when my phone buzzes in my pocket, and I have a good idea already as to who's texting me.

CUPCAKE: It's not what it sounds like.

I stare at the text the entire ride down the elevator, only managing to tap out a reply when I'm pacing through the lobby of Jack's building.

ME: Don't even sweat it. None of my business anyway.
I'll check in tomorrow about outing ideas. Good night!

It's not at all how I feel, but it's not like I can demand he tell me what other women he's had over—who they are, what they are to him, why they were there. It's wholly not my business and definitely not my place.

And that, if I really take the time to analyze it, is exactly why I feel so shitty right now.

Twelve

IAN

Even sitting off the ice and lacing up my skates, I'm second-guessing my idea to bring her here. And on top of that, I'm second-guessing the fact that I'm second-guessing my idea to bring her here. I have to remind myself that this isn't actually a *date*—even if the amount of nervous sweat I'm producing under my hoodie says otherwise.

Delilah has been distant in the last few days; I've wanted to try to explain what she heard from Jack more than once since she walked out of the apartment, but not only would I not know where to start, I also worry that she meant what she said that night. That she's not actually worried about it. That it's just *me* obsessing over what she might be thinking.

Skates laced, I lean back on the bench and scan the indoor rink, noting the decent amount of people currently occupying the ice. Enough that there will certainly be pictures taken of us, but not so many that I'll feel like we're under a microscope. The nostalgia of being here again washes over me like a wave, bringing back memories of skinned knees and too many bruises on a much smaller me, my dad off to the sides barking at me to *do it again, and right this time.*

My phone buzzes in my pocket, jarring me from my memories, and a twisting feeling settles in my gut when I pull it out and see my mother's name. We've talked here and there since I got back into town, but I've yet to go and see her. Something she hasn't let me forget. Taking a deep breath, I answer her call and bring the phone to my ear.

"Hey, Mom."

"Ian! Sweetheart. What are you doing right now?"

"Me? I'm . . ." I frown. I can't really tell her what I'm *actually* doing, which is stressing out about a "maybe, maybe not" date with a woman I can't stop obsessing over. I clear my throat. "I'm at the rink Dad used to take me to."

"Oh, your father loves that place. Is he with you?"

My nose wrinkles with distaste; my father hasn't been anywhere near the ice with me since I was at least fifteen, and as much as I wonder *where* he is, since my mother doesn't seem to know, I don't comment on that either.

"No, I'm meeting a friend."

"A *girl* friend?" Mom teases.

"Mom . . ."

"Don't think I don't surf the web, too, son. I've seen the pictures of you and the Baker girl. Delilah? She's so gorgeous. She was always a cute kid, but my, what a looker she grew up to be."

I swallow around the lump in my throat; my mother has no idea how much I'm struggling with that very fact. "Yeah," I say. "She has. But you know it's all a stunt."

"I don't know," Mom says slyly. "Those pictures looked pretty convincing."

I snort. "That's the point."

"Mhm." Her tone suggests she still isn't quite convinced. "Whatever you say."

"I *say* we're just friends," I stress, the words sounding weak to my own ears.

"You should bring her to dinner. Oh, that would be lovely. I could make my chowder, and we could—"

"No," I say quickly, *too* quickly. I can hear the way my mom pauses, can practically see the hurt in her expression. It makes me feel even more shitty than I already do. "I just mean . . ." Fuck. I wish I could tell her everything. It would be nice to have someone else to comb over all the complicated feelings I'm having, but I know that's a road I can't go down. Not when I can't tell her the *entire* truth. "I just mean . . . I don't want to put any pressure on her. She's already helping me out."

"Oh." My mother does her best to hide her disappointment, but I hear it. How much more disappointed in me would she be if she knew everything? "Well, that's okay. Maybe later, yeah?"

"Sure," I say, not sure if I actually mean it. "Later."

"Well, I just wanted to check in with you. I miss you, son. *You'll* come see me soon, at least, won't you? I know you've been busy, but your old mother misses her boy."

A painful squeezing sensation spreads through my chest, and I close my eyes against its sting. "I miss you too. I'm sorry I've been so busy. I'll come visit soon, okay?"

"I'll hold you to that," she chuckles. "I love you, Ian."

My voice sounds a little too thick when I answer, "I love you, too, Mom."

We say our goodbyes and I stow my phone back in my pocket, the added layer of guilt over my mother only worsening my nerves. There are so many anxious thoughts rolling around in my head, so many people to potentially disappoint that I can hardly keep up with them anymore. My mother, Lila, Abby, my *father*—not that it would be anything new with him—it makes it hard to breathe sometimes, the weight of it. It makes me wish things were different.

"Only you would suggest ice skating on your day off as an outing," I hear behind me, followed by a soft chuckle.

I turn my head to see Lila approach, her hair tucked under a pink knit cap and a pensive look on her face. Those anxious feelings are still swirling inside, but at the sight of her, strangely, they almost seem to settle. Her small smile seems to almost knock away the cobwebs forming on my brain, and even if those doubts and fears still linger, they feel less overwhelming when she's here.

It makes the feelings I keep having for *her* even harder to ignore.

"Too on the nose?"

She shrugs one shoulder, plopping down beside me on the bench and shucking off her shoes so she can don her own skates. "With you? I don't know. It kind of feels right."

I watch her tie her laces as a silence settles between us, and I can feel it, the awkward air still lingering that I'd hoped would have thinned since I last saw her. It feels like too much, seeing the obvious disappointment she's carrying; I've disappointed so many people in my life, and Lila is someone I desperately don't want to add to the list. She doesn't look at me throughout her entire task, keeping her eyes on her skates until they're firmly in place. Then she stands, testing her balance before moving toward the opening that leads out into the ice.

Only then does she turn back toward me, that same dull expression on her face that feels so unlike the Lila I know. Like she's doing her best not to let her emotions show. "You coming?"

I can only nod dumbly, rising from the bench and following after her as she glides out on the ice, moving leisurely as I fall into rhythm beside her. We make an entire circle around the rink in silence before I can't take it anymore, clearing my throat and hoping I sound more casual than I feel.

"Your skating has definitely improved," I say, going for teasing.

She snorts under her breath. "Yeah, well, the last time you saw me in skates, I was still wearing a training bra."

Keep your eyes on the fucking ice, Chase. You already know she's well outgrown those. You have no reason to confirm it again.

"Right," I answer with a weird laugh that sounds nothing like mine. "I guess it has been a while."

"It's been a while for all sorts of things," she says cryptically.

I slow my pace. "What does that mean?"

"Nothing," she says quickly, skating ahead and forcing me to catch up to her.

"Have you been avoiding me?"

She frowns. "I haven't seen you. How could I avoid you?"

"I don't know. You've seemed . . . different."

"Have I?"

I grind to a halt, grabbing her wrist and forcing her to stop skating. "Lila."

"Ian," she counters almost petulantly, her chin tilting up and her eyes narrowing.

"Listen," I huff. "I don't really know how to fix whatever I did, but I don't like this weirdness. I *do* know that what you heard from Jack the other night isn't at all what you think it was. I'm not seeing anyone. I haven't seen anyone since Mei. I'm definitely not bringing random women over to my place. Jack's place. Whatever."

She purses her lips, averting her eyes. "I told you, it's none of my business."

"Isn't it?"

Her eyes snap up to meet mine, her lips parting.

Fuck.

I don't even know what I'm doing. Maybe she really doesn't care. Maybe I really have been worried for nothing. Why don't I know which option sucks more?

I watch her features shift numerous times before settling onto something more *her*—her lips curling in a soft smile as she nods. "I believe you." She laughs then. "Dork."

The knot in my chest slowly begins to unwind. I shoot her a grin back.

"Excuse me. Out of the two of us, I am definitely not the dork."

"Keep telling yourself that, Cupcake."

I let her wrist slide through my fingers so she can start moving again, and out of the corner of my eye I can definitely notice people stopping to stare and even some blatantly taking photos.

"I think we can expect more photos on the internet soon," I mutter.

"That was sort of the point, right?"

"Still feels weird."

"At least there's not *too* many people here." She glances my way. "Why did you pick this place again?"

I feel my ears heat beneath my hair. "I used to practice here a lot as a kid with my dad. He had me out here every weekend and most days after school running drills."

"Really?"

"Mhm."

"How come I never knew that?"

"I don't know . . ." I shrug. "When I was with you guys, I didn't really like bringing up my dad."

"Is he still . . . ?"

"A giant dick? Yeah." I laugh bitterly. "Not that anyone else knows that. He's the perfect father and husband as far as the rest of the city is concerned."

"I don't know," she muses. "I've always thought he was kind of sleazy-seeming."

I smirk. "Oh, have you?"

"It's the eyes," she says seriously. "You can always tell."

"We have the same eyes," I remind her.

She turns her head, her lips curling and her expression warm as she says, "No, you really don't."

I don't know what to say to that, since I can't really think over the current pounding of my heart, so I just clear my throat, nodding instead.

She catches me off guard when her fingers suddenly brush against my hand, curling around my larger ones in an attempt to hold them. I glance down at her hand, pausing on the ice. Her lips quirk as she cocks a brow, her index finger drawing a slow circle over one of my knuckles and causing a shock of awareness to prickle over my skin.

"This okay?" she asks, her gaze teasing. "Don't want to do anything you can't handle."

I scoff, spreading her fingers and lacing them together with mine until I can feel the warmth of her palm in my grip. I give her hand a squeeze, trying to look as if the simple weight of her hand isn't enough to make me feel restless, like it doesn't make my heart race.

"I told you," I say evenly, "I can handle whatever you can."

I feel her give my hand a squeeze back, and it doesn't escape me how *not* weird it is, what we're doing. I clear my throat, trying to distract myself from how much smaller her hand is than mine, how holding it makes me want to hold all of her.

"Mei never liked him either," I say offhandedly. "My dad."

Immediately, I feel Lila tensing, her grip on my hand going stiff. "Oh?"

"Yeah, even when we were just dating, she said he seemed like he was just putting on an act."

"I see."

A quick glance reveals her expression to be thoughtful, her nose wrinkling slightly and her brows turned down as she watches the ice in front of her as she glides forward.

I slide my thumb against the back of her hand. "What is it?"

"Do you still love her?"

The question takes me completely off guard. "Mei?"

Lila just nods.

My mouth opens and then closes, trying to formulate an answer to her very complicated question.

"I—" I frown, thinking. I can practically feel the tension in Lila as she waits for whatever it is I'm going to say. There's no reason for me to be so invested in the fact that *she* seems invested, but I am, I realize. I really am. "No," I say finally. "If I'm being honest? I'm not sure we ever loved each other like that. She was my best friend. We helped each other through a lot of shit. I loved being there for her, and she felt the same for me. I think we both thought that was a good enough reason to get married."

Lila is still watching the ice. "Oh."

I don't know what compels me to keep going, but I can't stop now. "Her parents are . . . very old-fashioned. They're very openly against homosexuality. Mei kept her bisexuality a complete secret because of that. I was the only one who knew." I consider for a moment, remembering. "Looking back . . . I think she agreed to marry me because she thought it would be enough for her to be with someone she loved even if only as a friend. I think she thought that being with me would help her forget the part of herself she was hiding."

"But it didn't?"

"Does it ever? Hiding a part of yourself does nothing but tear you up inside. You can't really live if you're only doing it halfway."

I notice her breath catch when I look at her, her eyes widening. "I . . . Yeah. That's true, I guess."

"It got too hard," I tell her. "Being together knowing we would never feel *that* way. I wanted Mei to go out there and find someone she could be *in* love with, not just love. You know?"

"So when you split . . ."

"Totally amicable," I say. "We're still very good friends. The best, really. I love her new wife." I grin. "Most days."

"Wow, that's . . . a lot to process."

"Why is that?"

"It's just not what I imagined in my head when I thought about your marriage."

"I'm sure with nothing but those fucking pictures to go off of, it was hard to really come to any other conclusions. I mean, the entire internet is still convinced I was cheating on her the entire time."

"I never believed that," she says firmly, slowing her pace. "Never. You would never do something like that. You're too steady for that."

"You hadn't seen me in years at that point," I mumble. "How could you know that?"

She bites at her lower lip, looking shy all of a sudden, which is very unlike her.

"Because I've always seen you," she says softly, so low I might almost miss it. "Always."

I swallow thickly, at a loss. "Lila, about the photos, they were actually—"

She shakes her head, cutting me off. "You don't have to tell me anything, Ian. You don't owe me that. Not me or anyone else. I know who you are."

God, I've never wanted to spill my guts to someone more than I do at this very moment, but rationally, this probably isn't the place to reveal *all* my secrets.

"Thank you," I say instead, sounding breathless. I feel that way, so I suppose it makes sense.

I tug on her hand, forcing her to stop, just holding it between us. I can't help but stare at the sight of our clasped hands, waiting for the feeling to hit me that there's something off about it, that there's something not quite right, but it never comes. I hold her tighter, pulling her hand to my chest and holding it over my heart as I try to figure out how to tell her what I'm feeling. She looks down at our joined hands, then back up at me with surprise. But then I'm rewarded with her slow, sweet smile, and her fingers give mine a squeeze, and suddenly I realize I'm not looking at her at all like she's Jack's little sister, I'm not thinking of her like the girl I adored as a kid—no, right now she's just . . . Lila. Lila with her perfect smile and her soft heart and her softer mouth that even now draws my attention.

Which reminds me.

"Lila."

We're both still now, just standing in the middle of the rink while God knows what is captured around us.

I watch the delicate line of her throat bob with a swallow, her face tilted up as she looks at me expectantly. "Yeah?"

"Was there really someone?" I can't take my eyes off her, scanning her face for signs of a truth that I now realize I'm desperate to know. "Someone you used to want. Someone that didn't see you."

She takes a deep breath, releasing it slowly before, "I think you know the answer to that."

My chest swells, and the urge to get closer to her is overwhelming, like a wave pulling me under, and she's the air.

"And if . . ." I clear my throat. "If they saw you now? Would it be too late?"

Her lip is trembling, but her eyes . . . Her eyes are fucking *shining*.

"I think . . . you know the answer to that too."

"I see you, Lila," I tell her quietly.

Her hand trembles in mine. "Took you long enough."

"What do we do now? I don't—I don't know what happens from here."

Her mouth tilts in a sensual curve, and she closes the distance between us, the warmth of her body chasing away the chill of the ice beneath us.

"Well, considering how long I've been waiting . . . I think now? Now, you take me back to your place."

"Jack isn't home," I rasp. "Physical therapy."

Her smile is almost predatory now. "Oh, I know."

It's crazy, it's ill-advised, and I have *no* idea what I would even begin to tell Jack, what he would say, but still . . . all I can think about right now is what her mouth tastes like.

And I fully intend to find out.

Thirteen

DELILAH

have wanted to kiss Ian Chase for a long time. I've had a long time to think about how it might go. Like, a *long* time. An *inordinately* long amount of time.

Which means that standing in an enclosed space with him on the ride up the elevator to his and Jack's apartment is both torture and an utter thrill. Questions ping around my skull like a pinball game seeking a high score, wondering if I should have kissed him on the ice, wondering if I should kiss him *now*, wondering how much convincing it would take to get him to throw me over his shoulder and carry me into the apartment caveman style before having his way with me.

Like I said, a *very* long time.

He seems as nervous as I am, at least, sneaking glances at me just like I am at him every other second, the ding of the changing floors only making the charged energy between us more palpable the closer we get to his. I keep waiting for him to say something, but we've both been quiet on the way over, neither of us in a hurry to break the electric silence that hums between us.

So it's a bit of a surprise when his hand curls around mine again just as the doors open to his floor—a good surprise, a fucking *fantastic* surprise even—tugging me out into the hall and practically pulling me down it as he stomps toward his apartment. He doesn't let go as he fishes his keys from his pocket, as he uses them to let us inside, still holding tight when he closes the door behind us and locking it.

And then he does absolutely nothing.

He just continues to hold my hand, staring at it with his lip between his teeth.

Fuck, he isn't changing his mind, is he?

"Ian?"

He peeks up at me, brow knit together. "Is this a bad idea?"

"What?" I try not to let the way that question punches me in the gut show. "What do you mean?"

"It's just . . . we've been friends for so long, Lila. I know we drifted apart there for a while, but you and Jack and Bea were always home to me growing up. I would never want to risk messing that up somehow."

"Oh." I avert my eyes to the floor, hoping he can't see how crushed I am. "I understand. If you don't want this anymore, I totally get it."

"No."

The force of his tone takes me by surprise, and by the time I pull my head up to meet his eyes again, his free hand has darted out to let his fingers cup my chin. His expression is serious, his gray eyes boring into mine with an intensity I've never seen from him. At least not directed at me.

"No?"

"Let me be clear," he says firmly. "I have been thinking about this for a lot longer than I probably should have. Fuck, since the moment you waltzed back into my life. Do you know how shocked I was that day in the studio? That the girl I cared for so much growing up turned into this gorgeous woman I suddenly couldn't stop thinking about? Because I haven't, Lila. I don't know what it means, and I don't know if it's a good idea, but I haven't stopped thinking about you for weeks now. And I can't think of a single fucking thing I want more than to know what your mouth tastes like."

The air got trapped in my lungs somewhere around: *gorgeous woman*—and even when it's clear that he's done speaking, it takes me several seconds to remember to let it out. I exhale shakily, feeling my pulse pounding in my ears as the warmth of his fingers leaves a wake of fire along my skin.

"Do *you* think this is a bad idea, Ian?"

His eyes roam over my face, settling on my mouth. "Probably," he says quietly. "You should probably say no."

"Do you *want* me to say no?"

He studies me for a long moment, one where the seconds feel like minutes and I can feel the weight of each one before finally, "No. I don't. I want to take you in the other room and find out if your mouth is as soft as it looks."

"Well." My lips quirk, and I reach to wind my arms around his neck. "What are you waiting for?"

Nothing, and I mean *nothing*—not years of want, not daydreams of the dizziest fashion, *nothing*—could prepare me for the way his mouth fits mine. He surges down to meet me in a way that matches the desperation I'm feeling, his hands reaching under my thighs and hoisting me up into his arms as if I don't weigh a goddamned thing.

He makes a soft, hungry sound deep in his throat when I tease my tongue along his lower lip, letting them part as he sucks on it like it's candy, making my toes curl. I distantly register that we're moving, but barely, too consumed by the way his hands are drifting to palm my ass, the way he tilts his head to deepen the kiss like he can't quite get enough.

I hear the creak of his bedroom door before the sharp slam of it as he kicks it shut behind us, and then I let out a surprised cry when he drops me into the middle of his bed. He only gives me a second to be caught off guard before he's crawling over me, letting his body cover mine as his fingers tangle in my hair to cradle my nape.

He lifts his head, his rich, red hair falling around his face like a curtain and his eyes dark with lust in a way I don't even think my *wildest* imagination could have ever gotten right, his throat bobbing with a swallow and his hips pressing against mine. "Is this okay?"

"Ian, I've wanted you to kiss me since training bras, remember? Fucking get down here."

My hands curl over his shoulders to drag him back down to meet my mouth, closing my eyes and reveling in the sensations of his warm lips and his soft tongue and the tiny grunts that resound in his chest when I arch into him. His beard scratches against my skin lightly, making me wonder how it might feel elsewhere, which in turn makes me shiver. He's still cradling my head with one hand, maneuvering me however he wants as he kisses me senselessly, but I feel his other hand press against my side, ghosting along my curves with gentle fingers as he maps the shape of me. Even through my clothes, his touch makes me shiver, makes me tilt my hips up to meet yet another surprise, one that I also could never have really imagined correctly.

Because Ian Chase is hard. He's hard for *me*.

And I can see on his face the second that he realizes that I know it.

"Sorry," he rasps, his lips still resting against mine. "Can't help it."

"Oh?" My mouth curves into a sly grin, and I roll my hips just for fun. "You can't?"

"*Fuck*, Lila."

His large hand applies pressure to my waist, effectively pinning me against the bed as his eyes flutter closed. His breath leaves him shakily as he grinds down against me, drawing out a quiet moan from my throat as tingles spread through my belly.

"You like that, sweet girl?"

Oh wow. My imagination should be fired for never offering up that little gem.

I lift my leg to press my thigh to his hip, bringing him closer. "Do it again."

"Greedy," he murmurs, swiveling his hips so I can feel every delicious inch of him rubbing between my legs. "Like that?"

"Feels good," I groan. "Would feel better without all the layers."

He does it again, and my legs wrap around his hips like they have a mind of their own.

"Lila," he says in a sigh, almost like a prayer. His face burrows into my neck, his tongue flicking out to taste me, his clothed cock still grinding in a way that might drive me insane. "You always smell so sweet. You fucking *taste* sweet. I want to taste you everywhere." His hand snakes between us, and I gasp when I feel the heat of his fingers sliding against the denim between my legs. "Especially here."

The mental image of Ian's head between my thighs makes goose bumps crop up over my entire body, a needy sound escaping me as I tilt my hips up to meet his next slow thrust. Ian shakes against me, his breath leaving him in a ragged pant.

"Gonna make me come in my pants like a fucking teenager," he grunts.

"Mm." I let my fingers tease through the ends of his hair, tugging it and forcing a soft moan from his lips. "Honestly, with as many times as I've come in my pants while thinking about you, it feels pretty fair."

Ian shivers. "You really are a brat, aren't you."

"Oh, you have no idea," I practically purr, kissing one corner of his mouth. "What are you going to do about it?"

"I can think of several things," he says roughly, hissing when my teeth scrape over his earlobe.

"Gonna punish me, Ian?"

"*Jesus.*" His big body *shudders*, and I feel a rush of excitement flood through me. "Are you looking to get punished, Lila?"

"I just want your hands on me," I tell him, trailing my lips along his cheek, the soft scrape of his beard tickling me, until I seal them against his, letting myself fall into the weight of his kiss for another long moment. "I'm not particular on where or how."

He pushes up, his palms flattening against the mattress as he stares down at me, and in the dying light that peeks in through his blinds, I can make out the soft spray of freckles across his nose, his cheeks. I can see the way his tongue sweeps out to wet his lower lip. The way his eyes are heavy with want in a way that makes my stomach clench.

"You're going to ruin me. Aren't you."

My smile is soft now. "I sure fucking hope so."

My fingers curl in his shirt, trying to pull him back down to me, and I can just feel the plush curve of his lips brushing along mine when a door slams somewhere in the house.

We both go very still.

"Ian?" Jack calls. "Yo, Ian, you home?"

"Jack," Ian hisses.

I grimace. "Fuck."

"What do we do?"

"Well, we definitely don't let him know you're home."

"Hey, Ian," Jack calls again. "Did you leave your shoes in the middle of the hall?"

Ian winces. Clearly neither of us was thinking about shoes when he was carrying me to his room. I can only hope mine are somewhere by his bed and not out there.

"This is definitely not how Jack needs to find out about this," I whisper. "If he sees us in here practically dry-humping each other, he's going to be apoplectic."

"I'm not really interested in being shouted at by Jack with a hard-on, anyway," Ian says with a grimace.

"Well, say something!"

"What do I say?"

"I don't know. Anything that will make sure he doesn't come in here."

Jack's voice is closer now. "Ian?"

"Uh, yeah!" Ian shouts, panic in his expression. "I'm here, man. I'm just . . ." He looks at me helplessly, and I shake my head, no less lost. "I'm naked in here."

Jack's voice is right outside the door. "Like . . . just hanging out? Naked?"

"Um, yeah. Just decompressing, you know?"

"Huh." There are a few seconds of silence, and then, "That's cool. Sometimes I like to eat in my room naked. Inner caveman time, yeah?"

"Uh . . . yeah," Ian says with a frown.

I can feel my face scrunching with distaste.

"Cool," Jack calls. "I'm just going to take a shower. Let's order Thai after."

"Sounds good," Ian shouts back.

Neither of us breathes as Jack's footsteps move down the hall, only risking words when we both hear the bathroom door shut.

"I did *not* need to know that about my brother," I groan.

Ian pushes away from me, but he doesn't look happy to do so, which does make *me* happy to notice. "Not really something I want to imagine either."

Ian rises to his knees as I prop up with my hands braced behind me, the heaviness of the moment Jack just interrupted making itself known as we both stare at each other.

Ian's jaw works. "To be continued?"

"Yeah?" I ask, beaming.

"You better fucking believe it." He scowls. "Maybe just . . . not while your brother is home."

I sit up properly to pull him to me, capturing his mouth in a long, slow kiss that feels as dirty as it is sweet, and packed full of promise. "Deal," I say after, a little breathless.

"Deal," he echoes. "Now let's sneak you out of here before Jack tries to whoop my ass one-handed."

"I might actually like to see that," I tease.

Ian snorts. "I'd hate to hurt your brother. I kind of like him."

"What about me?"

We're both standing after I put my shoes back on, and he pauses from straightening his clothes to peer at me, his mouth forming a grin that's almost boyish, one that makes my chest feel tight. He grabs my hand to pull it to his mouth, letting his lips brush along the back. "I kind of like you too."

"Ditto," I answer dazedly, feeling very much like my crush— my *first* crush—just made out with me on his bed.

He tugs my hand, moving toward the door. He peeks into the hall to check and make sure that it's still empty before pulling me through the living room to the front door, pausing with it open to haul me against him for another kiss that has me pressing up on my toes, toes that are now curling in my shoes.

"Text me when you get home," he murmurs when I finally break away.

I grin up at him. "Are you asking me or telling me?"

"Telling," he answers firmly, reaching around to give one sharp slap to the side of my ass. "Brat."

He shuts the door then, leaving me half-shocked and whole-horny, rubbing lightly at the denim covering the skin he just *spanked* in the hallway outside my brother's apartment. Honestly, that part isn't really even registering in my mind.

It's far too occupied wondering when I can get him to do it again.

Fourteen

IAN

I didn't think there was anything in the world that could dampen my excitement for today. I haven't stopped thinking about Lila in days; her warm mouth, her soft curves, her quick wit and her kind heart and all the things that make her inherently *her* have been at the forefront of my brain since she snuck out of the apartment the other day, mostly because it feels surreal that I've gotten to experience it all. That I still can, because for whatever reason, this woman who is out of my league in a dozen different ways wants *me*. Has for a long time, to hear her tell it.

That's a heady thing, for someone who's not even sure if they're worth wanting that much.

So needless to say, I've been in a great mood on the way to the studio this morning. With her flirty texts to keep me sated in the days since I've seen her—we've both been busy between my practices and her meetings—there hasn't been a thing to bring me down.

Of course, one phone call would change that.

I'm walking into the studio when I answer the call, on purpose this time, if only because I'm curious why he would be calling, given that things are going exactly the way he wants them to, and as far as I know, there's no reason to criticize me.

"Hello?"

"What is this shit with you and the Baker kid's show?"

I bristle immediately. "Excuse me?"

"Once was one thing," he says. "I get good publicity, but you don't need to become some cheap commodity. It sends the wrong message."

I pause my steps, my mouth parting in surprise.

Really? The wrong message?

"That's rich," I snort. "Coming from you."

"Watch your fucking attitude. Don't forget who you're talking to."

"Is there any reason you called? Not that it's not always a pleasure to catch up."

"All right, smart-ass. Don't forget that I'm still the one who calls the shots around here. Just because you used your mother to worm your way back onto the team—"

"I didn't do shit," I growl. "*She* wanted me back, and in case you forgot, she has just as much say in what happens with the team as you do."

"She does," he answers, his voice icy. "As long as you don't fuck things up. You *know* what will happen if you decide to play hero."

I *do* know, unfortunately. It's the only reason I'm even still entertaining his bullshit.

"I *got* it, Dad. I've already agreed to the episode. I can't back out now. You wanted me to do everything Leilani said, remember? This is what *you* wanted."

"I didn't want you to be at some damned cable show's beck and call."

"Well, it's done. I'm not canceling."

"If you want to keep pissing your career down the drain with mediocre gameplay and stupid fucking career decisions, playing the trained monkey for that dumb girl, then you—"

"Shut the fuck up," I hiss, surprising myself. I've never really talked back to him, not in all the years since he's been doing his best to control every part of my life. "Don't talk about her. You hear me? Don't you ever fucking talk about her."

My father makes a disgusted sound. "Please tell me you aren't fucking around with the Baker girl. After all the shit that went down with you and Mei, you really think it's a good idea to have another public—"

"I said," I manage through gritted teeth, *"don't* talk about her. Remember, *Dad*, it's your ass I've been protecting by keeping my mouth shut. Your stupid fucking legacy. If it wasn't for Mom, I would—"

The rest of what I'd been about to say falls flat when I catch sight of soft brown waves and a smile that brings my anger from an inferno to a simmer, swallowing down the rest of my vitriol and deciding that Bradley Chase isn't worth my time right now.

"I have to go," I mutter into the receiver. "Don't call me if this is all you have to say."

I can hear him shouting even as I pull the phone away, cutting him off as I end the call before shoving the device in my pocket as Lila sidles up to me.

"Hey, Cupcake," she says sweetly, reaching out to hook a finger in my pocket.

She gives it a sharp tug, surprising me as she presses up on her toes to leave a brief kiss at my mouth. I find myself leaning into her as if instinctually, my eyes closing of their own accord as my hands unconsciously gravitate toward her waist.

I'm a little dazed when she pulls away—too quickly for my liking—but she looks perfectly composed.

"I thought I was going to have to send out search and rescue," she teases.

"Oh. Sorry." I frown, trying to shove thoughts of my father away. "Phone call."

"Everything okay? You looked sort of stressed out."

"It's nothing." I wave her off. "Just my father and his same old bullshit."

Her brow furrows. "Still being a dick?"

"On a good day."

Her hand finds mine, giving it a squeeze. "I'm sorry."

"Don't worry about it. We have an episode to do, right?"

Her lips curl. "Right. I hope you're ready to milk this shit, because Ava is on a rampage."

"Milk it?"

Her smile turns coy, and she tugs on my hand to drag me behind her. "Oh, you'll see."

— — — — —

"This is a joke, right?"

Lila looks absolutely delighted as she adjusts the pink chef's hat on my head, one that pairs nicely with the new *matching* pink aprons they had made for us—both embroidered with our names over the chest in a complementary purple.

"I think it looks cute on you," she says sweetly, stepping back to admire her work. "Very dignified."

I narrow my eyes. "I look like an idiot."

"But a very *cute* idiot."

I reach above my head, shifting the hat minutely so it sits better. "You're such a brat."

"Mm." She leans in, lowering her voice as she traces my name on the front of my apron with the tip of her finger. "But you like that about me."

I shiver lightly, mindful that there is an entire crew milling about the space, and that I can't pull her against me and kiss her senseless. Which is a real bummer, since she's entirely too close and entirely too sweet-smelling to resist.

"It has its merits," I murmur back.

"Maybe if you're a good boy today, I'll let you show me how much you like it."

She turns away then like she didn't just drop the sexual equivalent of the atom bomb at my feet, looking innocent as she situates her bowls and her ingredients. I sneak a peek around and make sure no one is watching us before I take a step to hover behind her, my body an inch from hers and my mouth at her ear.

"Maybe if *you're* good today . . . I won't have to spank the brat out of you."

I hear her breath hitch, feel the slight tremor run through her as her throat works, and then I hear her quiet, "What if I want you to?"

I'm about three seconds from spinning her against the counter and slipping my tongue into her mouth, crew and cameras be damned, and if it weren't for her friend Ava appearing in my peripherals, forcing me to step away from her quickly—I think I might have done just that.

"Oh, you guys look adorable," Ava says as I back away. "The hats were a great touch, if I do say so myself."

"I look like the pink version of the Swedish Chef," I grouse.

"People love the Muppets," Ava counters.

"Not me," I say with a slight shudder. "They're kind of creepy."

Lila giggles beside me. "Ian was afraid of Count von Count until he was thirteen."

"No, I wasn't. I just don't like puppets. Don't like the way they move."

"Uh-huh." Lila smirks. "You keep telling yourself that."

I huff out a breath. "Are we going to cook something?"

"We're almost ready," Ava says. "Lila is going to do her normal intro, and then she'll introduce you again. I want the two of you to really play this up. Like, we want the audience to be totally convinced you two are boning off camera even if you aren't."

I feel the tips of my ears heat, and Lila chooses that moment to inspect a bowl of what looks to be salt. Ava continues to run down the flow of the episode, but I'm stuck on *you two are boning*, my mind traveling back to the moment where we got dangerously close. Not that I've really *stopped* thinking about that moment since it happened. If I'm not worrying about whether or not we should cross that line, I'm desperate to hurdle over it like I'm in the fucking Olympics and she's the gold medal.

Which, to be fair, she absolutely is.

"—and if you have any mishaps with your hat, just call a time-out and we'll cut to adjust it. I definitely want you guys to keep them on the entire time. Really gives off a good vibe, I think."

I realize I zoned out for half of what Ava said, thinking about Lila. I hope there wasn't anything *too* important in there I missed. Ava heads back offstage, and Lila nudges me with her elbow before adjusting her own hat, which actually *does* look adorable on her. Go figure.

"Remember not to burn anything."

I roll my eyes. "I won't."

"Good boy," she coos.

My cock twitches. It's like a switch has been flipped, and now I can't turn it off. Is there anything Lila can do that *won't* turn me on?

She winks at me, and my poor dick gives another desperate jerk. Apparently not.

— — — —

This is the second time that Lila has asked me a question while we're shooting that I missed what she said. I don't think anyone can actually blame me, since watching her hands work is . . . distracting. She's so effortlessly confident in what she does, but just like when we were kids, she gets this little furrow between her brows when she's concentrating on the ingredients in front of her that is just as endearing now as it had been back then.

"Start again," someone calls from off set.

Lila grins at me. "You dozing off on me, Cupcake?"

"Just . . . really interested in the process."

I can tell by the way her teeth press against her lower lip that she knows *exactly* why I'm not paying attention, and that it has everything to do with her sweet voice and her authoritative command of her kitchen. She's just so in her element that it's hard not to get a little swept away by her. I find myself slightly aroused by it but also infinitely proud of her all at once, and it's a very confusing set of emotions to deal with at the same time.

Her smile brightens for a second, and then she collects herself, turning the mixer to a slow setting for a few seconds so she can start the segment again.

"Do you know why they call these choux pastries?"

She pronounces it like *shoe*, but that doesn't really help me out any. I shake my head. "Does it have anything to do with them being footwear at some point?"

"No." She rolls her eyes even as her lips curl. "*Choux* means cabbage in French."

My nose scrunches. "And?"

"*And*," she huffs with amusement, "the finished product looks a little like tiny heads of cabbage."

I can feel myself frowning. "Well, that sounds . . . appetizing."

"They're going to be amazing," she laughs. She gives her attention to the camera. "I promise you all, he's going to eat at least three when we're done."

"We'll see," I answer skeptically.

I listen as she explains the next bit of her process; she transfers the dough to a piping bag after laying out a parchment paper over her baking sheet and brushing it with water, and then I feel myself leaning in as she starts to dollop perfect little three-layered blobs that look weirdly like—

"Are they supposed to look like an, ah, emoji?"

Her brow knits. "What?"

"Those." I point to the blobs in question. "I mean . . . with the three layers and the little curl on top . . ."

Lila stares at her dollops intently for a few seconds, and then her eyes widen before she reaches to smack me in the chest. "They do *not* look like that emoji!"

"But you see it, right?"

"No, I absolutely don't."

I roll my eyes, even looking over toward the camera. "She totally does. You guys see it, right?"

The damn things look like poop emojis, and she knows it.

"You're such a—" She presses her lips together, narrowing her eyes. "Such a *bad* assistant."

"I think I'm the perfect assistant," I say confidently. I can tell by her expression she's not actually annoyed. "Probably the best you'll ever have."

The length of the moment where her eyes go round and her lips part is infinitesimal at best, and there's no way anyone else caught it, but *I* fucking did. I realize now how my words could mean something entirely different, and suddenly I'm not really thinking about pastries anymore, and by the way Lila's cheeks flush ever so slightly, I don't think she is either.

"Well," she says, clearing her throat. "That's why you wet your finger a bit." She dips her index finger in a small bowl of water, peeking over at me as she does it. "Helps smooth out the curls on top."

I watch her finger move in slow, rhythmic circles as she smooths the top of each little mound of pastry dough, swallowing thickly as my thoughts wander against my will to that same finger circling somewhere else. Preferably on my body. Would she tease me like that?

Lila's mouth hitches up on one side, and her eyes glimmer with mirth; she *knows* what she's doing, the brat. "Better?"

"I guess so," I manage.

"Just wait until they're done," she promises.

I do my best not to openly stare at her ass as she places the uncooked pastries into the oven, and then someone calls "Cut" from somewhere out of sight.

"So what now?"

She moves to the fridge. "Just need to get the pastry filling we made earlier so it can start thawing a bit. We want it to be nice and creamy when we fill the pastries."

Now, I've never been turned on by the word *creamy* before, but I guess there's a first time for everything.

"Looks good," I note as she sets the bowl down on the counter.

She smirks. "It *is* good, but you're a stickler for the rules, remember? We're not supposed to be eating anything with raw eggs in it."

"Mm. Someone did tell me to live a little."

"They did," she agrees. "Pretty sure that person never expected you to actually take them up on it though."

"I don't think I expected to take them up on it either."

Her fingers reach out to toy with the strap of my apron that lies against my chest, and I have to suppress the urge to shiver. "They're glad you did though. Actually, I think they would probably want you to cut loose even more."

"Oh yeah?"

"Mhm."

I lean in just a little, but even with the cameras off, I know I can't kiss her here. Instead, I reach past her, dipping my finger into the bowl of cream before bringing it up to my mouth to taste.

"I did hear that being bad can be worth it."

Her breath leaves her in an unsteady exhale, and I actually hear it catch when I reach past her again. I bring my finger to her lips this time, watching the soft curve of her mouth as I hold it close but not quite touching, lowering my voice.

"Open up," I murmur.

She doesn't even hesitate, letting her lips part as her eyes find mine to hold them. *I'm* not breathing as she licks at the very tip of my finger, feeling everything below the belt tingle with interest and then give a heavy pulse of desire as she sucks the entire digit into her mouth, making the sweetest, softest little noise. It's in and out in mere seconds, like it never even happened, but I feel the slick heat of her mouth for much longer. I want to feel that tongue on my lips, my skin, my *cock*—and the set of her fucking *cable show* is definitely not the place for it.

A throat clears nearby, and we both jump apart, catching her friend Ava smirking at us with one brow raised. "You guys ready to finish up?"

Lila still looks a little dazed, and I brush my thumb against her lower lip, clearing away the leftover cream that clings there before bringing it to my mouth to lick it away. I know people are watching, most likely speculating—but I can't find it in me to care right now.

"Lila?" She jolts a little at her name, like she's coming out of a trance. "You ready?"

"Yes," she says in a throaty voice that isn't quite hers but threatens to make me hard all the same. She says it again, surer this time. "Yes! We're ready. I'm ready." She blows out a breath, eyeing me. "You ready?"

"Whenever you are," I tell her with a grin.

I almost don't catch her muttering, "You'd better be."

She's already straightening her ridiculous hat that shouldn't be so fucking adorable and fiddling with her bowl of cream with a sweet pink tint still in her cheeks. Not that I'm judging, since I can feel the tips of my ears burning, making me yet again grateful for my longer hair. I definitely wasn't lying though—I'm ready to finish up here.

Mainly so I can see if I can get her to make that sweet little noise again.

— — — —

I really like Ava, I do—but with her loitering in the doorway of Lila's dressing room, resulting in me having to keep a respectable distance and pretend to be *very* interested in Lila's potted plant, is less than ideal.

"—and the ratings are going to be through the roof," Ava is saying. "I can feel it."

"If Ian in a pink chef's hat doesn't break the viewing threshold, then I don't know what will," Lila chuckles as she brushes her hair, peering in the mirror to make sure there isn't any stray flour anywhere. "Maybe Gia will get off our backs."

"You know she just answers to the guys upstairs," Ava points out.

Lila rolls her eyes. "Yeah, yeah."

"And how about you, stud?" Ava grins slyly. "Feeling happy about all the good publicity?"

"Well," I snort, "I haven't seen anyone calling me an adulterer in a while." Lila pauses in her brushing, catching my eye in the mirror as her lips turn down in a frown. Fuck. Definitely hadn't meant to bring that up. I avert my gaze, shrugging as if I'm not bothered. "Anyway, it's a nice reprieve, in any case."

"Right." Ava nods, her eyes darting between the two of us. "Well, I'd better go make sure the camera guys are doing okay."

I suspect she's only leaving because of my inadvertent attempt to bring down the mood, but I can't say I'm not grateful to finally be alone with Lila, whatever the reason. She's still eyeing me in the mirror, and I move closer, wanting to distract her from my pathetic past, wanting to stay in the little bubble we've made for just a while longer.

"You know," I tell her, toying with the knot of her apron at the back of her neck, "the apron might look ridiculous on me, but it's very tempting when you wear it."

Her brow arches as her lips quirk. "Is it?"

"Very," I say, leaning in close to press my lips to her throat. "And you always smell so sweet."

I hear her drop her brush back onto the vanity, and then her hand reaches up behind her until her fingers are teasing through my hair. "Do I?"

"Mhm. Everything about you is a temptation, Lila." When I peek up at her reflection, I catch her lashes fluttering as I brush my lips down the column of her neck. "But this fucking apron . . . The things I'm thinking about you and this apron aren't very sweet at all."

Her smile is downright wicked. "I like that."

"Do you?"

"Mhm." Her eyes flutter until she meets my gaze again in the mirror. "I've been wanting to tempt you forever."

"You're definitely making up for lost time."

"Mieux vaut tard que jamais," she hums.

"Fuck," I groan. How does her voice sound so much sweeter in another language? "Have I told you what that does to me?"

"I might have guessed," she teases.

"What does it mean?"

"Better late than never," she tells me. "More or less." She sighs softly when she feels my smile against her throat, her voice a bit lower when she speaks again. "What are you doing after this?"

I straighten, cocking my eyebrow. "I didn't really have plans. You?"

"I was just going home," she says. "I live nearby."

She says this slowly, like a suggestion, and heat courses through me. "Jack mentioned that, yeah."

"You could walk me home," she goes on quietly, her pretty pink tongue swiping at her lower lip, tempting me again. "If you want to."

And it's a suggestion that has more meaning than the obvious one, I think, one that I've both been obsessing about but that also leaves me slightly terrified, because what will that mean for us? What will it mean if we cross a line we can't come back from?

But her eyes on me are full of want that I know matches mine, and her chest rises and falls at a pace that tells me she's feeling as breathless as I am, that her heart is most likely pounding in her chest at a similar cadence to my own, and there's only one thing I know for sure.

"Yes," I answer quietly, coiling one silky strand of her hair around my finger and leaning in to inhale her sweet scent. "I want to."

And maybe it's a bad idea, maybe it's a *terrible* one, but the way Lila's mouth curves into a soft smile, looking at me like I hung the fucking moon . . . I find I simply don't fucking care.

Fifteen

DELILAH

It feels strange, foreign even, when Ian's hand finds mine as we enter my apartment building. It's a quiet thing; he doesn't draw attention to it, doesn't make a production of the act, but our fingers tangle and his grip tightens until it's definitely a *holding* type of situation, and what would teenager Lila think if she knew this was going to happen? How many afternoons did I spend daydreaming about this, just this? It fills my belly and my chest with all sorts of flutters that are mostly elation but at least a *tiny* bit of nerves—something that I find surprising, because I rarely get nervous about anything. Especially when it comes to men.

But this is Ian, my brain reminds me. As if I could forget.

"Building is nice," Ian comments as we ascend the stairs.

I scoff. "It would be better if they would fix the damn elevator. Stairs and I don't really vibe."

"Good for your heart," he says offhandedly. "Cardio is important."

I give him a sly smile. "I can think of a lot better ways to get your cardio in."

His cheeks flush and his eyes turn upward while he mutters something that might be prayers for some sort of guidance; I can't actually make it out. I love when I can rile him like this, when I can break through that composure of his. It feels like a secret side of Ian that's just for me.

We're stepping onto the landing for the third floor—one below mine—when he changes the subject. "Have you lived here long?"

"Since I moved back," I tell him. "I love the neighborhood, and it's so close to work . . . The place is small, but it's never made any sense to move. It's perfect for just me."

"I have to say, I am intrigued by what your place might look like."

"Why is that?"

"Do you still have your collection of porcelain cat figurines?"

I narrow my eyes. "Are you implying that the Porcelain Pride isn't amazing?"

"Oh God. You named it. Are there more? There have to be at least a hundred of them by now."

"I don't feel inclined to answer that."

"So, yes, essentially," he laughs.

I roll my eyes, pushing open the door to my floor and leading him through it. "At least they're organized now. They have their own special shelf and everything."

"I can't wait to see it."

"Unless it's to tell me how cool they are, keep your comments to yourself."

He makes a motion like he's zipping his lips, and I can't help the grin that spreads across my face. That fluttering sensation is back, intensifying when we get to my door. It's only just hitting me that Ian is *here*, at my *place*. It's only just occurring to me what will most likely happen after we go inside. What I have thought about happening for so long it's embarrassing, considering I've only been on his radar for a month, at best. A chilled sort of tingle spreads through my limbs as I dig in my purse for my keys, swallowing around a dry lump that's forming in my throat as I reach toward the knob to undo the lock. I get so far as sticking the key in the latch.

And then I fucking freeze.

I'm nervous, I realize. Actually *nervous*. Like, heart pounding, stomach clenching, full-on panicking with my key trembling in my hand and my dumb key chain with a mixer on it that says "beat it, just beat it" tinkling softly in the quiet space of the hall.

How the fuck can I be nervous? I've literally *dreamt* about this moment for longer than I care to admit. So long that I might as well have a goddamned play-by-play for it in every possible way that it could go.

But maybe that's the problem, I rationalize. I've built it up for so long, fantasized about what it might be like for Ian to be mine, *really* mine, and what if it's not what I expected? What if it *ruins* everything? Could I live with that? Could I really—

"Lila," Ian says softly from right behind me, where we're still lingering outside my apartment door. "Lila," he says again, his fingers coming to brush against the underside of my forearm that's still outstretched toward the lock. "You're shaking."

"I'm sorry," I splutter. "Sorry, I'm being ridiculous, I—"

"Lila."

His touch is heavier now, falling to my waist to urge me to turn, and when I force myself to look at him—at this boy who became a man while I wasn't looking but has always been larger than life in my eyes—I see everything I've ever wanted staring back at me in his warm, gray gaze.

"You know nothing has to happen here, right?" His hand lifts until his thumb strokes my jaw. "It won't change anything. It won't change a single thing about how I feel."

"It's not that I don't want you to come inside," I tell him, meaning it.

His head cocks slightly. "You can talk to me."

"I just—" I swallow, and his eyes track the movement, his palm becoming steadier as it cups my jaw. "I know that you know how long this has been a thing for me, but you don't *know*, you know?"

His mouth quirks. "I'm not sure that I do, no."

"I've just . . . Before I knew what it even was to feel something for somebody, I felt things for you. Whether it was just feeling safer when you're around, or looking for you when I enter a room, or doing whatever I could to make you smile because it made *me* smile when you did . . . It's *always* been you, Ian."

"Lila," he says, but words are falling out of my mouth before I can catch them now, and I hardly even know where they're coming from, since this anxiety attack seems to be slamming into me all at once.

"And I realize that isn't the case for you, and that this is all new where you're concerned, but it's not for me, you know? It's been on a back burner somewhere, sure, but it's never really been turned *off*. And what if we go there and you realize that you can't feel those things for me? What if I finally have you, and then I don't get to *keep* you? I just . . . I don't know what that would do to me, or to you, or hell, even Jack, and I worry that it makes me . . ."

I press my lips together in a frown, tipping my head down to stare at my feet. I take a steadying breath, teetering between feeling like an idiot for ruining what might be my one chance to *finally* have him and also being completely terrified that I'm *right* somehow, but it's his hands that draw me out of the maelstrom in my head. His calloused, rough hands that are so wide they almost cover both sides of my face completely when he cups my cheeks.

"That it makes you what?"

I gulp, my fingers reaching to grip his forearms as if that will somehow keep me steady when I feel so suddenly *un*steady. "That it makes me selfish," I whisper. "Because I still want it. I still want you."

Ian's eyes search mine, looking for my uncertainty, surely, and maybe even for reasons of his own as to why we shouldn't—so it's both a surprise and a relief when he leans in slowly, hovering by my mouth. "Do you trust me?"

"I—" It takes me a second to register the question, mostly because the answer is so obvious. "Yes."

He lifts me in one fluid movement, his hands coming under my thighs as he pulls me up to his body and presses me against the wall by the door to my apartment, holding me steady. Making me feel just a bit more so. His eyes flick to my mouth, and then back to mine like a silent question, and all I can do is nod, because I'll never say no to more of him.

Ian's kiss is like everything else Ian does—unassuming, but with a quiet strength that makes you want to fall into him, just like I've been wanting to do for most of my life. It's overwhelming that I'm getting to do so now.

"Lila," he says again, and I don't think I could ever get tired of him saying my name like that. Like it's important. Like it's his favorite word. "You're right. I don't know what it's like to want you that long. I've always loved you—"

He doesn't mean it like that. You know he doesn't.

"—and even if it wasn't in the same way, you have *always* been a part of me. Maybe it looks different now than it did then, because who we were then couldn't be what we could be now. It wouldn't have worked. For all sorts of reasons. And maybe that's the point, you know? Maybe we're exactly where we're supposed to be, because all I know is that while I may not have wanted you as *long* as you've wanted me, I can say with absolute certainty that I have wanted you as *hard* as a person can want another person. I don't know when you went from the girl I adored to the woman I can't stop thinking about, but you did. You've always been in my heart, but now you're in my head too. You're fucking *everywhere*, Lila. You're in so deep that I don't see how I could ever get you out." I don't realize I'm holding my breath until his soft mouth presses to mine again, only for a second before, "And I don't want to. The way I feel right now . . . I don't think I ever will."

Okay, maybe he didn't mean it that way, but that's still really nice.

My voice sounds small, unlike me, when I answer, "Oh."

"Just oh?"

My lips twitch. "I didn't think 'holy fucking shit' was an appropriate response."

"It could be," he chuckles. "If it's a good 'holy fucking shit.'"

"The *holiest* fucking shit," I say breathlessly.

"You're so weird sometimes."

"That's nothing new."

"How adorable I find it is."

My brow quirks. "You didn't find me adorable back then?"

"Sometimes," he admits. "But most of the time you were a pain in my ass."

My lips curl as I lean in, feathering my mouth against his. "Can I make it up to you?"

"Lila, I told you, nothing has to hap—"

I kiss him, *hard*—hard enough that his word morphs into a throaty groan that makes me tingle with something other than nerves. "Shut up and open the door, Ian," I mutter against his mouth. "Key is in the lock."

"I just don't want you to think I expect anything."

"After that little speech, I am not above sucking your dick right here in the hallway."

"*Jesus,*" he chokes out, keeping me upright against the wall with *one fucking hand* as he fumbles with the key sitting in the lock with the other one. "You can't say shit like that to me."

I let my mouth drift along his cheek, feeling his beard tickle my lips. "Why not?"

"Because it might have me doing something stupid."

"Like?"

"Like letting you suck my dick right here in the hallway."

"And that's a bad thing?"

He groans again just as the door swings open beside us. "Get your ass inside, brat. I have plans for it."

He releases his hold on me to let my body slide down his until I'm back on my feet, his forearm coming to rest against the wall by my head as he looms over me, tension in his features like he's struggling not to touch me. I like that. I *really* like that.

So maybe I make a little show of swishing my hips when I slide past him to duck into my apartment, going for a seductive look when I peek over my shoulder at him as he follows me inside, only to let out a sharp yelp when he swats my ass through my jeans.

"Not fast enough, Lila."

"I thought you wanted to see the Porcelain Pride?"

"Is that what you want to do right now?"

I make a show of pretending to think about it. "I don't know . . . It could be."

"I think you're trying to test my patience."

"Is it working?"

He looks deathly serious when he answers, "You're about to find out."

My eyes round as he starts toward me, and my heart rate doubles as I stumble away, going into a run toward my bedroom, hearing his heavy steps following close behind. A giggle that sounds almost like a scream leaves me when his arm slides around my waist just as I burst through my bedroom door, his solid frame colliding with mine.

I don't think I'll ever get over how easily he seems to be able to toss me around; Ian Chase treats me like I'm his own personal shot put, and he's going for the fucking gold medal. It feels like he barely puts any effort in throwing me onto my bed, crawling over me like a predator, with a look in his eye to match as his wide shoulders block my view of the ceiling. His gray eyes are darker now, like charcoal that's just been lit, with the way they seem to burn.

I let my fingers skirt over the toned expanse of his inked forearms that are braced on either side of me, keeping my touch light, teasing, just happy to be able to touch him the way I've always wanted to. I let them slip higher until they're smoothing over his biceps, his shoulders—curling my hands around his neck and lacing my fingers there.

I don't tug at him very hard, but thankfully he takes the hint, anyway. He lowers himself until his body is practically zippered to mine, and I can feel every hard inch of him against every soft inch of me and the contrast of it is wonderfully decadent. His lips mold to mine as my eyes flutter closed, opening for him without question as his tongue slips inside to explore my mouth. There's no one here now, I realize, no one to interrupt, no one to stop us from fulfilling every fantasy I've ever had, and the realization of that has me kissing him just a little more desperately, has my body pressing against his as if I can somehow get even closer.

This is actually happening, I think with wonder. *He's here. He wants me.*

It makes me feel a bit frantic.

My hand snakes between us, searching, seeking him out until I can feel the hot, hard length of him in my palm. He hisses through his teeth, breaking the kiss, his breath huffing against my jaw as his eyes press closed.

"Lila," he rasps.

My lips drag along his cheek. "Want you," I hum, sounding out of breath myself. "Please, Ian."

"You'll have me, sweet girl," he breathes against my skin just before his lips press a lingering kiss there. "But I'm not looking to do this rushed, and if you keep touching me like that, it damn sure will be."

"I meant it when I said I wanted to suck your dick," I say petulantly, feeling robbed of the opportunity.

"*Fuck,*" he groans. "Not this time. I'll never last through that. But I can do that for you."

"But I don't have a dick."

I yelp again when he swats the side of my ass. It's really becoming a thing for him. I wonder if he can tell just how much I fucking like it.

"Stop being a brat," he warns, "and I'll make you come."

Holy hell. I'm dreaming. This must be a dream. Maybe I've died, even. Is this heaven? Would there be talk of orgasms in heaven? Actually, I don't know if I want to go if there isn't.

He pushes up on his knees, reaching to wrench his shirt over his head and tossing it somewhere on the floor, and my entire brain turns into goo because *he has tattoos there too.* My eyes drink in the black-and-gray lines of script and some sort of claws covering the expanse of his left pec, leading right up to the tight, pink bud of his nipple that I weirdly have the urge to suck on. I'm too horny to function, probably.

"Your turn," he murmurs, fingers finding the hem of my T-shirt.

I'm worrying about what kind of bra I'm wearing, or if I remembered to shave under my arms this morning, and several other ridiculous things as he wrestles my shirt over my head, but when I see his mouth part, his throat work with a swallow, his eyes greedily taking me in wearing nothing but a bra—it's pink polka dots, turns out, which isn't terrible, all things considered—I forget to be worried about anything.

"Fuck, Lila, you're . . ."

He trails off, eyes still moving over my body hungrily, making me desperate for whatever he was going to say.

"I'm . . . ?"

He presses one thick finger between my collarbones, letting it drag slowly down over my sternum to the valley between my breasts as his breath stutters.

"Fucking *edible*."

Honestly not what I expected, but judging by the way everything between my legs clenches, I'm apparently a big fan of the descriptor. I'm about to tell him to get down here and taste me then, but he's already reaching for the button of my jeans, seeming in an awful hurry now, for someone who said they didn't want to do this rushed. He's so focused on the task of seeing more of me that I forget all about what's waiting underneath the denim, right up until he pauses with my jeans shucked around my hips, pulling one of his hands away to brush a thumb against the soft skin by the bone there.

The pad of his thumb traces the soft colors, sliding over the pink icing, the blue wrapper, lingering on the little red cherry on top, his eyes growing more and more hooded with every second. "You really do have one."

"I told you I did," I say hoarsely.

"A cupcake?"

His voice is tight. "When?"

"When I turned nineteen."

He presses against the cherry on top of the icing, flicking his gaze up to meet mine with an intensity that makes me shiver. "And were you thinking of me when you got it?"

"Maybe," I answer quietly. "Just a little."

"*Fuck.*" His entire palm covers the tattoo, his fingers wrapping around the fleshy bits of my hip and squeezing. "That shouldn't turn me on, right?"

"Kinda hoping it does, actually, since I'm wanting to get to those plans you talked about."

His body bends, and I suck in a breath, having no warning before his warm, wet mouth is pressing against the ink that his hand had just been covering.

"It does," he mumbles into my skin. "Everything about you does." He's tugging at my jeans again, dragging them down my legs with an urgency that makes my nipples tighten and my pussy throb. "Wanna taste you. Want to know if you taste as sweet as you look."

"O-okay," I manage, my skin feeling tight with anticipation. "No complaints here."

My jeans join his shirt on the floor, and my breath catches when he kisses his way back up my calf, against my knee, my inner thighs—pushing them apart before burying his nose against my underwear without any warning whatsoever to actually *inhale* me and making my back bow off the bed of its own accord. I don't think my brain was ever capable of imagining this—this *ferocity* that he seems to have in the need to touch me, taste me—but it's better than my imagination. It's better because it's *him*, because it's *real*.

"Is this okay?" he asks directly to the increasingly wet fabric between my legs. "Can I?"

So polite, my Ian.

I grin lazily. "Have at it, Cupcake. I was promised an orgasm."

"Thank fuck," he grunts.

He doesn't even bother to peel my underwear off, apparently too impatient for that; he hooks a finger under the elastic at the crease in my thigh, pulling it to the side and wasting no time sliding his hot tongue right through the crease of me.

"*Oh God,*" I moan.

"My name," he practically growls, surprising me in the best way. "You say *my* name when I'm between your legs."

"*Ian,*" I whine when he licks me again, humming against the most sensitive part of me before he swirls around the bud of my clit. "There," I sigh. "Right there. That's what I need."

He flicks my clit again. "Here?"

"*Yes*," I hiss through my teeth.

"Mm."

He wraps his lips around my clit to suck, and the urge to prop up so I can watch is too strong to resist. His eyes peer up at me as he alternates between long pulls with his mouth and soft swirls of his tongue, watching the way it drives me crazy.

He's making sounds I've never heard him make—soft grunts and chest-laden moans that I can feel on the most sensitive part of me, and I feel my thighs clenching against the softness of his dark red hair that tickles my skin. I can feel my mouth hanging open; I'm unable to look away from the sight of him between my legs but also physically incapable of forming coherent thought outside of *Ian is between my fucking legs*—and the way he laps at my pussy like he's trying to consume me is enough to have me hurtling toward something mind-blowing.

"I-Ian," I whimper, reaching down to card my fingers through his hair. "*Right there*. I'm going to fucking come."

His eyes shut tight as his hand slides under his body, and I can see his shoulders trembling, feel them quivering against my thighs as a tortured groan leaves him. I let out a whine of protest when he suddenly releases me, his forehead resting on my hip as ragged breaths puff against my clit, almost enough to finish me off but not quite.

"What the fuck," I pant. "Don't stop."

"Gonna come," he grinds out, his arm moving beneath him, and I realize he's *squeezing* himself to prevent it from happening.

"Fuck, your sounds," he rasps. "Your *taste*." He shudders again. "You're going to make *me* come."

I like that. I *really* like that. Ian Chase being so into eating me out that he almost comes in his pants? Yeah. Suddenly not as outraged at being left hanging.

I tug on his shoulders until he painstakingly crawls back up my body, melding his mouth to mine. I can taste myself on his tongue, and that knowledge has me shuddering too.

"I want to come with you inside me," I murmur. "Wanna feel that cock I've been dreaming about forever."

"*Jesus*, Lila," he groans. "Are you actually trying to kill me?"

"The French call an orgasm 'the little death,'" I chuckle softly. "La petite mort."

"Keep talking French, and I might still come."

I grin as I lean into his ear, whispering, "Je veux que tu me baise, Ian"

"*Fuck.*"

His hands grip my waist as he licks and sucks at the sensitive place beneath my ear, and he blessedly lifts his hips just enough so that I can reach between us to fumble with the button of his jeans. Every soft scrape of his beard against my throat has me trembling, a condition that we seem to share, if the way he shivers when my hand delves inside his pants is any indication. He's hard and so warm in my palm when I cup him through the soft cotton of his underwear, and I can't help but give his cock a slow stroke that has him tensing against me.

"Je veux cette grosse queue," I tell him softly.

He arches into my hand. "Tell me what it means."

"I want this big cock," I purr. "I was promised an orgasm, remember?"

I can practically hear him swallow, it's so loud. "Do you have condoms?"

"Bedside table."

There's a tension in his jaw when he lifts up and peers down at me, obviously thinking about the last time I might've used them, and sure, if it were any other man, I might kick his ass. But this is Ian, and I'm realizing that I like him jealous. I *like* him hating the idea of me with anyone else.

I lean up to kiss his cheek. "I haven't used them in a long time."

"I didn't say anything," he mutters sheepishly.

I feel my lips curl. "I know."

He rolls away from me with renewed urgency, and I take advantage of the opportunity to rid myself of my bra, tossing it to the floor.

"I wanted to do that," he huffs as his knee dips on the bed, sans jeans and condom in hand. "Fuck, look at you."

And he is. Looking at me. He presses his palm against the top of my belly, slowly pushing upward until his fingers are smoothing through the soft skin between my breasts.

"Fucking edible," he murmurs again.

And as if to prove his point, he leans in close until I can feel the warmth of his breath against my nipple, and it hardens in anticipation. The first flick of his tongue is tentative, like a tease, but just like when his mouth was between my legs, it takes him no time at all to wrap his lips around the stiff peak and suck it into his mouth, leaving me a moaning mess by the time he releases me with a wet *pop*.

"How do you want me?"

I blink dazedly, trying to process the question. "Huh?"

"You said you've fantasized about this." Another slow pull of his lips around my nipple before, "I want to make sure to get it right."

My mind flicks through a dozen scenarios that I've dreamt up over the years, feeling like a kid in a candy store with it being left up to me. Although, I think it's one of those situations where there's no wrong answer. But still, there's one picture that is solid in my thoughts, and if we are working through my list, it's as good a place to start as any.

"On top," I say breathlessly. "I want to ride you."

"You really are going to kill me with that mouth of yours," he huffs. "I don't know if I'm ever going to get used to it."

I sit up, smirking at him as I reach for his underwear. I tug at the elastic, pushing at his hips simultaneously to urge him to go where I want him. He falls down onto his back with the same eagerness he's given everything else, watching me through hooded eyes as I start to drag his boxer briefs down his thick thighs. I don't think I could ever be fully prepared for the experience that is seeing Ian's cock for the first time; it slaps up against his abs, hard and red and so fucking thick I press my thighs together in anticipation—and if I wasn't so desperate to have him inside me, I would definitely be pushing the "sucking his dick" issue.

Later. Definitely later.

"You look pretty edible yourself, Cupcake," I tease. I hold out my hand, gesturing to the condom he is still holding. "Gimme that."

He passes it to me wordlessly, never taking his eyes off what I'm doing. I can feel the weight of his gaze as I tear open the wrapper with my teeth, biting gently at my lip as I concentrate on rolling it over his thick length. His large hand wraps around the base, giving himself a slow, lazy stroke when he's fully encased, still tracking my every move as I push up on my knees, grinning at him as I shimmy out of my underwear. His fingers curl around my hip—and it turns me on even further that he can encompass me entirely, given how generous my hips are—to steady me as I lift my leg to straddle his waist, my heartbeat thumping away in my ears as his eyes drift between my legs.

"Fucking hell." His palm slides across my hip bone, his thumb dipping between my thighs to slip between them to tease my clit. "Look how wet you are." His thumb glides through my folds in a slow back-and-forth, his breath punching out of him like it's a chore. "Is that for me?"

My lashes flutter as I nod, sucking in a breath. "Mhm."

"Come here, sweet girl," he hums. "Wanna watch you sit on my cock."

I brace my hands on his abs that feel like granite under my fingers, imagining for a moment tracing each groove with my tongue. Something else for later, I think. I rock my hips back and forth so that I can grind down on his cock without actually taking him inside, delighted that his gasp is as loud as mine.

"Lila," he murmurs. "Need you."

It's a *good* sort of overwhelmed that I feel, hearing that—the elation of knowing he *needs* me, that he *wants* me—threatening to fill me up to the point of bursting. Even more so than I know he's about to. He's still holding his cock with one hand, but the other wanders, teasing the soft curves of my belly and the supple skin of my thigh until every inch of me feels like one big nerve, over-sensitized to the point of almost being too much.

"Watch me," I tell him, reaching between us to brush my

fingers against his. I take over holding him steady, catching his gaze as I notch him right where I want him. "*Watch.*"

And he does—eyes fixed on the place where he slowly starts to slip inside—the delicious stretch of him filling me, causing me to clench around him involuntarily as a ragged breath falls out of my mouth. I take him inch by inch until I can feel the soft hair of his massive thighs against my ass, supporting my weight, and I can't help but circle my hips experimentally, just feeling him.

Ian's head tips back then, his lips parting. "*Fuck.*"

"Mm. You like?"

He grits his teeth. "You're lucky I haven't come already."

"I'll take that as a compliment."

"I'm begging you to move," he groans. "Put me out of my misery, Lila."

I lift up just a little, dropping on his cock as the slap of skin rings through the air. "Like that?"

"You're being a brat again," he says through gritted teeth.

A breathy laugh escapes me. "I think you like it."

"Yeah?" He grips my hips with both hands, his molten gaze tilting up to find mine. "I think you like being one."

The sharp *smack* takes me by surprise—slightly harder than the others, but that could be because it's bare skin. Whatever I'd been about to say dies on my tongue as a garbled moan tumbles past my lips, my pussy clenching hard around the throbbing weight of his cock that's buried inside me.

"*Ian.*"

"Like that?" he says, echoing me. "You like that, sweet girl?"

My movements are instinctual now, my body lifting from his cock without thought before slamming back down as I nod frantically. "Do it again."

"Yeah?" Another loud *crack* rings through my bedroom as his palm lands against the rounded curve of my ass, making it tremble as I start to find an actual rhythm. "You want me to spank the brat out of you?"

"Need it," I sigh. "Need you."

"You have me, sweetheart," he coos, landing another smack. "You've got all of me."

My head falls back when he tilts up his hips, bracing his feet on the mattress beneath us to gain some leverage as he starts meeting my thrusts.

"It's too much," he groans. "You feel too fucking good."

"Don't stop," I plead in a low whine. "Please don't stop."

"Not until I feel you come on this cock," he grates. "Want to feel your sweet little pussy soaking me."

For the love of all that's holy—praise be to the dirty talk gods.

"Then fuck me harder," I tell him, sounding out of breath and much less teasing than I intend. "I can take it."

Another smack to the ass for my efforts, and I actually *tremble*.

"So fucking beautiful," he mumbles, his thumb dipping between my legs again to circle the throbbing button of my clit. "Need to see you come. Can you come for me? Wanna feel you."

"Right there," I whimper. "Keep touching me."

His hips slam into me harder now, bouncing me on his cock and shaking the entire bed with the force of his efforts, and I have to actually hold on to his waist just to keep myself steady. I feel that hot pressure building between my legs, hurtling toward the precipice of something earth-shattering.

"You're getting so tight," he gasps. "So fucking tight. Are you close?"

I nod quickly, eyes shut tight as I chase after the orgasm that is *right there.* "Yes, just—Don't stop. Keep—Right there, I—*Holy fucking shit,* I—"

My entire body curls inward when I come, my forehead resting against Ian's chest as I shiver and shake. His still-thrusting cock means that it goes on and on and on, so much so that it almost feels like dying, but in the very best way.

Little death is right.

I'm still shaking when I feel his rhythm falter, his hips stuttering and his arms coming around me to hold me tight as he fucks into the wet mess he's made, his lips resting against my forehead, his breath washing against my skin there.

"Fuck. *Fuck, Lila.*"

He gets so tense beneath me, when he comes undone, his fingers clutching me so tightly I imagine there might be bruises tomorrow, but I *want* that. I want the reminder of what we've done. I want the proof that this is fucking *real.*

We both lie still after, catching our breath, time passing at an unknown pace. I can't say when it is that my melted brain registers the slow stroking of his fingers up and down my spine; maybe it's when his lips start to press lingering kisses down the side of my face, maybe that's when I come back online.

"Wow," I laugh, my voice sounding scratchy and not quite like me. "That was . . ."

"Fucking amazing," he finishes.

I grin into his chest. "Yeah?"

"Gimme a bit, and we're doing it again."

I lift my head, feeling a strange sort of thrill run through me. "Really?"

His brow scrunches. He looks so fucking delicious like this— sweat-slick skin and too-red lips and eyes that are a shade too dark with pupils that are entirely blown out—and it only occurred to me this very second that there was some deep, deep part of me that worried he would change his mind after. After we gave in.

"Did you think I wouldn't want to do it again?"

Did I? I must have, right? What other reason would suddenly make me feel so unsure?

"I . . . Maybe?"

He frowns, pushing up from the bed and bringing us to a sitting position without seeming to exert any effort whatsoever. It really is unfairly hot how easily he manhandles me.

"Lila," he says in a tone that almost seems chiding. "This wasn't—" He puffs out a breath, shaking his head. "This wasn't just sex to me. I couldn't do that. Not with you. I could *never* do that with you. This is . . ." His hand reaches until his palm covers my cheek, and my fingers drift there to hold it steady like they have a mind of their own. "This is so much more than that. Do you understand?"

I honestly can't say that I do, not one hundred percent, but the sincerity in his eyes, the absolute *truth* in them—it makes it hard to argue.

"Okay," I say quietly. "Me too."

He kisses me in that way of his—like he has all the time in the world, but he wants to use every second of it for *me*—slow, dirty, but with the promise of so much *more*.

"You've got bigger things to worry about," he mumbles, a smile in his voice.

I frown, pulling back. "What?"

"Well." He brings his finger to my lip, tracing the shape of it slowly as a devious grin spreads across his face. "We still have to tell Jack."

I groan as I slump forward, ignoring the tiny *oomph* Ian lets out when I cover him with my weight, dropping my face to his shoulder. Definitely was *not* anticipating the buzzkill that is thoughts of my brother after having dream sex with my dream guy.

"You ass," I grumble. "Way to kill the mood."

Ian laughs loudly, thinking he's funny, no doubt, the bastard, but I certainly don't. Probably. Mostly. Not even the tiny kisses he starts to pepper across my shoulder are enough to make me forgive him. Nope. Definitely not.

His tongue slowly traces the curve that leads up to my neck.

On second thought . . .

Sixteen

IAN

close Lila's bedroom door behind me quietly, not wanting to wake her. She dozed off in my arms after round two, and while watching her sleep like a creep is tempting, I imagine she'll be hungry when she wakes up. We did technically skip dinner, after all. Not that I'm complaining in the slightest.

I can feel a smile etched onto my mouth as fresh images of her above me and beneath me flit through my thoughts, half tempted to go back the way I came and wake her up for more. Now that I've had her, it feels like I might never get enough, and sure, that's a little scary, but it also feels . . . right, somehow. That's the part that is the most jarring about all of this, how *not* weird it is. I guess part of me thought that with our history, with the progression of what we were and what we're becoming—that it might be awkward. But I feel none of that. Honestly, for the first time in a long time, I feel . . . settled. Happy, even.

And I know it's all because of the gorgeous woman snoring softly in her bed.

I keep my steps quiet as I move toward Lila's kitchen, pausing for only a second to laugh at the glass display case just off the living room that does in fact house the Porcelain Pride with, well, *pride*—moving on after a few seconds so as not to rob Lila the pleasure of showing me her newest additions. I open up a few of her cabinets instead; I'm nowhere near Lila's level of culinary prowess, but surely I can whip up something that she'll eat, her constant worries of me burning something be damned.

I'm currently ignoring a text from Jack that's sitting unread on my phone, which is tucked in the rear pocket of the jeans I slipped back into; I don't want to lie to him by any means, but telling him about Lila and me should be a joint effort. She should have even more say about how it happens, I think, given that it's her brother. I want to believe that Jack wouldn't *actually* disown me for this, not with the way I care about Lila, but I can't pretend there isn't a niggling worry at the back of my mind, however small. I guess we'll cross that bridge when we get there.

I'm pulling a box of spaghetti out of Lila's pantry—there was some sort of leftover meat sauce in the fridge, and even *I* can use a microwave—when I feel my phone start buzzing with a call in my pocket. I dig it out and check the display before answering.

"Mei?"

"Hey, Ginger Giant."

I roll my eyes, amending, "Bella."

"What's up? My wife wants you over for dinner, for some reason."

"Maybe she misses me," I taunt. It's harmless, since Bella and I both know that Mei is head over heels for her, but it's still fun. "Maybe she's already tired of you."

"Hardly," Bella scoffs. "She'd miss that thing I do with my t—"

"*Bella*," my ex-wife hisses after what sounds like a small scuffle. I hear Mei sigh heavily, and then her voice is coming through the speaker. "For fuck's sake. Is it too early for divorce?"

"You love me!" Bella yells from the background. "No take-backsies!"

Another labored sigh before, "We just got back yesterday. I wanted to see how you were doing."

"I'm . . ." My mouth quirks on its own, thinking about the woman in the other room. "I'm great, actually."

"Huh."

"What?"

"You actually sound . . . happy," Bella chimes in, suspicion in her tone. "What's going on?"

"Am I on speaker?"

"Duh," Bella says, at the same time as Mei's, "Of course not."

"Wow," I laugh. "Smooth."

"Shut up and spill," Bella tuts. "Why do you sound so happy?"

"I can't sound happy?"

"Normally you sound like someone ate your puppy in front of you."

"That's a horrifying image," Mei says.

Bella snorts. "But am I wrong?"

"You do sound . . ." Mei trails off, as if thinking. "You sound different."

I pause after filling one of Lila's pots with water, weighing my response. "I've just had an . . . interesting month."

"Does that interesting month have anything to do with a hot baker?" Bella singsongs.

"Bella," Mei hisses. "We said we wouldn't pry."

"*You* said," Bella corrects. "I said no such thing."

"We're supposed to be a united front," Mei argues.

Bella's voice turns coy. "I can give you a united front if you want, baby."

"Ladies," I interrupt, not needing to hear their foreplay. "Focus."

"Right," Mei says. "Okay. So we *are* curious."

"I told you it was just a PR thing." It's not a lie, per se, but it's definitely not the truth. Not anymore. I'm just not sure how much I should say, given that Lila and I haven't discussed what we might tell people. If we're even telling people at all. "Our publicists put it together."

"Those pictures I saw looked downright saucy," Bella points out.

I frown. "Who says *saucy* anymore?"

"Me, motherfucker," Bella says, blowing a raspberry. "Don't deflect."

"I don't have anything to tell you," I say carefully. "At least . . . not right now."

"Hmm." Mei sounds thoughtful. "How about you invite your *friend* to dinner with us? I'd love to officially meet her."

My nose scrunches as I watch little bubbles start to form in the pot of water. "That won't be weird?"

"Only if there's something going on," Bella answers in an accusing tone.

Mei clucks her tongue. "No, not even then. It wouldn't be weird at all, because Ian would totally be honest about what we were to each other to anyone he cared about, *right*?"

"Right," I say immediately. I wince before adding, "If there was someone."

"Yeah, yeah," Bella huffs. "Bring the baker to dinner. Ha, baker. Get it? Because she's a baker, and her *name* is Baker . . ."

Mei sighs wearily. "Honestly, I love you, but sometimes I do question it."

"Sure you do." I hear the sound of Bella smacking a kiss on Mei. "Keep telling yourself that."

I hear Mei's voice more clearly, and it seems like maybe she's taken me off speakerphone. "We *would* love to see you," she stresses. "And any of your . . . friends. You know that, right?"

"Yeah, I know," I tell her. "I just need to make sure it's okay with my . . . friend. Before confirming anything, yeah?"

"I get it," she assures me. "Whenever you *confirm* things, let us know, okay?"

"You'll be the first," I say, which is probably true, outside of Jack. We'll have to play it by ear. "I gotta go, okay? I'll text you about dinner."

"Okay. Love you."

"Love you too."

I set my phone on the counter after hanging up, mulling over the conversation, wondering if Lila will *want* to tell people about us. Realizing that I *do*. I want everyone to know she's mine. I want to make sure that there's zero chance of anyone snatching her away. I've never been possessive before, but something about Lila fills me with an almost caveman-like feeling, one that has me wanting to wrap her up in my arms and stow her away somewhere.

Which I know Lila would one thousand percent kick my ass for, if I ever dared to try.

I shake off the thought as I dump the dry spaghetti into the now-boiling water, flicking my eyes to the counter when my phone starts buzzing again. I answer without looking this time—mostly because I'm busy looking for the salt container for the pasta, and

I assume it's Mei calling again to tell me something she forgot the first time, which she has a habit of—absently clicking the speaker button to give her a taste of her own medicine.

"What did you forget this time?"

"Ian?"

I pause, my hand suspended in midair in front of one of Lila's cabinets as I jerk my head toward the phone. I purse my lips, half considering pretending I'm too busy to talk. I don't exactly want anything spoiling my good mood, and this conversation definitely has the potential to do so. Which almost makes me feel guilty for even thinking it.

"Abby," I say finally. "What's up?"

"Nothing much," she answers quietly, but I know that's not the case.

She never calls me unless there is something, and I have often wondered if that's my fault.

I frown as I continue what I was doing, grabbing the salt and sprinkling some into the boiling water and giving the pasta a stir. "Sure about that?"

"I . . ." She blows out a frustrated breath. "I just talked to him."

"Never a good idea, in my experience," I mutter.

"Yeah, well." She really is too young to sound so weary. "I guess I'm a glutton for punishment."

"What did he say?"

"More of the same old shit," she says. "I just . . . I don't know why I keep wanting it to be different."

"Abby . . ." I pause, frowning. I know what she's feeling, but I don't want to be the one to completely snuff out her hope. "You're not going to find what you're looking for. Not with him. He's just not wired that way."

"I know that, I do, but—" I can hear her puff air from her nostrils. "It just sucks, you know? I didn't ask for any of this."

"I know you didn't," I tell her quietly. "This isn't your fault."

"And I'm sorry for dumping my problems on you," she barrels on. "I know it isn't your fault, either, and I know you definitely didn't ask for this any more than I did, but I—"

"Abby," I interrupt calmly. "Listen. You don't have to apologize to me, okay? I'm here for you. I'll *always* be here for you, got it? I care about you, and that means I want to help you when you need it. I know I haven't been very good about being there, but it's not because I don't—"

"Ian?"

I turn to look behind me with my mouth parted midsentence— a sleepy-looking Lila blinking at me from the attached living room with her arms wrapped around her middle and a puzzled expression on her face.

"Lila," I breathe.

Abby's voice sounds from the speaker on my phone. "Who's that?"

"Abby," I say, clearing my throat. "Can I call you back?"

"Oh. Um. Sure."

I probably seem like a dick leaving her hanging like this, but I don't know how much Lila heard, and the idea of her misconstruing whatever it *was* that she heard makes my stomach clench.

"Thanks," I tell Abby. "We'll talk soon."

"Okay."

I don't move even after Abby hangs up, still watching Lila as she eyes me curiously.

"Hey," I offer quietly. "Sleep well?"

"I slept okay," she says, her brow wrinkling. "You were gone when I got up."

"Yeah, I . . ." I gesture at the pot in front of me. "I found some sauce in the fridge, and there was pasta in the pantry, and I thought . . ."

Lila's mouth quirks. "Really pulling out all the stops for me, huh, Cupcake?"

"Right," I manage, relief flooding through me. Her joking is a good sign. "Only the *best* food that you mostly cooked yourself."

She bites back a grin, but there's still an uncertainty to her gaze. "I didn't mean to interrupt."

"You didn't," I tell her immediately. "You really didn't. That was . . ." I frown, wondering where to even begin to explain. "You see, that was actually—"

"Ian," she interrupts, holding up a hand. "You don't owe me an explanation. Seriously. I trust you."

A knot I hadn't even realized had been bundling up in my chest starts to loosen, a warm feeling flooding in its wake that feels too big for the short span of time since Lila has come back into my life. I nod slowly back at her, my tongue feeling too thick all of a sudden.

"Thank you," I manage hoarsely. "I'm glad that you trust me." I shift my weight from one foot to the other, realizing that I *want* her to know. She deserves that. "I'd still like to explain, if you don't mind. I think . . ." I nod to myself. "I think I'd feel better if I did."

"Okay," she says quietly, stepping across the living room and into the kitchen. She doesn't stop until she reaches me, pressing up on her toes and leaving a kiss at my cheek. "Finish the food, and we'll talk about it, okay?"

I wrap an arm around her waist, pulling her tight against me and pressing my nose to her hair just to breathe her in. "Okay," I murmur. "Sounds good."

She's smiling when she pulls away, saying something about freshening up in the bathroom, and I watch her the entire time she goes, trying to piece together how to lay all my secrets bare to the one person I worry about disappointing the most. But she deserves to know, I resolve. Especially if there's any hope to ensure this thing between us is lasting.

And I want it to be, I realize all at once.

Desperately.

- - - - -

Dinner is a quiet affair. I'm aware the entire time that Lila is giving me space, letting me approach on my own terms the subject of the phone call she heard; she's always so careful with other people. It has always felt like Lila can sense what others need more than they know themselves. When we were kids, it was as simple as a cookie after a hard test, or maybe even a dumb joke after a bad day—I don't think I ever fully realized the extent of how *good* she's always been at reading people, most of all me.

It just makes me appreciate her more.

"That was good," she says, dropping her fork onto her plate.

I can't help but laugh. "It was your sauce. I just reheated it."

"Hey, you didn't burn it."

I roll my eyes. "I rarely burn my food; you realize that, right?"

"Pics or it didn't happen."

"Right," I snort. I push the last bite I'm avoiding around my own plate, my jaw working as I try to figure out just *how* to broach the conversation I'm mostly sure I need to have with her. I *want* to have it, even. "So, about that call . . ."

"If it's difficult, we really don't have to talk about it."

She reaches across the table to place her hand over mine, and in that moment, I have a distant thought that it was inevitable that I end up here with her. How could I not, when she's always been so sure in her blind faith in me? Has *anyone* in my life ever had that for me?

"I want to," I say with confidence. "I do. It's just . . . I don't know where to start."

"Wherever you want," she tells me in a soothing tone. "I'll listen to whatever you want to tell me."

"Well, you know why I left for Canada."

"I know . . . as much as I can," she says carefully.

"Meaning you know what you read."

"I told you, I never believed that."

"And I believe that," I assure her. "But I know that you had nothing else to go on."

"But they had it wrong, right? You didn't cheat on Mei."

There's a certainty in her voice, but there's a question there too. Like some part of her is desperate for confirmation that her rock-solid surety of who I am isn't wrong. It's that soft question in her tone that makes me more determined to tell her everything.

"I didn't." My tone is quiet, mostly because I'm realizing this is the first time in years I've talked about this with anyone who wasn't directly involved. "Mei and I were already separated when those pictures came out. We had already figured out we didn't love each other like that."

"So that woman . . ." I watch her soft throat work with a swallow, her lips pressing together briefly. "Was that the same woman you were talking to on the phone?"

Even now, when her voice wavers, I don't see any hint in her eyes that she doesn't trust me. It makes me feel . . . whole. It makes me want to give her every bit of trust in return.

"It was," I say honestly. And when her eyes dip to the table, her head bobbing with a soft nod, I feel the words I've been keeping from the world tumbling out right after in a rush. "She's my sister."

Lila's gaze snaps up to meet mine, her mouth parting in surprise. "Your sister?"

"Half," I correct.

"So . . ." Her brow furrows, trying to puzzle it out. "So who—"

"My dad. My dad cheated on my mom when I was eight. Abigail is the result."

"Oh my God." Her hand squeezes mine. Like she wants to comfort me. Like I'm the victim. "How long have you known?"

"I found out that week," I tell her. "The week those pictures were taken. That was the first time I met her."

"Ian . . ." Her expression falls, and she looks almost pained. "Why didn't you tell someone? Why would you let everyone say those awful things about you all these years?"

A bitter laugh escapes me, and I shrug in defeat. "The same reason I do anything in life that doesn't feel right. My fucking father."

"Bradley?"

"My mother doesn't know," I explain. "I can't . . . I know that I should have told her, but I can't do that to her, you know? She's always . . . loved my dad. I don't know what it is she fucking sees in him, but it would break her heart if she found out. I can't be the one to do that to her."

"So you kept it a secret to protect your mom?"

"He told me she'd lose the team if she left him," I say quietly.

"Apparently, my grandfather wrote stipulations into his will." My lip curls. "He wanted to be sure the team stays with someone that 'knows what they're doing.' I guess he was just as much of an asshole as my father is."

"That's not fair," she says, outraged.

"It isn't," I agree. "My mother *loves* that team. It would kill her to lose it. She's been a part of it since she was a kid. I can't believe her father would do that to her. I'm not even sure she knows about it, honestly. Or maybe she does, but she's so sure about my dad that she's never worried about it? I just . . . I don't know. It kills me thinking that I could be the reason she loses everything. She would hate me."

"She wouldn't *hate* you," Lila stresses. "She's your mother."

"And Bradley is my father," I remind her. "It's never stopped him."

"So your dad used your mom as leverage, essentially."

"Among other things. He has ways of protecting himself. He's paying for Abby's education. Her mom was a waitress when they met, and she died when Abby was a senior in high school. That's the year I found out. My dad came to my apartment and basically told me, 'This is your sister, she's going to be staying with you until I can figure out what to do with her.'" I shake my head. "She was only eighteen, and she was so fucking scared. He just dumped her on me, Lila. This guy she didn't even know. She'd just lost her mother, and then she got dropped on my doorstep, and both of us had his threats hanging over our heads . . . I don't know. I couldn't risk having him ruin her life any further, so I . . . did what he said. I kept my mouth shut."

"Even when it ended up hurting you," Lila says quietly.

"I could have paid for her school, I know that, and I would

have been happy to, but . . ." I breathe out a sigh. "Abby still wants him to be her dad. I *know* that if we don't keep in line, he'll cut us both out of his life. I can live with that, but . . . I can't take away this hope she's clinging to that he'll come around and be the guy she needs him to be. I can't take away the only person she has left."

Lila's hand squeezes mine again, and she ducks her head until I'm forced to meet her eyes, and she gives me a determined look. "She would still have *you*."

"I know that, but I'm not her father. I'm just some guy whose doorstep she was dropped onto once who ended up leaving her behind like everyone else."

"You didn't leave because you wanted to," Lila says firmly. "Not really. You didn't *want* to leave her behind. You just protected her the only way you knew how. Didn't you. If you hadn't left, the press would have kept digging into her. They would have figured it out. You just wanted to *protect* her."

"How can you know that?"

Her smile is slow, sweet. "Because that's who you are, Ian. That's who you've always been. You make people feel safe." Her hand lifts from mine to cup my face, her thumb stroking the skin just above my beard softly. "It's how you always made me feel too."

I can't help but stare at her, at this woman who seems to see me as something better than I've ever seen myself—having to take a heavy inhale just to keep the emotions that threaten to overtake me at bay.

"He told me to take the trade," I whisper.

"What?"

"My father," I clarify. "He pushed me into the trade."

"He sent you *away*?"

"More or less," I say. "Told me that the team was better off without my drama. That *everyone* was better off."

"You should have told him to go fuck himself," Lila seethes. "The absolute nerve of that fuckhead."

Her cheeks are flush with indignant anger on my behalf, and weirdly, that makes some of my melancholy dissipate. "Maybe I should have," I muse. "But I guess I thought he was right."

"What do you mean?"

"Everything that was happening felt like my fault, somehow. I guess some part of me thought that maybe everyone really *would* be better off without me."

"That's bullshit," she practically spits.

I rear back. "What?"

"*None* of what happened was your fault, Ian. I mean, Christ. Your jackass dad has an affair, completely fucks off from the kid's life, dumps her on his *other* kid's doorstep to care for when it's convenient for him, then blames *you* when it all goes to shit?" She shakes her head. "Absolutely not. There's a villain in this story, Ian, but it isn't fucking you."

"Wow," I say thickly, emotion still clogging my throat. "I'm not sure I deserve the faith you have in me."

"I just *know* you," she says with a slight shake of her head. "I've known you since I was six years old. You met me before Jack. Do you remember?" I nod, watching her expression turn wistful. "I was crying at the bus stop because Jack was sick, and I was scared to get on by myself."

"You were so fucking little," I murmur. "Just this tiny little thing."

"You came right up to me, this huge kid with flaming-red hair and freckles looking like some sort of giant, and you squatted right down to my level . . . and you smiled at me."

I feel myself smiling now as I remember. "I asked you why you were crying."

"I told you it was because my brother was sick, and I was scared to sit by myself." Her smile widens, bright, like it's shining a light on all the dark parts of me. "Do you remember what you said?"

"I . . . I told you that there's no reason to be scared, because you have me now, and I wouldn't let you sit alone."

"I know you met Jack when you walked me home, and I know that you became best friends and all that . . . but I . . . It always felt like you were mine first. I guess it still does."

"Lila, I—"

"But from that moment on, I felt better when you were around. I always knew that as long as you were, nothing bad would ever happen to me. Because *that's who you are*. For me, for Jack, and for Abby, too, it seems. You spend so much time making sure that everyone *else* is okay, you don't take the time to make sure *you're* okay. The world won't end if you're okay, Ian. You know that, right?"

The warmth in my chest feels stifling; like the kind of heat that steals your breath, that makes it feel a little like dying slowly. I feel so many things, things that seem impossible, that seem too quick, and all of them begin and end with the overwhelming urge to hold her, so I give in to that feeling, I pull her from her chair and over into mine, letting her crawl into my lap as I wrap my arms around her like she's tethering me—and in a way, it feels like she is.

"I don't want to hurt anyone," I manage thickly. "It feels like

I'm trapped. Like no matter what I do, someone will eventually end up being hurt."

"You can't put that on yourself," Lila soothes. "You love hard, Ian. You always have. Anyone who knows you will know that you would never hurt someone you care about on purpose. You have to try and give yourself the same care you give everyone else."

I consider that, trying to remember a time in my life where I did what she's saying. When I worried more about myself than those around me. I realize I can't think of one. I've spent so long carrying different weights, holding them on my shoulders until it felt like I might be crushed . . . I don't even know what putting myself first would look like.

"I've never told anyone else but Jack about my dad's part in my leaving," I admit quietly.

She runs her fingers through my hair. "I'm glad you told me."

We're quiet for a moment; I'm letting her words marinate and she seems content to let me, and when she finally speaks, it's with a soft kiss to my temple. "Not sure my kitchen chairs are built for me *and* an NHL player."

"I'll get you stronger chairs," I mumble into her hair.

"Wow, we had sex one time and he's already trying to buy me *chairs*," she tuts. "You're smothering me."

"Two times," I huff against her throat.

"Mm. Two is the magic number for chair sugar daddies?"

I laugh as I give her ass a light swat. "Brat."

"You like it." She pulls back, her arms still looped around my neck and her eyes glittering with amusement. "Thank you," she says sincerely. "For telling me."

"I wanted to," I assert. "I . . . I trust you too."

"I'm glad," she whispers.

I pull her in until her lips meet mine, feeling that same sensation of being *settled*, *happy*—swelling inside to the point of bursting.

"So what would you get me if there was a third time?" she teases, nipping at my lower lip.

My lips curl, elation bubbling inside to have her here. That I finally *saw* her.

Too soon, my brain says, just as my heart whispers back, *Too late*.

Seventeen

DELILAH

So let me get this straight," Theo says, tapping his spoon against his coffee cup. "You're . . . dating Ian Chase?"

I purse my lips. Can I call it dating? I mean, I *want* to call it dating, but we haven't exactly discussed a label, so . . .

"We're . . . something?"

Ava snorts. "Something involving their genitals."

"Could you not be so crass?" Theo says with distaste.

Ava sticks her tongue out at him. "I once watched you make out with the drummer of a ska band in a dive bar after *Jägerbombs*, of all things, and you want to talk to me about crass?"

"Dee," Theo says calmly, "might I suggest again you find new friends? I'm only thinking of your image here."

"Says the man who tongue-humped a guy with a soul patch," Ava quips sweetly.

"Both of you need to keep your voices down." I glance around the busy coffee shop, noting the people milling about. "And can we not do this today? I'm still mildly freaking out about tonight, and you two are supposed to be comforting me."

"I'm sure it'll be totally not awkward at all to have dinner with your long-standing-crush-turned-maybe-boyfriend's ex-wife," Theo deadpans.

"Stop being an ass," Ava chides. "Ian told you that they weren't ever really in love, though, right? That's something."

"Not like *that*," I confirm. "But she's still important to him."

"She's also one of the most popular artists to come out of Massachusetts in the last twenty years," Theo notes.

"Thanks," I say dryly. "That's helpful."

"And *you're* a successful, young, *hot* baker with her own television show," Ava reminds me. "There's nothing for you to be intimidated about."

"I'm not . . . intimidated per se," I tell her truthfully. "It's more like . . . I want her to like me, you know? She's important to Ian, practically his best friend, so it feels like it would be a disaster if she didn't."

"Oh, shut up," Theo grouses, taking a sip of his Earl Grey. "You're sunshine personified, when you're not being a pain in my ass. It's impossible not to like you."

"Wow," I laugh. "Thanks for the glowing review."

"Don't hire your friends as your agent if you want them to blow smoke up your ass."

"Is it weird that his ex is going to know about the two of you before Jack?" Ava muses.

I frown. "Maybe . . . But I think I'd like a more solid definition of what this is between us before I involve Jack. He's already going to be weird enough about it as it is."

Ava narrows her eyes. "You don't think Ian thinks you two are serious?"

"It's not that," I start. "I just don't want to push it, you know? I've wanted this for so long, and it's like now that I have it, I'm terrified of jinxing it somehow."

"Well," Theo says, clucking his tongue, "the two of you had better be extremely careful until you get it figured out. If the media gets ahold of this, there's no taking it back."

"I know that," I tell him. "Which is another reason why I don't want to be too hasty. I don't want Ian to feel like he *has* to commit to anything if this blows up in our faces. I want to give him time to make sure that he really wants this without the internet picking apart his business again."

"Are you worried about all of that?" Ava gives me a concerned look. "I mean . . . He seems like a nice guy, but with everything that happened with his ex . . ."

I have to bite my tongue to keep from jumping to his defense; it's not my business to share everything Ian told me about what really happened all those years ago, which is why I can't come out and say that none of what people read is remotely close to the truth. Even if it kills me to continue letting people think that Ian could ever be capable of what he's been accused of.

"I trust him," I say instead. "He would never do anything to purposefully hurt me."

"Let's hope not," Theo says thoughtfully. "Because if this blows up as bad as his last relationship, it could be just as damaging for you as it is for him."

"What do you mean?"

"It's all fun and games to let the internet *think* the two of you are in some sort of situationship, but if they find out that not only is it actually happening, but then if Ian somehow bungles it all, you'll be nothing more than the dumb girl who fell for his bullshit again."

"Hey," Ava cries indignantly. "Don't be an ass."

"I'm just telling you how the good people of social media have a tendency to kick people when they're down. That's not to say it might not gain you some sympathy, but I've seen the dark side of the web too many times not to worry that it might not go the other way."

"He won't hurt me," I say again, firmer this time. "That's not who he is."

"For your sake," Theo answers with sympathy in his gaze, "I hope you're right."

There's a beat of silence that passes between us at our little table, the sounds of chatter and chimes of the nearby cash register filling the air as the three of us mull over Theo's words.

"Anyway," Theo goes on, clearing his throat, "I'm glad you told me. I will make sure to keep an eye on the gossip about you two a little more closely so I can stay on top of things."

I don't say that he's almost made me regret telling him at all, knowing that it would be stupid to engage in this thing with Ian without giving Theo a heads-up. It *is* what I pay him for, after all.

Ava shoots Theo a look, but blessedly changes the subject. "So what time is dinner tonight?"

"Seven," I tell her. "They live on the other side of town, so Ian is picking me up at six."

"Do you know what you're going to wear?"

"No idea," I sigh. "What do you wear when you're meeting your . . . Well, when you're meeting the ex-wife?"

"Something that accentuates your tits," Theo says flippantly.

Ava and I both turn our heads to gape at him, but he just cocks an eyebrow. "What? I may not be attracted to them, but even I know they're great tits."

"He's not wrong," Ava chuckles. "Might as well give yourself all the confidence boosts you can."

I shake my head at the both of them, grabbing my drink—yeah, it's the same one Ian ordered for me when we first hung out here, because I've started drinking them again like a total sap—fiddling with the straw as I try to quell the nerves that flutter in my belly when I think about tonight.

It's going to be fine, I tell myself. *It's a good thing that he wants me to meet her.*

Maybe if I repeat it enough times, I'll stop feeling like I might hurl.

— — — —

"Was it your intention to make sure I can't focus on anything anyone is saying tonight when you put on that dress?"

I can't help the grin that forms on my lips, catching Ian's disgruntled expression when I peek at him from the side while we're walking up the driveway. "You don't like it?"

"I like it too much," he mutters.

"My friends said it would give me a confidence boost to accentuate my best features," I tell him, gesturing at the scoop neckline.

Ian squeezes my hand, pulling it up to his lips to brush them against the back of my knuckles. "While it is a very good feature, I wouldn't say it's your best."

"Oh?" My chest flutters. "What would you say my best feature is?"

His lips quirk, his gray eyes playful. "I'll be happy to show you later."

"Are you *trying* to get me riled up before I meet your ex? Because that's low."

He turns my hand to press a kiss against my palm. "I'd call that karma."

"I'll show you karma, you—"

My words die off when the door we've just stepped up to swings open before we even have a chance to knock, a tall, willowy woman with jet-black hair and cheekbones that make her bright smile seem even wider beaming at us from the entryway.

"You made it!"

"Kind of the point of RSVP'ing," Ian chuckles.

The woman, who I know is Mei from her pictures, slaps him on the chest. "Don't be a jerk." She turns her attention to me, her smile widening. "And you must be Delilah."

"Dee is fine," I tell her. "Everyone calls me Dee." I peek over at Ian. "Except this one."

Mei's eyes have a knowing look about them, but she just gestures us inside. "Come in, come in. I hope you like empanadas. Bella is cooking."

"That sounds amazing," I tell her as we step inside.

Their house is huge; even the foyer is immaculate with its gleaming tiled floor and its high ceiling that boasts a sparkling chandelier. I can see a wide living room in the other room with cream-colored couches and warm-burgundy throw pillows, and I can only assume that the put-togetherness of it all is Mei's handiwork, given that she's the artist.

"Your house is beautiful," I comment, still looking around, a little awestruck. "Ian said you guys just moved in?"

"Just before the wedding," Mei tells me as we take off our shoes. "Bella insisted on doing a lot of the work herself, which meant it took a little longer."

"Your wife helped build it?"

"She's a general contractor," Mei tells me. "Which means she gave anyone we tried to source out jobs to hell if they didn't do everything *just* right."

"*Excuse me* for wanting to make sure the place was perfect," a slightly accented voice calls from the other room. Mei rolls her eyes as she takes off in that direction, and we follow her. A woman several inches shorter than Mei but with the same inky black hair is at the counter, arching a brow at her wife. "She likes seeing me in a tool belt, so it all evens out."

Mei huffs. "Bella."

"Is this your girl?" Bella glances at Ian, but then her dark eyes flick back to me. "What are your intentions with our Ian?"

"Bella!" Mei gasps.

I look over at Ian for help, but I notice he's covering his mouth with his hand like he's trying not to laugh, so I take a shot in the dark. "They're terrible," I tell Bella. "Just the worst."

Bella nods seriously, the slightest tilt to her mouth when she says, "I like her."

"You'll have to forgive my wife," Mei says exasperatedly. "She thinks she's funny."

"¿Perdón? No te ríes cuando uso mi boca para—"

"Callate," Mei hisses.

"I know enough Spanish to know I don't want her to finish that sentence either," Ian mutters.

"I wish I *didn't* know enough Spanish," Mei sighs, but there's a pink tint to her cheeks, so I have a feeling she isn't as irritated as she acts.

"I only know French," I offer. "So I'm blissfully in the dark."

"Oh, I've always wanted to learn French," Mei gushes. "Ian told me you studied in France?"

"For a few years. It was a great experience."

"I bet dirty talk is great in French," Bella sighs.

I can't help but laugh as I wind my arm around Ian's waist. "It absolutely is. Right, Ian?"

"That's it," Ian huffs, pointing between Bella and me. "You two aren't allowed to be friends."

"Oh, I think it's too late for that," Bella says with a grin.

I meet it with one of my own. "Much too late."

Mei goes back to chastising her wife with hardly any real bite, pulling Ian in for backup every so often, to no avail. I watch it all happen with a smile on my face, the nerves I've been carrying for tonight melting away when I realize that everything here is exactly as Ian said. That there's nothing between him and Mei but deep friendship, one that I can sense just by watching the two of them together.

"Dee," Bella calls, waving me over. "Come help me finish up and let the squares set the table."

Ian peers down at me as if silently asking me if I need his help, but I just give his side a squeeze before pulling away from him. "Gimme an apron, and I'm in."

"This was a mistake, wasn't it?" I hear Ian asking Mei as they leave the kitchen.

I hear Mei's answering sigh. "Yeah," she says. "Probably."

Eighteen

IAN

like her," Mei whispers to me, watching Bella and Lila chat animatedly about some movie they both like.

I peek over at her, noticing her warm smile as she eyes her wife with my . . . my Lila, and I feel my own mouth curling to match, a tightness spreading through my chest. I reach up to rub the spot through my shirt, nodding.

"I like her too," I murmur back.

Like feels . . . not quite right, but the alternative feels too much, too soon. Regardless of whether or not it feels right.

"I guess you bringing her here means that you clarified things?"

"Not . . . exactly," I tell her. "I mean, we've established that she's okay being here, with you knowing that we're . . . something, but as far as defining whatever *it* is . . ."

"Ah." Mei nods thoughtfully. "Well, if the way she looked at you all through dinner is any indication, I would say it's a conversation you should totally have."

"How did she look at me?"

"Exactly like you looked at her," Mei chuckles.

My grin widens. It's been a lot more satisfying than I thought it would be, having Lila here. Seeing her blend so well with these people who are so important to me but whom she has every reason to be less accepting of, if she wanted to be. I mean, I can't say that if she brought me to dinner with *her* ex I would be as cool as she's being right now. I know that I explained the history between Mei and me, but still, the fact that she's settled so easily into outright pleasantness with Bella and Mei takes a weight off my shoulders I hadn't even fully realized was there before coming here.

"You seemed different tonight," Mei says, drawing me out of my thoughts.

"Different?"

"Yeah," she confirms. "Different. A good different though. The last few years . . . It's always seemed like you've had your guard up. I don't think you were unhappy, per se, but you definitely had me worried sometimes."

"I didn't seem happy?"

"I don't know," she says with a shrug. "Maybe I was reading too much into it. You were always just so carefree in college. Do you remember?"

"I remember doing a *lot* of dumb things in the name of being 'carefree,'" I scoff.

Mei chuckles quietly. "Still. You were always smiling. It was infectious, you know? I guess it was just difficult seeing you go from that happy guy to the hardened one you've had to be these last few years."

"I hadn't noticed, honestly," I answer, my brow furrowed.

"No, I doubt you would," Mei sighs. "You've been too worried about everyone else. I just always worried that you weren't as okay as you let on."

My mouth parts as her words trigger a memory, remembering Lila saying something very similar the other night.

The world won't end if you're okay, Ian. You know that, right?

Have I really been so different these last few years?

"I didn't mean to be," I tell her. "I guess it was just . . . easier. Expect the worst so you can't ever be let down, right?"

"That's a horrible way to think," Mei chides. "Still. Tonight . . ." She smiles softly. "You seemed more like yourself tonight. The you I remember. You just seem . . . brighter. Around her."

I turn my head to catch Lila throwing her hands up, her expression equal parts exasperated and amused as Bella waves her hands around while yammering about whatever point she's trying to make. I realize that just *looking* at Lila puts me at ease, makes all the noise in my head quiet and all the worries I'm constantly juggling seem less important—and I wonder if it's normal to feel this way for someone so quickly, or if our history has somehow paved the way for these feelings. If the protectiveness and the friendship I've felt for her all these years were only holding the door for something more. If it was inevitable that I would wind up here.

Mei's voice interrupts my thoughts again. "Does she know?"

"She does." I don't have to ask what she means. "I told her everything."

"That's good," Mei sighs. "That's really good. How did that go?"

"It went a lot better than I ever expected it would. Lila was . . . She *is* amazing."

"I don't know why you always expect the worst," Mei tuts.

"None of what happened is your fault. I've told you that a thousand times."

"Yeah, well. Tell that to . . . pretty much everyone."

"I *tried*," Mei grumbles. "I would have said a lot more if you weren't so stubborn. I don't know why you work so hard to protect that bastard just because he's your father. He doesn't deserve it."

Yeah, pretty sure if Mei knew Dad pushed me into leaving, she'd be right behind Lila forming a line to cut off his balls.

"I don't do it for him," I remind her.

"I know, know," she huffs. "I just get so angry thinking about it."

"That's because you're a marshmallow."

"Shut up," she scoffs, elbowing me. "I am not."

Bella plops down on the couch beside her wife, throwing an arm around her neck. "What are we saying about Mei?"

"That she's a marshmallow," I tell her.

"Oh," Bella laughs. "Totally. Might as well put her on a s'more."

"I'm not a marshmallow!" Mei crosses her arms indignantly over her chest. "I can be a total bitch if I want to be." She looks to Lila pleadingly. "Dee, tell them I can be a total bitch."

Lila barks out a laugh as she sinks into the couch cushion at my other side. "Definitely not going to be doing that."

"Face it," I say, patting Mei on the shoulder. "You're soft."

Mei is still grumbling as Lila's hand slides over the top of my thigh, the gesture innocent, but the way it makes me feel decidedly less so. "Did you finally come to an agreement?"

"We agreed to disagree," Lila says, huffing air out of her nostrils. "Since Bella clearly has no taste."

"Um, excuse me," Bella quips back, sitting up. "I think I have more insight on who Ms. Swan should have been with. We *literally* share a name."

"The entire love story is for Bella and Edward! You can't argue with canon."

"I can when it's *wrong*," Bella grumbles.

I arch a brow at Mei. "Do you know what they're talking about?"

"*Twilight*," Mei sighs. "Trust me, I don't get it either."

"That's because your parents kept you from all the good stuff. I mean, if it was up to them, you still wouldn't know the benefits of boobs."

"I *have* boobs," Mei points out.

"I mean other than yours," Bella amends. "Who wants to play with a dick their whole life?"

"Um, I have no qualms with that," Lila says, raising her hand and grinning.

Bella waves her off. "We've already established we can't trust your choices."

Mei groans. "Can we talk about literally anything else? Whose idea was it to get all of us together like this, anyway?"

"Yours," Bella, Lila, and I say in unison.

Mei shakes her head. "I regret my decisions. Everyone go home now."

"Nah." Bella smacks a kiss on her wife's temple. "We still have Cards Against Humanity to play."

"That game is filthy," Mei grouses.

"Which is why it's so awesome," Bella says.

I turn to find Lila watching the two of them bicker with a smile, her eyes meeting mine and looking like she's *genuinely* having a good time, which makes me relax even more. "Do I want to know what Cards Against Humanity is?"

"Don't worry, Cupcake," she tells me. "You're going to love it."

"If someone gets the one about Daniel Radcliffe's delicious

asshole," Bella tells us, "I promise you that card will be an instant win for any of my rounds. Fucking gets me every time."

"I'm sorry," I splutter. "*What?*"

Lila's head falls back in one of those loud laughs that I love so much, distracting me from my incredulity. She recovers only enough to tug on my arm to drag me off the couch, patting my forearm as Bella does the same to Mei and we all make our way to the dining room for what is apparently a hellish card game.

"This is going to be *so* much fun," Lila says, her eyes gleaming.

I'm a little suspicious of that, if I'm being honest, but seeing how happy she is, how *genuinely* okay she is with being here, with all of this—my past and my present colliding to make what is hopefully a better future—has that same tightness setting off in my chest. The one that feels both wonderful and terrifying all at once.

So I let her lead me into the dining room for the seemingly awful game, starting to come to terms with the fact that I would let this woman lead me anywhere. And what's more . . . I find that I'm entirely unbothered with the revelation.

—————

Mei and Bella's place is well outside of the city, which means that the drive back consists of a lot of two-lane highway with woods on either side. It's a far cry from the usual traffic in city limits. Lila has been chatting idly about the night—how good dinner was, how much fun she had with Bella and Mei—and I've been content to mostly just listen, distracted by the gentle circling of her fingers where they've come to rest on my knee.

"—and Bella told me she even wrote fan fiction for Bellice back in the day," Lila snorts. "She wouldn't tell me her username, but I'm going to get it out of her."

"And Bellice is what exactly?"

"The ship name for Alice and Bella," she explains, as if this is obvious.

I nod dumbly. "Right."

"We are *so* watching these movies the first chance we get," she says firmly. "I need you on Team Edward with me."

"Yes, dear," I tease.

She flicks my knee. "Shut up."

"But you had fun?"

She must sense the slight hint of worry still lingering in my voice, because her palm settles back against the denim of my jeans, squeezing my knee through the fabric. "*So* much fun. They're really great."

"Good." I blow out a surreptitious breath. "That's good."

"Aw, were you nervous? Was this like 'meet the parents' for you?"

"You've already met my parents," I remind her.

"True." She squeezes me again. "I really did love them. I had an amazing time."

"I'm glad," I tell her honestly. "I was a *little* nervous. I was afraid it was a stupid idea to even ask you to come."

"Why?"

"I don't know . . . I mean, I know I explained how things were between us, but I kept thinking it was still a dick move to ask you to have dinner with my ex."

"Ian," she says, her tone firmer. "I told you that I trusted you. If you tell me I have nothing to worry about, then I'm not going to worry. Okay?"

Tension uncoils in my belly. I have to grip the steering wheel just to keep myself from slamming on the brakes and launching myself into her seat so I can cover her mouth with mine. I mean, I've always known that Lila was too good for this world, but I'm starting to wonder if she's too good for *me* as well.

I blow out a breath. "You don't," I answer, "have anything to worry about." I can't help the strangled laugh that escapes me. "God, Lila. You keep being so fucking perfect, and you're going to have to pry me off of you with a goddamned crowbar if you decide to get rid of me."

"Mm." I can just make out her biting her bottom lip when I glance at her from the side. "I kind of like the sound of that, actually."

"What, prying me off with a crowbar?"

"More like you being so close I would even need to in the first place."

"You can't say shit like that to me when you're still wearing that dress, and I can't do anything about it."

Her hand slides further up my thigh, her smile turning coy. "Who says you can't do anything about it?"

"Lila."

I groan just as her fingers tease the shape of my cock through my jeans. Her touch is still slight, teasing, even, but the slow back-and-forth of her finger tracing my length that is rapidly filling has my head spinning.

"I cannot guarantee a safe drive if you keep touching me like that," I warn her.

She squeezes me, and I suck in a ragged breath. "I trust you. Just keep your eyes on the road."

"You really expect me to be able to keep my eyes on the road when you're undoing my fucking zipper?"

"Mhm." And she means it, apparently, since she's working the panels of my fly apart, slipping her fingers under the waistband of my boxer briefs. "I want to play, and you have to drive."

"What if I want to touch you?"

"Later," she murmurs. "This is about you right now."

I don't know why that one sentence gets me so unreasonably *hot*—but the low rasp of her voice telling me that this is about *me* as she pulls my cock out has me visibly tense and noticeably sweating.

Her thumb teases my slit to collect the splash of pre-come there, circling it around the head of my cock as my hips shift up of their own accord as if seeking more of her touch. She squeezes me gently as my hands tighten on the wheel, feeling like I'm taking the world's dirtiest driver's exam with the way my eyes are forcibly focused on the road ahead and my palms are sweaty as they grip ten and two.

A pathetic sound escapes me when she lets me go, but a peek in my peripherals has me almost choking on my own tongue when I notice her licking her palm. Her eyes connect with mine just as the slick pink dips back into her mouth, her lips curling at the corners with a smirk.

"Eyes on the road, Ian."

"Fuck," I hiss. "You know when I get you back to your place you're going to get it, right?"

"Oh, I'm counting on it," she practically purrs, the wet warmth of her hand circling around my cock again. "But first."

My head tilts back minutely to rest against the back of the seat, still peering at the road through hooded eyes when she gives me a slow stroke from root to tip. I have to bite my lip to keep from gasping when she does a little twisting motion over my glans, milking out more of my pre-come and using it to ease the glide of her fist as she slides back down.

"Lila. *Fuck.*" I press harder on the brake as I glide onto the shoulder, putting the car in park and white-knuckling the steering wheel. "You're trying to kill me. Literally."

"Couldn't focus on the road?" she teases me hoarsely, rolling her wrist in a way that has my eyes wanting to cross as she pumps me steadily. "Fuck, you're so hard."

"You're enjoying this," I manage through gritted teeth. "Aren't you."

"I am," she admits.

"You like touching me knowing I can't do anything about it?"

She does that twisting thing around the crown of my cock, and my mouth falls open on a shaky exhale as my hand reaches to cover hers—not taking over, just feeling her movements.

"I do," she purrs.

"You want me to come in your fucking hand?"

"Yes."

She starts to stroke me in earnest, my cock leaking into her fist with every crest of her hand, but it still feels like it's not quite enough. My pulse thumps in my ears like a roar, and I'm grateful for the empty highway; the last thing I need is for someone to pull over and check on us. When I glance at Lila, I notice the way she's watching me intently, her face lit by the soft glow of the dashboard and her expression rapt, like she's turned on just by the sight of me unraveling.

It makes me lose my head a little.

"Spit on it," I groan.

I feel her hand still, hear her shaky inhale. "I can use my mouth—"

"No." I'm already shaking my head. "You put your mouth on my cock right now, I can't guarantee I won't haul you into the back seat, and we don't have time for that. Not here." I curl my fingers tighter around her fist, squeezing my cock through her grip. "But I can pretend." I drag her hand in a slow upstroke, my abdomen tensing with the sensation. "Make it wet, sweet girl."

"Jesus."

"My name," I remind her. "You say *my* name."

"Ian," she whines.

I place my hand over hers, gripping my cock by the base and holding it straight up. It takes all my willpower to refrain from doing exactly what I want to and *actually* drag her into the backseat, and when I hear the sound she makes when she does as I ask, when I feel the warmth of her saliva dripping down my cock and onto our joined fists—I almost lose it.

"Fuck. *Fuck.*"

She's pumping me harder now, her hand still covered with mine as I guide her strokes. My grip isn't all that tight, this is her show, after all, but I like feeling her soft skin against mine, love the way the delicate lines of her knuckles work under my palm.

"When I get you home," I grate as she shuttles her fist up and down my cock again and again and *again*. "I'm going to peel that fucking dress off you." My jaw goes slack for a moment when she leans over and spits on me again—a wet, sloppy sound ringing in the small space of the car as she strokes my cock. "And I'm going to fuck you until you forget your name."

"That's a tall order," she breathes, unsteadily, like it's hard to find her voice.

It turns me on to no end that she seems to be as affected by touching me as I am by *having* her touch me.

"*Fuck*, Lila, keep doing that." My eyes drift closed as my head tilts back against the headrest. "I'm going to fucking come. Make me come, sweet girl."

"Ian," she whimpers.

"Are you wet?" I bite at my lower lip, feeling my orgasm building like a hot pressure at the base of my spine but wanting to savor it for a bit longer. "If we weren't out here on the road, could I pull you across this seat and drop you right onto my cock?"

"Yes," she groans, her forehead pressing against my arm, which is moving in time with her hand that's wrapped around me. "I want that."

"You'll get it. I'm gonna come in your hand this time, but later it'll be in that hot little pussy of yours."

"Are you close?"

"Mhm. Keep twisting like that. *Mm.* There you go. Just like that. Good girl. Sweet fucking girl. Fuck. *Fuck.* Right—Keep— *Fuck. Fuck. Fuck.*"

My cock bucks against her palm, spurting out so hard that she barely has time to catch it in her fist; I don't even want to think about where in my car it might have landed—that's a problem for tomorrow me. Blood rushes in my ears as colors flash behind my lids, my eyes still shut tight and my breath leaving me in deep, rough pants while my lungs feel like they're on fire.

I'm still breathing hard when my eyes flutter back open, noticing that her hand is still stroking me idly, covered in my come. It might be one of the hottest things I've ever seen, but it also wakes my brain up a little, and I sit up straighter.

"Shit." I hold her hand tight so that I can try to keep from getting it all over her, reaching across us with my free hand to riffle through the middle console until I come back with some of the mandatory stowed napkins from random fast-food places. "Here. Sorry."

"Are you kidding?" I flick on the overhead light just to be met with her flushed cheeks and her even more flushed chest—her breasts heaving like she's as out of breath as I am. "That was hot as fuck."

"I'll say," I murmur, distracted by the pretty picture she makes all rosy and satisfied-looking while she cleans my come off her hand. "You almost made me pass out."

"And you stopped the car," she tuts. "You were supposed to keep your eyes on the road."

"I wasn't willing to risk crashing us for that orgasm, as amazing as it was."

"Sounds like I wasn't doing it right."

I snort, leaning over the console and wrapping my fingers around her neck to pull her in so that I can bring her mouth to mine. I take one long, bruising kiss, nipping at her lower lip for good measure before pulling back.

"I meant what I said, brat," I tell her. "It's my turn when we get back."

"I guess that depends on how long it takes you to get us home," she says sweetly, leaning back into her seat. "If you take too long, I might have to just start without you over here."

Her smile is wicked, making me want to spank her ass just as much as it makes me want to kiss her again.

I speed the entire drive home.

Nineteen

DELILAH

The picture Ian's sent me has me grinning like a fool as I hunch over my phone in a lonely corner on set; I'm still surprised he sent one when I asked. He's out with Mei and Bella for brunch, and I wish I were with them, but as much as I'd like to brush off filming to spend more time with my hunky ginger, I know that Gia would skin me alive if I tried. Especially with numbers finally starting to creep back up.

I'll never tell him that I'm saving the photo as my wallpaper, but I'm assuming he'll figure it out soon, anyway. He looks so cute with his mouth turned down in a deep frown, his brow knitted together as he holds up the bright pink cupcake for the camera.

CUPCAKE: Bella is never going to let me live the "cupcake" thing down. You know that right?

ME: I take it brunch is going well?

CUPCAKE: Bella had about two more mimosas than she needed, but yeah it's been good. We have to come back here soon. You'll love the scones.

My heart flutters at him casually making something-akin-to-date plans; it's been two weeks since we started . . . whatever this is, and I still haven't gotten used to the idea of it. Mainly because it still seems surreal that after all the time in my life I've spent wanting him, I actually get to *have* him.

ME: Are you doing anything after?

CUPCAKE: Just hitting the gym. I'm waiting outside with Mei now while Bella pulls the car around and then I'm heading that way.

CUPCAKE: When do you think you'll be done filming today?

ME: Midafternoon at the latest.

CUPCAKE: Jack is going out with Sanchez tonight.

ME: 😑 That always ends well.

CUPCAKE: At least the arm is already broken. What more can he do?

ME: He's got another arm. Two legs. Who knows with Jack. You didn't want to go hang out with them?

CUPCAKE: Actually . . . I was hoping I could sneak a certain brat over to my room.

More flutters, but in my belly this time.

ME: Oh yeah? And do what?

CUPCAKE: Come over when you're done and find out.

I bite my lip to hold back my grin as I stare at the text; I might still be struggling to get used to it, but I sure as hell enjoy the easy flirtation that we've fallen into. Teen me is practically dancing around her bedroom to Katy Perry circa 2012.

"God, you are killing me with all that giggly shit," Ava grumbles as she sidles up beside me to get to the coffee maker. "You're going to rot my teeth out if you don't stop being so sweet."

I shove my phone in my pocket, reaching for an empty cup. "I don't know what you mean."

"Please. I caught you staring at your dressing room mirror yesterday, smiling to yourself while 'Enchanted' was blasting."

"I was just happy for Taylor's version," I mumble.

"Uh-huh." She rolls her eyes as she stirs her creamer into her paper cup. "Sure you were. I happen to know for a fact that you're a 1989 stan."

"Taylor is Taylor," I hmph.

"But it's . . . going well, right?"

I hate that she's right; my mouth immediately turns up, and it really is ridiculous how giddy just thinking about Ian makes me.

"It is," I tell her.

"But you still haven't told Jack?"

"No," I sigh. "I'm going to. When I figure out how to approach the subject without him going all alpha-hole big brother on me."

"I would pay money to see that."

"Honestly, so would I," I laugh. "If it weren't going to be directed at me. Can you *imagine* how insufferable he's going to be when he finds out I'm sleeping with his best friend?"

"Oh, he's *never* going to let you live it down once he stops being weird."

"Exactly."

"Probably be weirder to keep *not* telling him though," she points out.

"I know, I know. I'm going to tell him soon. Ian is just stressed out about training camp right now, and everything is already a lot for him right now, I don't want to add an overprotective Jack to the mix."

"Oh God. You are so smitten." She raises her voice in a terrible impression of mine. "*Ian* this. *Ian* that."

"Shut up," I grouse.

"You *lurve* him," she teases.

And it's a joke, I know that, but the way my stomach tightens is no laughing matter. I won't pretend that it hasn't been . . . intense, being with Ian after wanting him for so long, just like I also won't pretend that *like* has felt like too small a word for what I've been feeling for him. Not that I would ever tell him that. I won't risk scaring him off when I just got him.

I bump her elbow with mine. "Don't you have something to be doing?"

"Yeah, making sure your show is perfect."

"Well." I make a shooing motion. "Go on then."

"Wow," she laughs. "Yes, queen. Right away, queen."

"Fuck off," I snort.

"Text your boyfriend for me and tell him to stop distracting you. He can sext you later."

Boyfriend.

That word makes my belly clench even more. In a good or bad way, I can't be sure.

I watch her give me a flippant wave over her shoulder as she carries her coffee away, the word *boyfriend* still bouncing around my head. I like the way it makes me feel, I decide. Maybe too much. I pull my phone back out, pulse still racing slightly as I shoot off another text.

ME: You're on, Cupcake. 😏

When Ava finds me again after filming, the concerned look on her face is a far cry from her teasing attitude earlier. She's chewing on the end of her nail when I spot her crossing the set to where I'm taking off my apron, her expression the one she only wears when she's delivering bad news.

"What's wrong?"

She scratches at the back of her neck. "It may be nothing."

"If it was nothing, you wouldn't look like that."

"Well," she sighs, letting her hands settle on her hips. "Gia wanted me to send you to her office."

"Okay? Why is that a problem?"

"She sounded . . . weird."

"Weird how?"

"Well, she asked me if I had seen anything online about you today."

"About me?"

"You and Ian."

"Why would she . . . ? Wait. Did you see something?"

"Not before she asked."

I'm already pulling out my phone. "What is it?"

"Dee, maybe you shouldn't—"

I'm already googling our names, hit with multiple headlines from only an hour ago immediately after clicking search.

HAS HOCKEY'S HEARTBREAKER DONE IT AGAIN?

HOCKEY'S HEARTBREAKER MIGHT BE BREAKING IT
OFF WITH BAKER

IAN CHASE AND MEI GARCIA—ARE THEY GETTING
BACK TOGETHER?

My first reaction is pure confusion, especially since I just spent a great night with Mei and Bella last week and can confirm that she and Bella are still very much in love and that there is absolutely nothing between her and Ian. I click one of the headlines, finding an attached picture that does the opposite of what I suspect Ava is waiting for—I laugh out loud.

"This is nothing," I tell Ava, who is looking at me like I've grown another head.

"He's kissing her," Ava says incredulously.

I roll my eyes. "On the *cheek*."

Ian is wearing the same thing he was wearing a few hours ago when he texted me the photo of him with the cupcake. In it, he's clutching Mei's elbow on the sidewalk, his lips pressed gently against her cheek while—I assume—he's telling her goodbye after their brunch earlier.

"You're not worried about this?"

I shake my head; I can't tell Ava *everything* about why this picture doesn't make me upset, because most of it isn't my story to tell, but I'm relieved that I can stow my worry, at least.

"I promise you," I tell her. "This isn't a thing. They had brunch earlier."

"Just the two of them?"

"No, Bella was there, too, but even if it was, it wouldn't matter. There's nothing between them, and I trust him."

Ava is still looking at me like she's not entirely convinced, and while I can't exactly blame her, since she doesn't have all the facts, it's still mildly irritating for someone to be doubting Ian.

"Wait," I gasp, remembering one of the headlines. It said Ian had "done it again." Which means now the entire fucking internet will be shredding his character again without knowing what they're talking about. "Fuck," I huff. "You said Gia wants to see me?"

"Yeah." Ava nods. "There's a lot of rumors circulating already about him cheating on you or something."

"They don't even know we're together for sure!"

"You know that doesn't matter to social media."

"What a fucking nightmare," I groan.

"Gia wants to make sure you're okay, and, well, you know. See what your next move is."

"My next move?"

"Yeah, I mean . . . you and Ian were doing this for good press. If this negative stuff keeps blowing up, it might have the opposite effect on your ratings."

"I'm not—" I feel my face flushing. "I'm not going to stop seeing him."

"That's not what I'm saying. I just . . ." She heaves out a sigh, crossing her arms. "Just go talk to Gia. I'm only the middleman here."

"Fine."

I nod distractedly, already dusting off my shirt and turning away from her, hearing her voice call after me, "Let me know how it goes!"

My mind is racing all the way up to Gia's office, both at the prospect of having the same conversation with her that I just had with Ava as well as with worry for how Ian is doing, if he's seen the news yet. I hate the idea of him having to see people slandering him again, and I can only hope that he hasn't checked his phone in a while, which is a huge possibility, given how little he uses it.

I don't bother with knocking when I reach Gia's office, immediately rushing inside and finding her scowling at her desktop before she looks up at me. "There you are," she says. "Have you seen it?"

"I have," I tell her, dropping down into one of her office chairs. "Ava told me."

"Do you have any insight on this? Is something going on between Ian and his ex-wife?"

"No," I say with more force than I mean to. "There's nothing going on between them."

Gia frowns. "How can you be sure? I know you're friends, but he might not tell you about something like that if he were—"

"There's *nothing* going on between them," I huff.

Gia eyes me carefully, pressing one perfectly manicured fingernail to her bottom lip. "Is there something I should know about?"

"I—" I consider, chewing on the inside of my lip. Personally, I don't think it's the network's business what Ian and I are or aren't to each other, but considering that the only reason we even *started* this was because of their ideas, I guess I owe them something, at least. "Ian and I have . . . gotten closer. Since he came back to town."

"Are you two in an actual relationship?"

"I don't know if I would call it that," I tell her. I *want* to call it that, but I need to check with Ian first. "But we're close enough that I can tell you there's nothing going on between him and Mei. I mean, we just had dinner with her and her wife last week. Together. I *knew* he was out to brunch with her this morning. Hell, her wife was there! The cameras just didn't catch that."

"Are you sure it's a good idea to get . . . closer to him?"

"This entire thing was your idea!"

"Well, not mine *personally* . . ."

"You know what I mean." I can feel myself scowling, too, now. "What, I can pretend something might be going on between us, but it's a bad idea to let something actually happen?"

"I told you," she says carefully. "We would never try to tell you who to date, Dee. I'm just thinking of you. I don't want you to get hurt."

"You mean you don't want the ratings to get hurt," I mutter bitterly.

"That's not fair," she tuts.

I blow out a breath. "You're right. I'm sorry. This is all just so frustrating."

"I know." Gia nods like she actually understands, and that

makes me feel a bit better. "Listen, you know I don't give a shit
what you do in your personal life, but the guys upstairs . . . Well,
I told you, all they care about are numbers. I won't sit here and lie
to you and say they won't care if Ian suddenly becomes poisonous
to your image."

"I still won't stop seeing him," I tell her vehemently.

Her eyebrows raise. "So you *are* seeing him?"

"I don't know. I just—Fuck. Whatever we're calling it. I'm not
stopping."

"Again, I can't tell you not to," she says. "I just want you to be
fully prepared for what that might mean."

"Okay. I hear you. I do. I need to talk to Ian about this. I need
to go make sure he's okay."

Gia studies me for a moment, sympathy shining in her eyes. I
kind of hate it. I hate that everyone thinks Ian is the type of person
who would hurt me. I want to shout it from the rooftop how great
he is, but I know I can't do that while he's still keeping secrets to
protect his sister.

So I keep my mouth shut.

"Was that all you needed?"

Gia nods. "Be careful, Dee."

"Thanks," I answer wearily.

I don't say anything else as I push up out of my chair, leaving
Gia behind in her office and heading straight for the back doors
so I can get out of here. I don't bother calling Ian as I go, wanting
to get to him as quickly as possible. I'm honestly hoping he hasn't
seen anything yet. That way I can break it to him gently, tell him
to avoid the internet for a while. The less he sees, the better.

I just have to get to him first.

— — — —

I know I've failed the moment Ian opens the door to his and Jack's apartment. His expression is tense—his eyes haggard-looking and his mouth pressed into a tight line as he lets me in.

"Hey," he says, moving aside to shut the door behind me. "You're early."

"Is Jack already gone?"

Ian nods. "He wanted to hang around after . . ." He clears his throat. "I convinced him to go. Told him I wanted to be alone for a bit."

"Do you want to be alone?"

He immediately shakes his head. "Not from you."

"Okay," I say with obvious relief. "So you saw, then."

"Jack has Google alerts set up on me, did you know?"

"Jesus," I sigh. "I love my brother, but sometimes I want to kick his ass."

"He means well," Ian says, moving to the couch and sinking down onto it. "Does the network know?"

I nod grimly. "Gia called me into her office after we got done filming."

"I'm sure they advised you to jump ship," he says woodenly.

"They can't do that," I argue.

He purses his lips. "They can strongly suggest."

"It doesn't matter. I wouldn't, anyway. There's nothing going on. You didn't do anything wrong."

"Tell that to the rest of the world."

"I don't *care* what the rest of the world thinks."

He eyes me sadly. "Maybe you should."

I rear back, my mouth parting in surprise. "What?"

He runs one large hand over his face, his chest rising and falling as he exhales slowly. "I don't know. I just hate the idea that you're being dragged into my shit."

"I knew that was a risk when we started this."

"I know that, I do, but . . ." His head drops to the back of the couch. "I fucking hate it. Even more than seeing them talk about me. They're acting like you're *naive* for even starting something with me to begin with, given my history. They don't even know for sure that anything is going on between us, and now they're judging you for the relationship you *might* be having with me? It's so fucked up, Lila."

My heart swells at his obvious concern for me, and I scoot closer, wrapping my arm around his middle and letting my head fall to his shoulder as I squeeze him. "I know it is, but it's not *your* fault. It's really not."

"It feels like it is. Sometimes. I mean, it feels like everything I touch ends up tainted somehow. I can't seem to turn my fucking head without disappointing someone."

Despite the defeat in his tone, I feel his arm wind around me to hold me closer, his temple resting against my hair as his body releases some of the tension it was holding. I place my hand to his chest, rubbing slow circles over his T-shirt in what I hope is a soothing motion.

"It's going to be fine," I assure him. "It will blow over."

"That still doesn't solve the entire issue," he says quietly. "What happens when we . . . confirm the rumors? If that's even something you want to do. I could definitely see why you wouldn't."

"What?" I pull back, jerking my head away from his shoulder to look at him. "Of course it's something I want."

He looks genuinely surprised. "It is?"

"Are you kidding? Do I need to ask Alexa to play 'Teenage Dream' for you? How can I express more than I already have that I'm literally living a dream come true right now?"

His throat works with a swallow. "I guess I keep waiting for the other shoe to drop. It doesn't feel real sometimes."

"It's real," I urge. "At least to me. Is it real to you?"

"Of course it is," he says without any hesitation. "Lila, being with you . . ." He shakes his head. "It's fucking real."

"Then we're fine," I assure him. "Everything is going to be fine."

"How can you be sure?"

There's uncertainty in his gaze, as well as something that looks suspiciously like fear, and I realize that despite him suggesting the idea that it might be easier for me to walk away, he's actually terrified that I might. It makes it that much easier to hold on.

"I can't," I tell him honestly. "I can't be sure of *anything*— that's what my life has taught me. I learned that when I was six." My chest squeezes at the thought of my parents, their loss an old wound that rarely acts up anymore, but thinking of them now, considering the idea that there might be a future out there where I could lose Ian too—it's enough to make me emotional. "But if nothing else, it's taught me when something is worth holding on to." I tighten my hold on him as if to prove my point, leaning in to let his lips brush against mine. "You're worth holding on to, Ian."

"So are you," he says shakily, his lashes fluttering when I let my mouth move against his.

I keep my kisses light even as a smile touches my lips, shifting so I can crawl into his lap, straddling it as I wind my arms around his neck. "Then hold on to me."

"You really want to do this?" His hands settle at my hips, squeezing gently. "With me?"

"Ian."

He shakes his head. "Right. Dream come true. I forgot. You're obsessed with me."

"Shut up," I laugh, pinching his side until he squirms. "Like you aren't obsessed with me too."

He's laughing with me, even when one of his hands cups the back of my head, the other reaching to tilt my chin up with his fingers so that he can bring his mouth back to mine. "I'm definitely obsessed with you."

"Really?"

I wish my voice didn't sound so unsure; I hate sounding so needy with him, but I can't help it. Ian wanting me like this . . . It's *everything*.

"Really," he murmurs, his lips feathering against mine. "I'm days away from doodling your name in my notebook. Teenage Lila has nothing on middle-aged me."

I grin so hard it makes my cheeks hurt, and it's on the tip of my tongue—words that have no business being there. Words I struggle to bite back.

"Middle-aged," I laugh instead. "Don't worry," I tell him. "I still think you're hot"—I lick at his lower lip, humming in my chest—"for an old man."

Ian growls, and suddenly I'm underneath him on the couch.

"I'll show you 'old man.'"

Twenty

IAN

I close my eyes as I move deeper into a stretch; the slight burn radiating in my thighs is almost enjoyable, like my body knows it's nearly done with the strenuous part of the day. Coach is still yelling at Rankin at the other end of the ice, but a few other guys and I have already started cooldown stretches. Coach apparently woke up this morning with every intention of making sure the entire team went home with sore muscles and ringing ears— probably because we're so close to the start of the official season. Jankowski is practically lying face first on the ice ten feet away, Sanchez doing similar stretches to me as we all try to work out the tension from a hard practice.

I can't help the way I glance over at her. I've found my gaze straying to the stands several times during practice; at least two of the times Coach yelled at me were because I was too busy watching her as surreptitiously as I could—almost like my eyes gravitate toward her without my permission. Her hair is flowing over her shoulders in a cascade of soft waves today, and I know from experience how silky it is when I tangle my fingers in it. Her sweater looks soft too—pastel pink with little hearts patterned all over in a slightly darker hue—hugging every swell and curve in a tantalizing way that makes it almost impossible to focus on what I'm *supposed* to be doing.

She's watching me, too, now, her head nodding slowly at whatever Jack is rattling off in her ear, but her eyes are fixed on me as I tilt my hips deeper into the ice, my thighs spreading wide until my groin almost touches the floor. I've never really thought about how it looks; it's muscle memory at this point, but honestly, with the way Lila is watching me stretch—her teeth pressed against her lower lip subtly and her arms crossed tight over her chest— my thoughts definitely wander down a dirtier path.

I smirk as I roll my hips, catching sight of her mouth parting even from this distance. I know she's thinking about last night, how I had her under me in a position similar to this in my bed, and I can't pretend I'm not remembering it too. I thought things would be more difficult when faced with our first hurdle with the disastrous photo and accompanying internet mob over the photos of Mei and me, but I should have known better than to doubt Lila. She's proven to be far more than I deserve at every turn, after all. Her reassurances made me feel that same comforting sensation of being *settled* that I've begun to associate with her, and I'm starting to realize that it is *just her*. That she just makes me feel this way.

I'm grinning when I finally push back up to my feet, raising my arms high over my head for one final stretch before I break from the rest of the guys to skate over to the edge of the rink where she and Jack are sitting. Jack is still rambling on— something about Florida's new center, I think, from what I catch at the tail end—only trailing off when I brace my arms against the bottom of the railing where the floor to the bleachers sit.

"Having fun?"

Lila shrugs one shoulder. "If Jack has his way, I'll be starting my own fantasy league this year."

"I hope I'm one of your top picks," I tease.

She tilts her hand back and forth. "Eh."

"Brat," I laugh.

Her teeth press against her lower lip again, so quickly I might miss it, and I have to tear my eyes away before Jack catches me staring for too long.

"You were looking a little slow in that second set of speed drills," Jack says with a frown.

"Thanks, honey," I scoff. "Glad to have you in my corner."

He rolls his eyes. "Dude, I'm just saying."

"Well, stop fucking breaking your shit so you can get out there and keep me on my toes."

"Only a few more weeks," Jack grumbles, rubbing his sling, neon orange today. "You sore?"

I shrug. "He worked us hard today. I could probably stretch a bit more, but I'm ready to get out of these fucking skates."

"Stretch," Lila snorts. "If you can even call that shit stretching."

Jack wrinkles his nose. "What?"

"I mean, honestly." Lila chuckles, her brown eyes sparkling. "What are you stretching when you hump the ice like that?"

There's no reason at all why the word *hump* should be even remotely enticing, but coming out of Lila's mouth . . . Yeah. I'm glad that my lower half is hidden by the wall and a shit ton of gear.

"It's for your groin," I tell her, biting back a laugh. "It's important."

"Your groin is important," she deadpans, and I can tell by her expression that it's taking everything she has not to crack up. "I can't believe you just said that with a straight face."

"Groin injuries are super common," Jack says with a furrowed brow. "Half the shit you do out there involves your groin."

"The groin is very important," she says with her best impression of a straight face. "Gotcha."

My lips curl in a smile that I can't stifle, covering my mouth with a hand as a laugh snickers out of me, Lila devolving into a fit of giggles not long after.

Jack shakes his head. "I'm supposed to be the immature one here. Get your own thing."

"Someone's grumpy today," Lila says with a mock pout.

I reach over and rub the tip of his shoe. "Do you need a hug, honey?"

"I hate you guys," he grumbles. "Stop being so . . . coupley. It's weird."

I wince, covering it immediately with a cough so I can pull my hand back to cover my mouth, my eyes darting to meet Lila's for only a second as I notice hers rounding.

"I have a meeting to get to," Lila says, clearing her throat as she stands from her seat. "But you guys are looking good out there. You're going to kill it this year."

Weirdly, this just makes Jack look more grumpy. Still, he offers his cheek so Lila can smack a noisy kiss there, making me jealous that I can't press up on my toes so she can lean down and do the same for me. She crouches and wraps her knuckles on my helmet instead, flashing me a grin. "See you soon, Cupcake."

I force myself not to stare as she walks away, knowing that the jeans she has on will be hugging her perfect ass in a way that will have me wanting to crawl over the railing and trail after her like a cartoon hound dog, keeping my eyes on Jack instead, where it's safe.

"It's still weird as hell watching you two pretend to be a thing," Jack says when she's gone. "You're both so chummy lately."

I keep my expression blank. "What do you mean?"

"I don't know," he says. "I mean, you guys just hang out all the time now."

"We're supposed to, remember? It's part of the plan."

"Yeah, I guess. I just don't remember her coming to so many practices before you came back home."

Guilt eats at me. I don't like keeping things from him, but it's not really my place to decide when we tell him. I won't do that without Lila agreeing that it's okay. I love Jack, but I . . . Well, Lila's feelings come first. Even more than mine.

"We're supposed to be seen together," I remind him.

"In public!"

I arch a brow. "This is technically public."

"It's just weird."

I frown at his frustrated tone, sensing something else bothering him. "What's really got you all twisted up? You've been off today."

"No, I haven't."

I roll my eyes. "You've been moody since breakfast, so spill."

"Fuck, I don't know." He rubs a hand down his face. "I guess it's just hitting me that I won't be starting the season with you guys. It fucking sucks, man. All because of my own stupidity."

"Shit happens," I tell him. "You'll be back on the ice in no time."

"Dude, we have the charity game coming up next week. It'll be the first one I haven't played in since I signed with Boston."

I frown. "Charity game?"

"Don't tell me you forgot. We always get together during the last week of training camp."

"Shit, I really did forget." I feel nerves flutter in my stomach. "I don't know if I should go to that."

"What? Why the fuck wouldn't you?"

"I mean . . . It's not just our guys that play in that. I assume Logan and Oscar still come? Lyle?"

"Yeah, but you know those guys."

"I *knew* those guys. Outside of playing against them during the season, we haven't exactly hung out much."

"Oh, fuck off. They'll be ecstatic to play with you again."

I can feel myself frowning, not so sure about that. It's been years, after all. I'm practically an outsider.

"Dude, wipe that look off your face," Jack chides. "You're going to play, and it's going to be a great time. Everyone will be stoked to see you, okay?"

I feel my ears heat. "This was supposed to be a pick-me-up for you, not me."

"Yeah, well. Stop being a baby then. Let me do the wallowing."

"You don't have to wallow," I tell him reassuringly. "You're going to be back killing it before you know it."

"We don't know that," he says quietly. "I just . . . What if this is my last year? What if I end up wasting part of it because I was fucking dumb?"

"You decide when you're done," I say calmly. "You finish when you're ready. Just because I'm thinking this might be my last year, it doesn't mean it has to be yours."

"I guess." He nods morosely. "It just sucks."

"Hey." I reach over and tap the toe of his shoe again, waiting for him to tilt his head up to meet my eyes. "I hate that you won't be out there with us that first game too. It's going to suck without you, man."

"Because I complete you, right?"

His more Jack-worthy shit-eating grin spreads then, and I almost sigh in relief to see him coming out of his mood. Seeing Jack down is like watching a puppy cry or something. "Practically my better half," I say seriously.

"I knew it," he sighs. "My sister will be so heartbroken when she finds out you're in love with me instead."

"We'll have to let her down easy," I chuckle.

"Thanks, man," he says more quietly. "I guess I was kind of in a funk today."

"I get it," I tell him. "I'd be the same way."

"Don't *you* get in a funk about the charity game. It's going to be a blast. All right?"

"Fine," I grumble.

He nods again, taking a deep breath before blowing it out. "Okay. Enough of this feelings shit. I'm going to go tell Rankin he was slower than your old ass."

"We're the same age," I call after him, already flouncing away from me.

He flips me the bird over his shoulder. "Not in spirit!"

I shake my head, turning back toward the way Lila left and wondering where she got off to. We were supposed to meet up after practice, so it's throwing me that she suddenly "has a meeting."

Jesus.

I give my own thoughts a mental eye roll. I might as well just get myself a collar with her name on it, for as whipped as I am.

Not that I mind, I admit to myself.

I push away from the railing and start to skate back to the ice entrance, ready for a hot shower and some fresh clothes that don't smell like they've been soaking in ball sweat. I'm sure Lila will text me whenever she's done. There's no need for me to get all mopey about it.

I *can* be away from her. Sometimes. I managed it just fine before.

I'm the first one in the locker room; usually, there are already a few guys in here cracking jokes or snapping towels at one another's asses, but right now, the room is quiet. I start pulling off my gear by my locker, down to my compression shorts and top, stretching my arms over my head before rummaging around in my bag for my phone. I can hear someone coming down the hall as I thumb it open, noticing a text from Lila waiting on me from only ten minutes ago. She had to have sent it as she was ditching me and Jack.

"Dude," Sanchez calls from the doorway as he passes through it. "Is your ass sore? Mine feels like it's going to fall off. What's that about?"

I turn my head to smirk at him from over my shoulder. "Better hit the foam roller tonight."

"Fuck, I guess." He blows me a kiss. "Wanna come do it for me?"

I roll my eyes. "You wish."

"Nah, I know you got somebody willing to handle all your sore muscles now."

"Dude, fuck off."

Sanchez cackles. "I saw you making googly eyes at Dee on the sidelines again."

"Jealous? I can make googly eyes at you, if you're feeling left out."

"Uh-huh." He winks at me. "I'm just saying I got money on this whole charade, and you better not let me down."

"How much?"

"Enough that I better be right."

A chuckle escapes me. "Losing would teach you to mind your own business."

"Yeah, yeah. We'll see."

He whistles as he saunters off to the next row of lockers, and I turn back to my phone to swipe open the text Lila sent me, immediately frowning in confusion when I notice what it says.

LILA: Come to the last shower stall when you see this. Hurry.

The fuck? I lean back to peer down the line of showers, not noticing anything out of the ordinary. Is she . . . ? There's no fucking way.

I strip off my compression shirt in a hurry, tossing it to the bench and snatching a towel from the rack without even bothering with my shorts as I stomp down the row at double speed. I can hear other voices filing into the locker room behind me, my heart thumping a heavy beat behind my ribs at the implication of her texts, because there's no way that she would—

A hand shoots out from behind the first curtain that sections off the cramped changing area before the second curtain of the actual shower, and suddenly I'm being pulled into the already-small space, crowded against a soft body attached to a devilish smirk and sparkling brown eyes that look up at me with mischief.

"What are you doing?" I hiss.

She runs a finger down my sternum, weaving the tip between freckles there. "Being bad."

"You know there's like six other guys out there, right?"

"Mhm." Her fingers toy with the edge of my compression shorts, the material hiding practically nothing with the way my dick starts to harden underneath them. "You'll have to be *very* quiet."

I can literally hear some of the guys laughing only a stall or so away as showerheads start to turn on, and I've never done anything so reckless, but the thought of it alone has me hot all over. I push my fingers into her hair just as hers curl into the waistband of my shorts, my lips grazing her ear.

"I can be quiet. Can you?"

"Mm." She pulls out my cock, giving it one slow stroke from root to tip. "My mouth will be busy."

"*Fuck*," I huff.

I kick out of my shorts and proceed to strip her out of her clothes with an eagerness that might embarrass me if I weren't so fucking turned on, pushing her past the shower curtain and closing it behind us as I turn the water on without thinking. It's cold as it hits my back, and I let out a shrill yelp that has Lila slapping a hand over her mouth to stifle her laugh.

"You okay over there, man?"

"Yeah," I call back immediately to Jankowski. "Jumped in too quick. Cold-ass water."

"That's one way to shrivel your dick," he snorts.

Lila is shaking with silent laughter, and I smirk as I pull her into me, letting my stiff length slide against her increasingly wet body as I toss back, "I'm good."

I bend to capture her mouth, slipping my tongue past her lips as her hands glide over the hard planes of my chest and up over my shoulders. My fingers dig into the wet flesh of her hips, pulling her as close as she can be as I kiss her senseless.

I make a soft sound of protest when she pulls away, but it dies quickly when she brings her finger to her lips, her smile wicked as she signals me to be quiet just before she drops to her knees. The sight of her there has me feeling light-headed—her palms smoothing over the tops of my thighs and her fingers teasing my hip bones as my aching cock strains only inches from her face. It's something we haven't done yet, mostly because anytime I'm able to get her naked I'm too impatient to be inside her to even entertain the idea, but seeing her like this now . . . I'm wondering if maybe it's because some part of my mind wasn't sure I'd survive the experience.

An assumption that is given more weight when my knees threaten to buckle the second her little pink tongue licks along the head of my cock.

I have to bite my lip to hold back the groan that threatens to escape when she closes her lips over my crown, swirling her tongue around and around while her lashes flutter closed. I force my eyes to stay open even when they want to droop, not wanting to miss one second of Lila's gorgeous mouth sliding over my length. I can feel the flat of her tongue cradling the bottom of my shaft as she takes me deeper, and watching my inches disappear between her lips has my stomach clenching with want and my balls drawing up tight as if I'm already in danger of coming right down her throat.

I can hear the guys chatting among themselves as she sucks me down, having to slap a hand over my mouth to suppress a moan. Her eyes drift open lazily when she wraps her fist around the base of my cock to meet her mouth, twisting her fingers and moving with her lips as she draws back up the entire length of me. Her wrist flicks so that she squeezes just beneath my glans as her tongue licks over the sensitive slit at the head, and my fingers slide over her temples as if they have a mind of their own, my hands settling to palm her head without really realizing that I'm doing it. Lila makes a soft hum in the back of her throat as she pushes back down my cock, her nails of the hand that isn't on my cock digging into my thigh and her fist working in tandem with her mouth as she manages a nod as if to let me know that it's okay.

"Yo, what do you think, Chase?"

My hips stutter, my body going still. "What?"

"Florida's new center," Sanchez calls. "You think he's really as much of a wonder kid as Jack says he is?"

Fuck.

My brain has no higher function right now. I'm pretty sure Lila is seconds away from sucking it right out of my dick. I'm definitely not equipped for actual conversation.

"I—" Lila chooses this exact moment to tighten her lips around my shaft, dragging up my length slowly. "He seems . . . pretty good."

"I saw some footage," Rankin adds from nearby. "The dude can move."

"Helps that he's built like a tank," Jankowski says. He chuckles, raising his voice. "Hope you can handle him, Ian."

"I can—*fuck.*"

"Dude," Jankowski calls with concern in his voice. "I was just kidding."

"No, I—" I tilt my head down to watch as Lila locks eyes with me while pulling my cock nearly into her goddamned throat, a playful glint in her gaze that has me clenching my jaw. I fist her hair, holding her there for a second as her eyes flutter. "I can handle it," I say a little more evenly. "It'll be fine."

I let Lila go, her lips puffy and her eyes red as she pops off for a second to catch her breath. Even with how wrecked she looks she offers a lazy grin, looking entirely too pleased with herself.

Brat, I mouth.

She flicks out her tongue, tracing it back and forth across my cockhead before giving it a teasing kiss.

"Old Man says he's fine," Jankowski laughs. "We can rest easy tonight."

They all start talking about something else, but I don't catch a word of it, too fixated on the temptress currently on her knees while almost bringing me to mine. My head tips back when she finds a rhythm; the slow, slick slide of her lips and tongue working me over becomes a steady back-and-forth that my hips chase with aborted little thrusts as my mouth falls slack with pleasure. My fingers tighten in the wet strands of her hair, gripping it in my fist as I give her a tentative thrust that pushes deeper, pushes just a little harder.

I'm rewarded with that same soft hum that barely makes a sound but that I can still feel vibrating along my shaft as it threatens to drive me crazy, and it's enough to make me a little greedy. My next thrust is too much for her; I can feel her throat spasm and the barely-there gag is only just hidden by the stream of water that falls over us, but it's enough to make me pause, pulling out of her mouth completely and peering down at her with concern.

I mouth: *I'm sorry*—but she's already shaking her head, her smile smug and her hands running up and down the wet muscle of my thighs. She tugs on my hips and urges me to turn, pulling me down onto the shower bench so that my jutting cock is inches from her mouth as she leans over me. Her nails rake over the tops of my thighs as she curls her body to let her lips trail down my shaft, her face teeming with mischief as she flashes me that same grin. I watch her pull back just to bring a finger to her lips to bid me to stay quiet, my brow furrowing with question only for her to immediately show me exactly why she had to warn me in the first place when she cups her breasts and leans in close to let my cock slide between them.

I breathe in harshly through my nostrils, the noise seeming to echo in the shower stall as loudly as the pounding of my heart, and I actually have to clap a hand back over my mouth just to keep the sounds from escaping when she leans over and pulls the head of my dick into her mouth while the rest is enveloped in the soft, wet tunnel of her perfect tits. I watch with what have to be crazed eyes as she presses the slick mounds tight so that I can feel every inch of her as she works them up and down, her mouth following the rhythm they set as she takes every inch not encased in her as deep as she can.

I want to watch every second; I don't want to miss a single moment of what's happening, given that it's the most erotic thing I've ever experienced, but I physically *can't* hold my eyes open as she starts to move faster, as she sucks me harder. My hands scrabble to grip the edge of the shower bench to keep me from sliding off—something that becomes increasingly more possible as my thighs start to tremble and shake.

I can feel that hot pressure building, can feel the heat of it flooding my balls and rushing through my cock as it actually *swells* in her mouth, and Lila never stops, never slows down; the slide of her breasts and the warm suction of her mouth work together to drive me right to the edge, teetering at the precipice of something that actually has my toes curling and makes my knees feel weak. I open my mouth to say something—to warn her maybe, to whisper that I'm close—but my tongue feels tangled and my throat feels dry, and words simply won't come.

I reach out to palm her head and give her a weak shove, just something to let her know how close I am, but Lila bats it away in a second and returns to her efforts. My eyes flutter open as my teeth press against my lower lip, watching my cock slip between her breasts just to disappear into her mouth again and again and *again*. My heels slip against the tile at my feet, shifting restlessly as I gulp down labored breaths, and I think my eyes actually cross when she pushes me deep again, the head of my cock nearly in her *throat*—and that's all it takes to push me over the edge.

I bring my fist to my mouth, biting at the fleshy part below my thumb to stifle the moans that are burbling in my throat, my cock pulsing against Lila's tongue and flooding her mouth, her throat, pouring straight into her fucking stomach as she takes everything I have. She's still sucking me, but it's languid now, almost sweet— her tongue petting the throbbing skin to work me through an orgasm that has me seeing stars. I don't know when I actually start seeing color again, when sounds start bleeding back in, but when I finally manage to look down between my legs, Lila's teasing tongue at the crown of my cock and her blown pupils peering back at me cause a flare of new arousal to burn in my stomach.

I'm surprised she doesn't make a sound when I wrench her to me, when I flip her so that she's the one seated, and I'm the one at her feet. I push up until my lips are at her ear, keeping my voice low enough so that the others all around us will hide it.

"Are you trying to kill me?" I nibble at her earlobe, enjoying her shaky exhale that comes after. "Did you want them to hear? You want them to come in here and see you with my cock in your mouth?" She trembles against me, and I let my tongue trace the shell of her ear. "You want everyone coming in here and seeing exactly who you belong to?"

"Ian," she breathes.

"Maybe they still will," I purr. "Maybe I can make you scream loud enough that everyone comes running."

I enjoy the hushed whimper that she can't hold back when I throw her legs over my shoulders, diving between her thighs to suck her clit into my mouth with every intention of making her see a few stars as well.

I don't tease her; I'm too fucking wound up to even entertain the thought—pushing two fingers deep inside her as I latch my lips around the slick little bundle of nerves. Her thighs press against my ears as her fingers tangle in my hair, but I enjoy the sting as she pulls roughly at the wet strands, like she can't help it, like she's losing herself in what I'm doing to her. I start to pump my fingers in and out, imagining that it's my cock sinking inside her, laving my tongue against her clit as I draw it deeper into my mouth, as deep as it will go.

My cock twitches with interest as she starts to roll her hips, bracing herself with one hand on the bench as she rides my face, chasing after the sensations of my mouth devouring her pussy like it's my last fucking meal. And it *feels* like it is. Every single time with Lila feels like some sort of life-altering experience—the world fading away outside of the way she feels, the way she tastes, just *her*.

I curl my fingers when they slide deep, rubbing that spot inside that has her head falling back and her mouth falling open, never faltering the rhythm of my lips even as my jaw starts to ache. I feel her tensing against and around me, feel her heels digging into my back and her hips circling as she chases after the end, and my groan is soft against the softer flesh in my mouth, just low enough to let her know that I want her to come all over my face, that I want to swallow her down like she did me.

I hear my name on a sigh, so slight it's almost lost to the stream of the shower, like a breath or a whisper, like she didn't mean to let it loose. It's just a precursor to the trembling that starts in her limbs—her pussy contracting around my fingers and a warm gush flooding my lips as I lap a long, wet stripe between her legs to collect every drop of my reward. I don't stop until she's forcibly pulling me away, coming easily when she tugs me up by the hair, bracing myself with my hands on the bench so that I can capture her mouth as she shivers through the aftershocks of her orgasm.

I can taste both of us on her tongue, our flavors blending together almost enough to get me hard again, and if we were home right now, there's no doubt in my mind I'd be balls deep inside her in a matter of minutes. Perhaps the only downside to this entire encounter.

She's grinning when she pulls away, her eyes glazed and her smile dreamy as she blinks dazedly. I watch her mouth shape the word *good* like a question, and I shake my head with a quiet chuckle as I reach up to press my fingers to her chin, pulling her in for another soft kiss.

"Perfect," I whisper in her ear after. "You're fucking perfect."

She kisses my cheek lazily, her lips lingering as her fingers trail down my ribs, the tickling sensation doing nothing to stanch my growing arousal, my building need to have her again that I'm trying to tamp down. At least for now. Especially when I can hear showers beginning to shut off around us, voices fading away. I know if we stay in here for much longer, people will start to wonder what the fuck I'm doing in here.

I keep my lips close to her ear when I ask quietly, "How did you plan to get out of here?"

"I didn't think that far ahead," she whispers with a soft chuckle.

I shake my head as a barely-there snort escapes me, pulling her up to her feet and into my body just to enjoy the slick curves of her body against mine.

"You'll have to wait here until they clear out," I murmur.

She shrugs one shoulder. "I can do that."

"I still have to shower."

Her smile is impish. "That means I get to wash you."

"There's no way I won't get hard again if you do that."

She pushes up on her toes, her lips feathering against mine as she whispers, "Oh, I'm counting on it."

It's insane that it was only a few weeks ago that I asked her if she was going to ruin me.

It's even more insane that it only took a few weeks for her to thoroughly do so.

Twenty-One

DELILAH

S top being nervous," I mutter, pinching Ian on his side.

He hisses, his nose wrinkling as he peers down at me. "I'm not nervous."

I roll my eyes as I watch him immediately turn back to watch the small crowd filing into the stands around the rink; Jack worked with the Druid's PR team to have the annual charity game moved to the rink at the orphanage last summer, something I was stoked about since it will mean a great time for all the kids, but it also means that many more eyes on the ice to watch what I'm beginning to suspect is a real source of anxiety for Ian.

"You know the guys are going to be happy to see you, right?"

He shakes his head. "Most of these guys I haven't spent any real time with outside of the rink since I got traded."

"So? People fall out of touch all the time. It just means you've got a good place to pick back up from."

His teeth worry at his lower lip, his arms crossing tightly over his practice jersey as he considers. It's honestly cute on him, these nerves; he looks like someone waiting for their first date, which is adorable on a man who looks like a ginger, freckled Thor.

I bump his hip with mine. "It's going to be great, Cupcake. Jack will be there."

"Where is he, anyway?"

"Running late, as usual," I say with a shrug.

"Ian!"

We both turn our heads toward the little voice, spotting a familiar head of blond curls bounding our way. Ian's face lights up immediately, his prior nerves melting away when he spots Kyle coming down the steps of the bleachers two at a time toward the landing where we've been lurking.

"Hey, buddy," Ian says, crouching to meet Kyle on his level. "Good to see you again."

Kyle's expression looks stern for all his seven years. "You haven't been back."

"Oh." Ian's eyes round, his face flushing with guilt. "I haven't. I've been pretty busy with training camp."

"I guess that makes sense," Kyle grumbles.

Ian stands, clapping a hand on the boy's shoulders. "But I tell you what. How about I get you tickets to our first game? And then the weekend after that, I'll come back by for more practice, yeah?"

Kyle's face pinches like he's trying to maintain his stoic facade, but I can see the way his lips twitch with the ghost of a smile. He purses his lips together for a beat like he's considering, finally bobbing his head with a nod.

"Okay," he says. "Yeah. That would be cool."

"Awesome." Ian flashes Kyle a bright smile, and my heart does a little flip-flop when the boy grins back at him. "You'd better go get your seat. I'll try to come say hi after."

"Okay!"

He waves at us both before taking off toward the steps again, and I poke Ian's arm. "See? Someone's already excited to see you."

"I wish everyone were that easy to please."

"I don't know . . . You do a pretty good job pleasing *me*."

He glances at me from the side, with heat in his eyes, the weight of his heavy stare something I can feel all the way down to my toes. "Be good, and I'll please you again after this."

"Promises, promises," I laugh.

He angles his body as if he's going to drive his point home, and my heart hammers in my chest in a Pavlovian response to the anticipation of any sort of Ian's touch.

"Ian!"

Our heads turn to spot the small woman waving wildly from the entry, her face lit up and her silvery hair bouncing behind her in a long braid. The man behind her looks decidedly less friendly, his sharp features hardened and his frown practically etched in.

Jesus, he looks so much like Ian.

It's the first thought that hits me, but even as I think it, I immediately question whether or not that's true. Sure, there can be no doubt that Ian is Bradley Chase's son with their matching hair and builds and similar features—but there's a coldness to Bradley. Something opposite of the warmth Ian radiates. He must get that from his mom.

Ian's mother reaches us and throws her arms around her son's waist, beaming up at him. "Oh, honey. I am so glad you're here! I have so missed seeing you play at these."

"Mom," Ian greets fondly, wrapping his arms around her shoulders to give her a squeeze. "Glad you could make it."

"Well, it wouldn't do for the owners to stand up their own event, now would it?"

Bradley's tone is just as chilly as his expression, and I can't help but wonder what Christine sees in him.

The woman in question smacks her husband's chest. "Oh, don't start. There will be no sniping from either of you today, got it?"

"Delilah." Bradley regards me curtly. "So nice of you to host the event."

"It was mostly Jack's doing," I tell him as politely as I can manage. "But I was all for it, of course. The kids don't have a lot to look forward to."

Christine reaches to squeeze my hand. "It really is so lovely. All the work you've been doing here."

"Thank you, ma'am," I reply with a lot more warmth than I afforded Bradley.

Christine waves me off. "Oh, none of that. I mean"—she winks at me—"you *are* dating my son."

"Christine," Bradley says tersely. "You know that's just for show."

"Mhm." Ian's mother looks coy, shrugging. "I guess an old woman can dream, can't she?" She places her hand on Bradley's forearm, glancing at him with a fond expression. "My romance with Ian's father was such a whirlwind—" She gives me a pointed look. "I mean, the owner's daughter and the star player? It was the talk of the town for such a long time. I've always wanted that kind of love for my son."

Yuck. If she only knew.

Bradley looks unaffected by her reminiscing, but Ian looks tense. I can see the muscle in his jaw ticking, and I wind my arm around his waist, giving him a subtle squeeze of encouragement. That seems to snap him out of his reverie.

"You should probably make your way up there," Ian says, looking only at his mother as he does his best to ignore Bradley completely. "The game will be starting soon."

"I'd like to speak with you after," Bradley says pointedly.

Ian barely spares him a glance. "I have plans after. I will call you when I can."

I can tell that his father would like to say more, but Christine is already tugging on his arm. "Come, come, let's get our seats before we're hounded by some reporter you'll have to schmooze." She pauses to press on her toes, kissing Ian's cheek. "Good luck out there."

"Thanks, Mom," he murmurs back.

We watch as she pulls Bradley toward the risers, and despite her best efforts, they *are* stopped by what seems to be a reporter, Bradley's entire demeanor changing as he dusts off a megawatt smile that feels forced. Or maybe that's just me.

"God, look at him," Ian grumbles. "I bet he's telling them all about all the 'good work' he does. As if this was even his idea." He rolls his eyes. "This game was always my mom's baby."

"He really knows how to turn it on for the press," I notice.

"Yes," Ian agrees. "He's very good at faking being a good person."

I can sense the slight air of defeat in his tone, and I know that he's allowing himself to be dragged down in memories, ones that will do nothing but threaten to ruin this day for him. I have every intention of leaning in to tell him exactly what I think of Bradley Chase and give him a much better occupant for his thoughts, me mainly, but before I can even open my mouth to speak, I feel strong, thick arms circling my waist, picking me clear off the floor as I yelp in surprise.

"Little Dee!" I'm spun around, feeling disoriented for a second before I'm plopped back onto my feet. "What's up, Baker?"

"Logan?"

He flashes me a bright white smile, reaching out to pinch my chin. "Miss me?"

"Like a hole in my head," I laugh.

He clasps a hand over his heart. "You wound me."

Logan Thomas went to college with Jack and Ian, but got drafted to Tampa Bay in his senior year. He never misses our annual charity event, usually crashing with Jack while he's in town. I wonder how that will work now that Ian is there.

Speaking of.

I peek back at the man in question, noticing a tightness to his jaw, his fists clenched at his sides as he watches me with Logan. Part of me wants to tell him to knock that shit off, but a much more feral part of me secretly likes seeing him wound up over me.

"Ian, you remember Logan, right?"

This seems to snap Ian out of it, his eyes blinking a couple of times before he *really* gives his attention to the man who's joined us. "Lo?"

"Ian! Fucking hell, man. Get over here."

Logan pulls Ian into a bear hug, Ian pausing for only a moment with surprise before he returns it full force. I notice his lips turn up in a smile as he wraps his arms around the other man, the tension leaving his face as they clasp each other tightly.

"How long has it been since you've played one of these," Logan asks. "Six years?"

"Almost seven," Ian tells him.

"Fuck, man. We missed you up there in ice land. It's good to see you without having to shove your ass into the boards."

"It's really good to be back home," Ian tells him. His brow cocks. "And when have you ever shoved me into the boards?"

"I see your memory has worsened with age," he laughs. Logan's warm, umber eyes flit between the two of us, deep dimples etched into the light brown skin of his cheeks with his mischievous smile as he crosses his corded arms over his chest. "So what's this I read about the two of you being a *thing*?"

"Oh," I start, my eyes darting to Ian for help.

I forget that not *all* the hockey players in our lives know that this thing between us is for show. Or rather, that it used to be. Since it's not *actually* for show now. But I guess it still is to everyone *else*? Except for people like Logan, who didn't know the truth to begin with. Jesus, we really need to put a label on this thing before I break my brain.

That thought gives me pause, but since I'm just standing here with my mouth hanging open, I shove it away.

"It's complicated," Ian says for me, scratching at his beard in what I've come to recognize as an anxious gesture. "You see—"

"We are," I blurt out. "A thing."

I can practically *feel* Ian's surprise projecting from his eyes to the side of my face, but I just reach out and lace my fingers in his, not allowing for him to second-guess.

"That's awesome," Logan says with a happy grin. "Look at you, Dee. Making good on that puppy love."

I feel my cheeks heat. "Shut up."

"What?" Ian cocks his head. "You noticed that?"

Logan rolls his eyes. "Pretty sure the guys on the space stations noticed it."

"Fuck off," I mumble.

Ian surprises me with a loud laugh, his fingers squeezing mine as he flashes me a teasing smile. "Aw. You really were obsessed with me, huh?"

"Getting less so," I huff.

"Don't worry, Lila, your secret's safe with me."

"All right, all right," Logan laughs. "Enough with that cute shit. Some of us single people can't take it."

"What happened to Serah?"

Logan rubs the back of his neck. "Didn't work out."

"Aw." I frown with sympathy. "I'm sorry."

"It is what it is," he sighs.

"Yo! Logan! Ian!"

There's a small crowd moving toward us from the entrance area, my brother and a few other of their old college buddies making their way inside toward the ice. I see at least two players who they didn't meet until later when they were drafted, but no one that Ian doesn't know, I think, thankfully.

Which reminds me that I'm still holding his hand.

I let go without making a thing of it, not quite sure that *this* moment is the right one to unload everything on my brother, but when I meet Ian's gaze, I don't miss the flash of displeasure there. It's definitely a discussion we need to have. Soon.

"About time you showed up," Ian greets my brother, letting the moment roll off his back. "I wasn't sure who was going to lead the cheerleading squad."

Jack snorts. "I was out getting my bloomers resized. They didn't have any big enough to fit my dick."

"Gross," I groan.

Oscar guffaws. "That's not what Lyle's mom said."

The player in question punches Oscar on the shoulder, and I feel myself smiling. These guys are idiots, but I sort of love them.

One a bit more than the others . . .

Ian looks almost nervous again—so minuscule in his features that someone might miss it, but I don't. It's in the slight tic in his jaw, the wary set of his eyes, the press of his mouth. It makes me wish I were still holding his hand. I watch the way he eyes the other players, guys he hasn't seen in years off the rink, not since everything went down with him and Mei, and I know that he worries about how they see him. What they might think of him now. I know it because it's all we talked about last night, cuddled in my bed while I ran my fingers through his hair. I'm willing to beat down any man who has something negative to say about him— regardless of how much bigger and stronger than me they are— but, as it turns out, these big dummies have a way of surprising me. In a good way.

Oscar's eyes light up. "Ian!"

I watch a repeat hug performance like the one Ian and Logan had a few minutes ago, and it takes no time at all for the other guys to follow suit—each one embracing their old friend like no time at all has passed. I can see the way each interaction melts more and more of the stress he's been carrying, his entire body becoming more relaxed with each *Dude, how have you been?* and clap on the back.

I linger at the edge of the tiny crowd, content to watch him, but I catch his eye amid the conversation, noticing the glint there, the hint of solidarity that only exists between the two of us. It makes me feel a bit surer about my blurted acknowledgment of what we are. Makes me realize how *good* it felt for someone else to know, someone who had no stake in what we are other than being happy that we are. It makes me want to feel that a hundred times over, to let the entire world know.

"All right," Jack interrupts, checking his watch. "Everyone needs to head back to the locker room and suit up so we can get out on the ice."

"Oh," Lyle snickers. "Should we call you Coach Jack today?"

"If it will make you move a bit faster," Jack answers sweetly. My brother aims a finger in my direction. "Ava is looking for you." He jabs a thumb over his shoulder. "She went around the other way. Somewhere back there."

"I'll find her," I tell him.

Jack squeezes Ian's shoulder even as the other guys start to file into the double doors that lead to the hall where the locker rooms are. "You good?"

"Yeah," Ian says, looking like he means it. "I am, actually."

"Good." Jack nods. "Coming?"

Ian eyes me briefly. "I'll catch up."

I don't miss the way my brother's gaze flits between us, a wrinkle forming at his brow, but he seems to dismiss it for now, following after the other guys through the doors.

Ian immediately blows out a breath when they're gone. "Fuck."

"I told you," I say, "that it would be fine."

"I just thought . . . It's been so long since I've spent any real time with any of them. With everything that happened . . ."

I reach for his hand again, not giving a damn who sees when I squeeze it with mine. We're supposed to be seen, after all, right?

"Anyone who knows you," I tell him firmly, "knows who you

are. No one who really knows you could ever think you're capable of the things people have said about you."

He nods, swallowing thickly. "I wish I had as much faith in me as you do."

"It's fine," I answer. "I have enough for the both of us."

His gaze lingers on my face, his jaw working. "You told Logan that we're a thing."

"Aren't we?"

"I hoped we were," he says quietly.

My lips quirk. "Then what's the problem?"

"He could say something to Jack," Ian points out. "You okay with that?"

"He's going to have to find out soon, anyway." I step closer, sliding my arm around Ian's waist. "I don't really think I can keep the way I feel about you a secret for much longer."

His breath hitches, and his eyes flick to my mouth, like he's considering taking it. "And how is that?"

"Hm." I throw caution to the wind, pushing up on my toes and brushing my lips gently against his in something that can barely be called a kiss but lights me up inside all the same. "Go win your game, and we'll talk all about it."

"Okay," he sighs against my lips.

I step back, beaming at him before I land a hard slap on his ass. "Get out there, Cupcake. I'll be watching."

The heat in his eyes as he leaves me could melt the entire rink.

— — — — —

The game has been a rush of excitement for both of the teams the various players have split into; Ian ended up on the same team as Jankowski and Rankin, joined by Logan, Oscar, and Lyle. I've watched them all laugh and smile between plays, each interaction bringing Ian more and more out of his shell and looking more at ease.

"Wait, so why did they blow the whistle?"

"Offside," I tell Ava.

"Is that why they're going back to the little circles?"

"Mhm. The player can't pass that blue line before the puck."

"This game seemed way more fun when the players could still beat the shit out of one another."

I frown, imagining Ian being mauled by another player. "Yeah, let's not hope for that."

"Your guy could handle himself," Ava says, snorting. "He's practically Wreck-It Ralph with red hair." She cocks her head, watching Ian as he blocks Connors on the other team from shooting a goal past Lyle. "Now I'm imagining him in overalls."

"Stop imagining Ian in things," I hiss, elbowing her in the side.

"I'm single," she huffs. "Let me live vicariously through the good dick you're getting."

"*Shh.*" I slap her knee. "There are kids around." I scowl when I glance back at the ice, jumping to my feet with dozens of other people around me as we all shout at the referee at once. "Dude, move! You're blocking the play!"

Ava eyes me with a cocked brow as I sink back down onto the bench, grumbling. "What just happened?"

"Ref got in the way of the play," I tell her. "Logan couldn't score because he was blocking the goal."

"You know this is a *friendly* game, right?"

"Shut up," I mumble.

"You're as bad as your brother," Ava laughs, pointing at the man in question, who is hanging over the boards at the bench, shouting at the referee. "Do you think he's going to start a fight?"

I watch as Jack waves his one good arm frantically, his face turning red as he shouts God knows what at the irritated-looking ref. "If he had both arms it definitely would have been a possibility."

"When will the cast come off?"

"It should only be another few weeks, so he should be playing by the second week of the season if nothing goes wrong."

"At least he won't miss too much."

"Thank God," I chuckle. "He'd be driving everyone up the wall if he missed much more."

"I can't believe he still hasn't picked up on what's going on between you and Ian. Are you going to tell him anytime soon?"

I bite my lip, shifting guiltily in my seat. "Yes . . . soon."

"Do you think he'll be weird about it?"

"Probably." I shrug. "But he'll get over it. He loves us both. He's not going to do something drastic like disown us over it."

"He loves you, you love each other . . . It's all very disgusting and cute."

I feel my face flush. "What?"

"Oh, come on." Ava rolls her eyes. "You've spent the first two innings of this game—"

"Periods," I correct.

"Whatever," she huffs. "You've spent the entire game watching Ian like he's got a golden dick and shits saltwater taffy."

"Well, that's utterly awful."

"But not incorrect," Ava laughs.

I press my knuckles to my burning cheeks, wondering if they're as red as they feel. I catch sight of Ian's bright smile as he claps

Logan on the shoulder after a successful play, gliding back down the ice effortlessly and looking every bit in his element. The things I feel for Ian aren't new, or at all a surprise, and they're definitely strong, but can I really say that I *love* him? Wanted him, dreamt of him, *burned* for him, yes—but love?

The crowd around me starts to grow restless as the clock ticks down the last sixty seconds of the game, interrupting my train of thought. The teams are tied right now, and if nothing happens, they'll have to go into overtime.

People are standing up again as the puck drops to the ice, the center for Ian's team, Oscar, slapping it away from Felix on the other team and pushing it toward the other team's goal. Ian and Logan work in tandem as the left and right wing to block Prescott from making a go for Oscar, and I can feel myself standing again as well, my heart thudding, as it seems like they might pull ahead.

"What's happening?" Ava stands next to me, grabbing my arm and shaking it as the crowd starts yelling again. "I don't know what the fuck is happening!"

"Oscar's about to try to score," I tell her, biting my thumbnail. "He's the one with the puck. Oh! That was one of the other team's forwards that just shoved him into the corner. They're battling now."

"Battling?"

"It just means the other team is trying to get the puck so they can—shit!"

"What? What happened?"

"Puck is loose—*someone get it!*" I wave my hands in the air as if anyone can actually hear me, adrenaline coursing through me. "Yes!" I shake Ava. "Ian's got it. *He's got it!* Oh! He just shot it to Jankowski, I think they could—*fuck yeah!*"

Our section explodes with noise when Jankowski shoots the puck right between the opposing goalie's legs as Ian's team takes the win at the last second.

"They won!" I shout to Ava, who is wild-eyed but smiling. "They fucking won!"

"There are children around!" Ava shouts back, laughing. "But fuck yeah!"

My heart is beating so hard in my chest that it feels like it might pound right through my rib cage, and I can feel my cheeks starting to hurt from the wide smile etched on my face. I'm still holding on to Ava as I watch Ian and the other players on his team crowd around Jankowski, shaking him and trying to hoist him up as if they've won a championship game and not a friendly charity match that didn't matter. The pure joy on Ian's face as he celebrates with his temporary teammates is infectious, and I feel it bubbling up inside me as if sharing it with him, ecstatic that he can have this moment after all the stressing he did over this game.

I notice his head moving when he breaks away from the other guys, his neck stretching as he peers into the stands as if searching. He skates closer to the rails as he continues to crane his neck this way and that, and it's then I realize that it's *me* he's looking for. I rush down the aisle and take the steps two at a time, barreling toward the railing and immediately dropping to my knees to duck under the lowest bar that opens up into the rink that's set lower than the stands. At this angle, Ian's face is almost level with mine when he reaches the edge, and in this crowd of so many cheering people, it feels almost like we're in our own little bubble.

"You won," I tell him, beaming. "You're supposed to be celebrating."

His smile makes my chest hurt, but his words make it feel like it's too full. "You're the only person I want to celebrate with."

"Yeah?"

"Always."

I know there're people all around us, but at this moment, I find I don't care. I spare one quick glance down the ice to confirm that my brother is lost to the sea of celebration, just one second before I bend until I can wrap a hand around the back of Ian's helmet, pulling him up to meet me as I crash my mouth into his. He doesn't hesitate to melt into the kiss, his fingers sliding over my knee and squeezing me there, tingles sparking along my skin where he touches me and spreading to fill me up. I realize all at once that there's no question. Not really.

Because I still want him, I still dream of him, I still *burn* for him—and I absolutely love him too.

Twenty-Two

IAN

I've been playing hockey for most of my life, but the high I feel after winning that game today is more potent than any I've ever experienced. Playing with my old friends, seeing the way they embraced me as if nothing's changed, as if I'm the same person they've always known—it's enough to make me start to think that maybe I am. That maybe I can stop dwelling on the opinions of strangers and cling harder to the ones that come from people who *actually* matter.

An idea that is a lot easier to entertain with the encouragement of the woman currently pulling me into her apartment.

"You were fantastic," she's saying between kisses as I kick her door shut.

I grin against her mouth, my hands circling her waist to pull her closer. "Yeah?"

"It's hot watching you play."

"Does someone have dreams of being a puck bunny?"

"Just yours," she hums.

I groan, slanting my mouth against hers and muttering "fuck" against her tongue. I hoist her up into my arms and carry her through the apartment, never slowing until she's flat on her back against her mattress. She's an absolute vision of soft swells, gentle curves, and long, silky waves spread out around her head, and the way she bites her lip when she looks up at me, looking so excited just to *have* me, sends a thrill coursing through my body.

"Fuck, Lila," I murmur, "I can never decide where I want to touch you first. You're too tempting."

Her lips curl. "Get down here and decide as you go."

I pull my shirt over my head as I obey, tossing it aside and making quick work of my jeans before crawling over her.

"You're too dressed," I note, sliding my hand under her shirt to caress her belly. "Let's fix that."

I realized quickly after the first time that I ever touched her like this that I would never be able to take my time getting her out of her clothes. Once I get even a hint of what's underneath them, it's like my mind goes into overdrive, needing to see more. Every part of her drives me wild—from her full, pink mouth to her wide, soft hips down to her cute, stubby toes. Sometimes when I look at her, it feels like Lila Baker was made just for me.

"Look at you." I slide my body against hers, grabbing a handful of one of her perfect tits and sliding my tongue across the column of her throat. "You're a fucking *dream*, Lila."

"*You're* still too dressed," she says breathily, her fingers tucking inside the elastic of my briefs. "Take these off."

"Why? Are you greedy, sweet girl?" I roll my hips, letting my clothed, hard length press against the juncture between her thighs. "You want this cock?"

"Preferably before I'm an old woman," she grumbles, her petulant tone less effective when laced with the thick arousal it carries.

"Mm." I peck a kiss at her cheek, lifting away from her. "Be right back."

I roll across her bed and wrench open her bedside drawer, reaching inside to fish out a condom. My fingers trip against the box as I curse under my breath, and I drag myself a little closer to get a better angle to reach for it.

"Um . . ."

I turn my head, catching sight of Lila biting at her lower lip and looking nervous.

"What is it?"

"I was thinking . . ." Her cheeks are tinged with a soft pink, her thighs pressing together restlessly. "Do we really need one?"

My cock throbs in my underwear, practically trying to jump out on its own to get to her. I swallow around a growing lump in my throat, my pulse pounding in my ears at the notion of feeling her bare around me.

"Are you sure?"

"I'm on birth control," she tells me, "and I'm negative, so . . ."

"So am I," I say immediately. She laughs at that, and I realize what I've said, adding, "Negative, I mean. Not on birth control."

"Right," she chuckles. "So, do you want to maybe . . . ?"

"Yes," I blurt. "Absolutely yes."

"You're sure?"

I reach for her hand, bringing it over to palm my hard cock, which is straining against my boxer briefs. "Just thinking about fucking you raw has me wanting to come, Lila."

"Fuck," she whimpers, squeezing me.

I'm moving to draw my hand back out of the drawer with every intention of doing just that, my fingers brushing against soft silicone that gives me pause. I peer over into her drawer, biting my lip as I notice what's waiting there.

"Hm." I wrap my fingers around the toy, pulling it out of the drawer. "Found a friend."

Her eyes round as she laughs. "Old faithful."

"Really?"

"Never let me down yet."

I run my finger over the small opening at the head, pushing it inside and feeling the soft pad at the bottom. "And what does this do, Lila?"

"You know what it does," she says with narrowed eyes.

"Oh, I do," I answer, closing the drawer and bringing the toy with me as I crawl back to her. "But I want you to tell me, anyway."

"It—*oh*."

She gasps when I wrap my lips around her nipple, sucking it deep into my mouth and swirling my tongue before releasing it with a wet sound. "It . . . ?"

"Sucks on my clit," she says breathlessly.

"Hm." I trail my lips over her belly, ducking my head between her legs and licking at her slit before doing exactly that, pulling at the sensitive bud with my lips for only a moment before letting go. "Like that?"

"Fuck, yes."

"I think you should use it," I tell her. "While I fuck you."

Her throat bobs with a swallow as she leans up on her elbows. "Yeah?"

"Mhm." I inch back up her body, brushing my lips against her mouth and licking at the seam there until she opens, tangling my tongue with hers so she can taste herself. "I want you to gush for me."

"Ian," she practically whines.

"On your stomach, sweet girl." I nip at her lower lip, placing the toy in her hand. "I want that pretty ass in the air."

She rolls over like she's eager for it, causing a giddy thrill to shoot through me as I kiss her shoulder, her spine—every bit I can reach while she situates herself on her stomach and props up on her knees with her chest against the bed so her perfectly round ass wiggles tantalizingly in the air. I palm it roughly as I sit up, bracing myself on my knees and squeezing the soft flesh there as she moans quietly.

"Jesus, you're already so wet for me," I purr, sliding two fingers between her legs to tease her slick folds. I ease them inside her gently, feeling a pulse of pre-come wet the front of my briefs as her walls ripple around the digits, imagining what it will feel like when I push inside her without anything between us. "You want my cock here?"

"Yes," she sighs, pushing back on my fingers. "More."

She turns her face against the bed, watching me with hooded eyes as I pull my fingers from her, bringing them to my mouth to suck them clean. "So fucking sweet."

She keeps watching me as I finally start working my underwear down my thighs, slipping out of them and tossing them away until there's nothing between us but the cool air and our skin. I actually *shake* when I tilt my hips to let my hard cock rock against the furrow of her ass, squeezing her to envelop me tighter as I imagine taking her there too. God, I want to own every part of her. Want to mark every inch until there's no doubt that she's mine. I've *never* felt the level of possession I feel for Lila, not for anyone else.

I grip my cock at the base and press it against her entrance, not yet pushing inside but instead rubbing the head up and down, slicking myself in the leaking mess of her.

"Fuck," I hiss, teasing her by *barely* dipping in before pulling right back out. "There's no way I'm going to last long when I get inside you. You're too fucking wet, too hot."

"Stop teasing and fuck me," she grits out, her fingers clutching the comforter.

I give her ass a sharp smack, shuddering at the low moan that tears out of her. "Settle, brat." I nudge at her entrance again. "Turn the toy on and use it. I want you messy."

Her hand that still grasps the toy slides down the bed to reach beneath her, and suddenly I hear a low thrumming of sound from under her body, feel her tense, and hear her gasp as she presumably situates it at her clit.

"There you go," I coo, rocking against her swollen pussy. "This pretty cunt is practically dripping for me." I push ever so slightly, watching her body give around the head of my cock as just the tip presses inside her. "I could slide right in."

"Do it," she moans. "Please, Ian. Need you."

And I do, finally—slipping deeper inside her, feeding her inch after inch of my throbbing cock as her walls clench around me, sucking me in.

"*Fuck*," I groan in a drawn-out exhale. My hips meet her ass, her body accepting all of me, and the feeling of being surrounded in the tight, wet heat of her without any barriers is almost too much. "You feel so *good*, Lila."

"Move," she urges, her pussy fluttering around my length as the toy hums between her legs. "*Fuck* me."

I grip her tightly by the waist as I draw out, watching every inch of my glistening shaft slide out reluctantly, her body gripping me like it doesn't want to let me go. I let the head of my cock linger at her entrance for only a moment when I'm all the way out, sucking down an unsteady breath before slamming back inside with a grunt.

"*Yes*," she gasps. "Fuck, yes."

I can *hear* how wet she is, each thrust offering up a filthy sound as her arousal coats my thighs. Her pussy clenches rhythmically as if trying to take me deeper, her hips pressing back against me as the sounds of slick skin meeting again and again fill the air.

"Fuck, sweetheart," I moan. "You hear that? How fucking soaked you are for me? Does it feel good?"

"*Yes*," she mewls. "Right there. God, you're right where I need you."

I thrust deliberately, feeling her tremble. "Here?"

"*Oh God.*"

"My name," I remind her. "Just mine."

"Ian," she cries. "I'm so close."

"I told you," I manage through clenched teeth, the sensation of her warm cunt squeezing me so perfectly making my balls draw up tight with impending release. "I want to feel you gush. Want you to soak my cock. I want"—I accentuate the words with a hard slap of my hips against her ass—"you fucking"—my head tips back as she pulses around me, her pussy so slippery that I'm on the edge of losing it—"*messy*."

"Oh God. Oh *fuck, Ian!*"

I hear the soft thump of the toy that still thrums quietly against the comforter, and then her hands are reaching back to grapple for my hips as she quivers—low, drawn-out cries falling from her mouth as she comes apart. She does exactly what I wanted; Lila fucking *gushes* for me—soaking my cock, my thighs—her orgasm dripping down to pool at my knees, which I'm braced on as I pound into her, chasing my own release.

"That's it," I rasp. "That's my sweet girl. I'm going to fill this pussy up. Gonna come so deep I'm there for days. I'm—I'm gonna—*guh.*"

My fingers grip her hips so tight they might actually leave a mark, and some primal part of my brain revels in the idea of that. It's the only part of my brain that actually seems to remain online as I press as close to her as I can, my balls throbbing and my cock pulsing deep inside her to flood her with my come. I imagine it seeping out of her after this, imagine pushing it back inside to keep it there, and that, too, has that caveman-like corner of my brain humming in pleasure.

I can do little more than slump over her when it's over, her back rising and falling with heavy, labored breaths that match mine as we both come down from what just happened. It's an absolute mess between us, exactly like I wanted, and without actually thinking of what I'm doing, I swivel my hips to stir her up inside, shuddering at the feel of her.

"You're trying to kill me," she groans. "I'm dead."

"We can get joint gravesites," I huff, still trying to catch my breath.

She snorts beneath me. "That's romantic."

I ease out of her, wincing when I leave the tight grip of her body, sitting back on my calves as I watch my come slide down her thigh. I give into my urges and place my thumb just under the thin stream, pushing it back up until my thumb shoves it back inside. Lila shivers, and I hold my thumb there as I lean over, pressing kisses into her spine.

"You really are a mess," I murmur.

"Who's fault is that?"

I smile against her skin. "You won't find any apologies here."

"Yeah, well. You get to clean me up."

My cock twitches, taking her words in an entirely different way from how she likely means them, and my smile turns impish as I skim my lips lower, palming her hips to hold her in place as I bring my mouth between her legs to nuzzle there, warming at the soft sounds that escape her when I slide my tongue through our combined orgasm, slipping it inside her before drawing it back out.

"Happy to."

─ ─ ─ ─

We're both boneless and spent as we lie on her bed some indeterminate time later, her head on my shoulder as my fingers lace through the tangled strands of her hair to gently separate them. Her arm is slung over my chest, her thigh cradling my hip, and her cheek resting over my heart, and that overwhelming, wonderful sensation of being so *settled* is so strong that I feel overflowing with it, like I might burst at the seams. And yet, despite being so full, I've never felt more at peace than I do at this moment.

"My legs are Jell-O," she mumbles against my chest. "Are you sleeping here?"

"Mm. Jack will wonder where I am."

She nuzzles my pec. "We should just tell him."

"We should?"

She lifts her head, propping up on her elbow and looking down at me. "Do you want to?"

"I want to tell fucking *everyone*," I say without missing a beat.

Her answering smile is breathtaking, and that swelling feeling brims with something else—something warm and consuming and new that has my breath catching.

God, I love her.

The thought hits me all at once, but strangely, it doesn't surprise me.

It was inevitable, I think, that she would mark me, that she would take everything, things I *want* her to take, things I want her to keep and hold on to. Everything I have. I never stood a chance against her.

Because Lila is like lightning on the sand—bright and powerful as it strikes, obliterating all the tiny grains of scattered pieces that feel so disjointed and unsettled and creating something new, leaving something more beautiful behind in its wake. That's what Lila's done to me. Taken all my pieces that didn't fit and molded them into something beautiful. Something that's hers entirely.

I manage a shaky inhale, the words there on my tongue but caught, worry about our history and our present and the short time that we've come back into each other's lives holding me back. I open my mouth to say something—what, I'm not sure—but Lila speaks before I can get the words out.

"So do I," she says warmly, tracing the freckles on my chest as her eyes follow the path of her finger. "I want to."

There are so many times in my life that I've felt undeserving, felt like I had to be better, that I had to be *more*, but right now, with her . . . I feel like I can just be. Like everything I am is enough, because Lila deemed it so.

"Then let's do it," I tell her. "Let's tell everyone."

"Yeah?"

"Absolutely." I place my hand over hers, squeezing it. "How should we do it?"

"Hmm." She purses her lips, considering. "Dramatic gesture? I'm a big fan of the kiss cams." I wrinkle my nose, and she laughs. "No?"

"I can't think of anything that makes me want to crawl into a hole more than being caught on one of those things."

"Fine, fine. We can do something simpler." She cocks her head. "Statement to the media?"

"Those always go well," I scoff.

She chuckles, leaning down and kissing the corner of my mouth. "It will this time."

"You think so?"

"Mhm. Because this time, I'll be right there beside you."

"Going to put a fish in everyone's locker that has something negative to say about it?"

"Absolutely I will," she deadpans.

A laugh tumbles past my lips, and I wrap my arms around her, pulling her into my chest and squeezing her tight just to feel her against me. Wondering how on earth I got so lucky as to find myself falling for the most beautiful girl I've ever known—inside and out. I just have to work out how best to let her know.

"But that'll be the easy part," she says.

I draw back to look at her, arching a brow. "It will?"

"Yep."

"What's the hard part?"

Her smile is full of mischief, reaching to tap the end of my nose. "First, we have to tell Jack."

I groan. That's going to be a trip and a half.

I eye Lila settling back into my arms, a soft sigh leaving her mouth and her entire body relaxing like she's exactly where she wants to be. Like *I'm* exactly where she wants to be.

I decide it's worth it. All of it. No matter what happens.

Because I'm never letting her go.

Twenty-Three

DELILAH

I should probably feel more surprised regarding the picture that is spreading across the internet like wildfire today, but honestly, I really don't. I think I knew when I kissed Ian after that game that *someone* would capture it, and maybe a part of me was fine with the idea of it. Rip off the Band-Aid, as it were.

My team, however, is currently in full crisis mode.

"I don't see what the big deal is," Theo is saying, and I'm reminded again at how grateful I am that he dropped everything to come to this meeting. "This is what you wanted, isn't it? You practically shoved this whole thing onto her."

"Now, now," Ben interjects, wringing his hands and looking as nervous as always. "We never made any statements regarding who Delilah should or shouldn't see in her personal life."

Theo rolls his eyes. "Sing that song for someone else, doll. We all know that you were happy to let her dally around with Ian Chase as long as it was doing good things for the show. Changing your tune now is hypocritical."

Ben's cheeks flush because of what I assume is Theo's flippant use of *doll*, which I'm sure he will second-guess later, but quickly recovers.

"No one is saying that Delilah has to make any sort of personal decisions here," he says carefully.

Theo scoffs. "Then why call a meeting over a picture? It's a fucking kiss. They weren't having sex on the rink."

Gia has been listening to this while rubbing her temples, her eyes shut and her lips pressed together as the two men argue back and forth. Her dark brown eyes open now to assess us, her fingers coming to rest on the top of her desk, lacing together as she seems to try to choose her words.

"Dee," she starts slowly. "I think the first thing we need to know is what is this thing between you and Ian? Is it something casual or . . . ?"

I straighten my spine, looking her in the eye. "No, it's not."

"So it's going to be something that will continue, then," she clarifies.

I nod. "It will."

Gia bobs her head as she sighs out a slow exhale, tapping one perfect nail against a knuckle of her other hand as she considers. I can see the gears turning in her head, and I know that this is her job, that her main priority is this show and the viewers it brings, so I do my best not to feel bitter about the way she's treating my personal life like a puzzle she needs to solve for her own benefit. She didn't sign up for this, after all, not really.

"As your friend," Gia says carefully, "which I would like to assume we are after all this time, of course I am happy if you are happy. It's clear that Ian means something to you, and as your friend and a fellow woman, I say hell yeah."

"But?"

"But unfortunately, I am also your EP, which means I have to look at this thing from all angles and be up-front with you about what it could mean. The fact of the matter is that while Ian's public opinion has drastically improved while the two of you have been . . . hanging out, there will always be the undercurrent of naysayers and ill will because of what happened before he was traded to Calgary."

"He *chose* to leave."

It's not the entire truth, but it's not exactly a lie either. But that's none of their business.

Gia holds out a hand, continuing. "Be that as it may, we can't change what people say about him. And I have to be real with you and tell you that there might come a time when that could hurt you professionally. I hate that this is the way it is, but unfortunately, it *is* the way it is. Public perception and social media are two sides of the same coin in today's world, and that means it would only take one viral post, one bad photo, to have your image tanking right along with his. You've done so well to maintain a high opinion with the public thus far, so I just have to ask you straight up."

I take a breath, nodding. "Then ask."

"Are you prepared for that? Is Ian Chase worth the possibility of losing all that you've worked for? Because it's possible, Dee. Flirting with the idea of something between you is one thing, but an actual relationship can be messy. Are you okay with the possibility that if things take a turn, it could hurt your image right along with his?"

I have to tamp down the immediate flare of irritation, reminding myself that Gia is just doing her job. Even looking out for me, in her own way. I know that my anger is not aimed at her, but at the people who have turned Ian into something he's not, based on a few measly photos that they don't even know the truth of. That he's had to carry the repercussions of a lie for years with hardly anyone in his corner. Remembering that makes my answer easy.

"Yes," I tell her firmly. "I'm okay with that. He's worth it."

Gia studies me for a long moment, her chin finally dipping with a nod as she leans back in her chair. "I will talk to the guys upstairs. See if there's a way I can spin this positively. I have to advise you—as your EP, not your friend—to tread carefully going forward, mainly because I would hate to see—as your friend, not your EP—everything you've worked for taken away from you because of a bunch of people making assumptions."

"I appreciate you being straight with me," I say honestly. "There are a lot of things regarding this matter that aren't my business to tell, but I can say with certainty that I trust Ian, and if something happens, I will be right beside him to weather it."

"We still have to address the pictures," Ben chimes in quietly.

Theo rises from his chair, crossing his arms over his chest. "Then address them. Tell them the truth, if that's what Dee wants. You set the world up for the possibility of something between them, so you should be fine with confirming that there actually is."

Ben eyes me warily. "And you're okay with that, Delilah? If we confirm?"

I remember the conversation from just last night with Ian, smiling softly to myself, confident that he would be okay with my answer.

"I am," I say. "Do it."

Ben looks less than enthused as he nods his agreement, but I notice a small smile on Gia's face as she bobs her head idly.

"Are we done here?" Theo reaches out to offer me his hand. "I have other meetings."

I let him help me from my chair, only half listening to Gia's and Ben's answers as I pull my phone from my pocket, glancing at the pictures I've already saved to my gallery again. Seeing myself kissing Ian from multiple angles is a little strange, but the way he looks at me just before I lean in, the absolute *adoration* on his face that is so evident even in a still like this . . . It fills me with confidence for my decision. It makes me one hundred percent sure that I would stand by him through anything.

I'm only half surprised to find Ava waiting in the hall for us when we step out of Gia's office; I'm surprised she didn't find an excuse to be in there for the meeting, honestly.

"Were you listening at the door?" I tease.

She rolls her eyes. "Duh. Damn thing is thick though. How did it go?"

"As good as can be expected," Theo answers for me. "They can't tell her not to date him, so there's really nothing they can do here but suck it up and get with the program."

"Love that for us," Ava says with a grin.

I notice the way it slips soon after as her eyes land on me, and she suddenly looks nervous.

"What?" I ask. "What is it?"

"Um . . . So Jack is here," she tells me. "He's in your dressing room."

"Yeah," I sigh. "That tracks."

"Yeah . . . I don't think I'll be attending that meeting with you," Theo says.

"Thanks," I snort.

Theo claps me on the shoulder. "You're on your own, kid."

"I can handle my brother," I say with what is mostly complete confidence. "Probably."

Ava looks sympathetic, but I tell myself that it's going to be fine. This is *Jack*, after all. My biggest cheerleader and my oldest friend. One of the very few people I have in the world.

With that in mind, I leave my friends behind, heading downstairs to find him.

Rip off the Band-Aid.

— — — —

Jack is pacing back and forth in my dressing room when I open the door, muttering to himself. I know from experience that he's most likely practicing every outcome of the conversation we're about to have, and if I couldn't see the frustration etched into his features, that would make me laugh. He halts midstep when he hears the door shut behind me, watching me lean against it, his brow furrowed.

"Hi," I say.

His fists clench, his phone in one hand. "Hey."

"You, uh, wanna sit?" I gesture to the small couch pushed against the wall. "Or did you want to yell at me standing up?"

More muttering under his breath, but he stomps over to the couch, plopping down on one side and patting the other aggressively to signal that I join him. I settle into the cushion with less force than he did, lacing my fingers together in my lap as I watch him chew on what are most likely a dozen different sentences as he tries to land on the one he actually wants to say.

I decide to throw him a bone. "So . . . I guess you saw."

"Yeah," he snorts. "I saw."

"You obviously have feelings about it."

"That didn't look like pretending, Dee."

I take a deep breath. "Because it wasn't."

"So you lied to me."

"Not on purpose."

"How long has it been 'not pretending'?"

"Not as long as you're probably thinking. It just . . . sort of happened. Hazard of the ruse, I guess."

"And why didn't you tell me? Why did you think you had to keep lying to me?"

"I . . ." My words trail off as I frown, considering that. It's a simple question, but my answer is less so. "Honestly? I just . . . I wanted him to myself for a little bit."

"That doesn't even make sense," Jack huffs.

"It does to me," I press. "Look, we both know that I was head over heels for him as a kid."

"Yeah, but that was only a crush."

"Maybe at first, but can we really say that? It never actually went away. The second I saw him again, I just . . ."

Jack eyes me, studying whatever he's seeing on my face. "Really? Why didn't you say anything? Why agree to this whole thing then? What if it didn't work out? That could have really hurt you, Dee."

"I know." The concern in his tone makes me smile, because even when he's irritated with me, he can't help but worry for me too. "I know that. But I couldn't help it. I mean, he was *right there*, and suddenly I had the chance to live out all my daydreams as a teenager, even if they weren't real. Maybe I thought I would get some closure out of it, I don't know. Plus, it's Ian. He needed my help too. There was no way I was going to say no."

"So when did things change?"

"I don't know if I can pinpoint the exact moment, not for him, anyway—" I cock my head, realizing something. "Have you said anything to Ian?"

"Yeah," he scoffs. "Fucker told me he wasn't telling me anything until I talked to you first." I can't help but grin, and Jack rolls his eyes. "Fuck off. I can't deal with the cutesy shit right now."

"Are you really mad?"

"I'm not . . . mad. Not about the two of you, at least. I mean, it's weird as hell, and it feels like my brother has been running around with my sister doing"—he shudders—"shit I don't ever want to know about, but I am a little hurt that neither of you thought you could tell me."

"Don't blame Ian," I say immediately. "He left it up to me to tell you."

"Of course he did," Jack grumbles. "Noble bastard."

"He would never intentionally do anything to hurt you," I assure him. "He loves you, Jack."

"Not as much as he loves you, apparently," Jack mutters petulantly.

The implication of that sentence makes my chest swell, but I brush it off for the moment.

"Wow, did I steal your boyfriend?"

"Actually, I changed my mind. I'm totally mad. I forbid you from dating."

I cock an eyebrow. "You really think you can forbid me from doing anything?"

"No," he sighs. "But it felt good to say."

"I'm really sorry that we didn't tell you sooner," I say, meaning it.

"Yeah, yeah. I get it. I guess. Maybe." He runs his fingers through his hair, glancing at me. "Is this . . . Is this like a real thing? Or some kind of fling?"

"It's real," I answer with full confidence. "I . . . I love him, Jack."

His brows shoot up. "Does he know that?"

"I haven't explicitly told him . . . but I plan to. Soon."

"This is so weird," he mutters.

"But he's better than Etienne, right?"

"The rat from Ratatouille would be better than Etienne," he huffs. "Like, straight up, hiding under your chef hat better."

I bark out a laugh. "Of all the French references that you could have used, that's what you come up with?"

"I have a condition," he says primly. "Don't make fun of my broken brain."

I roll my eyes. "It's not broken. It's wonderful."

"Don't try to butter me up."

I lean in close, pressing a kiss to his cheek. "I love you, too, you know."

"Yeah, yeah. I know. I love you, too, Dee." He wraps his good arm around me, squeezing my shoulders, making a disgruntled sound that puffs against my hair. "I'm going to need at least six months before I'm subjected to the two of you kissing in front of me."

"Two weeks," I counter.

"Three months."

"One month."

"Deal," he grouses.

"Don't be too hard on Ian," I urge, tilting my chin up to look at him. "You know he would never hurt you."

"I know," he sighs. "He's such a good friend. The dick."

"Speaking of—"

"Not on your life," Jack says, shoving me away. "As far as I'm concerned, you are both celibate and happier for it."

I laugh as I try to hug him again, fighting against his one-armed shoves to fight me off. We wrestle on the couch for a minute more—him poking me in the side and me trying to lick his cheek while he shouts about how gross I am—only settling when the sudden and constant pinging in his pocket finally has me pulling away with curiosity.

"Is someone trying to hunt you down or something?"

He shakes his head, fishing out his phone with his good hand and swiping it awake. His frown is immediate, and it's much more dour-looking than the one he wore when he was just here to gripe at me for keeping my relationship with Ian from him. The one he wears now makes my stomach twist.

"What is it?"

"Google alert," he says in a clipped tone, scrolling furiously as he skims whatever he sees there. "Fuck."

He shows me the screen, and one look at the headline has my heart thudding violently in my chest, and I'm already scrambling off the couch. "Where is he?"

"Home," Jack answers. "Should we—?"

But I'm already out the door, not bothering to say goodbye to anyone as the singular focus that drives me carries my feet one after the other. Only one thought in my mind dominating my every step.

Get to Ian.

Twenty-Four

IAN

LEGACY HOCKEY STAR BRADLEY CHASE'S SECRET
LOVE CHILD

THE CHASE DYNASTY CRUMBLES: DRUIDS OWNER
TELL-ALL

IAN CHASE HELPED KEEP HIS FATHER'S DIRTY
SECRETS FOR YEARS

WHO IS ABIGAIL THOMPSON?

MEI, ABIGAIL, AND DELILAH—THE TANGLED WEB OF
WOMEN IN IAN CHASE'S LIFE

It's the last one that puts me the most on edge, strangely. The other explosion of headlines I had the misfortune of stumbling across while thumbing through the photos of Lila and me kissing for the dozenth time are upsetting, sure, but it's the one that throws Lila into the mix that truly has my stomach twisting.

There are texts from her on my phone, her and Jack, so I know she's on her way here, but I have no idea what I'm going to say to her. What I'm going to see on her face when she gets here. Will there be disappointment? Exhaustion? Will I see that it's too much for her? Everything that's happening feels so reminiscent of years ago, and given that the *last* time my personal life was aired for the world to see led to me leaving the fucking country, I can't help but feel terrified at what this will mean for me. More important, what it will mean for me and Lila.

And could I even blame her if she wanted to put the brakes on things? She didn't sign up for this. She didn't *ask* for all the baggage that comes with being close to me. Already the media is speculating, tearing into her for just the crime of *maybe* being in a relationship with me, and it makes me sick, reading the things people are saying about her. Knowing it's *my* fault that they're saying them at all. They call her naive, they pity her for having to deal with my "lies"—hell, some have even speculated that she knew all along, and that somehow makes her just as tangled in the web of my father's twisted legacy as I am.

I fucking hate it.

I've been sitting here trying to formulate some sort of plan, even trying to discern how in the hell the media might have gotten wind of this after so long—coming up with nothing on both fronts. The only people I've told the intimate details of the entire truth to are Mei, Jack, and now Lila, and I trust each of them implicitly. I can only assume that somewhere, somehow, my father finally fucked up. That's the most satisfying option, anyway.

Speaking of the dick in question, there are several texts waiting for me from him as well. I've yet to answer any of them, mainly because I don't yet know what I want to say.

DAD: If you had something to do with this there will be consequences.

DAD: Who have you told?

DAD: If reporters come calling, say nothing.

DAD: I highly suggest you call me as soon as possible.

I drop my phone onto the couch, scrubbing a hand down my face. I feel the weight of his anger even from this far away. I don't know what it is about the man that reduces me to a child again, begging for his approval, but it's enough to have my stomach twisting into knots. Like suddenly I'm ten again and he's berating my form, telling me all the ways I could do better, *be better*—not that anything has really changed there.

And my *mom*. What the fuck am I going to say to my mother? I called her immediately after I saw the first article, and I've tried twice more since—but she isn't answering. Which only makes me feel worse. Is she disappointed in me? Does she hate me now? Do I deserve it?

I've spent so many years living my life trying to avoid this very thing to protect the people around me, and now it's out there, and it feels like every decision I've made in the wake of my nearly ruined reputation has all been for naught. What was the point of losing six years away from my best friend, my team, only to have it all come out, anyway? Now I'm here, at the end of my career, and everything feels as if it's all been for nothing.

Well, not everything.

The thought of Lila is my one bright spot in the dreariness of my own head, marred only by the niggling worry that this will somehow be a wake-up call for her. That she will see the shit show that is my life and decide it's not worth it, that *I'm* not worth it. Knowing the depths of my feelings for her, the thought is a terrifying one. It would have always hurt to lose Lila entirely, even in the years we grew apart, but now . . . Now it would be devastating.

I feel my heart pound in my chest—faster and faster until its racing rattles the cage of my ribs and thrums in my throat and my ears as panic starts to grip me, because what if she *does* leave? What will I do now that I know what it is to touch her, to hold her against me, to *know* her in ways that only come from love, just to lose her? I press my hand to my heart as if this will somehow soothe the thudding, my breaths coming out shorter and shorter as everything comes crashing down on me all at once as echoes of my father's words over the years ring in my ears.

Straighten up, Ian.

Honestly, you can do better than that.

Don't embarrass me, Ian.

Clearly, I was wrong to expect more from you.

You just love disappointing me, don't you?

It would be better for everyone if you just left.

I double over, letting my head drop between my knees as I try to suck in lungfuls of air that feel like they won't come, my vision blurring as an iron vise squeezes my chest until there's no room left, until the bones feel like they're breaking. There's a roaring in my ears, and beyond that there are other sounds I can't make out, a pounding that I can't discern whether it comes from the room or my own head—but then there is the distinct jingle of keys in the door, and quick steps across the carpet, and then hands on my shoulders, my chest, soothing me, pulling me in close as a soft, warm voice surrounds me.

"Hey," Lila says—because it's her, she's *here*. "I've got you. Shh. It's okay."

I throw my arms out and wrap her up in them, fisting her shirt to prove to myself that she's really here. It still feels a little like I can't breathe, but her distinct sweet scent and her soft embrace make the world feel a bit steadier, make *me* feel steadier.

"You're having a panic attack," she coos gently. "Just breathe, Ian. Breathe with me."

I close my eyes and bury my face against her throat, matching the rhythm of my breaths with hers and trying to focus on the steady *in* and *out* of air filling her lungs and mine. I don't know how long she holds me like that, or what all it is that she murmurs directly into my ear as she strokes my back, but at some point, sounds bleed back in, and things feel less like they're crashing down on me, and suddenly I can breathe again, can *see* again— and all I see is her.

"Lila?"

She cups my face in her hands, worry etched in her features. "I'm here. Are you okay?"

"I—" I swallow, my tongue feeling like sandpaper. "I think so."

"Oh, baby," she says in a broken voice, like she's on the verge of tears. For *me*. "I'm so sorry. So, so sorry. Do you know how this happened?"

"No, Lila," I choke out. "*I'm* sorry. I'm so sorry."

"Why?" Her brow furrows. "You have nothing to apologize for."

"Have you seen what they're saying?"

"I've seen enough," she says with disdain.

"Then you know what they're saying about you. I didn't mean to drag you into this. I would have *never*—"

"Ian."

"I understand if you need a break from this, from us, but—"

"Ian."

"I'll tell them the truth. I'll make sure they know this is all on me. I'll—"

"*Ian.*"

As her palm cradles my chin she actually *pinches* my cheeks, holding them between her fingers until my mouth puckers so that I physically can't say anything else. She looks irritated, which only makes me more anxious. Her hand relaxes against my jaw, her eyes contemplative.

"Do you know the moment I realized you had ruined all other boys for me?"

"I . . . What?"

"It was a random Wednesday. I was fourteen, and you and Jack were throwing that huge graduation party while Aunt Bea was visiting her mother."

"I remember," I say curiously.

"I was supposed to be in bed, but there was too much going on. The music and the lights and the laughter . . . I hung out in the hall outside my room just listening to it all for hours."

My mouth opens only to close, that night coming back to me hazily. "You said you had just woken up."

"Yeah, well, I lied," she laughs. "You had just come stomping down the hall all arms and legs, looking for the bathroom and almost tripped over me. What else was I supposed to say?" She smiles; it's slow, and sweet, just like her, and the knot of anxiety in my chest loosens a bit. "Do you remember what you did?"

"I made your ass go to bed," I scoff.

Her lips tilt up higher as she beams back at me. "That was after. You don't remember what happened before that?"

I frown, trying to recall, but in all honesty, there was a lot of beer our friend Paul had stolen from his dad's fridge involved that night.

"I told you I wanted to come to the party," she says, helping me out. "And you told me that was absolutely not happening, that I was too young."

"Okay?"

"So I did what I always do, I pouted, telling you I wanted to dance with everyone else, and that I wasn't going to bed until I got to dance to one song."

Sparks of memory tickle at the back of my brain, my mouth parting. "I danced with you."

"Right on top of your feet," she laughs. "It was awkward, and I have no idea how you even stood up for it since I'm pretty sure looking back you were hammered, but . . . God, Ian. I went to bed that night wishing I was just a little older, that there weren't so many years between us, because I was afraid I would never feel the way I did standing on top of your big-ass feet dancing to a bad pop song."

"Lila . . ."

Her thumb brushes across my cheek, and she leans in close, feathering her lips against mine. "And I haven't. Not once. I've never felt that way since. Not until you. Not until you saw me."

"Fuck, Lila." My voice cracks, emotion choking me. "What if I ruin everything for you?"

"Not going to happen," she asserts.

"How can you be so sure?"

"I'm not," she says easily. "I told you before that I know now that I can't be sure of anything, remember? But I *know* what's worth holding on to. You are. Nothing is going to change that for me. Do you know why?"

I shake my head, my heart thudding wildly in my chest again but for an entirely different reason. "Why?"

"Because I love you," she says softly, the words quiet and yet the feeling they invoke so loud that it has my ears ringing.

"You do?"

She looks so sure, so utterly at peace with this revelation that the stunned way it leaves me feels almost ridiculous. She nods, pressing another gentle kiss on my mouth as she breathes against my lips, "Completely sure."

"I—me too. I mean, I love you too. Fuck, Lila." I cradle her face, pulling her in to cover her mouth with mine, murmuring between frantic kisses as relief bubbles up inside and spills over. "The way you make me feel . . ." I shake my head, laughing under my breath. "It's like I spent my entire life blind until you walked back into it, and I finally *saw* you."

Her arms are around my neck, and her smile matches mine, and her kisses are seeking, joyous—they're a confirmation that everything that comes after this is just details, because this, this thing between us, that's what really matters. I pull her closer, so close that she's practically molded to my chest. I palm her head so that I can deepen the kiss, sweeping my tongue through her mouth as a happy sigh escapes her throat. I could do this for hours. I *want* to do this for hours. I pull her tighter, I kiss her *harder*, I—

"If I knew I was going to be accosted in my own home," Jack

grumbles, "I would not have given you the spare key to run off and fornicate on my couch."

Lila grins, pulling away from me, but just barely. "Do you hear something?"

"Hm. I don't think so."

"Oh, fuck you both very much," he huffs. I can hear him muttering as he toes off his shoes. "Fucking weird is what it is."

"Hi, honey," I call, finally untangling myself from his sister. I mean, it's probably the right thing to do. He hasn't tried to kick my ass yet, after all. "How was your day?"

"Don't you start with me, jackass," he scoffs. "The only reason I'm not crushing your thick-ass skull with my cast is because you have bigger problems at the moment."

"Not because you love me?"

"That's debatable right now." Jack points at Lila. "And you! We agreed one month before I was subjected to kissing."

"It isn't my fault you walked in on us," she laughs.

"Right," he snorts. "Heaven forbid I walk into my own apartment and not expect to see my brother tonguing my sister."

I make a face. "Please don't say it like that ever again."

"Oh?" Jack looks vindicated. "And why should you be comfortable?"

"We could go to your room," Lila whispers.

"I heard that!" Jack stomps over to the chair across from the couch, plopping down into it. "No one is sneaking off to do things I want to know nothing of until we talk about this. There are fucking reporters outside the building, did you know?"

"I saw them on the way in," Lila says with a wince.

"Fuck," I sigh. "What a shit show."

"Do we have any idea who leaked this?" Jack asks.

I shake my head. "No clue."

"Are we sure it wasn't your dad? Maybe he's hungry for some attention."

"Considering he's been sending me threatening text messages about keeping my mouth shut," I say, "I don't think it's him."

Lila bristles. "He has?"

"I didn't answer," I tell her.

She seethes, anyway. "That motherfucker. I should drive down there and kick his ass."

"Down, girl," I laugh, kissing her temple. "Let's not give the press any more fodder."

"But I mean," Jack goes on, in full detective mode as he taps his chin thoughtfully. "Who else even knows? Did you guys have a maid I don't know about?"

"No, we didn't—"

"Oh!" Jack barrels on. "Could it have been *another* jilted lover of your dad's maybe? Maybe she got jealous. Or maybe he's been paying her off, and he threatened to stop." Jack gasps, snapping his fingers. "Maybe there's *another* love child!"

"I don't think there are any more," I say, hoping I'm right.

"I don't know," Jack continues, still thinking. "My money is still on your dad. He's just the type to pull this shady shit. Maybe he made a deal with someone in the press for the story. Or *maybe*—"

"It wasn't him."

We all turn toward the quiet voice in the doorway, Jack frowning at the woman standing there, her gray eyes locked on mine and shining with guilt as she takes off her large sunglasses and pulls back the deep hood of her jacket—no doubt the reasons that helped her sneak by the horde of reporters outside.

I sit up straighter. "Abby?"

"How did you get in here?" Jack says.

She points back at the door. "This was open."

"That tracks," Lila mutters.

I'm standing now, taking a step closer to my sister, who is still looking at me warily. "What do you mean it wasn't him?"

"Because . . ." She bites her bottom lip, her eyes wide and searching and making her look so much younger than she actually is. "Because it was me," she says finally.

Everything is silent for a handful of seconds, and then:

"Oh shit," Jack whispers. "Plot twist."

Twenty-Five

DELILAH

Abby's admission is surprising, and not only just to me, if the look on Ian's face is any indication. His brows shoot up and his mouth parts, his eyes searching her face as Abby continues to stand there, seeming to almost wither under his scrutiny.

"You told them?"

Abby sighs as she turns and shuts the door, running her fingers through her long, strawberry blond hair as her eyes stay glued on her worn Converses. "I know I should have talked to you first."

"You're damned right you should have," Ian bites out. Ian is so rarely angry—at least that I've seen—that this new side of him throws me a little. "Do you have any idea what you've done? The problems this will cause for everyone? It's not just you who will be affected here. You get that, right?"

Abby nods glumly, trudging across the room and sinking into one of the lounge chairs opposite Jack. She seems so small like this, even being several inches taller than me, her willowy frame hunched over and her hands wringing in her lap. My heart goes out to her, and a strong urge to give her a hug overtakes me, but I know it isn't my place right now. That I have to let them figure this out on their own.

"I do," she says quietly. "And I tried to talk to you about it. I called you not long ago, remember? I told you how I was feeling."

Ian stomps across the room, dropping down beside me on the couch. His posture is tense, and I keep my hands tucked in my lap for the moment. "You never said you were thinking about going to the *press*."

"I wanted to tell you," Abby urges. "I was working up to it, but then you had to go, and you didn't call me back, and I . . ." She bites her lip, peeking up at Ian with weary eyes. "I'm sorry."

"Sorry can't take things back," Ian huffs. "Sorry won't stop the shitstorm that this is going to make for me and my mother. I know you don't know her, Abby, but you realize you just hurt her, too, don't you?"

"I know," she says. "I know that. But you don't know what it's like. You have no idea what it's like to be *everyone's* dirty secret. I have no one left, Ian. No one but you and Dad. You two are the only family I have, and the both of you have spent the entire time that I've known you wishing I didn't exist."

"That's—" Ian's mouth snaps shut, his eyes hard for a moment before softening slightly. I can see it, the minute that *my* Ian comes back to the moment—the kind protector I know him to be overriding his anger as his shoulders slump. "I didn't want you to feel that way."

"I know you didn't," Abby assures him. "You've done the best you can with me. I know you didn't ask for any of this, but you've always done your best."

"I just don't understand why you felt like this was your only option," Ian sighs.

Abby levels him with a hard stare, her gray eyes, which are so similar to Ian's, holding his. "And if I had told you what I wanted to do, what would you have said? Honestly? Would you have supported me?"

"I . . ." Ian shakes his head, looking down at his hands clenching his knees. I can't help but reach out, covering one with mine and squeezing it just to let him know I'm here in whatever way he needs me to be. He gives my fingers a gentle squeeze back, expelling a breath. "I don't know. I want to say that I would, but like I said, we're not the only ones affected by this."

"I know you wanted to protect your mom," Abby tells him, "and I'm sorry that I've ruined that, but the truth is, if I hadn't done this, I would have been a secret my entire life. I can't do it anymore. Even if it makes you hate me. I—I love you, Ian. I know that's probably weird for you, because you didn't ask for a sister, and I never wanted to let you down, but I've just been *drowning* in this secret, and I—"

Ian is off the couch and crossing the room before any of us can blink, and Abby lets out a soft *oomph* as he tugs her up from the chair and wraps his arms around her. My chest squeezes at the sight. I hear a soft sniffle from the slight woman in his arms, and then her hands reach to tentatively clasp at his sides.

"I don't hate you," Ian says quietly. "I could never hate you, Abby. Regardless of how we came into each other's lives, you're my sister." He pulls back, peering down at her. "And it wasn't *just* my mother I wanted to protect—it was you too."

Abby looks confused. "Me?"

"I know you still want things from our father that I've long since learned he can't give," Ian says gently. "I wanted to protect you from this image you had of him. I wanted to hope that he could be the person you wanted him to be. Eventually."

Abby's face crumples, her lip quivering as her eyes fill with tears. "But he won't," she whispers. "Will he? He doesn't want me."

"Sweetheart," Ian chokes. He draws her in close, squeezing her tight. I can feel my own eyes prickling, the emotion between these two siblings, the weight of everything they've suffered banding them together like this making me eternally grateful for having Jack all these years. Even when he was a complete dumbass, he's always been there for me. It's so gratifying to see Ian finally have a chance to be that for Abby. "I wish he could be," Ian says thickly. "I wish you could have that. I really do. You've suffered so much. You're twenty-five years old, and you've lived more life than most of us. It's not fair. It really isn't. I should have been there for you more. I was so busy waiting for our father to step up that I never even tried to do it myself."

"No," Abby argues, shaking her head against his chest. "It's not your—"

"But it is," Ian shushes her. "It's just as much my fault as it is his. I can sit here and blame you for what you did, but I'm just as complicit. I kept the secret right along with him. I did what he told me to do because I thought it was better for everyone, but lies never solve anything. Lying to save someone from pain only delays it. Eventually, that hurt always comes back around, and the longer you put it off, the more power it has."

"I'm sorry," Abby cries. "I'm so sorry, Ian."

"Shh." He strokes her back, and I can feel my own eyes

watering as I watch them. "Stop. I may not understand the way you went about this, but I understand why you needed to do it. It's something you never should have had to do in the first place."

"He's going to hate me now," Abby whimpers.

Ian presses his cheek to her hair. "No matter what happens, I'll be here. You have me. I won't ever abandon you. Okay?"

"Okay," she rasps, clutching him tight. "I'm sorry."

"Stop." Ian closes his eyes, blowing out a breath. "We both have things to be sorry for, but instead of dwelling on them, let's just try to be better, yeah?"

"Don't be sorry, be better?" Abby says with a watery laugh.

Ian smiles. "Put that on a T-shirt."

"Fuck me," Jack says finally, and honestly, I'm surprised he was able to keep quiet for so long. I love him, but subtle, he is not. "That was beautiful. Do we have tissues? I might need some therapy after watching that."

Abby lifts her head to give Jack a puzzled look.

"Ignore him, Abby," I tell her, shooting my brother a glare. "He can't help himself."

Jack pouts. "What did I do?"

"Sorry," Abby says again, wiping her eyes as she looks around the room sheepishly. "None of you signed up for this shit today."

"You're fine," Jack tells her, waving her off. "Our parents are totally dead. We get it."

I throw a pillow at him. "Jack!"

"What?" He ducks out of the way, looking genuinely confused by my outburst, which, of course he does. "I was commiserating!"

Abby is still gawking at my brother like he's from another planet, and honestly, I get it.

I'm just about to tell my brother off again when his pocket

starts going crazy, and he lifts his hips to dig for his phone with his good hand, frowning at the screen. He winces, peeking over at Ian. "It's Coach."

"Fuck," Ian huffs, untangling himself from his sister and running his hand through his hair. "He tried to call me earlier."

"Going to have to face the music sometime," Jack points out.

Ian nods. "I might as well get over there and explain."

"I can come with you," Jack says, shooting up from the couch. "I'm an excellent wingman."

"This isn't a wingman situation," Ian says.

Jack scoffs. "Sure it isn't, Goose."

Ian rolls his eyes before giving his attention back to Abby. "I want you to stay here. Don't leave the apartment until we get back. We're going to figure this out together, okay?"

"Okay," Abby says with a nod.

Ian turns toward me. "Can you . . . ?"

"I'll stay with her," I say without letting him finish. "You don't even have to ask."

Ian's smile is small but still enough to make my heart clench, and he crosses the space between us easily before leaning down to brush his lips against mine. "Thank you."

"So much for a fucking month," Jack mutters from a few feet away.

I ignore him, stepping closer and returning Ian's soft kiss. "I love you."

"I love you too," he answers, his lips curling into a full-blown grin against my mouth.

I smack his ass, continuing to ignore Jack as he groans. "Go get 'em, Cupcake."

Abby is staring at us when we break apart, her head cocked

with curiosity but keeping quiet. Jack shakes his head, glancing at Abby. "Yeah," Jack huffs. "It's a whole gross thing."

"Don't be jealous, babe," Ian calls, moving toward him. "I can give you kisses, too, if it helps."

"Get the fuck out of my apartment before I bash your knees in," Jack grumbles.

Ian chuckles, bending to fish his phone out of the couch cushions where it's fallen. He looks between Abby and me once more after he gets his keys from the bowl on the thin table in the entryway, and Jack steps behind him as they head for the door.

"You two will be okay?"

I peek over at Abby, who watches me nervously. I nod for us both. "We'll be fine. Go."

He shoots me another smile before they both head out, leaving me alone with Ian's little sister, who I haven't met before, watching her having an emotional breakdown only moments earlier. I can totally get why she's looking at me like she wants to bolt.

"Well," I say, "do you want food or sleep?"

Abby's brow wrinkles. "What?"

"When I'm having a bad day, naps and snacks always help. So which would you rather have first?"

"I . . ." She eyes me incredulously, but I just keep the pasted smile on my face, waiting for her answer. She looks shy when she admits, "I am kind of tired."

"Right." I nod, wrapping my arm around her—which is kind of hard, given that she's at least four inches taller than me. "Let's put you to bed, and I'll do what I do best when I'm stressed, which is bake. When you wake up, we'll get to the snacks."

Her eyes stay glued to the floor as I practically march her

toward Ian's bedroom, but after I tuck her behind the door, she utters a quiet, "Thank you, um . . . ?"

"Delilah," I tell her. "But most people call me Dee, except your brother. He calls me Lila."

"Lila," she says without hesitation, a small smile on her face that reminds me so much of her brother that it momentarily takes me by surprise. "Thank you."

I can see her sadness and her vulnerability coming off her in waves, and I decide right then that she and I are going to be friends. That neither of the Chase siblings are ever going to be sad on my watch.

"You're welcome," I tell her. I point to Ian's bed. "Now nap. That's an order."

She's still smiling softly when I leave her, and despite all the revelations that we've endured today, I feel . . . hopeful.

It has *me* smiling as I start riffling through Jack and Ian's cabinets.

— — — —

"So how did he take it?"

I have my cell propped between my shoulder and ear as I check the oven, the smell of baking dough permeating the kitchen as I decide to give the cookies another minute.

Jack makes a noncommittal sound. "I mean, there was some yelling, but from what I gathered pressing my ear to the door—"

"Wow, talk about professional boundaries," I snort.

"I don't think Coach was really mad *at* Ian but more *for* Ian."

"I mean, he's always been a bit of a closet softy," I point out.

Jack scoffs. "Tell that to my hips after a day of drills."

"That sounded entirely too sexual to be in reference to your coach."

Jack snickers. "Coach wouldn't know what to do with me."

"I don't think a retired porn star with a psych degree they got for shits and gigs would know what to do with you," I say, clucking my tongue.

"I choose to take that as a compliment," he says primly.

"You would." I check the cookies again, finally determining that they're done and pulling them out with an oven mitt to set the pan on the oven so they can cool. "So when are you guys coming back?"

"Soon," Jack tells me. "I think they're finishing up now. How is Abby?"

"She's been napping," I say. "I put her down an hour ago after you left. She looked like she needed it."

"You 'put her down'? She's not a toddler."

"Neither are you, but you're still a nightmare to deal with when you're tired."

"Yeah, yeah. She going to be okay, you think?"

"I think so," I say, only half-sure, really. "Maybe. I don't know. She's been through a lot."

"Yeah, but she's got us," he muses.

"Oh?" I lean against the counter. "Does she?"

"I mean, Ian is my brother, and he's now in some gross incestuous relationship with you—"

"Yeah, still not accurate."

"So I figure we can confidently assume that we're going to adopt the baby Chase sibling."

"She's twenty-five," I chuckle. "Hardly a baby."

"I know that. She's kind of hot in an Ian way."

"In an Ian way?"

"She looks a lot like him. Kind of weird. Confusing to my libido."

"You are so strange."

"You love me."

"For some reason."

"Hey, I think Ian's coming. We'll be back soon, okay? Hold down the fort."

"We'll be here," I tell him.

I set my phone on the counter, digging into a bag of sugar I pulled out from underneath the cabinet and sprinkling a bit on top of the cooling cookies to give them an extra kick of sweetness. I learned very early on that a little sugar can sweeten any bad times you're experiencing, and I figure Abby and Ian could use it.

"Those look good."

I jolt, dusting sugar all over the oven. "Abby!"

"Sorry!" She holds up her hands in apology, looking contrite. "I thought you heard me."

"It's fine," I say with a quiet laugh. "Did you sleep well?"

"Mostly. I do feel better after the nap."

"Told you," I tell her smugly. I point to the cookies. "And I'm just finishing up the snack portion of today's therapy session."

"They smell incredible," she admits, eyeing the cookies. "I watch your show, you know."

"You do?"

"Well, I mean . . . I started after Ian was on."

My lips curl. "That's sweet. He looked like the Hulk trying to handle teacups up there, didn't he?"

"Kind of," she laughs. "But it was fun to watch."

There's a fond look on her face, and I think it's safe to say that

Abby admires her brother more than she lets on. Not that I blame her. I pick up a still-warm cookie, testing that it's cooled enough that it won't fall apart before handing it to her.

"Here," I say.

She takes it gingerly, biting into it and moaning as her eyes close. "Holy shit."

"Yeah?"

"This is amazing."

"It's the touch of cinnamon."

"I can totally taste it."

I take a cookie for myself, moving to one of the chairs at the overhanging counter and taking a seat before patting the one next to me. Abby settles into it, taking another large bite of her cookie as a look of bliss spreads across her face.

"You look just like your brother," I laugh.

She peeks over at me sheepishly. "Really?"

"He also inhales my cookies like a starved coyote."

Her freckled cheeks tint in a blush, and she bites back her grin. "They're really good."

"I take it as the highest compliment."

"So . . . you two are dating?"

I consider this as I take another bite. "I guess so. I mean, we sort of just now put a label on it."

"Like recently?"

"Like last night," I laugh.

"Oh."

"But we've been . . . something for weeks now."

"I'm glad," she comments softly. She cuts her eyes to me. "That he has you. He deserves that."

"He has you too," I remind her. "He cares about you a lot. I know we don't know each other, and he only recently told me the entire truth of everything that's happened between you, but I can tell by the way he talks about you that he really cares."

"That's . . . good." She stares at the counter, her cookie forgotten in her hand for a moment. "I've always felt like I'm just a burden to him." She blinks then, shaking her head. "I don't know why I told you that."

"It's the cookie," I tease. "They're truth cookies."

"Must be," she mutters, taking another bite.

"You're not, you know," I say. "A burden to him."

"How can you know that for sure?"

"Because Ian doesn't think of people like that," I say confidently. "Not when he cares for them. He's just not that kind of person. He's always putting others before himself. It's just second nature for him to make sure everyone he loves is okay before he does the same thing for himself."

"I don't know if that makes me feel better or worse."

"It just is what it is," I say with a shrug, popping the last of the cookie into my mouth. "Ian's always been a safety net for people. Once you fall into it, he's gonna make sure to do his damnedest to hold you up safe and sound for as long as he's able."

"I've always wished we were closer," she sighs.

"Then why don't you tell him that? I know he would love to be."

"You can't know that," she mumbles bitterly. "I'm a mistake. Just some kid his dad had when he cheated on Ian's mom."

"You're his family," I say firmly. "I know we don't know each other well, but I can tell you that you're not a mistake. Not for Ian. If he says he loves you, then he loves you. If he says he wants to protect you, then that's what he really wants. Ian is . . ." I know my smile is dopey, but I can't help it. "Ian really is just that selfless. It would hurt him more for you to pull away."

"You really think so?"

I take a chance, reaching out to squeeze her shoulder. "I know it."

"I . . . Thank you. That makes me feel a little better."

"Plus, it's not just Ian. If you're important to him, then you're important to me. Same goes for my idiot brother, but I would totally understand if you don't want to capitalize on that one."

"Is he always . . . ?"

"Unhinged? Yes. But it grows on you."

A genuine smile touches her lips, maybe the first full one I've seen since meeting her. "Thank you, Lila. I can't tell you what that means to me."

"I know exactly what it feels like to think you're alone in this world, Abby, I really do, so trust me when I say that you are *not* alone." I squeeze her shoulder again. "We're all here for you."

Her eyes glisten, and her throat works subtly, but she just nods, popping the last of her cookie in her mouth in lieu of answering. "Fucking truth cookies."

"They're the worst," I laugh.

"They really aren't."

"Yeah," I sigh, taking my last bite. "I know."

Abby opens her mouth to say something, but a sudden pounding at the door has both of us jolting in our seats, heads twisting toward the sound.

Abby's brow knits. "Ian?"

"They have a key . . ." Another loud banging ensues. "Why would they . . . ?"

"Open the fucking door!" A sharp, angry voice calls. "I know you're in there."

Abby's eyes, full of panic, go wide, meeting mine. "It's my dad."

"How the fuck did he even get up here?"

"He has his ways," Abby mutters. "There isn't a string that exists that my dad can't pull. Doesn't help that people in this city treat him like he's the mayor or something."

My body goes on high alert. "I can ignore him. We don't have to let him in. We can wait for Jack and Ian."

Almost as if he can hear us, Bradley yells, "Ian! I'm not leaving!"

"No," Abby says, drawing in an unsteady breath. "Let him in. He's just going to draw more attention to us if he keeps yelling like that."

"Are you sure?"

She's already sliding off her chair. "I'm sure."

"Stay there."

I push past her, determined not to let Bradley Chase cause any more grief for the Chase siblings if I can help it. I steel all five foot four of myself before reaching for the handle, turning it, and pulling the door wide to reveal one angry, elder Chase.

"I want to talk to my son," he says curtly. "Get him."

"I'm failing to hear the request in there," I say coolly.

His eyes narrow. "I'm not here to play games with you, little girl."

"Never been very good at games," I say sweetly.

He pushes past me then, ignoring my sound of protest as he rushes into the apartment. His eyes scan the space quickly, settling on Abby, who is still frozen in the kitchen and pausing as confusion colors his features.

"Abigail?"

"Hi, Dad," she says meekly.

"What are you doing here? Where is Ian?" His eyes narrow yet again. "Did the two of you *conspire* to do this? Is this some sort of ploy to get more money? Because, I swear to God, I will fucking ruin the both of you."

Abby's face goes white, her skin paling so much that her freckles look starker, more noticeable. The entire effect makes her seem smaller, younger even. Her nonanswer seems to be enough for Bradley to come to his own conclusions, and his face purples with rage.

"Dad, I just—"

Bradley makes a disgusted sound. "I should have known. Haven't I done everything for you? Who pays for that fancy grad school? What, that wasn't enough for you?"

"I never wanted to—"

"Wanted to what?" He stomps toward her, shaking a finger at her. "You never wanted to be a total fucking disappointment? I thought *maybe* one of my children could do what they're fucking told, but you're both just complete wastes of time, aren't you? I don't even know why I bother. Your brother might be a fuckup, but I thought I could at least count on you to keep your mouth shut, considering you'd have nothing without me."

I can't take it anymore. I leave the door ajar as I rush across the room, ignoring the fact that Bradley might as well be twice my size as I give him a hard shove in the side to put myself between him and Abby.

"Leave her alone," I seethe. "You think you're some kind of big man coming in here and making threats? Throwing your weight around like we're supposed to be scared of some bitter old man who cares more about some dumbass legacy than his own children? News flash, Mr. Chase, your son is twice the man you ever were or could ever hope to be, and I barely even know your daughter but can confidently say that she deserves better than the likes of you for a father."

Bradley takes a menacing step, the vein at his temple throbbing as he sneers. "Who the fuck do you think you are? You think because you're fucking my son that you're important? You're nothing. Just some two-bit cake maker with a cable show no one cares about. Who the *fuck* cares what you think?"

A flash of movement in the open door behind us catches my eye, but before I can even register it fully—hands grasp the sleeve of Bradley's shirt, shoving him away as Ian's broad body slams into his, his normally happy face teeming with unchecked anger as he practically spits at his father:

"*I do.*"

Twenty-Six

IAN

The rage I feel at seeing my father crowd Lila as she shouts in his face in my defense is a living, breathing thing. It thumps in my ears and my blood and all through my body, so much so that not even the flicker of love that sparks from Lila taking him on for me can quell it. I barely register the moment in the time that it takes for me to rush my father, but suddenly his shirt is fisted in my grip and his body is up against a wall as I bump him with my chest.

"*I do.*"

He blinks at me, momentarily stunned, but he recovers quickly, his anger superseding any surprise I might have given him.

"Get off me, boy."

I fist his shirt tighter. "Apologize."

"Like hell I will," he snorts. "I don't give a damn about your flavor of the month. I care about the fucking mess you two have made. I *know* it was one of you." His eyes flick over my shoulder toward Abby. "Or both. If you think that *either* of you will squeeze another dime out of me after this, then you've got another thing—"

"I never wanted your money!"

I turn my head toward a heaving, red-faced Abby, her eyes wet and her fists shaking as she stares at our father. Her chest rises and falls with shaky breaths, her lip quivering as she goes on.

"It was never about your money," she says in that same exasperated tone. "I just wanted you to notice me. I just wanted you to be my fucking *dad*."

My father surprises me by laughing, the sound harsh and cruel. "You did this? Just you? Wow. I have to admit, I didn't think you had the balls. Do you even realize what you've done? You not only fucked with me, but with Ian too. Was it your goal to alienate *everyone* you had with this little stunt?"

Tears run down Abby's face now, and her crushed expression as she finally lets herself realize *exactly* who Bradley Chase is crushes me in turn. My chest squeezes as I watch Lila go to Abby's side, her hand curling around Abby's, and I'm so in love with Lila at this moment that it hurts.

"Why couldn't you love me? What did I ever do to you, Dad? You treat me like I'm just a—"

"Mistake?"

The cold tone my father uses to spit the word is gutting, and I hear Abby's sharp intake of breath.

"I treat you like one because that's what you are, Abigail. I didn't need the headache that came from being in your life when your mother was alive, and that's exactly what I told her when she let me know you existed. If she hadn't gone and made herself a nuisance one last time by up and dying, then I wouldn't be dealing with the full weight of my *mistake* right now."

I shove my forearm into my father's chest, gritting my teeth. "Watch your fucking mouth. You don't fucking talk to her like that. What is *wrong* with you? Abby isn't the mistake, *you* are. *You're* the one who made your choices, *Dad*," I sneer. "*You* cheated on my mother. *You* brought Abby into the world. *You* treated me like a fucking pawn to push around for the sake of your image my entire life. *You* turned your nose up at a chance for a relationship with the only child you have left who had any respect for you."

"I *made* you," my father seethes. "Without me, you'd be nothing."

"You didn't do shit for me," I bite back, shoving him harder. "You gave me hockey, and that's it. What I did with it was *me*. Just me. I don't owe you anything. You weren't there for me the entire time I was growing up unless it was beneficial to you, and now I don't have any reason to put up with you at all. Now that there are no more secrets, I can happily tell you that we are done."

"You're just going to stand there and take her side? She hurt your mother, you know. She's already kicked me out of the house. We were happy, and Abigail took that away from her. Are you really just going to let that go? Some fucking son you are."

"Abigail didn't do anything but quit accepting a life living under your thumb. It's what she should have done in the first place. It's what I should have *encouraged* her to do in the first place."

"And this sudden attack of conscience is worth your mother losing her owner's rights? Is it worth you losing your position? Because if you think I can't work around your contract, you've got another thing co—"

"*Enough*," I shout, leaning my full weight against him and bringing my face close. "It's done. I don't care what you do from here. You have no more power over me or anyone else. Understand? I should have never gone along with your lies. I should have never kept your secrets. I won't ever do it again. I'm going to let the world know exactly who you are, and I am going to smile the whole time."

I can see it, the moment my father realizes that the carefully crafted image he's shirked his entire family for over the years is slipping through his fingers, and I wish I could say it was satisfying. I wish I gained any sense of triumph from it, but all I really feel is sorrow. Sorrow for the life we could have had, for the father he could have been, for the sister standing behind me who I could have been better for, for the mother I kept the truth from when all it did was ensure her suffering was tenfold when she finally experienced it—especially knowing what she'll lose.

"I know people," my father says quickly, grasping for leverage. "I could take away your career in a heartbeat." He shoots a glare in Lila's direction. "Your little whore's too."

"Sir," Jack chimes in, choosing that moment to join the fray. "I realize that I have only one arm right now, but I will one thousand percent shove my foot up your ass if you even look at my sister again."

"I'm not afraid of you," my father hisses. "None of you." He levels his gaze with mine. "Without me, Abigail will have nothing. You think I'll keep paying for that fancy school she's going to? I won't shell out a *dime* for her. I won't—"

"You won't have to," I interrupt, giving him one last shove with my forearm to his chest before stepping away. I go to Abby, who is still trembling slightly, and throw my arm around her to give her strength. I can feel Lila on her other side, and the warmth she radiates gives *me* strength. I don't need this man who made me. I have everything I need right here. "I will. I've got more than enough to take care of her. She doesn't need you. *We* don't need you."

My father is fuming, his face red and his body shaking, and for a moment, he almost looks as if he might want to *lunge* at the pair of us—but he just stands there quaking with rage, his nose wrinkling in disgust and his mouth curling into a sneer.

"You're both the worst mistakes I ever made," he practically spits. "I'm sorry I ever gave either of you a minute of my time."

"And I'm sorry I ever let you take a minute of mine," Abby says quietly, her voice small but steady. Her hand reaches up to squeeze mine, which is curled around her shoulder, and she stands a little straighter. "I don't need you."

"Neither of us do," I agree.

"I think it's time for you to go," Jack calls from closer by the door. "Leave with some dignity, for Christ's sake."

My father looks from me to Abby to Lila and even to Jack, his confidence slipping away with every second as he realizes there's nothing here for him. I want to hope that he feels some regret throwing away the only family he has left, but I know better. I'm just above letting it affect me anymore.

"This isn't over," he growls, stalking away. "Not by a long shot."

"Tell it to the papers, man," Jack says cheerfully, bowing slightly as he gestures out the open door. "I'm sure you're going to be hearing from them a lot."

"Useless. All of you." My father stands in the open door, curling his lip. "You're all a bunch of fucking—"

Jack slams the door in his face, smiling blithely. He regards the rest of us. "Anyway."

I turn to Abby, who is swiping at tears still leaking from her eyes, wrapping my hands around her shoulders and looking her over.

"Are you okay?"

She shakes her head. "No, but I will be."

"I'm so sorry, Abby."

"He wasn't wrong," she hiccups. "Not totally. This will hurt you. Your mom too. I should have thought it through. God, did he mean it when he said she might lose her owner's rights? What the fuck? I could have done something different. I could have—"

"It doesn't matter now," I tell her. "It's done. What did we say about being sorry?"

She lets out a watery laugh. "Don't be sorry, be better?"

"Exactly."

"I have plenty of that to do too," I admit. "You aren't the only one who had a hand in hurting my mother. I have things of my own to mend."

"I didn't mean to hurt anyone," Abby says in a small voice.

"I know," I say, meaning it. "You should have never been in the position to do it in the first place. I should have never kept you a secret. You're an amazing person, Abby. Too amazing to live your life in anyone's shadow. Now you can live it as loud as you want, and I'll be right there with you, every step of the way."

"We all will," Lila adds, curling her hand over one of mine still clutching Abby's shoulders.

Lila's eyes meet mine, her smile bright enough to cast a light on the darkest parts of me, and I know right then that a future with her in it will be just as bright.

"I am happy to provide enthusiastic high fives and ill-timed comments," Jack adds.

Abby laughs again, her chin tucking into her chest. "God, this has been a weird day."

"And it's not over yet," I sigh, stepping away from her. "I still need to go check on my mother."

"Do you want me to come with you?" Lila asks, her voice full of concern.

God. I don't even know what I was doing with my life before she burst back into it. She's too good for me, more than I ever thought to hope for, but at this very second it fully hits me that she is *mine*, and I vow that she always will be.

I pull Lila to me, wrapping my arms around her and letting her immediate return of my embrace bring me strength and comfort. "I think I need to do this alone, but thank you." I pull back slightly, pressing a kiss to her temple. "Wait for me?"

That smile. That fucking smile. It's all I'll ever need for as long as I live.

She doesn't miss a beat when she says, "Always."

- - - - -

I hate this house.

I've hated it for a long time, but I hate it more now. Looking up at the extravagance of it all, the size that's always been too much for three people, let alone two now, and thinking of my mother inside, all alone and no doubt hurting, makes me feel small. Like I'm a child again.

I press the doorbell and wait anxiously on the porch, twisting my hands as I hear my mother's voice calling from the other side. Even through the door she sounds . . . tired. It makes my guilt worse, makes that sick feeling that's been building in my stomach more prominent.

She looks as tired as she sounds when she opens the door, her blue eyes so clear that they always seem to see right through me wet with old tears and red-rimmed over dark circles. It makes her look smaller than she is, more frail.

"Ian," she says wearily. She shakes her head. "Glad you finally came to visit."

"Mom," I try. "I'm—"

"Not here," she sighs, stepping away from the door and gesturing inside. "Come in."

I follow her through the house, watching her stop at the wet bar and pour herself a generous glass of wine. My entire life, my mother has been the picture of put together. Being the wife of Bradley Chase has meant she's *had* to be—so it's a little startling to see her in old flannel pants and a loose robe over a simple cotton T-shirt. Even on Christmas morning, my mother was always photo ready.

She carries her glass to the couch, taking a heavy sip before patting the cushion beside her. "Well, come on."

I step through the room carefully, as if I might set her off at any moment, bracing myself for her anger, her sadness, her *disappointment*—knowing I deserve all of it. I settle next to her as she takes another drink of wine, silence hanging between us as I try to decide what the hell I should say, how I should even begin to apologize.

"Well," she says before I figure it out, "I'd hoped you'd come to visit in better circumstances."

There's amusement in her voice, but like her face, it seems tired.

"I should have," I tell her honestly. "I wanted to."

She nods slowly, her gaze fixed on the opposite wall. "How much did you know?"

"I . . ." That panic that almost overtook me earlier claws its way up my chest, and I have to physically wrestle it down, knowing that my mother doesn't need any more to deal with right now. "Everything," I tell her in a small, guilt-drenched tone. "I knew everything."

"For how long?"

"Since . . ." I wince, preparing myself for everything I deserve her to feel toward me. "Since I left Boston."

She nods again, still staring at the wall. "I guess all of that makes sense now. I always wondered why you felt you needed to leave us. Why you couldn't just come clean about who that woman was." She shakes her head, smiling fondly. "I knew you would never do what they were saying you did."

"No, but I did something worse," I tell her. "I lied to you. To everyone, but more importantly you. I thought . . ." My voice cracks, and I have to take a deep breath. "I thought I was protecting you, and Dad, he—" I shake my head. "He told me to go."

She stills. "He what?"

"He told me the team would be better off if I left. That *everyone* would be better off."

"That conniving bastard," she hisses, crossing her arms over her chest. Her face pinches as she shuts her eyes, seeming to try to collect herself. "So all these years when you said you were happy there, that you didn't want to come back . . . ?"

I nod. "He was strongly against it."

"But you did, anyway," she points out.

"Eventually." I bob my head in a nod. "I wanted to finish here. At home. I decided it was worth risking his anger." I make a frustrated sound. "And now look what's happened."

"Ian," Mom sighs. "*You* aren't the one who made all these bad choices. Your father is."

"It doesn't matter. I'm as bad as he is. I chose not to tell you, and now you're suffering even more than you would have if I'd just been truthful. None of this is what I wanted. I never wanted to hurt you, Mom."

My mom takes another slow sip, her eyes faraway, as if she's thinking. She draws in a deep inhale just to expel it slowly, bobbing her head in a nod. "Sometimes hurt is inevitable, sweetheart. Heart pain is a wound just like any other, but lies are an infection. Sometimes they're deep enough that you don't feel that pain, not for a while, but they keep the wound from healing right, they bury deep and make that wound bigger and bigger until it's not a little cut anymore but a gaping, bleeding thing. Until it's so big you have to amputate."

"Mom," I choke out.

"Shh, Ian." She waves me off. "I'm not angry with you."

I wince. "You aren't?"

"Honey," she sighs. She turns to face me then, pressing her palm to my cheek. "No child should ever suffer the sins of their parents. What your father did . . . That should have *never* been your burden to bear. I'm sorry that it was. I'm so sorry you've carried this for so long. I can't imagine what that must have been like." Her thumb brushes back and forth across my cheek, not unlike she's done a million times in my youth, and relief bleeds into the guilt to form a confusing cocktail of emotions that makes it hard to breathe. "I'm not angry that you didn't tell me, because I understand it, I think, but I'm angry that it cost us years of the closeness we used to have. I've missed you so much, son. I've lost your father, and it feels like I lost you, too, somewhere along the way."

I reach to cover her hand with mine. "You haven't lost me. I've just been so afraid. I didn't want to disappoint you. I didn't want to disappoint *anyone*. I've hated every single second of lying to you, Mom. I thought I was protecting you. I thought—"

"Shh," she says again, my rising voice and quick breaths obvious to her. "It's okay. We all have a piece of blame in this."

"Mom, no. You don't—"

"Sweetheart." She chuckles. "I know who your father is. Sure, I didn't know *this*, but I've known for years what kind of man he's become. What that legacy of his turned him into." She looks away again, sighing. "He hasn't been the man I fell in love with for quite some time." She shrugs listlessly. "I've been holding on to something that's been gone a long, long time. Maybe if I'd let go sooner, you never would have found yourself in this position to begin with."

"No, that's not—"

"Shush, I said." She cocks a brow, eyeing me from the side. "This is what we're not going to do." Her voice is stern, and I sit up a little straighter instinctively. "We are not going to carry any more blame or guilt or whatever else you're feeling over this. Not anymore. You've no doubt had years of it, and I think that's quite enough suffering for one tragedy, don't you?"

"But I—"

"And also, we're not going to let this thing fester anymore. We're cleaning out all the infection. You're going to come see me, often, and you're going to accept my obnoxious calls checking in on you, and you're going to answer all my texts that have no real point to them. Yes?"

A watery laugh escapes me as her hand curls in mine. "Yeah, I can do that."

"And you're going to bring Delilah over for dinner," she says firmly. "I haven't had a proper conversation with her since you were teenagers, and I want to know what the woman you're seeing has been up to. You *are* seeing her, aren't you?"

"I . . . Yeah." Thoughts of Lila have a real smile tugging at the corners of my mouth. "Yeah, I am."

"Good." She nods, a tension in her eyes and a set to her jaw as she adds, "And I would like to meet Abigail."

I blink in shock, my mouth falling open as words fail me. When my brain comes back online, I manage a, "*What?*"

"I've been reading her story," Mom says softly. "That poor girl. She's been so alone in all this. I can't imagine. She's just as much a victim as the rest of us in this."

My chest swells with overwhelming love for my mother, so much that it almost completely swallows the guilt inside me. Almost. "She's . . . She's definitely had a hard time."

"Well, that's something we can all relate to, don't you think?"

"It is."

Mom smiles then, squeezing my hand. "I love you, Ian. You know that, right? I've loved you since the day I found out about you, and I've never stopped. I'm sorry that so much got in the way of that, but the beautiful thing about life is that no one moment can destroy us, not really, because there will always be another chance to make things right. I think this might be ours."

I wrap my arms around her then, careful not to jostle the glass she's still holding. I hear her set it on the coffee table before her smaller arms curl around my waist, the familiar scent of her perfume tickling my nostrils and reminding me of better times. Times that I hope we can get back.

"I love you, too, Mom," I murmur against her hair. "So much."

"I know, baby." She pats my back. "I know."

I hold her tight for a moment, content to breathe her in, before another thought strikes me, making me jerk backward. "The team. What about the team?"

"The team?" She cocks her head. "What about it?"

"He said . . ." It hurts to think about, and unsurprisingly, hurts even more to say out loud. "He said if you got divorced the team would go to him. That my grandfather wanted it to stay with someone more knowledgeable."

She blinks at me for a moment, and then she takes me completely by surprise by throwing her head back and *laughing*. "Is that what he told you?"

"I . . . Yes?"

"Oh, honey," she chuckles, looking genuinely amused for the first time since I walked through the door. "I hate to be the bearer of more bad news, because I'm sure that's just one more burden you've had to carry but . . . that's not true at all."

"It isn't?"

"No." Mom shakes her head. "Your grandfather *hated* your father. He didn't even want me to marry him."

My mouth gapes. "You're kidding."

"Nope. He made sure that *several* stipulations went into our prenuptial agreement that ensured the team would stay with the family if our marriage ever dissolved." She chuckles again. "I was so angry when he pushed me into doing that at the time, you know?" Another bewildered shake of her head. "I guess he knew what he was doing."

"So . . . you keep the team?"

"I keep it all," she clarifies, almost smug. "Your father will leave this marriage with only what he brought into it."

"Wow. That's . . . I feel bad for hating my grandpa all these years now. I thought he was a misogynist prick."

She reaches to pat my cheek. "I wish you could have met my father. He would have loved you. He was quiet, but so strong. Just like you, really."

"I don't feel very strong right now," I admit.

Her thumb strokes idly against my skin, her smile soft but still enough to pierce through the shadows hovering around my heart. "My dad used to say, 'Strength isn't measured by how quickly we pick ourselves up after we've fallen . . . A person's strength is determined by their willingness to keep going once they're back on two feet.'"

"I . . ." My eyes sting, and I swallow at the lump in my throat. "Yeah. Okay."

"You'll keep going," Mom tells me. "Even if it takes a while to pick yourself back up."

I bring my hand to cover hers, the warmth of her palm soothing me. "You think so?"

"Yep." Her lips tilt into a smile that is actually *hers*—the one that's brought me peace since the first time I remember seeing it. "And so will I."

—   —   —   —

I leave my mother's house—not completely free of my guilt, because I know that will take time—but feeling confident for the first time in maybe ever that there *will* come a time when I'm free of it. When, as my mother said, I will finally recognize this as my moment to start making things right.

Standing on my mother's porch, it's overwhelming how much there's only one voice I want to hear. One person I want to share everything that just happened with. I place the call with a soft smile on my face, and when her voice fills my ears, that same beautiful sensation of being so settled, one that only she brings, fills me up to the point of bursting.

"Ian," she says with worry in her tone. "Are you okay?"

My smile widens, remembering something she said not too long ago.

The world won't end if you're okay, Ian.

"Yeah," I tell her, meaning it, I think. "Yeah, I am."

Twenty-Seven

DELILAH

After everything that's happened today, it feels . . . nice. Lying here in my bed with Ian, his head on my chest as my fingers card through the thick, red strands of his hair. His arms are wound around my waist, tucked underneath me as his big body rests over mine, and I can feel the scratch of his beard against my collarbone, the tickle of his nose at my throat.

He's spent the last hour telling me all about his visit with his mother, and I was happy to let him talk through it, to just be here for him while he processes. It was clear to me from the moment he arrived that it was what he needed most, just someone to listen and assure him that it would all be okay. I'm realizing that this is something Ian has been sorely lacking in his life for a long time, and I'm perfectly content to fill that void for the foreseeable future.

"Can we just . . . never leave this bed?" he mumbles into my skin, breaking the comfortable silence we've been basking in.

I chuckle softly. "It's been a very long day."

"It has," he hums.

"How was Abby when you took her home?"

He nuzzles my chest, exhaling slowly. "I think she'll be okay. Eventually. I told her I would check on her tomorrow."

"I can come with you, if you want," I offer.

His lips feather against my shoulder. "I always want."

"How much shit did Jack give you when you told him you were staying over at my place?"

"He sort of just made a grunting sound and started cleaning the countertops."

"He'll get over it," I laugh. "He's not *actually* put out, but he wouldn't be Jack if he didn't give us a little shit for it."

"I can handle it," Ian says, pressing slow kisses up the curve of my throat. "I was yours first, remember?"

My lips curl. "You were."

"I haven't told you," he says, pulling back to look at me, the wispy gray of his eyes looking so soft as they peer up at me. "But thank you. For being there today. I know it had to be a lot for you."

"I'll always be there," I promise. "Wherever you need me to be."

"Fuck, I love you," he sighs, a lazy grin spreading across his face. "I love saying that too."

"I'm happy to hear it as many times as you want to tell me."

"I love you." He leans in, his lips skimming my jaw. "I love you." They slide higher, hovering against my cheekbone. "I love you." He leaves a soft kiss over my eyelid, trailing lower before his mouth is just a breath away from mine. "I fucking love you, Lila."

"Teenage me is screaming into her pillow right now," I chuckle.

I feel his lips tilt against mine. "I can make that a reality for adult you, if you want."

"Are you sure you're up for that?" I nip at his bottom lip. "You must be so tired. Probably past your bedtime."

"Are you seriously making an old joke right now?"

"Does that sound like something I would do?"

His hands skim my waist, his knees pressing into the mattress so that he can curl his body over mine. "You're being a brat."

"You like when I'm a brat," I say sweetly, licking along his lower lip.

"I *love* when you're a brat," he rumbles, his hands falling to the mattress to brace on either side of me. "Because it means I get to spank it out of you."

I thread my arms around his neck, capturing his mouth fully and letting his tongue dip past my lips to tease mine with a slow, languid kiss that feels as lazy as it is satisfying. Like it doesn't *need* to be more. Like just this is enough.

And it is, really. As much as I always want more of Ian—more of his touch, his body, his heart—little moments like this are quickly becoming my favorite. Moments when the boy who started as my friend and my safe place becomes the man who's now my future, my everything. I *live* for moments like this, and the knowledge that I might get them for the rest of my life is overwhelming, almost too much.

"I love you too," I murmur into his mouth. "Just in case that wasn't obvious."

"Oh, I know. Practically obsessed with me, remember?"

"Completely obsessed," I answer without a hint of shame. "Just wait until everyone finds out you're mine. I might put it on a damned billboard. Force you into every kiss cam at every damned game so no one forgets."

He makes a pained sound. "Anything but that."

"I'll think of less embarrassing options," I laugh. "Maybe."

He pulls back, grinning boyishly, one red strand of hair falling into his face. "Yeah, let's pretend like I wouldn't do absolutely anything you asked me to do."

"Well." I push his hair back, tucking it behind his ear. "I was trying to save your dignity."

He turns his face, reaching to grab my hand as he turns it to press a kiss into my palm. "Don't need it," he murmurs. "I'm happy to go half on the billboard."

"Yeah?"

"Mm. Yeah." He smiles against my palm, peeking back at me. "Because I want everyone to know you're mine too."

The emotion that swells inside me feels too big for my body; it feels like the impossibility of everything you've ever wanted but never thought you could have all culminated into one explosive thing that can't be contained by one person. And maybe that's why love is better shared, I think idly. Maybe love can only truly be held by two people, because it's too big for just one.

I pull Ian close, my eyes shiny and wet with happy tears. I hold him against me, the reality that I can do this whenever I want crashing down on me all at once, because he is mine. He really is.

"Well," I say shakily, "let's see what we can do about that."

It's been a week since the explosive day where all of the secrets Ian's been clinging to came to light, and the aftermath has been a lot less hard to deal with than we thought it would be. The general consensus of the public has been remorse for the years spent assuming the worst of Ian, many people even *commending* him for going to such lengths to protect his little sister.

Bradley Chase has been considerably less fortunate with public perception; I would honestly be surprised if he didn't move out of the city before month's end, with the way he's become something of a pariah now that everyone knows exactly what sort of person he is, and I can't find it in me to dredge up a single ounce of sympathy. It's not like he's shown any remorse, after all; the only contact he's attempted with Ian and Abby in the last week has been just as volatile and nasty as the day we last saw him. Thankfully, neither sibling has seen any reason to give him the time of day.

We decided to wait until after the Druids' first game to go completely official with our relationship, and sitting here in the crowd during intermission before the final period—after watching Ian play so fantastically with his teammates, looking so at ease and in his element—I think we made the right call. He didn't need any extra distractions today.

"He's doing really well," Abby says from beside me.

It was my idea to invite her along, both of our teams agreeing that a united front was the best way to go forward. Seeing how happy she's been watching her brother play, I think I made the right call. I had wanted to bring Christine with us as well, but she said she isn't ready to be out in the public eye yet. I can't really say that I blame her. Ian and I have been to her house twice this week, and she's handling it well, all things considered. I can only hope that with time, she'll be able to find happiness again. She's too lovely a person not to.

"He was so nervous," I chuckle. "I thought he was going to throw up last night."

Abby smiles. "You can't tell watching him play. Do you think they'll win?"

"It's close," I tell her honestly. "Pittsburgh is a great team, but we're still two points ahead. I think we have a good chance."

A small elbow digs into my side as a tiny body squirms on the other side of me, and when I glance down, I catch a pair of wide eyes as the boy sitting next to me says sheepishly, "Sorry."

"It's fine," I tell him, shaking my head. "Are you having fun?'

I'm rewarded with a toothy grin. "Yeah!"

I lean to glance down the row, noticing that the rest of the kids from St. Michael's are bouncing with just as much energy as the one beside me. I spot Kyle's blond curls further down, and when his gaze meets mine, he offers me an enthusiastic wave and an elated smile. My chest warms at the sight of them, even more so with the knowledge that despite everything that's happened, Ian didn't forget his promise.

God, I love that man.

"Is your brother always so . . ." Abby's voice has me turning toward her, catching the way her head tilts in the direction where Jack is practically yelling through the plexiglass at Sanchez. "He seems very . . . passionate."

A laugh bubbles out of me. "Hockey is his life. It's killing him that he can't play today. I imagine the bench-coaching helps him cope."

"Ah," she says. "I see." Her brow furrows, her lips turning down. "What's he doing now?"

I lean in my seat to catch sight of Jack in skates moving out onto the ice, holding a microphone as he glides to the center of the rink and does a little spin that seems completely inadvisable, considering he's only got one good arm.

"Hellooo, Boston," Jack calls, his voice booming through the arena. "Thank you for coming out to watch our boys play today. I know your *favorite*"—he wiggles his casted arm—"is down for the count right now, but it's so wonderful that you could show support for the rest of these chuckleheads."

A low current of laughter sounds throughout the arena, and Jack flashes a bright grin.

"Thankfully, since they knew you would all miss me *so* much, they let me come out here during intermission to do something fun." He points his mic to the jumbotron above him before bringing it back to his mouth. "I know, I know, kissing is gross, but sometimes lovebirds like to do it, so we're happy to indulge them."

A graphic with animated hearts and lips pressing together in a kiss flash across the jumbotron screen, dissolving in seconds to focus on an elderly couple somewhere in the crowd. The woman's cheeks pinken as the man beside her bursts into a smile under his grayed mustache, and he turns to give the woman a sweet kiss.

"Wow, gross, love," Jack comments. He winks at the crowd. "Just kidding. Do we have another one?"

An image of two men sitting together appears on-screen, the taller man's arm slung affectionately over the back of the other man's chair as their faces light up. The taller man tugs the smaller one to his side quickly, smacking a kiss on his mouth.

"Disgustingly cute," Jack sighs. "No, I'm not jealous. Shut up, all of you. Do we have time for one more?"

The laughter on my tongue dies when my own face fills the screen, confusion causing my brow to wrinkle. I turn to Abby, who gives me a head shake and a shrug as she sort of scoots away, and my mouth parts, about to tell my brother off, but he starts talking again.

"Oh no, is that my sister? She looks pretty lonely sitting up there. I know she's the lesser of the Baker siblings, but come on, surely there's *someone* out there who wants to kiss her?"

A tap on my shoulder has me jolting, and suddenly Ian is plopping down in the seat beside me, still wearing his full gear save for his helmet and skates. His hair is damp with sweat, clinging to his temples, but his smile is bright, his freckles more prominent on his flushed face as he settles close.

"What are you doing?" I hiss.

He shrugs one shoulder. "Putting up my billboard."

"You hate these things," I remind him.

"Yeah," he says, reaching out to cup my cheek. "But I love you."

He leans in, his kiss soft but lingering, making my chest flutter and my eyes drift closed as I lean into it. The roar of the crowd fades away as he draws back, leaving nothing but the two of us and his warm gaze, which shines back at me, owning me, claiming me, telling the entire world that I belong to him, and that he belongs to me.

It's something I used to dream about but never thought I'd have, and now we're here, practically in front of the entire world, and he's looking at me like I'm *his* entire world. If I could go back in time and tell a younger me that we would be here, that Ian Chase not only saw me but *loved* me too—I think that version of me might have laughed in my face.

The thought has me pulling him back to me, kissing him harder as the crowd goes wild.

"All right, all right." I hear Jack's voice break through the haze of our bubble. "That's quite enough of that. Can we please have our left wing back if he's done making out with my sister? Apparently, they're dating. Did we know?"

"I hate him," I grumble.

Ian chuckles softly. "No, you don't."

"No," I sigh. "I don't." I can't help but peck another kiss on his mouth. "Now go on. You have a game to win."

"Sweetheart," he says, smiling against my mouth. "I already won."

My cheeks hurt from my smile, my heart full and my stomach fluttering, and watching Ian go, knowing that when he's done here it will be *me* he leaves with . . . Well.

I feel like I won too.

Epilogue

IAN

Three months later

s this the last box?"

I glance around my now mostly empty bedroom, assessing. "Yeah, I think so."

"I guess I'm stuck with you now then," she says with a sigh.

I grin, pulling her against my side. "You were already stuck with me."

"I know," she says with a frown. "Such a burden."

"Such a brat," I counter, leaning down to press my lips to hers.

"Ugh," I hear from the doorway. "You live together now. Can we not do this in my presence?"

Lila ignores her brother, making a show of nipping at my bottom lip. "Do you hear something?"

"Mm, no," I hum, grinning.

"That's it," Jack grumbles. "I'm going to make a sex tape, and I'm going to send it to both of you."

"That's an odd choice for revenge," Abby adds, peeking her head around the doorframe.

Jack moves to give her room, rolling his eyes. "Well, I don't know what other options I have for getting the guy back for constantly sticking his tongue down my sister's throat in front of me." His expression turns thoughtful then, giving Abby a beseeching look. "Unless . . . ?"

Abby makes a face. "Not on your life."

"What? I'm hot!"

"And entirely too aware of it," Abby scoffs.

"Dee." Jack pouts. "Abby is hurting my feelings."

Lila rolls her eyes. "It's about time someone took you down a peg."

"I'm not really into pegging," Jack deadpans. "But never say never."

"Wow," I comment dryly as Abby and Lila make an *ack* sound in tandem. "I'm really going to miss interactions like this."

"Oh, shut up," Jack huffs. "You've spent more nights at Lila's than this place in the last few months. You might as well have already been living there. I don't even know why it took you this long to make it official."

"I didn't want you to miss me too bad," I answer, stepping closer to pinch his cheek.

Jack punches me in the shoulder. "I have both arms now, dick. I'll kick your ass."

"Sure you will," I laugh.

Jack throws up his hands. "You're all assholes."

We watch him stomp back toward the living room, Abby shaking her head before she regards us. "Was there any more?"

"Just this last one," I tell her, pointing to the box on the ground.

"I'll get it," she says, bending to scoop it up. "Actually, I'll make Jack carry it. Give him something to do other than bitching."

I hear her call his name as she makes her way back down the hall, the sound of them bickering immediately drifting toward my old room. Lila chuckles as she loops an arm through mine, shaking her head.

"Abby has certainly gotten used to Jack."

I nod thoughtfully. "I sort of love watching her boss him around."

"It's definitely new for him," Lila snickers.

I take another look around the bare room behind me, feeling a little nostalgic. This is where I first touched Lila, after all. The first place I called home after coming back to my old life. I can't help but think about how different things are now from how they were when I first arrived back in Boston—all changes that have been overwhelmingly good.

My father ended up moving; he moved in with some woman he's been seeing in California. We haven't heard a word from him since the day he stomped out of the apartment all those months ago, and honestly, I'm glad for it. I hadn't expected him to go as quietly as he did, but it seems Bradley Chase is smart enough at least to know when he's lost. I can tell that it still bothers Abby sometimes, but she's less than willing to talk about it, so I've been content to give her space on the matter while she comes to terms with her new life.

Another surprising thing that happened was how quickly the public did a one-eighty on their opinion of me; suddenly I'm some sort of hero, which is a moniker I don't really think I deserve. I share too much of the blame in everything that happened, I made too many mistakes. Not that anyone will let me wallow in those facts for too long. It helps that Lila's show is doing better than ever, one good thing to come out of the media frenzy we went through. With our official couple status and a partnership agreement between her network and the team for the next year, it seems that her numbers are something we won't have to worry about for a while. Between my mom and Abby and Lila, the women in my life refuse to let me beat myself up too much. I count myself extremely lucky to have them.

"Well, I guess that's it," Lila says beside me, pulling me out of my thoughts.

I nod, turning to press a kiss to her hair. "Guess so."

"We should hit a thrift shop when we're done here. Find a new member of the Porcelain Pride to commemorate. For you, of course."

My lips twitch. "Oh, sure, totally for me."

"You know I'm always thinking about others," she says sweetly.

"I know," I answer, meaning it. "We have time before dinner at Mom's tonight."

"Abby is coming, yes?"

"Yeah," I say with a smile. "She is. Mei and Bella too."

The biggest surprise of all, I think, is how close my mother has gotten to Abby. No one would blame her for taking a different approach to this young woman—who, one could argue, threw a wrench into her life—but my mother has taken to Abby like she was hers, and I can tell how much that means to Abby. How much it's helped bring her out of her own guilt.

"And then after," Lila hums, trailing a finger down the front of my T-shirt, "you and I can celebrate you moving in."

"Oh? Anything particular in mind?"

"It depends on how good you are."

I roll my eyes. "Such a brat."

"You love it," she chuckles.

I press my hand to her cheek, rubbing my thumb back and forth before tracing it along her lower lip, cataloging her features, the warmth in her eyes, her smile—storing them away so that I won't ever forget how lucky I am to be able to do so. How lucky I am to have opened my eyes and *seen* her—this woman who had me first, and who'll have me always—to be able to call her mine. Everything between us started as a game, and I can't pinpoint the exact moment that it changed, but I'm so grateful it did.

She's in my head now, in my heart, and I plan to keep her there for as long as she'll let me.

"I do," I murmur, leaning in close. "But I love you more."

I feel her lips curve against mine, and I know I'll never want for anything when she answers, "I love you too."

Because of Lila . . . I'm finally okay, and the world didn't end because of it.

In fact, it feels like it's just beginning.

Acknowledgments

My entire life, I have heard people say "the third time's the charm," but in the case of this book, there was a large portion of time while drafting it when that didn't feel like the case. This story is one that I took a chance on after being posed with the question: Do you think you would ever write a sports romance? For me, the stereotypical nerd whose only handling of balls comes from her own fictional works, it was a huge risk. I have cried over this book; I have *hated* this book; but now, while I am currently finishing up copyedits after having been away from it for a few months, I am finally able to look at it without the weight of the expectations I was putting on myself, and I have come to the conclusion that I might . . . love it?

This book taught me that pushing yourself is daunting; that trying things in a different way than you're used to might seem impossible at first, but in the end there's a good chance you'll be better for it. I learned so much about myself and my writing because of this silly little hockey story, and regardless of what comes next for it, I can be at peace with the knowledge that I am proud of that, at the very least.

But on to the important part.

I know you're all here to answer the question: Does Lana still require hand-holding and hair-petting to get by? Well, the answer to that question is abso-fucking-lutely. Always.

To everyone at Berkley and Penguin Random House—I feel so lucky to be a part of such an amazing team. This industry is forever changing, and with every book I put out there, it feels like my experience changes right along with it, and knowing that such a brilliant team is behind me brings me comfort constantly.

A special thank-you to my incredible editor, Cindy Hwang, who I am constantly bragging about to others because I often feel so lucky to be working with someone who not only encourages my nonsense but revels in it. I have heard horror stories about how a bad author/editor relationship can go, and each one makes me all the more grateful that I am one of the lucky ones. Cindy is the person who encouraged this sports-inept author to take a chance, and—after a lot of nights spent screaming into my pillow—I'm grateful for that too.

To the wonderful people at my agency, and my agent, Jessica Watterson, who has become a psychic of sorts when it comes to knowing the exact manic text that means she needs to drop everything and call to talk me off a ledge (which is needed more often than is probably acceptable); I sleep better at night knowing she's in my corner. And to two wonderful ladies who are unfortunate enough to also regularly put up with my nonsense: Andrea Cavallaro, who takes good care of my books and makes sure they are where they're supposed to be, and Jennifer Kim, who I will forever know as "Money Daddy" for, well, daddying my money. (Always my favorite emails, so sorry to everyone else.)

To my Bejeweled Babes, Jessica Mangicaro and Kristin Cipolla, who I refer to in my head as "the dream team." I am so grateful to have people on my team as funny, kind, and genuinely supportive of my silly stories as they are. (I am so sorry this didn't end up being the werewolf/hockey romance of your dreams, but never say never, right?)

To the incredible art team that is responsible for the jaw-dropping covers and promo art that never ceases to blow me away, with a special shout-out to Rita Frangie, for always knowing exactly what I want to squeal over even before I do, and to Monika Roe for making those squealworthy covers a reality.

A much-deserved shout-out to my daddy, Kristen, who spends many a day daddying me the way I deserve, which is to say she spends a lot of time combatting my awful brain and all of its tendencies to put me down frequently and viciously; I don't know what I would do without her. Honestly, we should all thank her for taking on the task of caring for and standing up to my brain, because otherwise there might never be any more books from me. It's a hard job, but there's no one else I trust more to do it. This journey I've been on has given me a lot, but Kristen is one of my favorites.

A special thank-you to my favorite authors who I am lucky enough to call friends: Ruby Dixon, Elena Armas, Tarah Dewitt, and Kate Golden. They are constantly taking time out of their own busy schedules to help reassure me, or listen to me rant about nothing, or simply make this experience a little less lonely, when it has a tendency to be just that.

To Dan, who has now embraced the glory of knotting but championed this hockey silliness first. You are my forever friend, and even when your taste is questionable, I still love you (even if we don't use the L word).

To Keri, the person on this earth who might actually complete me and who is always down for a long day of signing and playing assistant, or a longer conversation about nothing at all that never fails to be the highlight of my day. I am so grateful that our other halves used to wear eyeliner together, because it gave me you.

Thank you to the people who take time out of their day to play a part in spreading love for my books—booksellers, librarians, bloggers, journalists, reviewers, even people nice enough to send a kind DM on Instagram or tag me in a sweet comment—I literally wouldn't be here without you.

And on that note: to the READERS. It is still mind-boggling to me that there are so many people out there who are picking my books off shelves and reading words I wrote, and not only that, but getting excited by them! It's a concept I fear I will never fully wrap my head around, but in that same vein, I will *never* stop being humbled by it. You are the heart and soul of this industry, the reason it exists, and without you, we would simply be pages collecting dust. From the bottom of my heart, thank you.

Last but certainly not least, to my family, and in particular, to that one guy that gave me a ring once—I have seen all that you have done and all that you have sacrificed in the name of me pursuing my dream, and it is that kind of love that inspires me to keep writing about others finding their happily ever afters, knowing that I am living mine.

Keep reading for an excerpt from

Under Loch and Key

The next paranormal romantic comedy
by Lana Ferguson

KEYANNA

never imagined that my death would come by way of a sheep avalanche, but as I watch the tumbling mass of floof barreling down the hill toward the stretch of road I am currently stalled on—it occurs to me that it would at least be a *memorable* way to go.

"*Christ.*"

I scramble to get the door of my ancient rental open—the door being on the *wrong* side, relatively, I might add, which means it's in direct line of impact for the bleating army currently rushing toward me. I manage to snatch my backpack and duck out of the car and half stumble to a more safe area, but the sheep, being less murderous than I'd come to believe, actually start to slow as they spill around the aged blue Hyundai, voicing their irritation of the impediment it makes by loudly trilling more of the hellish sounds of loud *bahs*.

"Oi!" a voice calls from up the hill. "You all right, lass?"

I bring a hand over my eyes to peer up into the sun, noticing a man with graying hair waving down at me. "Fine," I call back. "They're not carnivorous, are they?"

"Not last I checked." He chuckles, trotting down the hillside. He notices my car in the midst of the sheep sea, quirking a brow. "Car troubles?"

"I *told* the woman at the rental place I wasn't good with a stick shift, but apparently it was all they had left."

"You an American?" He doesn't ask it like it's something to be offended by, but he does sound perplexed. "You're a right ways from the tourist spots, aren't you?"

"Oh, I'm here for . . ." I trail off, deciding it's probably a bad idea to vomit my entire complicated pilgrimage to a veritable stranger. "I'm here to visit family."

His eyes crinkle at the corners, a bright, expressive blue among the weathered lines of his face making him seem genuinely interested. "Is that right? And who might you belong to? I know everyone around these parts."

I hesitate, again considering the ramifications of telling a stranger about my spur-of-the-moment reunion with my estranged family before *they* know about it. In the end, I reason that if nothing else, there's a good chance I will reach my grandmother's house before this man can wade out of his pile of sheep.

"The MacKays," I tell him. "Rhona MacKay?"

"Oh, aye, aye, I know Rhona! Is she your granny, then? Would that make Duncan your da?" He squints as if trying to make the connection. "You've got the look of him. Didn't know he had any weans when he ran off to America."

I try to process all of this; I am deciding to take his stream of consciousness as overt friendliness and not some backhanded comment on my father's complicated history with his family. He must notice my stunned expression, though, because he waves a hand back and forth.

"Listen to me, babbling on. Sorry, lass. Don't get many newcomers in Greerloch." He wipes his hand on the front of his worn flannel shirt, extending it after. "Hamish Campbell. I live over the hill there with this lot." He nods back toward the still-bleating horde. "Pleased to meet you."

I take his hand, still reeling from the influx of conversation. People don't just *chat* like this back in New York. "I'm . . . Key. Key Murphy. Well, Keyanna, actually, but everyone calls me Key."

"Key," he echoes. "I like it. You remind me of Rhona now that I've had a proper look at you. You've got the eyes."

I don't exactly know how to feel about looking like a woman who hasn't wanted anything to do with me for my entire twenty-seven years, but I manage a tight smile regardless. "How nice."

He frowns at his brood, looking sympathetic. "I gather you'd like to be on your way, aye? Your granny is probably expecting you."

I don't correct him, giving a noncommittal shrug and a thin smile instead.

"Might take me a wee bit to get the herd to move along, but I can take a look at your car if you like? I'm right handy when I aim to be."

"That would be amazing, actually." I sigh in relief. "If it's really no trouble?"

"No trouble at all." He waves me off. "You just wait right there, and I will have you right as rain within the hour."

I glance across the rolling hills and lush green that spills all around us, biting my lip as I pull out my phone. "You don't happen to know how far"—I squint at the notes on my screen—"Scall-an-jull Cove is, would you?"

Mr. Campbell laughs. "I grant ya, that's a hard one. It's *Skallangal* Cove, love." He says it like: *Scall-an-gale*, which sounds much nicer than my butchered attempt. "You're after Nessie then, aye?"

"I . . . What?"

Another chuckle. "They don't call it 'cove of the fear' for nothing, lass. I've chased many a wean from that cove. Rocks are too rough there, you see? S'not safe."

"Oh, it was just a place my dad mentioned . . ."

"Oh, aye, I reckon he did. Duncan always claimed he saw the beast. Ever since he was a wee lad. Swore on it, if you got him good and steamin'."

"Steaming?"

"That's drunk to you, hen."

Hen?

Probably be here all day if I stop him for a slang lesson every time it comes up.

"You saw my dad drunk?"

"A time or two. Before he took off." Mr. Campbell scratches at his jaw. "I was sad to see him go. How's the auld boy getting along, then? He not come with you?"

I feel a twinge of pain in my chest; even after six months, it still hurts to think he can't be here with me. "He . . . passed," I tell him. "In the spring."

"Ah, lass." Hamish sighs, looking truly grieved by the news. "I am sorry to hear that. He was a good man, your da. We were mates when we were lads. I wish we hadn't drifted. Can I ask how he went?"

"Pneumonia," I explain. "He was diagnosed with Alzheimer's a few years ago, and he just sort of . . . degenerated. He came down with pneumonia after a bad winter, and he"—I have to clear my throat, feeling it grow thicker—"he didn't recover."

"Oh, hen." Hamish's blue eyes glitter with genuine emotion, which only worsens the pressure I'm feeling in my chest. Hamish reaches into his jacket pocket to retrieve a handkerchief, rubbing at his nose briefly before stowing it away. "I'm sorry, love. And your mum? We all heard the stories about how auld Duncan ran off with a wily American. Is she not here with you?"

He's determined to pick at all my scabs today, isn't he?

"My mother died giving birth to me," I manage stiffly.

Hamish blows out a breath. "Aye, I've really stepped innit, haven't I? Forgive me for being a nosy bastard." He shakes his head, clearing his throat as he gestures to my car. "How's about I get to work on this, then? There's some lovely views from the hill there"—he points across the lush green expanse stretching beyond the little knoll his sheep are currently crowding—"and your Cove is nigh a kilometer"—he turns his finger in the other direction—"that way." He winks. "If you're brave enough, mind you."

I chuckle softly. "I'm not afraid."

"Well, mind the rocks, would you? It really is unsafe. Keep to the shore, aye?"

"I will," I assure him. "And thank you for your help."

He waves me off. "Think nothing of it, lass. We're a close-knit group here in Greerloch, and you're family, apparently! Don't you worry, I'll have this fixed up within the hour."

He turns to shoo away one of the bleating fluff-monsters currently nibbling at his coat hem, pushing his way through the masses toward my poor, pathetic rental car. I watch him for a moment, wondering if it's *actually* wise to leave my car with some stranger, but honestly, what choice do I have? It's not like I can fix it myself, and my only other alternative is to lock myself inside and hope someone else comes along. I let my eyes sweep across the sprawling, endless green of the landscape, not seeing any signs of life outside of Hamish and his horde.

I guess that's what the rental insurance is for.

I turn toward the direction he pointed out, which leads to the massive hill that supposedly hides the way to Skallangal Cove, thinking that now is just as good a time as any. I hoist my backpack up higher onto my shoulders, taking a deep breath and letting it out as I turn toward the hill.

Onward and upward, I guess.

─ ─ ─ ─ ─

I doubt Hamish's "nigh a kilometer" more and more as I trek across the grass; the hill itself was a feat and was less of a "hill" up close and more of a small mountain, I think. My thighs burn with effort as I walk, and I'm sure my Apple Watch is probably organizing me a pizza party for the overage of steps I'm getting in today. But when I finally see the glittering surface of the loch coming into view, the sun shining onto the small waves and making them sparkle, I think maybe it was worth all the steps.

There are signs as I get closer—the standard KEEP OUT and DANGER posted along the barely-there path that leads to the rocky shore—but given that there isn't a single soul for miles, it would seem, I think I'm probably fine to explore a little. I mean, who's going to tell me I can't? Hamish's sheep?

There *are* a good number of large rocks jutting up at the water's edge, giving the shore a craggy effect that I can definitely see being a problem for kids wanting to adventure onto them. For a moment, I can only stare at the quiet rolling water that gently ebbs back and forth against the shore, and then I'm struck with a sudden memory that isn't mine—one that *feels* like mine for as many times as I've heard my dad recount it.

He was just there. Just beyond the shore. I'd slipped on the rocks, see? I thought I'd drown . . . but he saved me.

As a kid, the story of my dad's salvation at the hands of some mythical beast had been thrilling. I remember late nights of begging him to hear it "just one more time"—anything to avoid bedtime. Sometimes I can still hear his voice, soft and comforting as he lulled me to sleep. Still feel his fingers on my brow, pushing my wild curls away from my face as my eyes drifted shut.

In the end, his stories were all he had.

I drop my backpack onto the ground and start to dig through it, my hands shaking a little as I pull out the black capsule.

"Hey, Dad," I mutter, rubbing my thumbs across the sleek curve of the urn. "Look where we are." I straighten, holding the urn close to my chest as I turn back to the water. "I brought you back," I say to the air. "Just like I said I would."

A deep ache settles in my chest and lower in my stomach; I thought I would find more peace here, knowing I was giving him the send-off he wanted. I can't even be sure if this is what he *actually* wanted or if it was just more ramblings brought on by the slow loss of his mind, but it *feels* right, I think. Sure, he never spoke of his family, or of his life here beyond silly childhood stories—but I could tell he missed it. There was a sadness in his voice sometimes that I could hear no matter how hard he tried to hide it.

I realize after a few minutes that I'm just standing here; that I'm stalling, really. It's silly; I quit my job, flew across the ocean, practically uprooted my entire life just to come here, and now that I'm here . . . I'm not sure if I can do it.

The wind picks up, whipping my sun-blazed curls around my face, and I tell myself that it's just the brightness out here that's making my eyes water. I can *do* this, damn it.

I turn to try and scope out a good place; I've never spread someone's ashes before, obviously, but it doesn't feel very special to just walk up to the shoreline and dump my dad out onto the algae. Surely there has to be a better way.

With that in mind, I start pacing along the edge of the water, nearing the expanse of jutting rocks that the signs and Hamish and probably God at this point have warned me about. There's a relatively flat one only a few steps out, just a short climb and several hops away from shore. Surely I can manage that. I'm not a kid, after all.

I hold my dad tighter as I carefully step out onto the raised stone that leads toward the larger flat rock, hovering with one foot still on the shore as I test my balance. My sneakers aren't the best choice for this, and I'm wishing now that I'd read a few more travel blogs about dressing for Scotland. Not, I think, that any of them would have accounted for rock climbing on the coast of Loch Ness. I curl my fingers to grip my dad's urn as I blow out a breath, readying to step further onto the rocks and finish this so I can head off to meet the family. Something else I'm not sure I'm looking forward to.

I don't even make it another step before I'm yanked back.

"Hey!"

Something thick winds around my waist, hauling me backward, using enough force that I nearly stumble as I'm forced back to both feet on the shore. The thick something—an *arm*, I realize—lingers for only a moment before releasing me, and I whirl around with hot anger flooding my cheeks as I prepare to tell off whoever interfered.

And then, funnily enough, I seem to forget how to use words.

The stranger is . . . beautiful. Not the kind of beautiful that one might attribute to rare works of art or a sunset or anything like that. No. *This* man is the kind of beautiful that makes you think of sex and sweat and all sorts of other filthy things that are currently flitting through my thoughts.

He's taller than me even at my five foot ten—easily by six inches. His golden brown hair seems almost highlighted by the sun, but the stubble at his chiseled jaw is darker, adding a rough edge to the prettiness that his high cheekbones and straight nose give him. He's all soft mouth and broad shoulders—and *holy hell*, his pants can barely contain his thighs—but funnily enough, it's his eyes that hold my attention most. So blue they almost appear silver, they hold my gaze for more seconds than is probably appropriate as I struggle to think of something, *anything* to say to this ridiculously hot man that might sound halfway coherent.

"I—I'm—"

"Stupid," he finishes for me, his sinfully deep accent—a literal brogue that makes my skin heat—enough to make it take a few seconds for me to fully comprehend what he's said. "That's what you are."

My mouth gapes when it hits me, and I blink at him in a manner that is probably as stupid as he's just accused me of being.

What the *hell*?

About the Author

LANA FERGUSON is a *USA Today* bestselling author and sex-positive nerd whose works never shy from spice or sass. A faded Fabio cover found its way into her hands at fifteen, and she's never been the same since. When she isn't writing, you can find her randomly singing show tunes, arguing over which Batman is superior, and subjecting her friends to the extended editions of *The Lord of the Rings*. Lana lives mostly in her own head, but can sometimes be found chasing her corgi through the coppice of the great American outdoors.

VISIT LANA FERGUSON ONLINE

LanaFerguson.com
Lana-Ferguson-104378392171803
LanaFergusonWrites
LanaFergusonWrites

Ready to find
your next great read?

Let us help.

Visit prh.com/nextread